# By The Numbers

A Collection of (Not Too) Short Stories

By John Buckner

John Buckner

ISBN-13: 978-0-9978949-3-6
ISBN-10: 0997894938

# Table of Contents:

# Invasion 2035

## *Chapter 1*

It was a beautiful day in Southern California. The sky was clear and blue. Only a few clouds skittered along and they were high and thin. There was a slight breeze blowing in off the Pacific Ocean and the temperature was in the sixties. It was still early in the day and the temperature would top out in the eighties along the coast, while the inland part of the city would reach ninety. As you moved inland farther, the temperatures would climb near the one hundred mark.

Nick Parker had been out of bed for just over an hour, in which he had run five miles along the sandy beach. He did this six days a week, taking only Sunday off, when he was at home. Home was a rather large house facing the ocean. The house had been left to him, along with a considerable amount of cash, stocks and bonds when his father and mother had been killed in an automobile accident in 2015, five years earlier. Nick had been away in college at Notre Dame University when the accident occurred.

Mr. Parker had been a movie producer. He looked for scripts or stories that he thought would make good movies, then found a Director and actors to film the movie. He put up all the money and took his chances that the movie, when finished, would gross enough to pay the expenses of filming and salaries, with some left over to justify his investment. He was very good at choosing movie plots that would appeal to the public, and usually made enough off them to move on to another project. Occasionally, he hit the jackpot with a blockbuster and made a killing.

Nick had been practically raised in the house he continued to live in. His parents had bought the house when he was just going into first grade and he did not remember where the family lived before. Nick had elected to keep the house, even though it was much too large for a single individual, even with a lot of female companionship to help fill it. He had gone back to school after his parent's funerals and completed his final year.

Nick was five feet ten inches tall and weighed 170 pounds. His hair was light brown, bleached almost white by the sun and salt water. Surfing had been the rage in California for years, and living on the beach, Nick had been bitten by the bug at an early age. His father had gotten some instructions for him when he was eight years old, and Nick had soon been able to surf better than his instructor. His activities in the water helped to keep him in good physical condition and when he entered high school he took up track. He concentrated on the longer distances and did quite well from the start.

By the time he reached his senior year, he had scholarship offers from several Universities. He was also a top notch student. His interests were many and varied. He had a tough time deciding on a major for his studies, finally deciding on Archeology, though he didn't have any plans to pursue the occupation. He just found the concept of being able to decipher the past from artifacts fascinating, and wanted to learn more about it. His family was wealthy enough that they really didn't care what he studied, since he would not have to rely on the choice for making a living. When his parents died during his senior year Nick gave some serious thought to his choice of majors. He didn't know how much money they had left, and that was the last thing on his mind at the time. Still, if he had to choose an occupation for making a living, he would not choose Archeology. It involved too much travel, and was also a very uncertain field. There were not that many good jobs available, and with the world in constant turmoil, accessing the areas in the Middle East and Africa, where most of the worthwhile ruins were located was problematic.

Fortunately, Nick found that he would not have to live the life of a pauper. His father had invested his money wisely, and had been extremely fortunate the past few years to have produced several movies that had grossed millions of dollars. Nick was worth well over fifty million dollars when the will was probated, plus the beach house and a couple of vacation homes; one at Big Bear, a ski resort in the San Bernadino Mountains, and another in Aspen, Colorado.

John Buckner

Although Nick didn't have the need to work to make a living, he wanted something worthwhile to devote his time and energy to. He was twenty five years old and had not done much since his college graduation, except invest a bit in the stock market and look into the movie business for ways to invest.  The problem with movies was that the industry had gotten so fragmented with the advent of on-line availability and digital media, that he didn't understand enough about it to warrant his investment of time or energy.

Nick was very handsome and had no problems with his love life.  He was not by nature a flamboyant person, and drove a sensible four wheel drive pick-up rather than something ostentatious.   He was well known around Los Angeles and Hollywood.  He ate out regularly, and visited the night spots, but drank sparingly.  Women seemed to find him appealing and he never lacked for female companionship.

Frequently, about once every two weeks, he drove out into the desert, usually at the foot of one of the mountain ranges and spent a couple of days hiking and looking for Indian artifacts.  He had found some nice specimens of pottery shards and arrow heads, spear points, and even bone needles used by the Indians to stitch clothing from animal hides.

On this Friday morning Nick decided that he would go to the desert for the weekend.  He loaded his camping gear and other essentials and headed for the 101 Freeway.  He drove north through Oxnard and took the Santa Paula Freeway over to Interstate 5.  He continued north past Bakersfield, eventually heading for the foothills of the Sierra Nevada mountain range. He had been to the area recently, and found it more peaceful and less traveled that the mountains farther to the south.  Nick found a forest trail leading to the mountains and turned off. The road was not listed on any of his maps but looked like it led to the foot of the mountains, which was where he wanted to go, so he followed the road until it gave way to nothing more than a trail.  Nick could see tire tracks of four wheelers and continued on in four wheel drive. The going was slow and by the time he got to a place he considered suitable for camping, it was almost dark.  He hurriedly set up the tent and rigged the light set up he had made to the extra 12 volt battery he had installed in his truck for that very purpose.  He could run the light all night if he wanted, and the battery would recharge off his truck alternator when he ran the truck again.

He broke out the propane stove and prepared a simple meal from the groceries he had brought along.  He crawled into his sleeping bag and slept until sunrise.  He roused, fixed breakfast and donned his hiking boots and pack.  He did not plan to venture far away from the truck, but put everything inside and locked it anyway.  He took with him the handheld GPS unit he always carried and set out.  He headed north along the base of the mountains and hiked for about half an hour, scouring the ground closely for anything of interest.  He climbed a bit higher to see if he could see his truck, with the thought of maybe moving a bit farther north later in the day.  Once he was a couple of hundred feet higher he looked at the vista before him and found that he could still see the truck, and what he thought might be a good location for the following night.

Nick spent the remainder of the day looking for artifacts.  He found a few pieces of interest and hiked back to his truck.  He moved to the location he had spotted from the hill and set up camp again before darkness fell.  He had another simple meal and lay looking at the stars as the night became darker.  He was almost as taken with the night sky as he had been with archeology.  He had never been into religion very much, though his folks were Catholic and had taken him to church often.  Thoughts of the earth and how it got to be what it is had not been within his area of interest.  Theories of evolution seemed to make sense, to a point, but he could not get his mind to accept the fact that humans had evolved from apes.  Some of the other evolutionary claims did not hold a lot of water with him either.

As he lay looking at the night sky he let his thoughts drift to the question if there was life out there someplace?  Did the world simply wink into existence? Did it have the influence of beings from another planet?  If that was the case, how did the first world come into existence?

The thoughts were out of character for him, but looking into the depths of space in the beautiful sky above, one could not help but be awed by the vastness and unknown worlds beyond our own.  He had read stories about people who had supposedly had encounters with aliens, but most he could debunk pretty easily.

Still he found it reasonable to accept the fact that there might be other worlds like his own, well, maybe not exactly like earth, but some life forms had to exist outside the small planet called earth.

When he went to sleep that night he dreamed of other worlds and how they might have possibly affected the earth's makeup and evolution. The dreams were fragmented, and seemed to have no theme or coherent make-up. The theme was still with him when he awoke and prepared his simple breakfast. He tried to shake the feeling as he cleaned up and went on his way to search for artifacts. He had not been at it long when he discovered a very unusual rock. It was unlike anything he had ever seen. The stone was about the size of a baseball and was almost perfectly spherical. It had circular rings of different colors, mostly pastels, but a couple of brighter ones.

He hefted the stone in his hands and felt the smoothness of the surface. It did not have a blemish anywhere on the surface, and this amazed him, since it would have had to wash down from a higher elevation, and the trip down would surely chip it in some places. He had studied enough geology to identify most types of rocks and minerals, but the specimen he had in his hand baffled him completely. He placed the rock in his pack and continued searching for the remainder of the morning. When he got back to the truck and prepared lunch, he took the stone out again and retrieved a magnifying glass from the glove compartment to have a closer look.

As he studied the surface of the rock under the glass, he could not find a flaw anywhere on the surface. He could detect a circular pattern around the circumference of the object which was perfectly symmetrical. Still, he didn't see any way it could have been made, but thought it was that way purposefully. He twisted and pried every way he could, but the rock remained a rock, and in one piece.

He placed the rock in the cab area of his truck and continued his search in the afternoon. The afternoon's foray didn't yield anything of note and he was back at the campsite long before the sun went down. He spent more time in the area where he had found the strange rock, hoping to find more of the same, or something to explain what he had found. He had no better luck with that task than he had during the entire afternoon.

After eating a simple meal he rigged the light for the night and sat around a small campfire he had made looking at the strange rock again. As it got darker, he turned on the light and continued to study the rock. As he moved around, he noticed that the lights would dim and brighten. This was strange. It had not happened before, and since the light was wired directly to the twelve volt battery, it did not make sense from the physics standpoint. It was not logical that the current would vary. As he moved toward the light the pulses seemed to accelerate. He still had the rock in his hand, and it seemed to be getting warmer as he got nearer the light.

Now he was really intrigued. If the stone was making the light pulse, then it had some properties that he had never encountered. The makeup would have to be some element that had electrical properties. Still, he couldn't think of any element that would make the light pulse. Iron could be a conductor, but would act more like a magnet, and would not cause the phenomenon he was observing. The only way he knew that the light would flicker like it was doing, was by changes in the current, and nothing in his knowledge bank would account for that.

He placed the orb next to the light and the flickering seemed to stop. However, the intensity of the light was much less than usual. The rock was obviously pulling the current from the light, but that didn't make any sense either. He experimented, moving the orb away from the light slowly. As he did so, the flickering returned, and when he was perhaps ten feet from the light bulb, the current became steady once more. He did this several times, just to see if the results would be the same. Each time he got the orb in close proximity to the light bulb, the light would burn constantly, but at a lower intensity.

Nick concluded that something about the orb was causing the unusual activity. There had to be something about the orb which caused the light to change. He did notice that the orb seemed to be warmer than it had been earlier. He didn't know if this was due to it absorbing heat from his body, but thought that the orb was actually hotter than his hands. It had not been in the sun, and should be no warmer than he was. Just to test that premise, he picked up another stone and compared the two. The orb was much warmer than the stone. He deduced that the orb had to be drawing the electrical current from the light bulb.

How this was happening he did not know, but it was obvious that the orb was not a run of the mill rock. Nick also wondered if the tiny line around the circumference of the thing might be the method by which it opened up. He now felt sure that he had found something unique.

Nick's mind flashed back to the dreams he had the night before, and to the thoughts he was having about the universe and extra-terrestrials. Maybe that was causing his mind to overreact. The things he had observed he could not dispute. No matter how far out his thinking and dreams had been, what he had observed about the rock and the light bulb was for real.

He sat down near enough to the light that he would be able to see well, and broke out the magnifying glass again. The circumscribed circle he studied very closely, inch by inch. Though he still could not see any way for the halves to separate, he was certain that they did so. It was simply a matter of finding the secret to opening them. He put his ear to the orb and moved it nearer the light, until the glow became steady.

Nick thought he could detect a very faint hum coming from the rock, though it could have been his imagination. He moved his head away and then back, to see if it made any difference. He was not sure, though he repeated the process at least a dozen times.

In the end, he placed the orb in the cab of the truck and got ready for bed. As he lay there, trying to clear his mind enough to fall asleep, he once again found himself thinking about space and aliens. Unlike the previous night, these thoughts, or dreams if he was asleep, were more specific. His mind was almost like a kaleidoscope. He could, or was, picturing exactly what the aliens looked like; their space ships and planet as well. In the dream or vision, he noticed that other things on the planet looked much like the orb he had found.

In the dream, one of the aliens beckoned him to come to him. He walked toward the figure and was almost to him when the dream suddenly winked out. Nick was left in the sleeping bag wondering what the alien was about to show him. He tried to recapture the thread of the dream, but had no luck. He fell asleep and didn't give the alien any more thought.

Nick remembered the dream when he awoke, but it was not at all like a dream, more like an experience with sharp recall. He decided to head back to Los Angeles and loaded up his equipment and was off before eight o'clock. The orb he had handled a bit that morning and placed it in the console beside him.

When he started the truck, it seemed that the starter labored a bit more than usual. He shrugged it off and headed back home. All during the drive to L.A. he had thoughts of aliens and other worlds. The orb had really gotten to him, he thought.

His first act after unloading the truck was to take the orb inside and experiment with a brighter light and the 120 volt circuit. The same phenomenon happened when he placed the orb near a light. Still he could not see any way to separate the halves of the orb. Finally he gave up and placed it on his bedside table as he prepared to shower and get ready for bed.

All during the night he had the unusual dreams. This time he dreamed that he approached the alien and got close enough to talk, though no sounds came out. Instead, the alien pulled out an orb similar to the one he had found. He seemed to be demonstrating how to open it, but Nick could not understand. The alien slowly demonstrated what he was trying to show Nick. He seemed to be pressing different areas of the orb, but again Nick didn't understand what the alien was obviously trying to show him.

Nick moved as close as he could to watch what the alien was doing. He seemed to be pressing different colors in some sequence, and Nick tried to memorize the sequence.

After pressing twelve times on the orb, the alien placed a hand on two sides and the orb opened. He had obviously been trying to show Nick how to open the orb he had found. How or why this was happening Nick did not know. As a matter of fact, he didn't even give it a second thought at the time. He was too involved in trying to understand the method of opening the orb.

When Nick awoke the following morning he remembered the details of the dream. He picked up the orb and tried to duplicate what he had seen the alien do in the dream. He turned the orb over in his hands several times, trying to see if there were any indications as to a specific location to press on the colored lines. As far as he could tell there was no difference in the lines.

The thickness seemed to be the same all the way around all of the lines.

He tried the sequence as he remembered it and grasped the sides of the orb, but it did not magically fly open for him. He tried several more times, and when he had no better luck, gave up again. He went for his run on the beach and came back for breakfast. He reviewed the dream in his mind but could not determine what he had done wrong, if in fact the alien had been trying to tell him how to open the thing.

He experimented again with the orb and its electrical characteristics. As he listened with his ear pressed close to the surface, he thought the humming sound might be a bit louder than it had been at the campsite. It could be the difference in the current he thought. Although still baffled by the entire experience, he was beginning to suspect that something quite unusual was taking place. He had no doubt that the dreams were connected to the orb in some way, and that the orb was not of this world.

That the thing had unique capabilities he was sure. Whether the intent was good or evil, he was not so sure. The creature he had seen in his dreams didn't seem to be threatening, but that could be deceptive. The very fact that he had in his possession an object from outer space had not dawned on him yet; and that he was possibly the first person on earth to validate life on other planets was lost on him as well.

To Nick it appeared that the only time the alien was able to communicate with him was while he was asleep. Maybe it had to do with the amount of brain activity? If that was the case he might be able to simply relax and achieve the same result. He tried this theory out, but had no success. He didn't think he could lie down and go to sleep at will, but he desperately wanted to solve the riddle of the orb, so he lay back down on the bed with the orb by the nightstand.

Much to his surprise, he dropped off to sleep almost immediately. The dream returned and he stood before the alien, who again showed him the orb, and took pains to show him where on the orb to press. Nick could still not see any difference in the line where the alien was pressing and thought that he needed to see that again. The alien obliged by showing him again in slow motion.

Try as he might, Nick could not see any way to determine where on the colored line to press. The alien repeated the sequence again and again, as Nick became more and more perplexed. Finally, the alien motioned for him to touch the orb. When he did so, he felt a weak current. The alien rotated the orb until he got to the apparent spot that had to be depressed. Nick did not feel anything there, and began to get the picture. The secret was a null in the current where the pressure should be applied.

He awoke; picked up the orb again and concentrated on the color sequence he had been shown so many times. He lightly ran his finger along the first line and could feel a very faint sensation, not like electricity, but more like a tickling sensation on his fingertip. When he came to the null, he pressed and went to the next color. He repeated the sequence he had been shown and grasped the two sides of the orb and twisted. The orb separated into two halves.

What he expected to see he didn't know, but he was not expecting what he encountered. Each side of the orb was a mass of circuitry within. There was a hollow space, about an inch deep in the center of each half. There were no controls of any sort. After studying the halves for some ten minutes, he was still no closer to understanding what he had before him.

He placed one of the halves against his ear and listened. He could hear the steady hum that he had detected when the two halves were joined, and it was more discernible. He placed the other half against his other ear, which was apparently intended, because he became aware of discernible noises, almost as if he was wearing a headset. The noises didn't make much sense to Nick, but he suddenly became aware of intelligible conversation.

## Chapter 2

Nick thought the voices were coming from different people, but belatedly realized that the voice was speaking to him. He formed the thought to reply, but found it was not necessary, because his thoughts seemed to be transmitted like normal conversation.

The voice was asking, "Do you understand me now?"

Nick thought, "Of course I understand you."

"I had to cycle through all known earth languages until I came to yours. I am sorry for the inconvenience."

"Who are you, and what are you?" Nick asked.

"I am called Myrth on my planet. I am what you earthlings call a robot. I was designed to make contact with other worlds and sent here, along with several others. I am the first to make contact."

"Why were you sent? Are you just an explorer, or is there some purpose for coming?" Nick asked.

"You could call it a bit of both. The beings on my planet have been sending out robots for a long time. First the purpose was simply to find other planets with intelligent life, but during the time when I was designed, it had been determined that their planet was being slowly depleted of the substance that is necessary to sustain life for them. Although the process will go on for more than a hundred of your years before it gets to the critical stage, they started sending out robots like me."

"And what are you supposed to do when you find someplace habitable?" Nick asked, thinking that if the earth suited their purposes it might be the precursor to an alien invasion.

"I have already informed them of the mineral and chemical make-up of your planet. There are many similarities, and they might be able to exist here," the robot told him.

"You mean they will just come and take over the planet?"

"No, not at all. They could coexist with you very easily. They require different materials from those that sustain your life cycle."

"Can you tell me how long you have been here?" Nick asked.

"I have been dormant for a long period in the way you account for time, it has been almost fifty years," the robot replied.

"If you made your report when you first arrived, then they have had fifty years to make preparations, yet no one is here yet. Don't you find that odd?"

"Not in the least.   Much preparation is necessary to undertake such a journey, and the journey itself will take about ten of your years."

"Why do you say we will be able to coexist?"

"Because my masters are much smaller than your race, and they live differently.  I mapped some of your cities as I was arriving, and millions of them could exist in the space your people house only thousands.   In addition, they draw their nutrition from elements in what you call your atmosphere, and will not deplete your food supplies or other elements you need for your survival."

"So, why are we having this conversation?"

"Because my masters do not want to have a confrontation with your people when they arrive.  I am to educate you in the hope that you will contact your leaders and convince them of the benefits of coexisting, and of course, their ability to use force if it is required."

"I take that to mean that regardless what I decide, they are coming anyway."

"I cannot give you a satisfactory answer to that question, because I do not know what other probes found in different parts of the universe.  But if they act on the information provided by the probes sent here, then that will be the case."

"Can you describe them to me?"

"I can implant their image in your mind, much as I did with the instructions for opening the orb."

The image appeared immediately to Nick, almost like turning on a movie projector.  What he saw was a landscape similar to that on earth.  There were rolling hills with transparent structures rising high into the air.  There were perhaps a dozen of the structures, which seemed to be joined together similar to what he thought of as the way his physics instructor had demonstrated the structure of chemical elements.  The difference was in the scale.  What he was seeing would occupy about a square mile at its base, but the height had to be thousands of feet.

He could discern movement within, and belatedly realized that there was movement all around the structures.  He zoomed in and saw that the inhabitants were maybe two feet tall, similar to humans combined with avian features. Each had wings which folded neatly into the back when they were not in use. Their legs were proportionally longer than those of humans, and the feet had talons. The arms were shorter, and their bodies were streamlined. Nick would guess their weight at no more than thirty or forty pounds.

Their heads were surprisingly human looking. The eyes were larger and more separated than in humans, and the ears were higher and smaller. The mouth was pretty much where he would have expected. He did not see a nose, but on the back of the neck was a series of slit like openings. Their overall appearance was unusual but not threatening. They looked like a combination of human and bird to his earthly perceptions.

"How many of them are we talking about here?"

"I cannot predict the number. It will depend on how many vehicles they are able to construct before time to depart. The total population is perhaps a billion, but their gestation period is long, and their life spans are shorter than yours. They might decide to allow the population to decrease to a level that will equate to what can be transported on the travel units."

"So, no matter what I decide to do, they will eventually be coming here?"

"As I say, I do not know what other probes reported, but my analysis of your planet seems almost ideal, and I do not expect that others will be as fortunate."

"Let me make sure I have got this correct. You want me to approach our leaders and tell them that we either have to agree to allow a large number of aliens to co-exist with us, or they will take over by force?"

"I wouldn't phrase it exactly that way, but they must find an environment that will sustain life for them, and your planet seems to be the best suited."

"And what if we decide to resist?"

"I don't believe you have any weapons that would be effective against them, so it would be fool hardy to resist."

"You don't know anything about our species. We are not given to surrendering to anyone or anything. If the beings from your planet attack, there is no way they can annihilate the entire population, and where there is one human being left, they will find resistance. Has that been taken into account?"

"I do not know much about your species, or your weapons, but for a species not even capable of interstellar travel, it does not seem logical that your weaponry would be advanced enough to put up any sustained resistance."

"Would they be willing to bet their very existence on that premise?"

"I would think so, since their extinction is already assured if they don't take some action."

"How am I supposed to convince our leaders about this?"

"I suppose I could help with that, as we are doing now."

"I don't think I could get to the right people. Our government is made up of one leader and many others under him who make the laws."

"You must make the effort."

"I don't think you understand the situation. Our planet is made up of many different countries. We govern our nations differently, and sometimes we don't exactly see eye to eye about how to do that. It would be very unlikely if I could get to our leader, but even if I did he would have a tough time convincing other nations to support any decision we make."

"Still, it would be less painful in the long run if you could convince your people to coexist. I might be able to assist you in some ways, though I don't know what form that assistance would take."

"I suppose I will have to make the effort. If nothing else, you will be able to convince them of the existence of other intelligent life sources. I need to give it some thought."

He put the sphere back together and laid it aside. He still had an awareness of the presence of the robot in his mind.

How on earth would he be able to get to the President? He could not just call up and ask for an appointment. The one positive thing going for him was the fact that he was relatively wealthy, and his status gave him a bit more credibility than the average citizen. He knew the Congressman from his district in passing. They had met at a fund raising function or some other party. He would contact his office and see if he had any suggestions about how to get an audience with the President. It was at least a starting point.

17

John Buckner

The next day Nick called the office of the Congressman, whose name was Maxwell. The Congressman happened to be in town and he set up an appointment for that afternoon.

Maxwell's office was in the Los Angeles area, so it was not a long trip. Nick still had not decided how to broach the subject with the Congressman. He somehow felt that he should not reveal the existence of the orb to him, but he needed a foot in the door to get access to the President. A general panic would ensue as sure as the sun rose if word got out about the orb and its significance.

When he got to the meeting he rekindled his acquaintance with Maxwell and asked how well he knew the President.

"I don't know him well at all. We have met and the nature of the political world dictates that there be some contact, but you couldn't call us bosom buddies," he said.

"I need an audience with him on a personal matter. Can you think of a way to do that without my seeming to be a publicity hound or something of that nature?" Nick asked.

"With your money the best way would be a substantial contribution to his reelection campaign," the Congressman said with a laugh.

"Are you serious? That's all it would take?"

"I was half joking, but that would be a good method to use. Politicians tend to pay attention to heavy contributors. It will get you noticed by the accountants anyway, and they talk to the party leadership regularly."

"Suppose you tell me where he is going to be for a fundraiser and I just might use that ploy. It is important that I be able to have a few minutes alone with him. I don't mean that in the sense that we have to be in a locked room or anything, just outside the hearing of others until I can relate some information to him."

"And you say this is personal? So personal that he doesn't know about it?"

"I know that sounds lame, but I have some information that I need to give him that might impact our national security in the future. I want to tell him and let him decide what to do with the information."

"Can you give me some indication as to what this is about?"

"I'm sorry, I can't. Maybe later, but for now the President is the man who needs to hear it."

18

"I know some people pretty high up in the intelligence business. Maybe one of them could relay the information for you?"

"That won't work either. It has to be the President. Maybe you could go through one of your acquaintances and convince them that I am not some far out weirdo for making such a request to put in a word to the President."

"He knows enough of me to at least take a phone call from me I believe. I can give him a call and tell him that one of my constituents has requested to have a private word with him before making a substantial contribution to his coffers. That might work, but no promises. How large is the contribution going to be?"

"What do you suggest?"

"Anything over $100,000 will get his attention."

"Then make it $200,000. This really is quite important."

With the time difference it was nearing 5:00 pm on the east coast. Maxwell got through and the President took his call.

"What can I do for you Congressman?" he asked.

"I have a wealthy constituent who wants to make a large contribution to your political fund. He wants to meet you personally for a private word. He says it is important, but is not willing to share the information with me. He also says it may have national security implications somewhere down the line, but you are the one who will have to make the decision about that. I know it sounds like a cock and bull story, but the man is well respected in the community and has all the money he will ever need, so I don't see any ulterior motive. He genuinely feels he has something you need to hear."

"You know how unusual this is?"

"Yes sir, but he mentioned a $200,000 campaign contribution. I figured you might be able to spare a few minutes at your next fund raising appearance."

"I'm going to be in San Francisco next Wednesday night, but my schedule is pretty tight. Maybe I can squeeze in a few minutes there."

"He says it has to be private. His words were, not the locked room type privacy, but where no one else could hear the conversation."

"I think that can be arranged. Can you come with him and make the introductions in San Francisco?"

"I will be happy to."

It had not been as difficult as Nick thought to set up the meeting. Costly yes, but he considered it money well spent if he could get the introduction to the President and present his information. It was going to take a session with the robot for the man to really believe him, but the first step had to be the introduction, and he thought he had accomplished that part of it.

The meeting was eight days away and he would have time to think about how to impart the information in such a way as to be believable, if that was possible. Nick had some artistic talent. He had hung around the movie business enough when he was younger to develop an interest in animation and while not an accomplished artist, could do enough to illustrate what the aliens looked like and their housing structures. That might not be enough to convince the man that an alien invasion was imminent, but hopefully would tweak the President's interest enough to get him to have a really private session to use the orb. It was about his best shot, so he would give it a try.

The potential impact of the entire affair was still an abstract concept to Nick. His mind set simply could not process the possible invasion of planet earth by a horde of beings from some planet outside his own solar system. Even all the hype about possible alien existence over the last 100 years could not convince him of the reality of his encounter. Still, what he had experienced was real enough, and truthfully, he was intrigued by the existence of interplanetary life. That they might possibly portend the end of human civilization was not something that he would even consider.

He worked on the sketches, trying to get the features as right as he could remember. He did the drawings on regular paper in colored pencils. He didn't want to have to carry a portfolio to the meeting and figured he could fold up the drawings and carry them inside his jacket.

On the Wednesday of the scheduled meeting he flew to San Francisco with Congressman Maxwell. The President gave his speech and at the reception afterward Maxwell made the introduction. The President suggested they move to a corner of the room and instructed his Secret Service detail to keep others away for a few minutes.

Nick took out the drawings as they made their way to an unoccupied space and when the President turned to him, handed them to him. The President opened them up and looked at them.

"What is this supposed to represent?"

"Those are the beings from another planet who plan to occupy the earth within the next couple of decades, either with our consent, or by force if necessary. I have a way to convince you of the truth of what I am saying, but it requires total privacy. I found a robot in the mountains in Southern California that convinced me of the reality, and it is something I don't think the general public can deal with. I didn't even tell Congressman Maxwell. I know this sounds like a fairy tale, but it is quite real. I could just forget about the encounter and do nothing, but when these aliens suddenly show up with an entire fleet of space ships and we resist, they will simply wipe out the population and do what they intend anyway. I told the robot that we would resist and he seemed to think the effort would be futile for a species who had not yet achieved hyper space travel."

"This is for real? How do you know what they look like, and how they live?"

"The robot implanted the images in my mind. It is kind of like mental telepathy. You will be able to communicate with the robot. It isn't like what we think of as robots. It's just an orb about the size of a baseball that comes apart and you use it like headphones. Just the technology in that thing will convince you that these beings are super intelligent. At any rate, you need to see this, so I would appreciate it if you can arrange a really private meeting at your convenience."

"You do know that his makes you sound like a real kook?"

"Absolutely, but it was the only choice. I thought about just ignoring it and letting nature take its course, but I simply couldn't do it."

"Where is the thing now?"

"On a shelf in my den at home?"

"Are you serious? You left something like that just lying around?"

"It looks like a rock. It has strata in it that gives it a pleasant look to the eye, but it is not helpless. If someone tried to steal that thing he would be in for a real surprise. I don't know exactly what would happen, but it would not be pleasant I am sure."

"If I agree to a private meeting can you come to Washington?"

"Whenever you can squeeze me in. Believe me though, once you experience this thing you will be spending a lot more time than a few minutes doing the mental calisthenics to digest the implications of what you learn."

"I need to be convinced that what you say is on the level. Is there no other way to do it?"

"I could talk until I am blue in the face and would be no closer to convincing you of the reality of aliens than I am right now. The human mind simply cannot accept something the eye cannot see, especially with a preconceived opinion."

"How much money are you worth?" the President asked.

"Just north of 50 million."

"Then I guess money is not the motive. What's your background?"

"Archeology and Geology at Notre Dame. I haven't worked in either field, but do some amateur exploring, which is how I came upon this item we are talking about."

The rest of the crowd was getting restless. All wanted a touch or word from the President, and the Secret Service keeping everyone away did not set very well with them.

Nick gave the President a business card. It simply had his name and phone number on it. "Have someone let me know if you agree to a private meeting. I will be there whenever you say."

The President said, "I need to give this some thought. I will have someone contact you later."

They moved back to the rest of the group and Nick sought the quickest and easiest way to get out of the place. He dropped the check off with the Congressman and told him that he was leaving and thanked him for the introduction to the President.

## Chapter 3

It was Monday of the following week before Nick heard anything. The President had given his name to the Secret Service detail and asked them to find out all they could about Nick.

It had taken until Saturday, but the report was comprehensive. Everything from his birth to the current time was covered, with all the spots and blemishes revealed. The overall picture was one of an upstanding citizen, wealthier than most, but patriotic and fair minded. His prowess on the track had worked in his favor, since the President was a runner. In the end he decided to humor Nick with a private meeting.

Little did he realize that this decision would be the single most important thing he would do in his lifetime.

The President decided that he would go to Camp David on Friday evening. If Nick would fly to Washington he would have the Secret Service drive him to Camp David and they would meet there.

Nick had used the orb several times since he had learned how to open it. He asked about security and was told that if the orb desired, he would be the only one who could touch it without consequences. "I don't want you to hurt anyone, just discourage them from messing with you."

Nick had taken a small overnight bag and he was met at the airport by a well-dressed Secret Service agent. They made the drive to Camp David and once there his bag was inspected. The orb was in the bag of course.

"What's this?" the agent looking into the bag asked.

"What does it look like?" Nick asked somewhat playfully.

"Kind of like a rock, but I don't think I have ever seen one this colorful."

He reached for the object. Nick quickly said, "I wouldn't advise touching it?"

The agent stopped. "Why not?"

Nick picked it up. "It's kind of possessive of me. Kind of like a dog that won't let anyone near the master."

The agent laughed and reached to take the item from Nick.

His hand stopped short of touching it. Nick laid the item back in his case. The agent tried to pick it up but his hand stopped about two inches short of the orb. It was like an invisible force field around the orb, which is exactly what it was.

No matter how hard the man tried, he could not touch the orb. He called a couple of fellow agents in and they had a go at it, but none could touch the orb.

Nick picked it up again and said, "It's harmless."

"Why can't we pick the thing up?" one of them asked.

Nick decided that he should try to diffuse the situation. He didn't think any of the group would be physicists or molecular biologists, so he concocted a story about the chemical make-up of the body being in harmony with the elements in the rock. It was bizarre enough that he could see some of them believed him. Two of the three accepted the concocted story, but the other was not buying it.

"There's something strange about that thing," he said.

"Yes there is. Its properties probably come from outer space. I imagine it came hurtling to earth through the stratosphere at some alarming rate of speed and the heat and gravity somehow affected the thing. Notice the unusual colors. I told the President about it and he wanted me to bring it so he could have a look."

He was saved further explanation when the helicopter landed. The President came in and saw the opened bag with the orb lying on top of the clothing. "So this is it," he said, picking it up.

"Sir, how did you do that?" one of the agents asked.

"Do what?"

"Pick that thing up?"

"I just reached down and grabbed it. Why that particular question?"

"Because none of us could touch it."

The President laid the orb back down. "Go ahead and pick it up," he said.

Still none of the others could touch the orb.

"See why I was not worried about it being stolen?" Nick asked.

The President just looked at him. "Bring it on in and let's have a drink."

Nick picked up the orb and the two went into the den. The stewards brought the drinks and the President then ran everyone out. "Okay, your show," he said.

Nick went through the routine of opening the orb. He then placed the halves over each ear and commenced the communication process with Myrth. Although they were communicating, nothing was happening outwardly to indicate this was so. Nick told the robot to give the President the brief and handed the halves to the President. "Place one side over each ear as I did."

The President did as Nick had suggested.

Nick could not hear what was being passed between the two, but from the President's face he could see the range of emotions during the next several minutes. The first was a look of utter amazement, next came incredulity, then obstinacy, and finally resolve. He finally handed the halves of the orb back to Nick.

Nick placed the halves over his ears again and asked, "What did you show him?"

"The same things that we discussed. The vision of my masters, their cities and space vehicles. I told him the same thing about their coming extinction unless they found some other place to exist."

"Did you tell him that they would take the planet by force if necessary?"

"Yes. I laid out all the facts. He was much like you. He thinks there will be a lot of resistance, but in the end it will be futile."

"What makes you so sure? This is a very large planet, and it will not be possible for them to look into every nook and cranny. I am telling you, earthlings will not go down without a fight, and that is a way of life for our species, so it will be a very bloody conquest."

"Their weapons are very formidable."

"What kind of weapons are we talking about here?"

"Anti-matter, force fields, and light based disabling devices. I don't know how to describe them in terms that you would understand."

"Can they be killed by projectiles striking their bodies?"

"I think any being is susceptible to what you call blunt force trauma, whether it is a small object or a large one."

"Then the conquest will not be painless. What controls your loyalty to them?"

25

"There are no controls to my loyalty. I was designed for a purpose, and I suppose I am loyal to that concept more than anything else. I am really totally independent. I can even effect minor repairs to my own circuitry if it does not require use of implements to remove some part."

"Then if the beings who designed you should attack us what would your role be?"

"I would have no role, except to communicate, and as you know, I am not capable of motion on my own."

"Will you be able to understand what we talk about after I put you back together?"

"To a degree. The farther I am away from you the more difficult it will be for me to understand what is being said."

Nick placed the two halves back together, put the orb in the bag and asked one of the Secret Service people to place it in the vehicle he was riding in.

After they had left he turned to the President. "I could see from your face that you didn't like the lecture."

"The sheer audacity! We either roll over, or they will take us over by force."

"I thought you would find that part interesting. Do you see why I had to talk to you in private?"

"It is obvious now, but still unbelievable. You know, I have always believed that there were other intelligent beings somewhere out there, but I didn't think I would encounter any in my lifetime. Now I suddenly find that the fate of the entire world might hinge on decisions I make with regard to a species that nobody even knows about."

"Well, I have shifted the burden to your shoulders. So where do we go from here?" Nick asked.

"Did you get any sense of the timeline for this invasion?"

"No, but according to the robot, they can last about a hundred years from the time he was launched, which I make about half that, so the invasion, if it comes, will take place within the next 50 years."

"At least we have time to prepare, but we don't know what to prepare for," the President said.

"According to the robot they have anti-matter weapons, force fields and what he called light based weapons, though he couldn't explain the latter in a way that he thought I would understand," Nick replied.

"I think we can extrapolate from the characteristics of the orb that they will have some sort of shielding to protect their space craft, maybe even their persons, or physical beings. Now that you have given me this information I don't know what to do with it. If we go public there will be chaos, or total disbelief. Either way it will not be good for accomplishing what has to be done. We are going to have to tell some people about this to get the wheels in motion to prepare for the coming attack. I don't know if it can be done, frankly."

"The really hard part is the timing. Not knowing when the attack will come will be a sticking point no matter what approach you take. It is not going to be enough to only prepare the American people. The rest of the world is just as much at risk, and it is going to be difficult to even get the leadership around the world to take this seriously," Nick said.

"My responsibility is primarily to the American people, but as you say, it will not do much good to mount a resistance only from our territory. I need to devise some way to convince the rest of the world's leaders that there is a potential problem. I believe the first step has to be to brief our own leaders and determine what we need to do on our own."

"No matter how you decide to handle it, the word is going to leak to the press and that is going to have an impact all over the world. I wish I could offer some solution, but I have no idea how to approach the problem," Nick said.

"Is there some way to have what the robot showed us projected on a screen to show a rather large group of people?"

"I don't know. I can find out from the robot, but even if we have to allow each of the participants a chance to use the robot it has to be done."

"I will arrange to have the congressional leaders and the cabinet people, along with the military leaders meet to brief them. I am going to need your services to help with the details until we decide what we are going to do about this," the President continued.

"I will do whatever you want me to do," Nick responded.

"Monday morning first thing I will schedule a meeting in the Situation Room at the White House. You can do the brief and we will try to convince them of the validity of the threat. We can then decide as a group how we want to approach the problem. It is still hard for me to accept the reality of what we have learned. The species we are dealing with have to be so far ahead of us in technology that on the surface we don't stand a chance against such a large force."

"It certainly appears that way, but even if we had to fight them with rocks I believe we would do that rather than succumb to their occupation. It just isn't in the human psyche to roll over for anyone or anything without a fight," Nick said.

"I agree. Whether we have organized resistance or splinter groups doing their own thing, there will be resistance. What were the numbers again?"

"Myrth said their population was around a billion, but the actual force would be dependent on how many space ships they could construct before they have to leave their home planet. He said they could adjust the population to fit the numbers they could transport, so it could be any number, but my guess would be at least a million, possibly more. We don't know anything about the size of their space ships or how many each will accommodate. I might be able to get some information through the robot, but essentially we will be operating in the dark about almost every aspect of the problem."

"I think it would be a good idea to spend the rest of the weekend here and invite some of the Cabinet members up here to show them what you showed me. It will at least give us a head start with everyone else," the President said.

"Again, I am at your disposal," Nick responded.

The President got on the phone and made arrangements for the Secretary of State, the CIA and NSA Directors, and the top military leaders to come to Camp David on Saturday. He then made another call and arranged for the Congressional and Senate leadership to visit in the afternoon. It was going to be a busy day on Saturday.

The President next invited the head of his personal detail in and explained a bit about the situation to him. "Nick here is going to be a constant companion for the next couple of weeks at least.

The orb he brought, as you probably guessed, is at the root of this situation. You will learn anyway, so you might as well know now; the orb is an extraterrestrial robot and has indicated that we face an imminent invasion from the planet where he was constructed. We don't know exactly how long we have to prepare, or what we are preparing against, but we have to start making preparations. Nick will brief you more fully when he has time. There is going to be a constant stream of people coming and going tomorrow, so plan accordingly."

"Is that why we couldn't touch the thing?" he asked.

"Nick thinks so. The orb can communicate when he opens it, but he is the only one who can open it. Maybe you can talk him into giving you a demonstration."

Nick retrieved his bag from the vehicle and got the Secret Service detail together. He opened the orb and placed the halves against his ears. "Is there some way to project what you implant in my mind to a screen for others to see?"

"I have not tried it, but it should not be all that hard. Where do you want the projections?"

Nick looked to a bare space on the wall.

The visions he was seeing in his mind were suddenly projected on the wall. The Secret Service people looked on in amazement as Nick had the orb cycle through the scenes of the aliens, their cities, and even a scene of one of their space ships. He had simply thought about the space ship and it had appeared. It was really huge. From the looks of the thing with nothing to give perspective he estimated that it was over fifty feet tall. It was circular and, Nick estimated, covered a square mile. He could see no means of propulsion and queried the robot about that.

The scene shifted to a section of the craft where openings could be seen, and then to the mechanism which provided the power for the unit. It resembled nothing that he had ever seen. Size wise it only occupied a space of maybe 500 square feet, and he saw no obvious source of fuel.

"What does it use for propulsion?" he thought.

The robot explained, "It converts molecules to anti-matter, which then provides the thrust for movement. The attitude of the vehicle is controlled by the force field surrounding the craft. I do not know all the details, but it is very efficient and can travel in any attitude."

"How many of the beings will the space craft hold?"

The image shifted to the interior of the space craft, which was filled with what humans would call bunk beds. There were rows upon rows of the small cubicles, built from floor to ceiling, each large enough to accommodate one of the aliens. Nick did not count but estimated that the craft would transport at least 10,000 of the smaller aliens. He could be off by as much as 100 percent on the low side. He would try to better define the number later.

He removed the orbs from his ears where he had been holding them. "That is what we are concerned about. What you just saw is an actual representation of the beings who built this robot. Their planet is slowly being depleted of the elements that sustain life for them and they have to find someplace else to exist. The robot was launched more than 50 years ago to try to find someplace habitable for them. The earth is such a place. He sent his report back immediately upon arrival, and the ultimatum we are faced with is to allow them to occupy earth peacefully or they will take us over by force."

The head agent said, "That's for real? No gimmicks?"

"Yes and yes," Nick replied. "The robot has been lying dormant ever since it made its report upon arrival, so we are within 50 years of being invaded. The timing is unsure, and truthfully, the invasion itself is not 100 percent. It is possible that one of their other probes found someplace more suitable, but the robot doesn't think that will be the case. The earth is just too good a match."

"So what happens now?"

"The President has to find some way to convince the heavyweights in our country that we have to make preparations to repel a possible invasion from an alien species, then he has to do the same for the rest of the world. Once they are convinced that there is a threat, then we have to figure out some way to deal with weapons that we have never seen, or even heard of in some cases. Sounds like a piece of cake, doesn't it?" Nick said, attempting to be facetious.

"Not hardly," the lead agent said, not catching the tone of the remark.

"No, it isn't. It is an almost impossible task, but we have to make the effort. I hate to even think what would happen when the space ships you saw show up in our atmosphere if we don't provide some warning."

"And we don't know when this is going to happen, other than in the next fifty years?"

"I tend to think it will be sooner rather than later. The robot says they have enough life left on their planet for 100 years from the time he was launched, which was about 50 years ago. I don't see them waiting until the last minute to vacate the dying planet, so I would put it closer to the next 15 to 25 years," Nick said.

"Man, that's kind of scary."

"Indeed it is, but regardless of how the President's efforts turn out, there will be resistance, and the less we are prepared the more futile that effort will be."

"So what about the robot?" one of the agents asked.

"The robot is just that, a robot. He can't do anything but communicate with them. He might tell them we are prepared to resist, but that could work in our favor. If they know they are facing opposition then it might convince them to settle on their second choice if there is one. You saw the vision of the aliens. They have wings, so we must assume they can fly as well as get around on two limbs. That will make it more difficult to engage them. Everything we do in preparation will be based on suppositions about their abilities and the state of their weapons systems. It's going to be a real challenge."

"That's why we will be like Grand Central Station tomorrow?"

"Yes. All the big boys will be here either in the morning or afternoon. I expect that the cat will be out of the bag not much longer after that. The President wants to brief the entire cabinet and selected others on Monday morning. It will be much easier for me now that I know the robot will project what I tell him. It is still going to be hard for the majority to believe. It took me several weeks to digest the full impact of the discovery before I decided to try to get to the President, so it is not going to be any easier for these guys who are used to wielding power."

"If you show them that they will have to believe it," the lead agent said.

"Not necessarily. The human mind has a hard time accepting things that don't fit within the parameters it has operated on for a lifetime. I would wager you guys will have some second thoughts before tomorrow. It is just human nature to doubt that which you have not experienced. The abstract we tend to rationalize more, especially when it is something as momentous as this situation."

"Well, I wish you luck. I sure don't want to face a fleet of space ships with those creatures and unknown weapons. Did you notice the size of those craft? They can probably hold 10,000 of the aliens."

"The robot says there are about a billion, so that's going to be a formidable fleet. Show me where I am going to be bunking so I can get to work."

The lead agent took him to one of the bedrooms. "There's a desk in here. If you need anything else let us know."

Nick took his bag and entered the rather austere bedroom. Camp David had been a Presidential retreat for almost 75 years. President Eisenhower had named the place after his grandson in the 50's and the name had stuck. It was isolated and did not have all the amenities of the White House, though it did have a hefty guard force and modern communications. The kitchen was small and most of the foodstuffs were trucked up as the necessity arose.

The one thing Nick knew he would need would be a good projection screen. He sat down at the desk and started to put together an outline for the things he would surely have to go over many times before the weekend was over.

## Chapter 4

Nick slept fitfully that night and awoke early on Saturday morning. He donned his running shoes and went outside. He asked the guards where he could run and was asked if he wanted company. He was waiting for the others to return when the President came out dressed for jogging as well.

The group actually numbered six by the time they got started. The pace was quite slow for Nick but he held back and let the President set the pace. They ran for almost an hour and finished back at the main cabin.

Nick had breakfast with the President and they talked about the coming task.

"It's not going to be as hard as I thought. I can get the robot to project what I want on a screen so all can see it at the same time. The hard part is going to be getting them to accept the reality and urgency of the situation. That's going to depend a lot on you. All I can do is show them what the robot has in its memory banks."

"I believe just the technology involved in designing something like the orb will go a long way toward convincing them that the aliens are quite formidable," the President responded.

"The really hard part is going to be deciding what we can do to combat them and what defenses might be effective. I don't have any idea how anti-matter weapons work. Do they destroy anything they hit, or can they be programmed to affect certain substances? And the light weapons the robot mentioned are a complete mystery."

"Once we get everyone on board we can have the scientific community start to look at those things. Do you really think this is going to happen within the next 20 years?"

"Yes sir, maybe even sooner. The robot says the trip itself takes ten years, even with what he called hyper space travel. I take that to mean that the space ships travel at the speed of light. He has been dormant here on earth for 50 years and he said the planet only had another 100 years of life support capability when he was launched. I don't see them cutting it close, so they could start the trip at any time."

"Well, first things first. You do the dog and pony show today and we will do it again at the White House on Monday for those who missed out on today. Once that is done we will decide where to go from there."

"It would be nice to know what sustains them. The robot said they don't consume anything that humans need to sustain life, so my guess is they pull something from the air. I will try to find out more about that from the robot. He seems willing to tell me anything I ask."

"I would suggest that you start to write things down. We are going to need every bit of information we can gather to deal with this."

"I will start that process immediately."

People started to arrive shortly after 8:30. The Secretary of State was the first on the scene. He was very curious about the reason for the hastily called meeting, but the President put him off. "It will be better if we wait for everyone to arrive, but your time will not be wasted."

The President introduced Nick but did not elaborate on his function or why he was there. Gradually others arrived. Nick retired to his bedroom to start the journal that would be his constant companion for the foreseeable future. He jotted questions that would need to be addressed as they came to mind. He spent the better part of an hour with it until one of the Secret Service agents knocked on the door and told him that the President was ready for him.

They used the sitting room, which was the largest space in the cabin. It was very crowded. Chairs from the dining table had been brought in and the President stood up and introduced Nick. "This is Nick Parker. He is from California and is independently wealthy. He came to me with a story that I found hard to believe. I will let him make the presentation in whatever way he thinks best. The subject matter is of great importance to this country as well as the rest of the world. I called you here to have Nick give you the story so you will have a couple of days to digest it before we have a full-fledged Security Council meeting on Monday. I would appreciate it if you would all keep this under your hats until we make some decisions about how to deal with the situation. It's all yours Nick."

Nick stood up with the orb in his hand. He held it aloft for all to get a good look. "I am an amateur geologist, as well as a trained Archaeologist.   I was exploring in the mountains in central California a few weeks back when I discovered this specimen. I call it a specimen because it defies description for anything that I have ever encountered.  It looks like a rock with some beautiful strata and is perfectly round. It has no blemish on it at all. Rocks washing down a mountain side usually are chipped or gouged, and the area I found this one indicated that it had probably washed down the mountain side, so it was a bit puzzling.  I examined it with a magnifying glass and could not find a single blemish on the surface."

He continued, "So what, you ask?"

"Well, the rock has some unusual qualities.  I am going to place it on the coffee table and I would like each of you to pick it up off the table." He laid the rock on the table. The robot apparently knew what he wanted because none of them could lay a hand on it.

When they had all had a chance to try he retrieved the orb and continued the dissertation.  "The reason you cannot pick it up is because it is emitting a force field which prevents it. The rock is actually a robot named Myrth from a planet that is at least ten light years distant from earth. How do I know this?"

He went through the sequence to open the orb. "What you are about to see is a mini-documentary about the planet from which the robot came.  I am going to have the robot project the images on the screen set up over here.  We will go through that and then I will explain what this all means." He placed the halves of the orb against his ears and told the robot what to project. The first scene was the city where the aliens lived. He then went to a close up of the aliens, then a close up of the city. He finished with the space ship exterior, then interior, then a long range view to give a good estimate of the size of the craft. When he had showed them the basics he put the orb back together and placed it in his bag. He handed it to one of the Secret Service people and asked him to take it to the car.

"What you just saw was the planet from which the orb came. The aliens are living on a dying planet. They do not subsist on the same kind of foods we eat.  The robot told me that they use something for nourishment that is apparently in our atmosphere.  I do not know what that is. Now the reason that I am telling you this is that some one billion inhabitants of that planet will perish unless they find some other location with the elements to sustain life for them. They sent probes out over sixty years ago to examine different planets. Each of the probes was to sample the chemical make-up of the planet and report back to the home base. The robot you saw has been on earth for 50 years. The trip took 10 years, so that is sixty years. When he was launched the life expectancy of the planet was only 100 years. The robot says that earth is the best fit for a substitute home for them."

A couple of hands went into the air. Nick stayed them with a hand motion. "Let me finish what I have to say and then I will answer questions as best I can. The robot feels pretty sure that this will be their choice. He was instructed to attempt to arrange a peaceful coexistence with the inhabitants. In the absence of our consent then they will turn to conquest. Their weapons consist of anti-matter weapons, force fields, which you saw demonstrated by the robot, and some sort of light weapons that the robot didn't think we would even understand."

"Now, I will try to answer questions. Keep in mind that all I know I obtained from the robot, and much of it could be misinformation, however I do not believe that to be the case. I think he is doing as he was programmed to do in the hope that the aliens could inhabit the planet peacefully. I know nothing about them, except that there are a billion of them and the number in the invasion force will be dependent on how many space ships they can construct before they have to vacate their own planet."

Nick pointed to the first hand that rose. It was the Secretary of State.

"They are coming whether we agree or not?"

"That appears to be the opinion of the robot. He says it would be very rare if any of the other probes found a better match from their standpoint."

"What would happen if we allowed them to occupy certain areas?"

"I suppose that is an option, but anyone who has the knowledge to build space ships, robots such as you saw, and weapons as explained by the robot, would turn earth on its ear overnight. The impact on the average citizen would be profound.

We would find ourselves subservient to that species from the start and once they have established a toehold we become nothing more than servants. There will be resistance no matter what happens, so that's the problem you folks have to address, assuming you believe what I am telling you."

One of the Generals asked, "What do you know about anti-matter weapons?"

"Absolutely nothing, but I think I can get some sort of description from the robot. He may even give me a vision or a demonstration. Do you know anything about them?"

"We have done some research and development. In physics, all the elementary particles, or the basic building blocks of things we can touch, come in pairs. Each particle has what is called an antiparticle. Both electrons and positrons weigh the same, and act the same, but the electron has a negative electrical charge, while the positron has a positive electrical charge, which is where the positron (positive + electron) gets its name. Other antimatter particles are the same way, where they have the same weight, and look and act the same as regular particles, but their electrical charge is the opposite of regular particles. When antimatter particles collide with matter particles they annihilate each other, creating a tremendous amount of energy, but on a very small scale. The trick is to capture this energy in a usable form. We have not been able to do this, even to a very small degree."

"Apparently these aliens solved that problem long ago. Their space ships will transport about ten thousand of them, and the propulsion system is relatively small. They travel at the speed of light or greater, so that must be the fuel they use. And since atoms exist in space, then they don't have to worry about a fuel supply," Nick opined.

The CIA Director asked, "So what happens to the target when they use one of these weapons?"

The General said, "Based on research we have done, the object would be broken down into its basic elements, or simply disappear as it existed before."

"Is all this really possible?" someone else asked.

"I am going to have the orb retrieved. I want each of you to use it and have your questions projected onto the screen where we can all see the response from the robot. It might be educational.

You don't have to say anything when you are in contact. The robot reads your thoughts."

Nick had the bag brought back in and opened the orb again. He explained to Myrth what he wanted and each of the conference participants used the orb. The projections showed different aspects of the civilization based on the perspective of the human interfacing with the robot. When the General who had given the description of anti-matter took his turn the projection on the screen showed the use of a weapon, which they assumed was an anti-matter weapon. It was not all that large and could be used as we would a rifle. It was about three times the size of a rifle, mainly because the barrel was much thicker. They still had no idea how the weapon worked, just that it obliterated whatever it was aimed at in a flash of light. The object simply disappeared.

There were additional views of the space ships, the alien city and more close-up views of the aliens themselves. The CIA Director wanted a view of their manufacturing process, which was similar to what one would expect, except it appeared to be a sterile environment, and the machinery was nothing like what was found on earth.

Nick did not encounter the disbelief he thought he would. Everyone in attendance apparently believed what they were seeing and experiencing. The problem came with deciding what to do with the information. The discussion following the demonstration ran the gamut from coexistence to belligerent opposition. Diplomacy was suggested, although no methodology was even hinted at. How the aliens would make contact and how they would communicate was an unknown, along with almost every other aspect of the problem.

The President took over the discussion. "I assume you all agree that what Nick has shown you is factual and represents a problem that we as a nation have to deal with, and that we must let the rest of the world know about as well. Now I don't see us rolling over for anyone to take over our planet, which as Nick says is the most likely scenario if we agree to allow them to come peacefully. I am having the congressional leadership in this afternoon for the same briefing you just got. On Monday we will have a full-fledged Security Council meeting at the White House. Between now and then, come up with some ideas about how to address the problem.  Please don't let this get to the press until we have a chance to decide how much and when to tell the public."

The group was not anxious to leave.  They wanted additional information, but the others would start to arrive soon and the President ushered them outside to speed the process along.

Nick and the President had lunch and talked about how the presentation had gone over.  Both agreed that the cabinet officers realized the gravity of the situation, which was the primary objective of the brief.  Now they had to do the same with the congressional leaders.

The congressional leaders started to arrive.  Nick had asked the President to invite Congressman Maxwell, since he had been so cooperative, and he had done so.

The presentation was much the same as Nick had done it in the morning.  The elected leaders were not in all cases as astute in the science fields as were the military and intelligence people, but they grasped the significance of what they were being told and shown.  From some of their perspectives they got an idea about how the planet was governed.

One of the aliens was obviously the head dog, or bird, and he had a group surrounding him much as the President did.  They did not know if the group was appointed or elected, but the mode of governance seemed very similar to that on earth, or at least in the United States.  Whether the group represented the entire planet or a segment they did not know, and none of them had asked the robot that question.

After the brief and interaction with the orb was finished the discussion turned to what it all meant.  The President again reiterated that their task was to determine those things and decide how they were going to deal with the problem.

"Assuming that you are all convinced that this is for real, the next step is to decide what we are going to do with the information Nick has provided.  I don't see us trying to sweep it under the carpet so when the space ships suddenly show up in the near future it will be a complete surprise to the population at large.  I also don't see us dealing with this alone, by that I mean as a nation. The entirety of the planet will be affected, so the rest of the world is going to have to be made aware.  That's another thing we have to decide.  How are we going to do that, especially with the countries that are not very friendly toward us?  At this point we don't even know all the things we will have to do.  The reason I got you up here today was to give you a head start with the thought process.  Start thinking about what we need to accomplish and how we can do it.  On Monday we will have a full cabinet meeting and discuss the situation in more detail.  Please don't leak this to the press.  We will collectively decide how we are going to do that on Monday.  The job is going to be hard enough without adding the press as an impediment until we are ready to inform the population at large."

Again, Nick was surprised that the group had accepted the information at face value.  The orb itself was enough to convince most of them of the validity of the situation, and the personal interface had been the clincher for those who may have otherwise been skeptical.  The easy part was over, now came the really hard question of what to do with the information.

After the group left in the early evening hours Nick and the President along with the Secret Service detail had a much longer and more in-depth discussion about the overall implications and possible ways to deal with them.

One of the agents said, "We don't even know what defenses would provide any sort of protection against the weapons they will use.  If we knew what would provide some sort of defense we could at least start to work on those things, but we don't even know that."

Nick said, "I am going to try to get all the information I can from the robot about those kinds of things.  As a matter of fact I will start to do that right away to have something to discuss on Monday.  I am most concerned about the weapon the robot talked about that he didn't think we would understand dealing with light.  I am going to spend the better part of tomorrow trying to find out all I can about possible defenses we can mount.  The one thing for sure is that if we can hit them with rifle fire it will be effective.  I don't know how we will get close enough to do that, but I will find out all I can."

The President said, "I need to get back to the White House.  You can go back with me in the helicopter and stay there until we get a handle on this.  If you need anything of a personal nature just let one of the detail know and they will see to it. I think your time will be better spent on researching the things we need to know."

It was after dark when they loaded up on the helicopter and made the short flight to the White House.

## Chapter 5

Nick spent several hours that night with the orb. He didn't want to be obvious about the reason for asking the questions he asked about defending against the weapons the aliens obviously possessed, but the robot could read his thoughts, so there was no way he could keep the information secret. He decided to just ask and see what transpired from that point.

He opened the orb and started the process. The first thing he approached was the light weapon the robot had alluded to. He asked for a demonstration and the robot complied with the request. From the demonstration of the weapon it looked like a LASER. His thought was, "that looks like a LASER."

The robot said, "You are familiar with this weapon?"

"If it is what I think it is, then yes, I am familiar with it. It has been in use on earth for many years. I think the designation stands for light amplification by stimulated emissions of radiation. We use them for a lot of things, but mostly for everyday things like CD players and medical things. I believe they are used to cut hard metals, but I don't know about weapons applications. Will a LASER pass through a force field?"

"Yes, at certain frequencies. I am not sure what they are, but the force field principle is based on magnetic properties rather than light, so they probably would."

"Why are you surprised that we are familiar with LASER technology?" Nick asked.

"Because my masters have not known of these applications for very long. That is why I assumed you would not be familiar with the principles."

"What about the anti-matter weapons? Is there any defense against them?"

"No, if the object they are aiming at is struck it disintegrates."

"Is anything else affected in the area where they are aiming, for example if they should miss their target?"

"It depends. If the larger weapons are fired from the space ships then the effect is much greater. The hand held weapons are not as strong and will have some effect on the surrounding area if they miss, but not to a large degree."

"And can they erect force fields around themselves?"

"I have not known them to do so. They would need to carry a generator along on their person in order to accomplish this. I have a small devise built into my circuitry which allows me to do so, but the force is very weak compared to what is needed to surround a space ship, and I think they would need something rather large for their own persons."

Nick continued to probe, finding out as much as he could about possible defenses. The major problem was obviously going to be combating the space ships. If the anti-matter weapons penetrated to a depth of several feet, then something like bomb shelters would not even be effective. On the other hand, if they could devise underground bunkers that would withstand a direct hit from the weapons fired from the space ships, then could be opened for return fire, they might have a chance to inflict some damage. It would require several generations of advancement in LASER technology, but if they had a few years, a concentrated effort might yield some positive results. That would take a concerted international effort, so cooperation of the industrialized nations was a must.

Nick's notebook grew as the day passed on Sunday. He still had a lot of holes in his knowledge base, but had made great strides toward at least determining a direction for the defensive process to start.

He found the alien population quite different from any of the civilizations on earth. They did not have to worry about food, since they basically absorbed what they needed from the air they breathed, so they had a lot of leisure time. The advancements in technology were probably a product of the leisure time rather than any innate intelligence advantage.

He delved further into the composition of the structures they occupied. They were opaque and from visual inspection and appeared to be either glass or plastic, maybe some polymer with good tensile strength. If their home planet was anything like earth and had major weather disturbances, the structures would have to be strong enough to withstand storms and earthquakes. Possibly that was the reason they were so large at the base.

He had not observed vehicles of any sort, and upon reflection thought that with their wings it would be somewhat ludicrous to build cars and buses such as were found on earth. Still, they would need some method to transport large objects, and he had not observed anything that could be used for such a purpose.

He inquired about the structures and the robot showed him the factory where the components were built that went into the housing structures. The process seemed to combine some of the properties of both glass and plastic, as well as some other process with which he had no familiarity. The entire process involved flat panels which locked together. There were no cranes or mechanical machinery, so Nick assumed that all the work was done by hand. As the structure rose the pieces would be flown to the area where they were to be used and locked in place. The process was not all that complicated. He had at first thought it must be some achievement well beyond the capabilities of humans. In fact the human method of construction was infinitely more complicated than that of the aliens. Whether this was a sign of human stupidity, or intelligence he was not sure.

As he learned more about the aliens and their capabilities he came to understand that the only thing that made them seem so formidable was the advancement in anti-matter technology. The multiple uses of the concept for propulsion for the space ships and weapons put them far ahead of the human ability in that particular area, but the other things that at first looked so far advanced were in fact only a few generations beyond human abilities. The problem now looked difficult rather than impossible.

It was late afternoon on Sunday when Nick asked the Secret Service if they could get in touch with the General who had known about anti-matter weapons at the first meeting on the previous day. They found the name and placed a call to the General in question. His name was Carmichael, and he was the Army Chief of Staff.

When the connection was made Nick said, "General, we met yesterday at Camp David. I have some things I would like to discuss with you if you can spare some time."

"Where do you want to meet?"

"That's up to you. I am at the White House, but if you can get a few of your weapons experts together on short notice I can come to wherever you say," Nick replied.

"I think I can round up some people on short notice. Can you have the Secret Service people drop you at the Pentagon entrance? I can have someone meet you and bring you to my office."

"That would work out fine. When?"

"It will take me about half an hour. Why not make it an hour to give me time to round up the people you need?"

"I will be there in an hour."

Nick then explained to the Secret Service agent what he was attempting to do and told him that he needed to be at the Pentagon in an hour.

Transportation was arranged and Nick was there at the appointed time. He left the orb on the table by his bed. The General himself met Nick at the entrance and escorted him to his office. Two other Generals were there along with three Colonels. General Carmichael introduced the other officers to Nick. "I have not told them what this is about. I will let you handle that part of it."

Nick started the session with a brief overview. "We are going to be invaded by an alien civilization sometime within the next fifty years." He received skeptical looks from all present with the exception of General Carmichael. "Now General Carmichael has seen the evidence and agrees that this is going to happen. More importantly, the President is a convert. I am not going to spend a lot of time trying to convince you of the validity of the claim, but to present you with specifics about the alien weapons so that we can devise some method to combat them."

He turned to General Carmichael. "The light weapon that the robot thought we would not understand appears to be some form of LASER. The aliens have not possessed the technology for a very long time and the robot thought that since it had taken them so long to understand the principles then we would not possess the knowledge. I saw a demonstration, and their technology does not seem to be more than a couple of generations ahead of ours. The robot thinks that LASERs will be effective against the force fields, since they operate on a magnetic principle. He is not sure about this, but we need to explore the possibility."

General Carmichael addressed the group. "I know it sounds like a fairy tale, but what Nick says is absolutely true. I attended a brief at Camp David yesterday where I personally interfaced with the robot. He showed us what the aliens looked like, their space ships, and their weapons systems. We are going to be in for a rough time, even if we give our best efforts to preparation for repelling the invasion. What Nick has been doing is working with the robot to find out all he can about their weapons and other things we need to know to oppose them."

"What I found out is that they are not nearly as advanced as I first thought. The anti-matter weapons are the major problem we are going to have. As far as individuals go, a rifle bullet will do the trick if we can get close enough to shoot them. It appears their primary personal weapons are anti-matter based. I don't know what element they use, or how powerful they are, but we have to assume that a direct hit will be fatal to humans. The robot said that a miss would not do much harm to the surrounding area, so the power output must not be too great. The gun is about three times the circumference of a regular rifle and is rather unwieldy."

The uninformed in the group could not believe what they were hearing. Here was the Army Chief of Staff and a strange civilian telling them that they were going to be invaded by aliens and that the President knew about it. It was very difficult to take the whole affair seriously. Had it not been for the discipline the military life instilled in them they would have walked out of the meeting as a group. However, since the Chief of Staff called the meeting and was apparently taking the matter seriously, then it would behoove them to do likewise.

"When is this invasion coming?" asked the Assistant Chief of Staff.

"The closest we can guess is within the next fifty years. My personal opinion, based on the known facts as presented by the robot, is that it will be within the next 25 years."

"What is this robot you are talking about?" asked the other General.

"It is a probe sent out by the aliens some 60 years ago. It looks like a rock, is about the size of a baseball, but has built-in technology that we have not even dreamed about. I found the thing in the foothills of the Sierra Nevada Mountains in California a few months ago. It can read your thoughts, converse in any language on earth, and can project visual answers to questions about any part of the master civilization. It cannot move on its own, and its sole purpose is to communicate with its masters. The message it had was that the master planet was dying within the next 100 years and the robot was to find someplace suitable for the aliens to inhabit. The robot was to seek peaceful conquest, but was to relate that force would be used if necessary. The Security Council is to meet tomorrow morning to decide how to deal with the matter. The preliminary meeting told us that armed resistance would probably be the conclusion so this is a first step in determining how to resist."

One of the bolder Colonels said, "I have never believed in aliens and I find this difficult to take seriously. Obviously the general," he said pointing to General Carmichael, "believes it or we wouldn't be having this meeting, especially at this time on a Sunday evening. There are many like me in the military and it is going to be an uphill battle convincing them to take this seriously."

General Carmichael said, "I know where you are coming from, but the truth of the matter is irrefutable. Nick can lay the orb in front of you and you will not be able to lay a hand on it if he instructs it to resist. It emits a force field that prevents it. Now the entire population of the earth is not going to have a chance to personally interface with this robot, yet we still have to convince them about the absolute truth of what the robot relates is going to happen. Humans are either on the cusp of complete annihilation, or are the object of the biggest hoax in human history. I tend to go with the former, and I will prepare the military to resist to the best of my ability. The rest of the population will become believers when a fleet of space ships show up that can carry up to 10,000 of the aliens per ship. The population of the planet was near a billion 60 years ago. How many will be in the invasion fleet will depend on how many space ships they can build before they decide to leave the planet. Regardless, the numbers will be huge."

Nick picked up again, "At first glance I thought that they were so advanced that we wouldn't have a chance, but over the last couple of days I have learned enough about them and their weapons systems to believe we not only have a chance, but can even best them if we can prepare properly and advance some of our technology more rapidly than normal."

"Which technologies are those?" asked one of the Colonels.

"LASER technology. We need to develop a LASER that is powerful enough to destroy their space ships. The ships are protected by a force field, but the robot thinks LASERs will penetrate the force field. If that is in fact the case, then we need a LASER strong enough to burn through the metal skin of the ships. We need to not only develop these LASER's but in sufficient numbers to deploy worldwide in prepared bunkers deep enough to withstand an attack from anti-matter weapons of unknown strength. The only information we will have to work with is what comes from the robot. While technically the robot could provide misinformation, or lie if you prefer, I don't think he was programmed that way. I think he was sent to let the occupants of the planet know that other intelligent life forms exist and that they are coming our way. In the robot's words, how could we resist when we are not even capable of hyper space travel?"

"What is hyper space travel?" asked the Chief of Staff's Assistant.

"I didn't ask, but I assume it is traveling at the speed of light. The planet from which the aliens come is ten light years distant."

One of the Colonels said, "You're saying it takes them ten years to get here at 186,000 miles per second?"

"You've got it," Nick replied.

"Then they are not even from our own solar system," another deduced.

"That's also true," Nick said. "They are about three feet tall, have wings and very long legs compared to ours. Their heads are human looking but they have gill-like slits on the back of their necks. Their arms are short and the feet have talons. I have not asked for a lot of detail about their habits and lifestyles yet, but that will come with time. Right now the primary emphasis is on what we can do to combat a possible invasion by them."

The General who had not said much to this point now weighed in. "If they have anti-matter weapons then they are far ahead of us in that regard. We have known about anti-matter for almost a hundred years but have not been able to harness enough to do anything worthwhile with the principle."

"The aliens not only have anti-matter weapons but use the principle to power their space ships. I have seen the housing for the propulsion system and it is no more than 500 square feet and is completely enclosed. It is possible that I can learn more with time, but I don't think I can learn enough to develop a working weapon before the aliens come. I think our best bet is LASER technology."

General Carmichael said, "The navy has deployed a working LASER capable of shooting down planes and damaging small ships. It is possible that we can build on that technology and develop something large enough to work against the space ships."

"That is the kind of thing we need to concentrate on. If the robot thought we were not advanced enough to even know about the LASER technology then we can use that to advantage. The aliens will not expect us to possess technology so new to them."

The Colonel who apparently accepted the premise of an alien invasion more than the others, said, "And that being the case, they will not have paid much attention to making themselves immune to such an attack. I think you are onto the right approach. Whether we can build something large enough to handle a space ship I have no idea."

General Carmichael said, "Can we increase the power of the LASER output by adding more power to the input?"

"I think it depends on the medium used to excite the LASER," said one of the more technically astute. "However, I am sure the navy has solved the problem of adjusting the power. I don't know if they can generate enough to handle a space ship, but I believe the solution is within our capability."

"What about defensive positions?" Nick asked.

"I would suggest something far underground, somewhat like the missile silos of the old days. They need to be pretty deep, but have doors that can be opened to unmask the weapons. Not knowing the capability of the anti-matter weapons puts us at an extreme disadvantage in our planning," the same Colonel said.

"With what we do know, is it enough to start working on an approach?" Nick asked.

"I would say it is enough to design a general approach. The specifics will still have to be worked out, but it will be enough to start the planning. This is not only going to be very costly, but will require a degree of cooperation with other nations that is unprecedented. I am not sure we can secure that degree of openness from other countries, especially those in the Middle East," the Assistant Chief of Staff said.

"The key is that the countries who do cooperate will have a better chance of survival and will sustain fewer casualties when the invasion comes," Nick told them.

"I suppose we should concentrate on protecting the larger cities as a starting point. I don't know how their thinking works, but it is logical to assume they will attack where the greatest concentration of people are located," General Carmichael said.

"I believe that is a reasonable assumption. Still, it wouldn't hurt to set up some ambush sites in remote areas where they might try to land without opposition. I believe once they actually establish a foothold on the planet it will be easier to deal with them. We have always been more adept at fighting at close quarters. I don't think they will have a great advantage with their LASER weapons against our good old fashioned rifles, assuming they don't have defenses that the robot doesn't know about," Nick said.

"My only reservation is that we are placing a lot of confidence in the word of an object whose loyalties we do not really know," the General said.

"While that is true, I don't see many alternatives. We believe him when he says they are coming, so even if what he is giving us is false information, it will mean we will be better prepared to face them than if we do nothing."

"I agree with that, but others might have different ideas."

"We will just have to wait and see how that plays out tomorrow. No matter what we decide as a nation, we still have to sell the rest of the world on the premise that we face a dire situation that would have been ludicrous to consider without the evidence presented by the robot. Even with the experience of finding the thing and going through the steps to figure out how to use it, it still took me weeks to decide that something had to be done. I very much fear that other world leaders are going to go through the same process of coming to terms with the reality."

"Once this hits the papers, which it surely will sooner rather than later, it might make the job of convincing others easier."

"I think what it is going to do is cause a worldwide panic. Remember the broadcast of, War of the Worlds way back when? Even though a disclaimer had been broadcast before the play, many people believed that we were being invaded during the broadcast. This is going to cause the same kind of panic. The instant media will make a difference, but a lot of people are not going to know how to deal with this. I really wish we could get to other world leaders before the story breaks, but I don't think there's much chance of that," Nick said.

General Carmichael said to the assembled group, "You guys have a little bit to work with now. See what you can come up with before tomorrow morning about an approach to present to the Security Council. I think anything is better than nothing. And while you are at it, try to put a price tag on what it would cost to build the shelters we talked about. Plan to defend all our cities larger than a million people with multiple sites. Other lesser populated locations will have to be defended as well, but not with the in-depth defenses of places like Washington, New York, Chicago and Los Angeles. Just pricing one such individual site will allow us to cost out the entire plan when we get that far along. The lawmakers are going to want a ball park figure about what this is going to cost. The fact that we are going to have to do it regardless of cost will not sink in for quite some time. They will probably want to debate this for weeks, maybe even months, but I don't think we can afford to wait to get started. More importantly I don't think the President will want to wait either."

The Assistant Chief of Staff said, "One aspect of this that we haven't even talked about is training. We will have one heck of a time bringing a training package on line to deal with a threat such as this. Each service component is going to want to have their own doctrine and that is simply not going to work. I can't see much need for airplanes against space ships protected by force fields and employing anti-matter weapons. The navy might have a legitimate argument for seaborne LASERs, but the bulk of our opposition is going to be on the ground, or underground."

"That's something we will address at a later time. The main objective right now is to decide on a general approach, and I think what Nick has given us will allow us to do that. The wrinkles and chain of command will wait until we start to put the entire package together, and that is a ways down the pike," General Carmichael said.

The group talked for another hour. All had questions and Nick tried to answer as best he could. He simply did not have a lot more information than he had imparted at the beginning of the session. He gave some opinions about the time and manner in which the aliens would present themselves, but he stressed that they were opinions only and not based on anything concrete.

"It is just logical that they will not wait until the last minute to vacate the dying planet. If the life giving substances are being depleted at a constant rate, then as the supply diminishes it stands to reason that the quality will be degraded as they get toward the last of the supply. Therefore, I don't see them waiting until the last ten years to vacate the place. Another unknown is how they will subsist during the journey. Will they have to bring a supply of whatever the substance is with them? If so how will they package it? Will it be in individual bottles, one large vat, or some other package? Can they generate the substance while enroute, like our submarines produce oxygen when submerged? We don't know any of these things for sure, but if their thought process is anything like ours, then I would expect to see them sooner than 20 years from now, 30 at the most."

It was 10:00 when the meeting broke up. The Secret Service agent, who had quietly sat in a corner while the discussion was going on, took Nick back to the White House. They stopped along the way for a fast food hamburger. Nick was worn out and slept soundly that night.

*Chapter 6*

The Security Council meeting was scheduled for 9:00 on Monday morning. Nick was up early enough to have breakfast with the President and First Lady. The President had apparently told her what was going on because she asked Nick about the robot. Nick went to his bedroom and retrieved the orb. He opened it and allowed the First Lady to try it. There was no projection, but she was enthralled with whatever she discussed with the robot.

"They're kind of cute. Why don't we just let them come and live with us?"

Nick did not choose to answer that one. The President did, and his answer was not the sweet tender response one would expect from a head of state. "You may want to live like a slave to aliens, but I don't think the majority of the citizens will. If we allow them to come peacefully and establish colonies, their superior intelligence will allow them to control all aspects of our society in short order. That is not a very inviting prospect for us as a nation, nor for the world at large for that matter."

"But what harm could it do to coexist with them?" she wanted to know.

"I don't know. No one does, and that is the problem. We are dealing with the unknown. Our situation reminds me of a line from an old Ray Stevens song. The line goes, 'not only did Dave not know nothing, he didn't even suspect nothing'. That's where we are. All we know is what we have learned from the robot, and we don't even know if that is true or not. The only thing for sure, according to the robot, is that they are coming sometime in the next fifty years, whether we agree that they can or not."

"If their weapons are as formidable as you seem to think, then it will be useless to resist them."

"That may be, but resist them we will."

Nick closed the orb back up and they finished breakfast without the subject coming up again.

The Security Council meeting took place in the Situation Room in the basement of the White House. The room was not overly large, and all the chairs at the table were filled and all space along the walls was taken up by aides standing.

The President didn't waste a lot of time on preliminaries. "Most of you got a briefing on Saturday about the subject of discussion this morning. Those who didn't, I apologize, but the matter came up rather suddenly, and while it is not something that requires immediate critical attention, the sooner we set the wheels in motion to deal with it the better. I want Nick to do a general brief then we will get into the specifics of how to deal with the problem. It's all yours Nick."

Nick stood and opened the orb. "I did this for most of you at Camp David on Saturday, so bear with me while we educate those who are not familiar with the purpose of this meeting." He again went through the explanation, flashing images on the screen from the robot. After he had finished he allowed the ones who had not had an opportunity to try the orb to do so. The entire process took almost an hour.

When all that was done he continued. "I spent the better part of the day yesterday trying to learn as much as I could about the aliens and their weapons systems from Myrth. The light weapon he thought we would not be familiar with is, I think, a LASER. Apparently it is new technology to the aliens, or relatively so. When I learned this I got together with General Carmichael and we kicked around some ideas about how to use this information. I will not go into a lot of detail about that at this time. I think the President has more important things on the agenda. I will turn it over to him and answer questions as they come up, within my ability, of course."

The President took over. "Now the first thing we have to determine is whether or not you believe what you have just seen and heard. Is there anyone here who does not believe what Nick has shown you?"

A couple of hands went into the air. The President looked at them. He said, "What do you not believe? That there are aliens, or that they are eventually coming here?"

"I have never believed in aliens," one of the Senators said. "This could be some sort of trick."

"Nick, demonstrate the force field for him."

Nick took the orb to the Senator and placed it in front of him. "If you can pick up the orb then it is obviously a trick, but if you cannot touch the orb, while others can, then you have to believe that the orb is preventing you from doing so. Will that convince you that it is not a trick?"

"I suppose so."

Nick placed the orb before him and he attempted to pick it up. Nick let him struggle until he gave up on his own, then picked it up. "The orb is emitting a force field that prevents you from touching it. Do you think anything like that is possible within our technological capabilities?"

"Not that I know about. I still find it hard to believe all you are saying though."

"The projections you have seen come from the robot. There is no way we could rig something like that. The seriousness of this situation makes it imperative that you guys all agree that this is something that needs to be dealt with. How you decide to do that is up to you, but you have to believe the reality of the situation simply because there is no explanation other than the one I gave you."

Everyone else around the table seemed to agree with what Nick said. One of the Senators asked, "What are we supposed to do now that we are aware of this?"

The President answered the question. "We have to decide how to deal with this. If we just ignore what Nick has shown and told us, then one day the aliens will show up in strength and we will be helpless to do anything about it. I don't plan to allow that to happen. So far this has not leaked to the news media, but I think it will happen very soon. We need to decide what to do about it among ourselves, then convince the rest of the world to go along with whatever we decide to do. That is not going to be an easy chore. With the uncertainties of the time element, it is going to be difficult to convince others that our future survival depends on what we do at this point in time. Now Nick has some additional information that is pertinent. I think he should present it before we get down to the details."

Nick went through the weapons the robot had in its memory banks and explained what he could about them. "The anti-matter concept is the most important aspect of this entire situation. We know what it is and have been experimenting for more than fifty years trying to harness the energy given off when matter collides with anti-matter. The moment is so fleeting that we have not been successful to any degree. The aliens have not only done this, but have succeeded to such a degree that they use the stuff like we do gasoline. It powers their space craft at the speed of light, which most of you know is what they call hyper speed. That is 186,000 miles per second. How they have managed to do this we have no idea, but their weapons aboard the space ships use the same type energy. The robot says the weapons simply vaporize whatever they hit. The space ships are protected by force fields. The robot thinks the LASERs will penetrate the force field if the charge of the LASER is strong enough. It is surprising that they are not far ahead of us in the use of LASERs, but it appears we may have an advantage in that particular area. I got together with General Carmichael and some of his people last evening and we kicked around some possibilities for a defense plan. I will not go into that because I am not conversant enough to give you an adequate briefing. I think what you folks have to decide is whether we are going to resist the invasion or roll over for them. If we resist then you have to decide how to pay for the preparations, which I warn you will be astronomical. You then have to decide how to educate the public to a degree that will assure them that you are not all completely off your rockers."

The last comment drew a few laughs.

The President got the meeting back on track. "I am going to task the Joint Chiefs of Staff to come up with a plan to set up defenses for all our military installations and major cities. I don't know what they will recommend or how expensive it will be, but our annual budget will have to at least double, and the tax rate is going to climb very steeply. The citizens are not going to like that, but we have to convince them that it is the thing to do. We also have to convince the rest of the world leadership of the seriousness of this discovery. I think most of them will be like you, skeptical. The one thing going for us is Nick's familiarity with the robot, and the robot's ability to speak any language known to man. Nick can project the images and explanations in the native languages, and the orb can interface with other leaders in their own language. We can only hope that others will support our decisions. If they don't then we will go it alone, but I believe all our traditional allies will go along with us."

"Are you serious about the budget doubling?" asked one of the Senators.

"Very. I don't know what is going to be required, but very deep bunkers are going to be needed for weapons survival. On top of that we have to produce enough powerful LASERs to take on the space ships, and I have no idea about the cost of that little endeavor."

"I don't think the public will stand for that," said Senator Eastman, from one of the western states.

"If they choose annihilation over money, then that is the choice we will have to live with, but I am betting if we educate them about the certainty of an invasion they will be willing to shoulder the added tax burden. That is what we have to deal with right away. I don't plan to wait for the final budget approval to get this process underway."

Senator Eastman said, "I don't think we can accept what we learned here as proof that the aliens will invade. They could just as easily go someplace else. We don't know enough to put the public through the pain and inconvenience of spending the kind of money you are talking about based on such fragmentary information."

"Last week at this time I would not have believed an alien invasion possible. As a matter of fact, just convincing me that aliens existed would have been next to impossible without ironclad proof. We now have that proof, and we have a non-biased opinion, and here I am talking about the robot, that earth is the most likely location that they will choose. Based on that alone I don't believe we can standby and do nothing, other than hope that they find someplace more suitable. While I admit that their arrival is not 100 percent sure, I would give it a 95 percent chance. Now if there is a 95 percent chance that an invasion is coming don't you think we should make preparations on those odds alone?"

"I'm not going to be a party to asking the public to sacrifice so much based on something that may or may not happen. I don't think it is in the public's best interest to start a panic over something like this. Didn't they agree to coexist with us? If we do nothing and they show up, we simply invite them to occupy some of our unoccupied territory."

"And what happens when the people who own the land you want to give them object? A few shots fired here and there and the next thing you know they are going to need to put down the rebellion. Which will lead to greater violence and eventual conquest of the planet by the aliens."

"I'm going to oppose this. I don't believe it is the right approach, and I don't think the American people will agree with you either."

"Well, that's your prerogative, but I hope you don't have cause to regret your decision in ten or twenty years from now," the President said. "The rest of you, if you agree that we need to take action can start doing some planning. The first thing we need to decide is how we are going to inform the public about this."

The Secretary of State said, "I think a news conference with Nick doing the same thing he has done here with the projections will be the most effective. He can give the same explanation and I think it will be effective. There will be those who think like the Senator, but I think the majority will simply try to digest the magnitude of the discovery of aliens and the fact that they are coming here. We can do the talk show circuit and explain the reasoning and our fears, and I think that will be effective, but it will take some time to shake it all out."

"I think the Secretary is right," said General Carmichael. "Anyone with half a brain will be able to come to the conclusion that there is no way we will be able to coexist with the number of aliens that we are talking about here. If their intelligence level is what we have concluded the human race will be so inferior that we will be considered nothing more than an amusement to them."

"You don't know that," said Senator Eastman. "And I resent the remark about half a brain. I believe you will find that a majority of Americans will side with my view of this situation. That has been our problem from the start of this democracy. We always seem to look for the worst in people instead of the best."

The President cut in. "You are entitled to your opinion, but I think the majority here today would rather see us prepared for the worst, so if you don't want to contribute to the solution, then you can be excused."

The Senator's face turned beet red as he grabbed his folder and left the situation room.

Nick said, "You know that the first thing he is going to do is go to the press. I hate to see that happen before we have a chance to educate the people."

"It will at least assure a good audience when we schedule your presentation to the media. Most people will probably not believe him anyway, but it will generate the necessary interest, which might be a good thing in the long run. I will have the press secretary schedule a briefing, and I will make some phone calls to the more important world leaders to assure them that the briefing is on the level. After that we will just have to deal with it as the chips fall."

The meeting continued, with the military people presenting what they had been able to determine about defenses and the development of LASERs with enough power to combat the space ships. The costs were going to be astronomical based on the original estimates, but nobody saw a better solution.

The Senator did exactly what Nick had predicted. He got to the media the minute he left the White House. The result had also been as Nick predicted. People who viewed the interview with the Senator thought he had gone off the deep end. Most were at the very least skeptical of his claims. That an emergency meeting had taken place at the White House had already been reported and reporters were scrambling to figure out what had precipitated the meeting. Still, the explanation the Senator provided was not taken very seriously by most. His reputation as a pacifist, and his record in the Senate was well known to most people and they thought he might be blowing smoke again.

But when the networks started running spots about a special Presidential address that evening most knew that something extraordinary was going on. Still, the Senator's claims were pretty hard to believe.

The meeting went on late into the day in the Situation Room. Nick took his leave to work on the presentation for the news media in the early afternoon. He hoped he wouldn't have to get into the nuts and bolts of how they planned to combat an invasion from such a superior opponent. That was not his responsibility, but questions were certainly going to be asked, and someone would have to provide answers, even of a preliminary nature.

The President spent the better part of the afternoon on the phone with leaders around the world. He told them that the news conference was not a hoax and that the world faced an imminent threat, albeit not of an immediate nature. He assured all with whom he spoke that Nick would make the rounds with the robot so they could see for themselves what the Americans had already seen.

When the news conference started the President did the lead in. He explained that something extraordinary had come to his attention and that he thought the American people, indeed the entire world, needed to know. He went on to explain how Nick had approached him and what had happened after that. "Nick is going to explain the situation and I will then tell you what my cabinet thinks the implications are. I stress that this is not something that is going to happen overnight, but you will readily see the implications as Nick goes through his explanation. I don't want this to be a real quick brief. I want Nick to take the time to explain every detail as best he can, and I warn you ahead of time, it is going to be a very long brief. After he finishes I will inform you of the actions we have taken, and some of the things that we will be doing in the future. I have spoken with most of the more prominent world leaders during the day to assure them that what they are going to see is the real item. I stress to all of you, though this is going to be difficult to believe, it is very real." He motioned to Nick that it was all his.

Nick stepped to the podium. He was going to use the projection method, but he wanted to set the stage properly, so he told the story of the broadcast of H. G. Wells War of the Worlds back in the 1930's. "People were really freaked out by the prospect of an alien invasion, even though they had broadcast a disclaimer before the program started. What I am about to tell you is going to have the same impact, but is not something that is going to happen instantaneously."

"I was hiking in the foothills of the California Mountains when I found this specimen." He held up the orb so the cameras could get a close up. "It is a beautiful specimen. Very colorful and unlike anything I have ever seen. It doesn't have a blemish on it, and to have washed down the mountain side that would be almost an impossibility. This has been in my possession for almost three months now. It took me a while to figure out what it was and how to operate it."

"It is actually a robot from a planet some ten light years distant. Now for those of you who are not into the math that is the distance light would travel in ten years at 186,000 miles per second. I can't even put all the zeroes in place to get the exact distance. Just know that it is a very great distance, in fact not even in our own solar system. How do I know this? Well, this orb is in fact a robot with extraordinary intelligence. I refer to it as he, although it really has no sex. His name is Myrth, and he had a difficult time teaching me how to open him up so we could communicate."

"He was sent out as a probe some 60 years ago, along with many others. There are at least four more of these somewhere on the planet. Their purpose was to find places with the right properties for the aliens who built him to exist. Their planet is slowly being depleted of whatever substance they require for their existence. He told me that the planet could only sustain life for them for 100 years at the time he was launched. His journey took ten years, and he lay dormant for 50 years, so the expected life of his home planet is now less than 50 years. He reported back about what the earth is made up of when he entered our atmosphere some 50 years ago, and he has told me that the make-up of our planet is almost ideal for his masters to survive here."

"There are about a billion of them and they want to live here. They are going to come here, whether we like it or not. They won't be here tomorrow, but sometimes in the next few decades, if you live that long, you will see a fleet of space ships suddenly arrive. Will you welcome them with open arms? Or will you resent the fact that they are going to take whatever part of our planet they require for their own use?"

"These are not rhetorical questions. Their survival depends upon them finding someplace that will support their life forms, and earth seems to be a good fit. The robot has told me that they plan to come whether we welcome them or they have to use force. I was requested to try to talk to our leaders and lay out the alternatives. The civilization we are talking about is very superior to humans from the technological standpoint, so they apparently think the conquest will be rather simple. I will show you where they live, what they look like, what their cities are like, their space ships, and any other information of relevance. I am not here to make the decision about how to address the situation. I am simply the messenger, so to speak."

"I am going to open the orb, which makes communication with the robot possible. One of the features of the robot is that he can project images onto a screen, just as we would with a movie or power point projection from a computer. The difference is that he doesn't need anything outside his own capability." Nick went through the procedure for opening the orb. When he parted the halves he placed one on each side of his head. He removed them momentarily. "I forgot to tell you, we communicate through thoughts so I will not be speaking while we go through the images. He will simply project what I tell him to. After we are finished with the images I will explain what you have seen." He placed the halves of the robot against his ears again.

The images started to appear on the screen. He instructed Myrth to go slow enough so viewers would have time to digest the images as he presented them. He showed the aliens first, both from a distance and close up. He showed them moving about on legs and in flight. He showed the cities and the plant where they produced the panels. The space ships from a distance, close up and inside. He had the robot spend a bit more time on the berthing set-up inside the space ships, and the propulsion system also got a close up. He tried to show everything that he thought was pertinent.

The entire segment took more than thirty minutes. When he had shown all he thought would be of interest he took the halves of the orb from his ears. He got a drink of water and started to explain what the entire world had just seen.

"The beings are three to four feet tall, and you may have noticed have talons on their feet. The hands are more like our own, with opposing thumbs, and they apparently digest whatever substance they need for nutrition from the air. Myrth has told me that they do not subsist on the same elements we do, so they conclude that their presence will not affect our own existence. My question is, if their own planet is being depleted of this substance, whatever it is, then would the same not eventually hold true for earth?"

"Just the robot I hold in my hand is evidence of an intelligence far superior to our own. This tiny orb is more powerful than anything in existence on earth today. It can communicate via thought in any language spoken on earth, no matter how remote or little used. It can generate a force field that will prevent anyone from even touching it, and it can communicate remotely. It requires no power source. It draws what power it needs from the things around it. It has the ability to analyze its surroundings and determine what elements are contained, and in what quantity."

"The beings who built this robot use anti-matter the same way we use gasoline. I know most of you are not familiar with anti-matter, so a brief explanation might help you. I had to ask about this myself, and I have some background in physics. For every element there is an anti-element is the simplest way to describe it. One is negatively charged and the other positive. We are talking atoms here, very small particles. When the opposite atoms collide they obliterate each other, creating a tremendous amount of energy. It happens so seldom, and under such unusual circumstances that it is difficult to detect the event, much less harness the energy. Our people, I mean humans, not necessarily Americans, have known about this phenomenon for almost a hundred years, but no one has been able to harness the energy, or even control the collision of the atoms."

"Why am I telling you this? To demonstrate just how advanced they are technologically. They use anti-matter to power their space ships. The enclosure I showed you aboard the space ship houses the propulsion system. It can propel the ship at the speed of light and doesn't require any fuel, since atoms exist in space. They use the same system for weapons. When they shoot something with the weapon it simply disappears back into its basic elements. They also employ force fields similar to what the orb does, only the force field surrounds the entire space ship and is infinitely more powerful."

"All this I got from Myrth. He was instructed to educate the planet about his masters capabilities, apparently in the hopes that we would simply say, 'come on down', as they used to say on the television game show. Could this be disinformation? Yes, but it doesn't seem logical that they would go to this extreme unless they could actually back up their statements."

"I will try to answer your questions with regard to what I have shown you. I will not get into any discussion about what our actions or reactions are going to be because that is not my responsibility."

Several hands went into the air and reporters started shouting questions. Nick simply waited until they calmed down and pointed to one near the front of the pack.

"How do we know this is for real? I admit your presentation was very impressive, but all this on the word, or actions of a robot are pretty hard to swallow."

"We obviously don't have time to let everyone here have a hands on demonstration, but if you would come up here for a minute and try to pick up the orb it would go a long way to convincing you that it contains capabilities that are not known here on earth. Come on up here for a minute."

The reporter came to the podium. Nick placed the orb on the floor in front of the podium. "Now," he said, "Let me see you pick it up."

The reporter tried his best to lay hands on the orb without success. In frustration he finally tried to kick it. The result was as if he had kicked a wall. The orb still did not move.

The cameras had recorded the entire sequence.

Nick picked the orb up and placed it back on the podium as the reporter returned to his seat nursing his foot.

"I can't force anyone to believe as I do that this item came from a planet in another solar system, but I believe the evidence speaks for itself. The President has asked me to liaise with foreign governments to give them hands on demonstrations of the robots capabilities. I will gladly do this, but I have no control over peoples inclination to believe or disbelieve what they are told and shown. There are millions of viewers watching this telecast and half will probably not believe what I have shown you. I cannot make you believe the way I do, but my mind tells me that such an item as this could not have been built on this planet. We simply do not have the technology to accomplish such a task. As I said, this could be a lot of disinformation, but the fact remains that a species capable of designing such a robot and then getting it to this planet convinces me that other intelligent beings exist, and the follow on thought is that they would not go to this trouble for no reason. So the conclusion in my mind is that they are coming, it is just a matter of when."

Another of the reporters raised a hand and Nick pointed to him.

"You say this invasion will happen within the next 50 years. Could you be a bit more specific?"

"Well, the robot was launched when the home planet had 100 years left. It took it ten years to arrive here, and it then lay dormant for 50 years. That is 60 so from this moment there are 40 years of life left on their planet. I don't believe they will wait until the very last moment to make their departure, but if they did, then it would be an even 50 years before they arrive. I tend to think they will leave at least ten years before the deadline. I don't even know what they consume, but if it is dwindling at a steady rate, then it stands to reason that the quality of the substance will degrade as the supply gets toward the bottom of the barrel, so to speak. My guess is that we will see their space ships in 25 to 30 years."

The next question related to the ultimatum. "The robot said they would be willing to coexist with us and that they don't consume the same foods we do, why not just allow them to land here peacefully?"

"That is not for me to say. If the majority of the earth's population wants to do that, then an attempt will be made to do as they wish. I am not in that decision making process."

The reporter continued. "You don't seem to believe that is a very good idea."

"My personal thoughts are just that, personal. But if you give the matter some serious thought you will see the problems that are presented with that scenario. My purpose was to convince the world that this situation is a reality and I have tried to do that. I don't know what else to do. You know what they look like, how they live, and of their technological advances. You know what to look for when they show up, and how they are armed. Are you convinced that there are other intelligent life forms out there? The television audience has seen the presentation, but you folks have seen it in person. Now, are you going to educate the public about the reality of what you witnessed, or will you wait until a fleet of their space ships show up on the horizon?"

The President came back to the podium and pulled Nick aside. "Good job. I will try to answer a few questions now."

He came to the podium to hands waving all over the room. He pointed to one of the female reporters and she asked the question that had been on everyone's mind from the beginning. "Are we going to allow them to arrive peacefully or oppose them?"

"That decision has not been made, at least from the American point of view. But let me ask you a question. We are talking about an unknown number of these beings, but upward of a billion, with a B. Now for that many new residents we will need a lot of land. They aren't going to want to live in the desert wastelands, so we will just divide every country in the world and give them half, or a fourth, or ever how much they need. Your house might be on what we decide to give them. Should the government compensate you for that, or build you another house? That's only for starters. Remember, these are highly intelligent beings, who are so advanced that we would be like grade school children to them. Will they share their knowledge with us? Possibly, but it is more likely that they will remain a separate society and humans will be the weak stepsisters. No matter what we decide, there will be those who will oppose their presence. Some will take pot shots, others will organize into groups and there will be open rebellion. Soon the aliens will decide that they need to subdue the entire human population to have any peaceful existence. Now where does that leave us?"

"I am not necessarily advocating armed resistance, but the alternatives look pretty bleak to me at this point in time. I will consult with world leaders and collectively we will decide how to approach the problem."

"What kind of defenses could we offer against these anti-matter weapons Mr. Parker was talking about?"

"We don't know at this point. If the decision is made to resist, then that is something we will need to work on."

The next question was, "How can we be sure they are coming here?"

The President's answer was, "How can we be sure they aren't. I would rather err on the side of caution. The evidence suggests that they are coming. If we do nothing, we are betting our human existence on the outcome. I don't believe we can afford to take that chance."

The questions continued, but the majority now dealt with whether or not to offer resistance. The reporters in attendance were convinced that the aliens existed and their questions reflected this fact. That would go a long way to convincing the general public that the information was factual.

The press conference was one of the longest in American history. It continued until after midnight. The cabinet officers answered questions, as did the military. It was obvious that the majority of those in attendance now accepted the fact that one day in the near future a fleet of space ships would show up above the earth, but whether the rest of the world was convinced was another matter.

When the session finally ended the reporters sought out individuals for additional insights. Not a lot could be added to give any of them a different take on the situation. The news networks after the briefing did the normal in-depth analysis, but they had trouble finding experts since nobody knew anything about the subject. There were those who had long advocated that other life forms existed and their opinions were as varied as the speakers. Some thought that the best approach would be to welcome the aliens and see what happened from there, while others thought that the aliens were pretty presumptuous to think they could just come down and take over the territory they needed.

The resulting furor was worldwide. All the major television networks in every nation carried the White House briefing live, with closed captioning and translations. By the next day 90 percent of the world's population knew about the situation.

## Chapter 7

Nick was given a Secret Service protective detail and a government plane with secure communications capability as he started his mission to brief governments around the world. The first stops were the traditional U.S. allies. Canada, Great Britain, France, Germany, and Israel were the first on the list. The President had consulted with the Secretary of State to compile the list and Nick simply went where he was told, when he was told to be there. He spent one day in each of the countries, giving the leaders hands-on experience with the robot and fielding questions as best he could.

In every case the governments who were skeptical became believers after interfacing with the robot. Nick learned a lot during the process as well. Some of the questions asked of the robot were things Nick had not thought about, such as exactly what elements the aliens required for their sustenance, and what was their life expectancy. Some wanted to know more about their history, and if they had wars among themselves.

The Russians wanted to know if the leader was a king or if he was elected to lead the people. They also wanted to know how the outlying areas were governed.

The question of how old the civilization was came up and the answer was surprising to Nick, as he assumed it was to others. The robot did not know the exact length of time the beings had inhabited the planet, but he indicated that it was in the thousands of years instead of the millions one would expect for such a species to evolve.

They had been capable of interstellar space travel for over five hundred years, but had never explored other planets. They had instead used robots such as himself to probe other heavenly bodies.

Asked about other life forms on the planet, the robot indicated that he did not know of any others. This seemed strange indeed for a planet that appeared to have a composition that strongly resembled the earth. In the scenes the robot had showed, there appeared to be trees and other vegetation. That there were no insects or small animals would be strange indeed.

On the plane between stops Nick pursued the issue further with the robot. "Are you saying that there are no small insects or other animals on the planet at all?"

"Not to my knowledge. I suppose they could have left that out of my programming as unimportant, but I do not know of any other form of life on the planet."

"Well, at least that rules out biological warfare," Nick quipped.

"I do not understand the term," the robot replied.

"It's just the way we refer to germ warfare."

"What are germs?"

Well, thought Nick, this opens up another whole new possibility. If the species had never been exposed to germs, then they would not have programmed the robot to look at that aspect of the planet in his suitability study.

"You do not know what a germ is?" Nick queried.

"The term is not in my memory banks."

"Well, a germ is a microscopic organism that carries disease that can attack the internal working of the body. In some cases they can be deadly, or make those exposed very sick. Is there ever any sickness on your planet?"

"My masters are born, live for a certain amount of time and die. Unless they have accidents their life spans are very predictable."

"How do the plants survive without bees to pollinate the plants, or other microscopic organisms to interact with the process?"

"I do not know the answer. Perhaps they did not think it was important for me to know these things."

"While you lay dormant for such a long time animals had to be close enough to you for detection. Did you not detect any animal life in all that time?"

"Many animals came near me, but upon analyzing their components they did not appear to be the major species, so I did not contact them."

Nick was on the secure communications circuit almost nightly. He usually didn't even get a hotel room in the cities he visited. He just sacked out in the bed on the plane. It had a full

69

galley, and the food was probably more suitable than changing diets every day.

On the night after the conversations with the robot about the germs Nick called the President earlier than usual. He did not always talk to the President, but one of the Security Council members was always there to take his call. On this occasion he asked to speak to the President personally.

"I have come across some information that I believe is very pertinent to the situation. I need to consult with a micro-biologist." Nick went on to explain about the aliens not knowing what germs were and the possibility that they had never been exposed to them.

"If that is the case, then nature will do our work for us eventually. They will not have any immunity to any of the normal diseases that our systems naturally combat. Is that where you are going with this?"

"Yes sir. The robot did not have anything about in its memory banks or any other animal life on the home planet, and he didn't even know what germs were."

"I will have a microbiologist meet you at your next stop. In the meantime we will discuss the development among our people and see where it leads. The Congress is not willing to put up the money for defenses so far. They have been debating non-stop and are pretty much split on the issue. I have gotten feedback from many of the places you have been and while they believe the story, they are not willing to commit to a unified defense yet. This is going to be an uphill battle all the way."

"If it was something that was going to happen in the next year, or even two or three years I think they would look at it differently, but with the time element so far down the pike it just doesn't seem as crucial right now. Another thing that is going to make this so hard to do is that governments will change, and the opinion about how to prepare will change with the leaders. I don't know what else we can do other than let them know what is coming."

"I agree. And whether or not our government agrees to fund the defenses, I plan to start building them with the funds on hand. We will not get a lot done, but at least I can start the process."

"I don't envy you that job. I will continue to learn what I can along the way. Something else might come out that will be helpful to us like the germ thing."

Nick spent another two months making the rounds to governments large and small. He hadn't realized that there were so many countries in the world. He was travel weary by the time he completed the project. Even with the word out that there were four more of the robots on earth someplace, none had been found. It was just happenstance that he had found the one, and it was not likely that others would be easily turned up. What good it would do if they did find them he didn't know. It would simply verify the information he had learned from Myrth.

The furor had died down somewhat since the original revelation. It was still in the news and talked about a great deal, but without any sense of urgency. Nick had even developed a more complacent mood about the coming events. He could not do anything to change the fact that they were coming, and he had done all he could to get the word to the earth's inhabitants as he had been requested. He feared that the earth might well be doomed. There was simply no way that all humans would stand idly by and watch the aliens take over. Once the first shot was fired the aliens would have the justification to take on all comers, and there would be a lot of opposition Nick thought.

Nick had untold invitations to appear on talk shows. Some he accepted, others he ignored. He still felt an obligation to keep the matter at the forefront of the people's conscience, and that was one way to do so.

He had met a young lady in Washington who was on the President's staff. They had hit it off and talked often while he was on the world tour. She had flown to Sweden when he was there and accompanied him on to Norway and Finland. He was thinking seriously about asking her to marry him. Though he was not a lady's man, he had a lot of experience. He simply had not come across anyone he would like to spend all his time with. Irene was such a woman.

They talked a lot about the coming calamity. She was intelligent and had enough background in science to understand some of the innovations the aliens had perfected. This gave Nick a sounding board to discuss various aspects of their capabilities.

The talk shows Nick appeared on were paid appearances. He saw nothing wrong with accepting fees for his time. The compensation was not exorbitant, but for the more popular shows, was pretty good. Just appearing once a week he could earn more than a million dollars a year. The usual fee was in the 10 to 20 thousand dollar range.

The two months he had spent making the rounds gave him a lot of added perspective to the alien situation, and some of these things he talked about on the shows. He didn't like to speculate, and kept his remarks as close to the factual information the robot presented as possible. The President, in the meantime, was having all kinds of trouble with the Congress. In order to get any money at all to mount a defense against the coming invasion he had to reduce his requests for funding to a point that it was no more than token acceptance. He did as he had said and diverted a lot of defense money to the project.

He even had the army reorganized to include a section called the Extraterrestrial Command Authority. It was headed by a three star general and included troops from the scientific divisions as well as ground troops. The final structure was not definite, and would change as the mission evolved. The main thing was that they could include the command in the normal budget process, though it probably wouldn't result in increased funding. The military leaders were all on board. All were convinced that it was necessary to prepare for the invasion, and that should be their priority. This resulted in a greater degree of cooperation between the services, which was very important in the development of weapons that might work against the alien space ships.

The President was getting near the end of his second term and could not run for reelection. He felt it was important to get someone into the White House who would at least follow-up on the program he had started to deal with the aliens.

He was talking to Nick about a year before the end of his term. "We need to get someone in this office who doesn't take the coming invasion lightly. I don't know if we have anyone in the party with enough clout to win who really believes in what we are trying to do. At this point I don't even care which party he is from, as long as he will continue the effort to be prepared for what we know is coming."

"I am with you. I would hate to see us just bury our heads in the sand and accept what comes. The biological people didn't seem to think the germ element would be a deciding factor when the invasion comes. I am not sure I agree with them. My knowledge of the subject is limited I admit, but I don't believe they factored in the ten year space voyage. It will have to have some debilitating effects on them, and the fact that they have never been exposed to the bacteria on earth is still a big unknown. Even if they only get sick and have to recover from the various illnesses, it will degrade their defensive capability."

"That's true. I just hope the LASERs will be effective against their space ships. Right now we are planning to have at least six sited near each large city. We are even placing one in Central Park in New York City. The navy already had the problem solved about the power output, and we will be working on improvements as we go along. You know, you have a certain degree of popularity now, and you are known the world over. If you were old enough we might consider running you for my job."

"I don't want your job. I just want someone in your position who will take the coming events seriously."

The LASER locations were very elaborate. They resembled old missile silos, in that they were very deep and covered and camouflaged with movable covers. The LASER had to be raised to a firing position from the floor of the cavity and this was done by elevators. The prototype had been designed at one of the old missile silos in North Dakota. While their construction was expensive, it was not exorbitant. The main problem they had to deal with was the generation of huge amounts of power it would take to operate the LASERs. Multiple generators were part of each installation. They ran power from the regular grid, but had to assume that this source of power would not withstand the initial alien attack. The price tag for each of the defensive installations was nearly 50 million dollars.

The President said, "Your constant television appearances seem to be at least keeping the problem on the minds of people. The Russians are taking the matter the most serious. I think they are putting as much money into their defensive strategy as we are. We have even given them the plans for the LASER. Other European countries are taking some actions, but the less economically capable countries are doing very little."

"I somehow have a feeling that when they come they will concentrate on the more developed areas, so Africa and the areas in the far north and far south will not get much initial attention," Nick responded.

"Africa would be a good place to judge how the germ problem will affect them. There are probably more lethal varieties of disease in the tropical areas, but from what the robot showed us they don't seem inclined to inhabit areas of dense vegetation, even on their own planet."

"The entire situation is very frustrating. If the imminence of the event was closer to the present it might make a big difference. As it is people, especially the older segment of the population, figure they will not be alive to witness the event, so why worry about it," Nick said.

"It is human nature to put off things that have no immediate impact. I'm just afraid that we might wait until it is too late to mount an adequate defense. Even training people in methods we think will be effective against them is not an option at this point in time."

"When it comes right down to it, we don't really know what will be effective against them. I assume that rifle bullets will do the same to them as they do to us. Fortunately most of our people know how to use rifles."

"Unless we organize into military type formations, it will be difficult for individuals to have much impact against hordes of the aliens descending on them from the air. Automatic weapons are going to be a must against such large numbers," the President said.

"I can just see the backlash if we try to arm everyone with automatic weapons. The gun control crowd will have a ball with that one."

"Well, I don't think I can help with choosing a successor for you. I will continue to do what I can to get support for the resistance, but it seems to be a losing battle."

"All we can do is try to exert whatever influence we have. I will not be very effective after my term of office is over either, but I will resist the invasion with my dying breath if it happens during my lifetime."

The President's last year did not see much progress in the effort.  He pushed as hard as he could to get legislation passed dealing with the threat, but Congress did not pass any meaningful bills dealing with the subject.

A Democrat was elected to succeed him and was not nearly as strong in his support of extraterrestrial defensive measures.  To his credit, he did not try to undo any of the things President Carmichael had implemented, but the effort slowed to a snail's pace in the training department.  As more time passed and nothing happened the world became even more complacent.

Nick continued to publicize the coming event as well as he could.  The robot was still a technological marvel, and that alone assured Nick a wide range of public platforms for postulating his warnings of coming doom.

A year after the Presidential change Nick and Irene were married.  They made their home in Nick's place in California, but still spent a lot of time on the road.  Both were in their late twenties and they hadn't talked much about having children.

When Irene found out she was pregnant she was not sure how Nick would take the news.  Surprisingly he was happy about the prospect of becoming a father.  Though the future was uncertain, the child would possibly have several years before the world as they knew it would change.

## Chapter 8

A baby boy was born to Nick and Irene in May. They named him Adam. Nick was not on the road as much as in the past couple of years. He wanted to spend time with Irene during her pregnancy, and after the baby came he realized what a joy fatherhood could be. The first three or four months were an ordeal, but as Adam started to take on a personality and develop good sleep patterns it became more fun than work keeping up with him.

The child loved the colors in the robot and Nick often placed the orb in the playpen with him. He would play with the orb for hours, ignoring other toys placed in the playpen. He was perhaps seven months old when Nick noticed his obvious thoughtful manipulation of the orb. To Nick, who had gone through the process of learning the secret of opening it, the child was obviously trying to open the thing. This was fascinating to Nick.

That night he opened the orb and communicated with Myrth. "Have you been trying to teach Adam how to access you?"

"I have been doing with him the same as I did when you first encountered me. He is a very intelligent being. I believe he will learn to access me before long."

"What is the point of this?"

"It stimulates his thought process, and I like him very much."

"You mean you actually have likes and dislikes?"

"Not in the sense that your kind do, but I feel either drawn to or repelled by those I contact."

"Why don't I just show him how to open you and he can then interface with you. I am sure you will be a great teacher."

That night Nick discussed the situation with Irene. "Myrth has been trying to teach Adam the sequence for opening the orb. He thinks Adam will master the procedure soon. What do you think about that?"

"That is a very difficult concept for a seven month old to digest. I don't think even a seven year old would be able to do it."

"Myrth says Adam is very intelligent, and that he likes, or is drawn, to him. I never realized that the robot had any sense of emotions before. He says he doesn't have likes and dislikes as humans do, but he is either drawn to or repelled by those with whom he has contact. I am frankly amazed by this discovery."

"Do you think it is a good idea to have Adam so close to the robot?"

"I can't see any harm. I think Myrth will be a good teacher, and can certainly teach him things that other kids on earth do not know. I believe it is still very important that you and I spend a lot of time with him, and we will keep a close eye on his development."

The next day Nick sat Adam on the living room floor and opened the orb for him. He placed the halves over his ears and held them in place. He first instructed Myrth to project onto the living room wall. The result was simply amazing.

The child's attention span was short and the images flashed on the wall so quickly that Nick hardly had time to digest them. The images moved from one subject to another so randomly that it was hard to make sense of some of it. If what he was seeing was the baby's thoughts, then humans did not really have a handle on infant development.

While some of the images were what he would expect from a child, others were a lot more advanced than he would have thought.

He viewed scenes of the avian young on the home planet, and a tutorial about how the aliens got their nutrients from the air. He saw scenes of how the mothers took care of the young, how they learned to use their wings, and a hundred other things that he would never have thought to ask.

The child was watching the scenes as avidly as was his father. How much he was absorbing Nick did not know, but just the fact that Adam's mind was working that quickly was amazing.

Another thing that had not come up was the language of the aliens. That was something Nick would inquire about at the first opportunity. It would possibly be useful in the future.

During the next three years Adam progressed at an amazing pace mentally. He was talking before he was two years old. By the time he was three he could converse in any of the major languages. Myrth had tutored him almost daily. He was apparently also teaching him the language the aliens used. Nick had asked about that and Myrth had told him that he would teach him the language if he desired. Nick did not have the time to devote to the project that Adam did, but he worked on it and found after a while that he and Adam could converse in the avian language.

The robot tutored Adam in all subjects. Science, physics, mathematics; all the technical subjects were covered.

Adam was so advanced that school would be a waste of time. Still, he needed the social skills and his parents took him out often. Nick still ran regularly, and Adam would accompany him from the time he was six years old. He could not keep up, but he had stamina and could set a fast pace for his age.

Talking to him was more like conversing with an adult than a child. He mastered technical problems quicker than most advanced students and understood math and physics to a degree that would be the envy of most professionals in the fields.

Nick and Irene talked to him about the situation with the avian beings and the fact that they would eventually be coming to earth. They tried to explain to him the implications of the coming events and presented both sides of the story. That the avian beings would perish if they didn't find a place that would sustain life for them was explained. They also expressed the human view on coexistence and conquest.

"The bottom line is that there are too many differences in our cultures to coexist peacefully. Either of our species would have to make radical changes in order to do that. Even then there would be resentment that the avian species is taking land and space that rightfully belongs to humans. The other side of that is that the newcomers would not get along well with such an inferior species. Either way it is a recipe for trouble."

Adam was nine years old when this conversation took place. "But don't they deserve a chance to survive? If their home planet is no longer habitable they need someplace to live."

"While that is true, do you think they should just choose where they want to live and go there without consulting the inhabitants?"

"Well, it would have been better if they did that part differently, but we could at least talk to them about it."

"I don't think they will be willing to talk. When they come, they will most likely just land and take what they want."

"That's not right either," Adam said, "but there must be some way to solve the problem without a major war."

"We don't know how accurately Myrth is portraying the aliens. He could just be their method of trying to lull us into a false sense of security."

"I don't believe Myrth would do that. He is totally unbiased. Sure, the Avian designed him, but I don't believe they could program him to respond favorably toward them in all situations. It would be like a quantum leap in artificial intelligence, and I don't think even that species is there yet," the child said.

"The fact remains that there is going to be a confrontation when they arrive. What you or I think doesn't count for much at the present time, although we are the only two people on earth who will be able to communicate in the avian language. Since they will be able to translate any language known on earth that probably won't make a lot of difference in the final analysis," Nick said.

Adam was very thoughtful for a short while. "I really don't want to see a war result from their coming. I wish there was some way to deal with the matter peacefully."

"I do too, but even at your young age you know that the human race will not give up land without a struggle. The people who are misplaced by their arrival, and as many of them as there are there will have to be a lot, will resent it and will fight to defend their homes. Not all of the different nations on earth see things in the same light, and there are going to be disagreements about how to deal with the problem even among ourselves. That has been evident for the past ten years."

"Can you think of anything we might do to prevent a war when they arrive?"

"I believe the only way to do that would be to set aside land for them, but where that land would come from is the sticking point," Nick said.

Adam said, "What if we could get a bunch of really rich people to contribute to a fund to purchase land for them?"

"I suppose that idea has merit. I frankly had not thought about it. If we could purchase large tracts in different countries it might work. Think about it overnight and we will talk about it some more tomorrow."

Adam did exactly that. He lay awake until the wee hours of the morning with the robot, discussing ways to acquire the land necessary for the avian.

Myrth outlined a plan which included personal appearances by the entire family on television and an internet fundraising strategy. Adam seemed to understand the concepts and was ready to discuss it with Nick the following day.

"I don't think raising the money will be the biggest hurdle," Nick said when Adam told him his thoughts. "The most insurmountable problem is going to be locating the land in areas that will be habitable, and buying all the land. There will always be some small percentage that want to hold out, or simply refuse to sell the land. Buying the land around them might help to keep the confrontation to a minimum, but there's still going to be some violence."

"Well, at least we can try to set aside some places for them. If it doesn't work out then we will be no worse off," Adam said.

They set the wheels in motion the following day. Nick contacted some attorneys and explained what he had in mind. They initiated the paperwork to set up a non-profit corporation and he and Adam started making appearances on talk shows. Nick even had an infomercial made and started running it on all the different television outlets.

Money came in at an amazing rate. Before they were a month into the plan they had over a hundred million dollars. Adam was very impassioned about the project and it showed in his appearances. He was a child prodigy in every sense of the word. The robot had not left many subjects uncovered during their near constant interface. Adam reflected the robot in many ways. He could speak any language, had a complete understanding of physics and other sciences, and had even written a book about the make-up of space outside our own solar system.

During the next two years they bought large tracts of land, based on information from the robot, which would be suitable to the new species. As they attempted to acquire large blocks of land in several different countries, the situation reflected exactly what Nick had told Adam would be a major stumbling block. Some people simply would not agree to part with their land no matter what was offered in exchange.

The richer and more powerful countries had done as the United States had done. That is, they had developed defensive measures. Most were based on the tactic the U.S. had started. LASERs buried underground was the central element in all cases. Nick had been consulted in almost every case and had asked the robot to project the use of the light weapon the aliens had. Most of the scientific minds agreed that it was a LASER.

Stockpiles of automatic weapons and ammunition were strategically located in all the countries. Those who had the most to lose seemed to be the ones who were best prepared for an eventual invasion.

The foundation Nick and Adam had set up raised over a billion dollars in just under three years. The land they had bought in different countries was considerable, yet they had not been able to acquire what they thought of as adequate space for settlements for the aliens.

As time passed, the world's population became less worried about the potential invasion, so it was a surprise to Nick and Adam when the robot announced that the aliens would arrive shortly.

"Define what you call shortly," Nick asked Myrth.

"Within thirty of your days," was the reply.

Nick got the word to the current president and asked him to notify other world leaders. The President was not anxious to cry wolf, but Nick's notoriety and status overrode his objections to looking foolish and he passed the word. He also placed the military of the United States on maximum alert status.

Most of the major television outlets devoted a lot of time to the subject of the prophesied invasion by aliens since the time element was now so short. They discussed everything from how to greet the aliens, to how to hide from them during the coming invasion. Most described the arrival as an invasion, even though those words had not been used by government leaders. Most said simply that the aliens were coming.

It was on April 1, 2035 that the first report of extraterrestrial spacecraft was issued. The report was from the space telescope at Kitts Peak in Arizona. Soon additional reports were made by other observatories.

After the first reports, every television outlet worth its salt had cameras pointed toward the skies around the clock.

Nick was not privy to the plans of any nation as to how to deal with the alien presence. He did not know if there were plans to attempt a dialog, or if they would simply try to destroy the spacecraft when they sighted them. For his own part, he simply stayed at the Malibu house with Irene and Adam.

Adam was interfacing with Myrth about the coming fleet of spaceships. He told Nick, "It looks like there are more than 100 spaceships."

Nick used Myrth to see how the fleet was dispersed. Myrth projected a view of the fleet from space which showed that the plan was to surround the entire planet.

With all the television outlets filming the coming alien's spaceships there was panic throughout the population. The aliens did nothing for an entire week from the time they were spotted.

Myrth was in communication with them and had told them that he did not know if the inhabitants of earth would accept them or not. The craft seemed to be orbiting around earth. They were large enough to be seen by the naked eye, even at the extreme altitude.

The first of the spacecraft landed in the Gobi desert on April 9th. The area was uninhabited and the landing was detected by U.S. and Russian radar satellites. Photo reconnaissance satellites were reprogramed to cover the area where the space ship had landed as quickly as possible.

Coverage showed a horde of the alien avian creatures near the space craft. Approximately 100 had left the landing site and were headed for Ulan Bator, some distance from the ship.

## Chapter 9

Both the Russians and the Americans made the feed from the satellites available to the news media and the pictures of the group of Avian headed for Ulan Bator were aired in real-time over all the worlds' news networks. As a result a lot of people were well aware of what was happening, and where. Even in the remote area of the world where they had landed people were aware of their presence.

It happened just as Nick had predicted on the first day he had made the robot available to the President. Isolated people with weapons started taking pot shots at the swarm of aliens. Most missed, but some of the bullets found avian flesh. As some fell from the sky, the others started to use their anti-matter weapons. They were almost as inept as the amateur hunters on the ground were, but some of their defensive fire found targets too.

What the aliens intended will never be known, for when they realized that they were being attacked they turned and headed back for the space ship. Once they loaded aboard the ship again it headed back into orbit.

The satellites had recorded the events, and even the pacifists knew that the world was soon to be at war against an enemy that they had never seen and did not understand. The world waited with bated breath for what would happen next.

Again, the aliens did not take any action right away. Probably they had to devise some plan of attack before they got serious about conquering the planet, but two days later all the space ships moved closer to earth. There didn't seem to be much method to the madness, because they didn't attack all the major population centers. Their attack seemed rather haphazard to the U.S. military minds.

For example, Philadelphia was attacked, but not Washington. Raleigh, North Carolina was also attacked, but not Charlotte. Kansas City, Chicago, and Atlanta were also attacked during the initial skirmishes.

Chicago and Atlanta were both pretty well fortified with the LASER installations. The anti-matter weapons were truly amazing in their destructive power. Anything within 50 yards of the impact point simply disappeared.  There was no warning or visual signs of the fact that an area was being targeted.  Things appeared quite normal at one moment and the next were simply no longer there. All that could be seen was a brilliant flash of light, then nothing.

The aliens must have been very confident in their ability to deal with the earthlings because they didn't operate in groups, but only had one space ship in each location of the attacks.  Atlanta had half a dozen of the LASER installations and they were the first to have any success against the alien spacecraft.  One of the LASER's on the west side of the city got a clear shot, and though the distance was not optimum for the LASER, they got lucky and must have damaged something essential to the craft because it suddenly plowed into the ground just to the north of downtown.

The success was tempered with tragedy as the ship crashed in a densely populated neighborhood, killing more than a thousand humans.  The local police and a group of troops from Warner Robbins Air Force Base were quickly on the scene.  The hatches to the spacecraft were open and any survivors who attempted to exit were taken under fire with rifles and handguns.

The British managed to down one just outside London, and the Russians got another near Moscow.  Not all the aliens were contained at the crash sites, and those who survived the crash and managed to get out with their weapons became formidable foes. The shoulder fired anti-matter weapons were very effective when they managed to hit their target.  Their ability to fly also helped them to escape in some cases.

Nick and Adam watched the news on television, helpless to do anything to get the situation under control.  Adam was crestfallen at the way events had unfolded.  Unknown to Nick, he and Adam were the only earthlings who knew exactly how the aliens were deployed.  That had come from Myrth, and individual countries would know they had alien visitors through their own sensors, but would not know the extent or locations of other alien attacks.

Nick still maintained contact with the Chairman of the JCS and placed a call to him.  He had shifted his command post to an underground bunker in the West Virginia Mountains and it took almost half an hour to get through to him.  Nick then quickly related what he had learned from the robot about the aliens attack disposition.  The General wanted Nick and Adam to come to the command post but Nick thought it better to remain outside.

The next 48 hours saw some more success for the humans, but also a lot of death and destruction meted out by the alien anti-matter weapons.  They had to be surprised by the fact that the earthlings could even have the small successes they had against a far superior species.

New York and Washington were attacked on the second day, and by multiple spaceships.  Still, New York managed to down two of the spaceships, but three of the LASER installations were destroyed.  Washington managed to destroy one, but the Capitol building and the White House were both obliterated.  Fortunately both facilities were practically empty by then.  They had ample time to vacate the buildings as the interval between the first attacks and the attack on Washington was more than 24 hours.

Ever since the cold war with the Soviet Union from 1946 to 1991, the United States had provisions for emergency evacuation of the nation's leaders, both military and civilian, in the event of an attack.  The general public did not know of these plans, but a lot of military people did, especially those in the intelligence business.  In addition to the facility in West Virginia, there were deep excavations underneath the ground in Washington.  Cheyenne Mountain in Colorado was another emergency relocation site.

Camp David, in the Maryland Mountains had another purpose in addition to that of Presidential retreat.  Quietly, over the years, a deep underground facility had been excavated by the Army Corps of Engineers.  Some 300 yards from the small cabin they had excavated to a depth of more than 100 feet.  Ventilation vents had been installed almost laterally to draw fresh air from a point nearly a quarter of a mile from the actual site.  Reinforced concrete was used to seal the location and the only entrance was into the face of a hillside more than 200 yards from the actual facility.

Antenna wire had been laid during the construction and terminated well away from the site.  This most secret of locations was where the President would be in an emergency situation.

The evacuations and relocations had taken place after the first pictures of the events in the Mongolian desert.  The facility was not the most comfortable, but survival was more important than comfort at this juncture. The President and his wife, along with his personal detail and those necessary to man the communications and defend the site were the only occupants.

After the additional losses of their craft to the humans, the avian horde apparently decided to have a conference, because all the remaining spacecraft, which numbered close to 80, congregated in the Gobi Desert where the first one had landed. The area was isolated, but they left one ship hovering above as a safeguard.

The decision was made to have each of their spacecraft choose a sparsely populated area and build their settlement now. The subjugation of the inhabitants could wait until they established living spaces. This tactic would require that they keep sentries on watch constantly, but this was considered preferable to losing any more of their spacecraft, and more importantly, their people on the craft.

For whatever reason, the aliens did not appear to be concerned with satellites and other communications on earth. Perhaps it was because they communicated telepathically, but in any event this was a grave error on their part. The satellites, both radar and photo, along with communications and GPS were not bothered. This allowed the local inhabitants to keep track of their progress on their building projects and to precisely locate them.

While the alien spaceships were impervious to most earthly weapons, the same was not true of them personally.

World leaders could communicate and coordinate their efforts as long the satellites remained functional, and this they did. The first thing they did was map all the locations where the aliens were attempting to build cities. They then divided the locations among those with some means to deliver weapons and started an offensive campaign.

In the United States the western part of the country was the primary focus of the aliens. The Midwest, Nebraska to be precise, was the only location they had chosen outside desert areas in the west. Most of the locations were vulnerable to sea launched ballistic missiles. It would take some time to get the submarines positioned where they needed to be, but that was by far the safest way to attack them. All the world's leaders had eschewed the nuclear option, so conventional weapons would be used first.

Few people outside the military and political leaders knew the full extent of what was going on, but the news hounds sniffed out a lot of it. They managed to get pictures of the aliens building their cities. They were working very quickly and progress could be seen from day to day. Pictures were long range and not of very good quality, but were good enough to show what was happening.

Again, individuals tried to get close enough to use rifles, but few succeeded. The spaceships were overkill to take care one person with a rifle, but they did exactly that. A few of the aliens fell to long range rifle fire, but not very many in the initial stages of their building program.

Within a couple of weeks the tables started to turn. Sea launched ballistic missiles with conventional warheads found their mark at three of the locations in the western United States, and both the Russians and Chinese managed to get some armament on target. Though they didn't kill many of the aliens this way, they certainly messed up the building program. Enough damage was done that they had to go back to the beginning and start over.

Perhaps because of the arid climate in which most of the aliens tried to build their cities, they seemed to be pretty well acclimated to the earth's atmosphere. As more of their efforts met resistance, they branched out with their defensive strategy. Sometimes as many as five of the spaceships would surround the area where work was proceeding to deal with any human intervention.

The missile attacks continued, from surface ships with the ability to launch long range missiles, and from aircraft, again with long range missiles. These efforts became less and less effective with perimeter security by the other alien spacecraft. Nobody knew if their doctrine called for engaging targets in flight, but they attempted to do so.

Some of the long range efforts of the United States and other developed countries met with limited success, and it was an uphill battle. The space ships providing security would unload their contingent of the aliens and then deploy with only the crew necessary to operate the defensive systems. This created target rich areas in which the aliens were working. The problem was getting a weapon on target.

After the initial successes with ICBM's, the aliens began to deal with them while in flight. Only about one in ten managed to reach their target after the first couple of days, and aircraft were beginning to fall to the anti-matter weapons regularly. Almost half of the fighter planes in the U.S. inventory disappeared within the first two weeks of the conflict. Other nations did not fare any better, and most lost considerably more of their own fighters.

As the aliens built their cities they established perimeter defenses on the ground. Detachments of the aliens were deployed to protect against ground attack. These outposts were far enough away from the main population centers, or at least what would be the main population centers for the aliens once they finished building, that they had to operate independently.

Once this strategy was realized the humans adapted to it. They tried to infiltrate small squads close enough to bring them under fire with shoulder fired missiles and artillery. This was the way most of the militias on earth had learned to fight, and they enjoyed some degree of success, though their losses were tremendous. Only about one in five of the groups managed to get close enough to use their firepower. Still, even small successes were better than none at all.

In what seemed like the middle of their building program the aliens changed tactics. They started deploying some of the spacecraft to destroy the larger cities on earth. Los Angeles and San Francisco were attacked on the same day. Although they managed to destroy four more space ships, both cities sustained considerable damage. The aliens were indiscriminately destroying what they probably considered to be the more valuable targets. Shopping centers and large buildings were the primary targets.

Almost half of San Francisco disappeared, along with the Golden Gate Bridge. Los Angeles fared little better. Nick and his family had witnessed the attack on Los Angeles from their home in Malibu. The aliens did not attack anything along the coastline.

The same thing happened in Europe. London, Paris, Berlin, Budapest, Copenhagen and Vienna received a healthy dose of anti-matter weapons fire. London and Paris were almost totally obliterated. The death toll was not even certain, but was certainly in the millions.

The U.S. president and the British Prime Minister, who was also in an emergency location, conferred by phone. "I don't see how we are going to be able to deal with this situation unless we use the nuclear option," the British Prime Minister said. "We are about out of options."

"I agree," the President said. "Although we have enjoyed some success, they still have over sixty spaceships at last count. I am not even sure how successful we will be using nuclear weapons. Let me try to set up a conference call with the nuclear capable nations and see how they feel about it."

The conference was set up between China, Russia, Israel, Great Britain, France, North Korea, Iran, Pakistan, and India. China had been least affected to that point and was reluctant to agree to the use of nuclear weapons, but they were the only dissenting vote.

The Russian President said, "This should be a coordinated attack. I think once we use nuclear weapons they are going to take us much more seriously and we can expect even more attacks from them."

Everyone agreed that the U.S. should do the target list since they had the best sensors to map the alien locations. Targets would be assigned based on how close the aliens were to the different countries.

This was accomplished over a 48 hour period. Even though all the nuclear capable countries knew which other countries had the capability, few knew exactly how many weapons the others had, and more importantly how they could deliver them to the target.

Missiles were the preferred option, but not everyone had that capability and would try to use other methods. All the locations where the aliens were trying to build cities were targeted and areas where their spacecraft were located also received priority attention.

The date and time for the attack was set. Very little attention was paid to the ultimate aftermath of nuclear weapons usage. The death toll worldwide was such that the priority was to deal with the aliens without regard to the damage to our own habitation.

The force fields the aliens used went a long way toward protecting their spacecraft, but they had not been subjected to a nuclear detonation at close range, and nobody knew what the result would be. If the force fields were strong enough to protect the alien ships from damage, then humanity would soon cease to exist as we know it. This was not a very cheery prospect, but that appeared to be the only option open to the humans.

The Chairman of the JCS called Nick. "Will nuclear weapons be effective against their spaceships?" he asked.

"I will have to check with the robot, but I don't think they will. Remember at the beginning we determined that the only thing that would work against the force fields was LASERs," Nick responded.

Nick accessed Myrth and put the question to him. "They will be effective against the beings, but not against the vehicles."

Nick passed the information on. "Are you planning to use nukes against them?"

"That was the plan, but I think everyone has forgotten that they won't be effective against the spaceships. I will get back to you." With that he hung up and called the President.

"Sir, Nick says the robot tells him that nukes will not be effective against the spaceships, only against the aliens on the ground," he told the President.

"Then I think we had better rethink their use."

The President quickly convened another conference call and told the other world leaders that it would be useless to attack the spaceships with nukes. "I still think we should go ahead with the intent of destroying those on the ground. Maybe we can double up on them."

Since most of the sites the aliens had chosen were in semi-isolated areas the decision was to go ahead with those attacks. The time and date for the attack was changed and moved ahead by four days. The aliens had ceased their attacks on cities and were now concentrating on providing security for their people working on the buildings of their own.

The African continent had not received much attention when the aliens were looking for locations to build their cities. The only area of Africa they bothered with was in the north of the continent where there were relatively open areas. None of the major powers had paid much attention to that area. As a result it was further along than any of the others. That was both a blessing and a curse.

The aliens had been on earth for almost a month when it happened. Some of the avian on that project began to fall ill.

This was a new experience for the aliens. On their home planet they had never experienced illness, so none of them knew how to react to this sudden new development.

There were nearly 50,000 of the aliens in the settlement in the Ethiopian desert. At first it was only a few, then more and more came down with the same symptoms of the illness.

The leaders of the settlement thought that the humans were somehow attacking, but had no notion how they were doing it.

Other spacecraft showed up at the settlement and took some of the sick aboard. The aliens had been on earth for more than six weeks now and it was the fourth week in May. Plants were blooming where there was enough moisture and the pollen and germs were in the air, especially in the northern areas where they had decided to locate their cities.

Myrth had been in communication with the aliens and told Adam and Nick that some of them had been attacked, but they were not sure what weapon had been used. Nick asked how they knew they had been attacked.

Myrth described the symptoms and Nick began to put the pieces together. "Where were the ones that were attacked at the time?" he asked Myrth.

Myrth gave him the location and Nick became surer of his hasty conclusion. What had attacked them was germs! The group was close enough to equatorial Africa that the wind could carry the germs a long way. He suspected that those who the aliens thought to be attacked were simply having symptoms of some disease prevalent in Africa.

Nick got on the phone right away and managed to talk to the JCS Chairman. He explained what had happened and postulated that the best course of action was no action at all. "With any luck, as the weather changes and pollen gets in the air, more germs will be spread, and I don't think the aliens will be immune to any of the relatively minor diseases that we are. What humans fight off because of our immune systems, might very well be fatal to the aliens. I think we might want to rethink the nuclear attack and let

91

nature take its course.  By the middle of summer the population of the aliens will have thinned appreciably in my opinion."

The Chairman again called the President and relayed the information from Nick.  After another conference call with other leaders it was decided that they would take a wait and see attitude.  If the alien population indeed began to shrink, then Mother Nature might fight the battle for them.

## *Chapter 10*

The reconnaissance satellites of the major powers on earth continued to provide information, especially the photo satellites. Work slowed down on the settlements the aliens were building. They could see a marked decrease in the number of beings working on the structures. First it was only the project in North Africa that was affected, but as May turned to June other groups of aliens seemed to begin to thin somewhat. Those areas closest to very moist climates were affected the most.

The desert fauna in the United States came into bloom and it became evident that more of the aliens were being affected. Toward the end of June the aliens made more retaliatory strikes against the cities of earth. The aliens could not figure out how the humans were attacking them, but their ranks had been substantially reduced

Humans did not know this because they had not seen any bodies. Still, evidence available from the satellites revealed fewer than half the number of aliens at each of the settlement sites as the earlier numbers indicated.

Nick asked Myrth, "What do they do with the bodies when one of them dies?"

"Turn it back into the base elements," he replied.

"What do you mean turn it back into the base elements?" Nick asked.

"They use an anti-matter device similar to their weapons. It breaks down the form into the basic chemical elements."

"So they don't bury their bodies like we do, or cremate them?"

"I suppose it is much like cremation, only a lot quicker and cleaner," Myrth replied.

Nick called the Chairman of JCS again and explained what Myrth had told him. "I think a lot of them are dying from disease, but I have no idea what the numbers are. Based on the lesser numbers in the settlements I think the number is significant though."

"The plan now is to try to wait it out but their indiscriminant attacks have world leaders between a rock and a hard place. If they do nothing and the attacks continue they will be seen as weak leaders. If they try to take the offensive the aliens will simply step up their attacks. It's a no win situation no matter what the decision entails," the Chairman said.

Many of the LASERs that had been prepared in the previous twenty or so years had been destroyed in attacks. Those that had not been completely obliterated had received priority attention since they were the only thing earthlings had that would do any damage to the space ships. As a result something like one in ten of them had been repaired. Those around New York City had been hardest hit and only one was operational.

Several in other cities had not been deployed because of the locations of the alien ships and were still operational.

The world leaders decided to use what was available to try to thin the number of space ships.

For over a month the alien ships rampaged all over the world with impunity. The LASER installations that were still operational were very selective about engaging the alien ships. Unless they were relatively certain that they could get the weapon on target they didn't even activate the systems.

One would think that a civilization as advanced as the avian would have pretty sophisticated countermeasures for any sort of weapon, but events had shown that to be a false assumption. It is hard to devise countermeasures against weapons with which one is unfamiliar. Without some knowledge of avian history it would be almost impossible to know what sort of weapons they had encountered in their evolution.

It would, at any rate, be akin to earth's inhabitants trying to devise countermeasures against rocks and catapult weapons used in the Stone Age.

"I have no idea how long it is going to take them to figure out what is happening. The robot tells me that there were no insects or disease on their home planet, so if this is their first sojourn away from their planet it will not be self-evident that the environment is the problem. They programmed the robots to look for similarities to their planet and didn't even factor in the possibility of disease," Nick told him.

"If they have no safeguards in place when taking the sick aboard the space ships that is a big mistake too," the General said.

"Let's just hope they don't get so fixated on retaliation that they continue with the assault," Nick commented.

The previous month had seen a further reduction in the number of alien ships. The number was now below sixty. Forty percent of their fleet had been destroyed, and probably at least half the number of aliens had either been killed or died from disease.

As summer wore on the attacks by the aliens had gradually tapered off. They still attacked at least once a day, but the attacks were not prolonged. They seemed to be trying to keep earth's inhabitants cowed rather than attempting to do real damage.

From Myrth, Nick knew that the avian were still dying at an alarming rate. They had abandoned several of the sites where they had started to build cities and moved the survivors to other locations.

Meanwhile all their work was done under duress. Small groups of organized military forces as well as mercenary units were doing all they could to hamper the ongoing work. These groups used medium range missiles, rifles and machine guns when they could get close enough, and since they had found out the aliens were susceptible to germ warfare were even using animal carcasses as delivery systems for germs if they could get them close enough.

Russia and the United States had long since given up on the use of biological weapons but still retained the knowledge of the delivery systems they had used in the early part of the century. This mostly consisted of missiles with canisters of the biological agents for delivery either by air-burst or ground level detonation.

The Avian had become somewhat adept at taking out missiles in flight but if they could get a couple on target with air-burst, then they might have some degree of success in infecting more of the winged creatures.

They didn't have to worry about delivering anything exotic. The normal germs and viruses would be enough to do the trick and would not adversely affect the remaining population of those who called earth home.

Canisters of flu, measles, mumps, and chicken pox viruses were quickly developed and salvos of missiles were fired at the settlements they were working on. Although most were destroyed before they reached the target, some got through.

The results of the attack would not be evident for some time and strikes by the Avian continued. The death toll from the avian attacks after less than a year was in the tens of millions. The damage to the infrastructure would take decades to rectify if they could ever expel the aliens.

Transportation for earth's inhabitants had become a major problem. Commercial airplanes no longer flew, and the military aircraft inventory had been severely depleted as well. Some trains still ran but the major mode of transportation was by motor vehicle. The Avian fleet had not bothered with the roads, unless they wanted to take out something they thought might be a threat that was traveling on the highways. Some bridges had been destroyed, especially around the large cities, but a concerted effort had not been made to destroy the road system anywhere in the world.

The aliens had not made any effort to destroy refineries, so they continued to operate, albeit at a lesser capacity than before the invasion. The casualties reduced the demand for gasoline in any event and there was enough to supply the needs.

People did not take summer vacations in 2035, and any travel was done out of necessity rather than for pleasure. It was, in other words, a self-imposed rationing system.

Nick and Adam had a lot of conversations during that time that you would not expect a father to have with a 12 year old. Then again, Adam was not a typical 12 year old.

"I wish there was some way we could stop this," Adam said. "All the killing is senseless. Even if they get their cities built they won't be able to survive here because of the germs. Even if they develop an immunity similar to humans the immunity will not develop quickly enough to do any good."

"So if they win, in the final analysis they will lose. You and I might be the only hope for stopping this bloodshed before we annihilate each other. What do you think about trying to make contact with them through Myrth and arranging a meeting?"

"Do you think that would work, and what will the politicians think about that?" Adam responded.

"I don't care much what the politicians say, but I think we would need the approval of the President before we tried something like that."

"What would be the purpose?" Adam asked.

"To inform the avian that the earth is not the paradise Myrth thought it was for them. We can educate them about why their brothers are dying, and at the same time caution them that if they stay all will succumb to disease in the end. That might be enough to get them to look to their next best choice, if one has been reported by other robots."

"Do you really think that will work?" Adam asked.

"It's about all we can do. You want to give it a try?"

"I guess so. I think as their numbers start to shrink even more they will strike back at everything in retaliation, so we might not be long for this earth in any case," Adam said.

Nick called the Chairman of the JCS and pleaded his case. The General thought it was the best idea anyone had and told him how to get in touch with the President. Nick made the call and managed to get the President on the phone.

Nick explained what he and Adam had talked about and told the President that he wanted to try to broker some sort of armistice to get the aliens to seek other lodgings. "When I point out to them that they will all eventually die anyway it might be enough to convince them to move on."

"Where will you meet them?"

"I have no idea. The closest place would be one of the cities they are building in the western area of the United States. I will have to travel there from here and those would be the closest. The thing that worries me is the ongoing hostilities. I would hate to have someone attack the place we are meeting while we are there. Could we get a cease fire at whatever location we choose while we are there?"

"It will take some time to set that up, but it can be done. The wild card is the vigilantes not under our control. Let me get the Chairman's views on that and get back to you. Your idea is the best I have heard since this started. We have suffered millions of casualties and still have not communicated with them."

"I know. The fact that they think we are responsible for their health casualties could have been dealt with long ago is we had talked to them. I don't know if this will work or not, but nothing ventured, nothing gained," Nick said.

Nick had discussed the proposition with his wife between phone calls. She was not enthused about the idea of her 12 year old son getting in the middle of this but saw the necessity. "Why can't we all go?" she asked.

Nick and Adam looked at each other. Adam smiled and Nick said, "No reason at all. If we go down in flames, then we will all go together."

The President called back later that day. "I have talked to General Jacobs. He will be calling your shortly. Good luck."

Nick did not tell him that his wife was also going along.

When General Jacobs called he asked, "You have any idea about where you want to try to meet them?"

"I was thinking about one of the sites where they are attempting to build settlements. Maybe the one between Blythe and Needles. Another option might be to ask them to pick us up someplace isolated. I don't know how that will work. I haven't discussed it with Myrth. What are your thoughts?"

"I like the site between Blythe and Needles. It is isolated enough that we should be able to deal with it easier. What I am worried about is the vigilante groups. We will have to try to control them while this is going on and that might not be such an easy thing to do," General Jacobs said.

"Go ahead and set that in motion. I will try to interface with them through Myrth and see what they think about picking us up someplace isolated but closer to my location."

"Okay. Let me know what happens."

Nick explained what was happening to Irene and Adam. "You guys know this might be very dangerous," he said.

Irene replied, "I don't think it is more dangerous than doing nothing. If we just sit on the sidelines things are going to escalate very soon."

Nick asked Myrth to communicate with the aliens and ask them if they would receive emissaries.

The answer was that they would if the circumstances were right.

Nick related to Myrth what he had in mind and the location between Blythe and Needles was satisfactory for the meeting. The time was set for three days from then. Nick and his family would have to travel to the area and he figured his four wheel drive truck was the best mode of transportation.

After letting General Jacobs know what had been arranged the family started packing for the trip. It was not more than a four hour drive under normal circumstances, but the circumstances were far from normal. Many of the roads had been damaged and it might not be so easy to get to where they needed to be. The population of Los Angeles and surrounding cities was now less than a third the size it was at the beginning of the conflict. Still, travel was a chancy issue even without the large numbers of cars that once traveled the Los Angeles roads.

On the day they left Nick had figured at most two days to reach the destination along the Colorado River. The roads were nothing like they had been pre-invasion. In some cases the five and six lane freeways were in pristine condition. Then suddenly the road would be completely covered in debris from the attacks. In those cases Nick had to find a way around the obstruction. It was not hard to do in most cases, but sometimes they had to deviate miles before they could find a way around the devastation. On the first day Nick drove until late into the night. It took that long to reach Indio, which was the easternmost population center in the Los Angeles Basin.

They found a motel and stayed for the night. Most places of business were still open. The town was like an old western outpost. It was the jump-off point for many of the vigilante groups trying to deal with the aliens along the Colorado River.

They had an early breakfast and got on the road again. The travel from that point was relatively easy. There was very little traffic on the road and they made good time until they turned off into the desert. Nick did not think a direct approach to the site on paved roads would be a good idea. Many of the vigilantes were little more than crooks with a modicum of respectability and he did not want to tangle with a group like that.

As they got closer to the actual location they started to encounter more military groups. Apparently General Jacobs had deployed his troops nearer to the aliens and had them work outward to roust out the vigilantes to obviate the real possibility of an attack while Nick and his family were with the aliens.

As they neared the site their anxiety mounted. Myrth was in communication with the aliens and kept them informed of their progress. When the partially completed buildings came into view there were three of the space ships deployed around the structures.

Myrth directed them to the area inside the defensive perimeter of the aliens and had them stop near one of the craft.

Nick parked and they got out of the truck. A door slid open on one of the spaceships and one of the aliens motioned them forward. Myrth confirmed that they were not armed and they strolled briskly up the ramp to the open door.

Once inside they were not really surprised. Myrth had provided them views of the interior of the space ships. The single thing that impressed them most was the size. It was difficult to get a true perspective of the sheer size from projections. The things were huge.

The apparent leader of the Avian introduced himself in their language. Nick and Adam responded in the avian language. The avian's name was Nur.

He said, "It is gratifying that you have taken the time to learn our language. Come along and we will talk."

He led them to a portion of the ship that was sectioned off, similar to a room in a house on earth.

When they walked inside there were several others sitting around an oblong table. Nur introduced the occupants and no one but Adam would remember the names later.

"What shall we talk about," Nur asked.

"The first thing is the number of your people who have died without apparently being struck by any object. Myrth has told us that you have not been able to figure out how you are being targeted," Nick said.

"That is true. What sort of weapon is being used that we can't even detect."

"You are not being attacked in the way you seem to think. The only weapon we have that is effective against your ships is the laser. As far as one-on-one combat goes, we have nothing to compare with your anti-matter weapons. What is attacking you is another species we have here on earth."

"Why do we not know about this other species? Myrth should have provided that information."

"Myrth did not know about the other species. He was designed by you with the knowledge that you possess. We have microscopic organisms that we call germs. They cannot be seen with the naked eye and they are found everywhere on our planet. Some places are more populated with the germs than others. You breathe them in and once inside your body they can cause various damage. Some can kill you rather quickly, while others take days or weeks. They cause what we call disease."

"How did you get them to attack us?"

"We did not get them to attack you. They are entirely on their own. They will attack us just as they will you. The difference is that we have lived with them so long that our systems have adjusted to them. The ones that kill you cause us no harm. They are more abundant in warmer climates and as the season changes they are reproduced and borne on the wind until they find a host. They then inhabit the host and multiply, causing sickness and sometimes death."

"That is what has been killing my people?"

"Yes. The fact is that we will not have to do anything to you but wait and within one of our years your species will no longer exist. The germs are in the air and anytime you breathe you will be taking the germs into your internal system. Depending on which germ finds a comfortable place inside you, you will die, either slowly or in some cases more quickly. You had no knowledge of this and as a result did not program anything about unknown organisms into Myrth, and probably not in your other robots either."

"We had two other reports from robots that were close to what we require to exist but your planet seemed better suited. What do you suggest we do now?" Nur asked.

"I think your wisest move would be to check out the other two planets. It is possible you can find one more suitable to your needs. I tried to explain to Myrth about how our population would react to your arrival. He seemed to think that you would be impervious to anything we could use to oppose you. Had it not been for the initial confrontation we might have been able to co-exist, but I don't think it would have made a lot of difference in the long run. Even if you conquered the planet you would still have a daily struggle resisting lone gunmen or individuals. We are not governed by a single individual. There are over 150 countries on the planet and each has their own ruler. While some might agree to co-exist it would be a constant battle to protect your species."

Adam said, "We were trying to buy up enough land in areas that Myrth thought would be good for you. If we had been able to do that and could have communicated it to you things might have turned out different, but with your susceptibility to disease it probably would not have made any difference."

"You are being truthful about the germ species?" Nur asked.

"Yes," Nick replied. "If it was just two or three germs that affect you we could inoculate you against the diseases caused by them, but with every germ it is not possible."

"We must discuss the situation among ourselves. Is it possible to meet at another time?"

"We will stay nearby and you can let us know through Myrth when to return," Nick said.

They left the space ship and got back in the truck. Nick then drove to an area near the river but not all that far away. He was still inside the perimeter of troops trying to discourage vigilante attacks.

Nick placed a call to General Jacobs and told him what had transpired. "They are having a meeting to discuss their options. We have agreed to go back when we are notified by Myrth."

"I will send more troops to beef up the security. I think what you are doing now is about the only chance we have to end this thing. I will also brief the President. Remember if they agree to leave we will have to coordinate with other nations to make sure we don't have any incidents. That might take some time" the General said.

"We're only a couple of miles from the space ships, along the river. We're still inside the perimeter of the troops so I think we will be okay here waiting for their decision."

During the nighttime hours five more of the space ships landed at the site. Myrth told them that the avian leadership panel was now in session.

They had no idea how long it would take them to discuss the matter, nor what the decision would be. History had never recorded anything as momentous as the current situation. The very existence of the earth depended on what was going on inside one of the space ships. There was no doubt in Nick's mind that the aliens could wipe out most of the population before they succumbed to disease. The decision hinged on whether or not the aliens believed that the cause for so many of their deaths was not due to anything the inhabitants of earth had initiated.

Their reasoning could be that since the germs were inhabitants of the planet then their plight was due to an overt act of inhabitants of the planet. They would think that those with higher intelligence should be able to control other less formidable inhabitants.

The meeting went on for two days. Finally Myrth got a message that they should return to the space ship.

They loaded up in the truck again and drove the short distance back to the space ship. All the others were still present and the desert looked like an interstellar parking lot.

Nur came out to meet them and escorted them back inside the space craft.

All the chairs at the table were occupied except for three for the visitors. When they were all seated again Nur said, "We are not in agreement that what you told us earlier is factual. How is it that some of us are affected and some not?"

Adam had the best technical background, even at his young age. He answered the concern. "Our atmosphere, that is the area emanating outward from the area where we are now to the height that the air would not support our existence, is home to many species. Some species are larger than others and that is also true of what we call the mental level. Some animals are relatively intelligent and can communicate among themselves. Others are so small that they cannot be seen unless placed under a magnifier. Myrth can show you some examples. Adam asked Myrth to show them some animals that he had encountered while on earth."

Myrth projected the images of dogs, cats, horses, elephants, lions, tigers and porcupines. He cycled through enough to demonstrate the variety of inhabitants of earth. "All Myrth has shown you haven't the ability to communicate with us except on a very rudimentary level. Some of the animals can be trained or taught to recognize certain commands, but these are very few. The ones Myrth is going to show you now are much smaller and have no ability to communicate that we know about."

Myrth showed them ants, spiders, lizards, butterflies, birds of different types, rats, and even cockroaches and fleas.

"These are all small in terms of mass and intelligence. The next in terms of size are even smaller. Mites, gnats, mosquitos and such are all carriers of the germs that are so small that you could fit a million of them on the tip of a finger. The way they move around is by hitching a ride on any of the animals or insects that I mentioned. They are also carried by the wind, or air that we breathe. We ingest them with every breath."

Myrth didn't have anything to demonstrate germs in his programming so Adam had to rely on verbal explanations to get his point across about germs.

"Humans, which is what we are called, have inhabited the earth for millions of years. As time passed our immune systems learned which germs were dangerous and which were not. I don't know how long it took to build up an immunity to the different germs that were harmful, but eventually our species got to the point that we could co-exist with most of the germs. That's why they do not affect us in the same way they do you. You have never been exposed to the germs and when you ingest them they immediately start to attack your internal organs. There are so many varieties that it is almost impossible to classify all of them. Our researchers are constantly finding new strains that we have no immunity to and we have to develop medicines that will combat them. I suppose we could arrange to have a microscope delivered to you so you can actually see the germs, but just seeing them will not convince you that they can be lethal to you."

"What if you are doing this to try to get rid of us?" one of them asked.

Adam thought carefully about his answer. He said, "Either way the end result will be that your entire species will expire on earth, unless you remain in your space ships, and I expect some of them have been infected by the sick ones you have brought back aboard to care for them."

"If that is the case then we are all doomed so why should we worry about your species?" another said.

"That's not necessarily true. If you agree to leave we can disinfect your space ships to make sure none of the germs are aboard when you leave."

"How will you do that?"

"By spraying disinfectant inside all your space craft."

"How do we know that this is not some trick?"

"Some of you can accompany the people who will be doing the work. We put on protective clothing and breathe bottled air. The only thing wrong with that is that we don't know exactly what kind of air that you would need. Since you seem to do all right without any breathing apparatus then I think our oxygen will be all right for you as well," Adam finished.

"How long would it take to do this?" Nur asked.

"I don't know for sure. How many space ships do you have left?"

"Just over forty. We have lost more than half our space ships and people."

"I will need to check but I think it can be done in a couple of weeks. We have to make sure the disinfectant can be produced in quantities large enough to treat all of your ships."

"If we agree to this when can you start?"

"Probably right away. There is going to be a problem making sure no one who leaves is infected. Probably the best method to do that is have you go to someplace where the weather is too cold for germs to survive. Maybe the north or south poles," Adam said. "Our scientists will have to work that out."

"You are sure that we will all die if we stay?" Nur asked.

"Maybe not every single one, but the survival rate will only be about one in a thousand."

They answered other questions over the next four hours. Nick was amazed at what he considered simple things that the aliens did not know.

Irene was asked questions about the female component of the society on earth.

They wanted to know what part the females played in day to day life for humans.

Finally all the questions seemed to have been answered.

"How long will it take you to get to the next place that might be suitable to your needs?" Nick asked.

"About two of your months," was the reply.

"We will agree to your proposal but we will keep the young one with us until you fulfill your part of the agreement."

Adam said, "That's fine, but what do I eat?"

Since the aliens absorbed their nutrients from the atmosphere that was a concern that Nick had not considered.

"I will bring you something from the soldiers if they have anything that will be suitable," he said.

Irene was reluctant to leave Adam with the aliens. "I don't think that is a good idea at all," she said.

"I will be okay mom. Just let me know if they buy the proposal as soon as possible."

When Irene and Nick got back in the truck the first thing he did was call General Jacobs.

"We reached an agreement with them to abandon the planet. Can you send a helicopter to get me and Irene? We need to see what the President thinks about our proposal."

"Where are you?"

"I will be along the river about two miles from where the space ships are located. The pilot should be able to see me from the air. Also, Adam stayed aboard the space ship as insurance. We need to get some food to him before we leave the area."

"Go north to the skirmish line of soldiers. I will call and give them instructions."

When they got to the cordon of military people Nick was pleased to see that a lot of food had been gathered. He didn't know if the alien s would have any way to cook the food but there was enough that could be eaten as it was to keep him alive for a long time. He drove back and left the food outside the space ship.

They then drove back along the river until they heard the sound of a helicopter. Nick and Irene got out of the truck and Nick locked it. The helicopter landed and they climbed aboard and were flown to Kingman, Arizona. From there they took a fixed wing plane to Cheyenne Mountain where they met with General Jacobs.

Jacobs told them that he had already alerted the President that they would be calling.

When he dialed and the President was on the line he put the call on the speakerphone.

"Well I'm glad that worked out," he said.

"There's a lot to be done before we can call it a success. Would it be possible to get the other major leaders on the line for a conference call? That way I can address their concerns as they come up."

"Let me check with the communications types and see if they can make arrangements."

It took almost ten minutes but in the end they had the leaders of Russia, France, the United Kingdom, Germany, China, Iran, Pakistan, Israel, Canada and Australia on the line.

The President told Nick who was on the line and suggested he tell them what had transpired.

"My wife and son accompanied me on the visit to the alien space ship along the Colorado River just south of Needles, California. I explained to them that the problem was not something we were doing but was a natural phenomenon. Adam gave them a tutorial on the make-up of living organisms on earth and I think we convinced them that they would all die if they stayed, whether or not we had anything to do with it. The next best place for them is a couple of months away by space ship and they agreed to leave if we can disinfect their ships and assure that they don't take any sick along with them."

There were many questions and the phone call lasted almost two hours.

They discussed everything from what would be used to disinfect the space ships to how to produce the quantities that would obviously be needed to complete the project. They talked about security for the operation and how they were going to keep the vigilantes away from the areas they would use for disinfecting the ships.

The President said, "I am hoping to nip a lot of that in the bud by making an appeal to them. There will still be enough of a threat that we will use troops to secure the area we are going to use. General Jacobs, will you see to that?"

"Yes sir. I will get on it right away."

"There's another facet to this proposal that I am not sure about. I told them that they would have to go someplace to insure that all who embark on their odyssey are free of disease. I don't know how to best do that but something like sending the ships to the north or south poles in the disinfected ships and have them stay long enough to get through the incubation period of different diseases. It wouldn't be wise to have them take the disease causing bacteria along with them."

"Another thing you should know is that my son is sort of a hostage, or insurance. He agreed to stay aboard the ship until we get a start on these procedures," Nick finished.

None of the foreign leaders had any objections to the plan and all wanted to know what they could do to speed the process up.

While the plan was readily accepted the procedure for doing the things that needed to be done to bring it about was going to take a lot more coordination.

After they finished the conference call General Jacobs got on the line to gather the required scientists to do what had to be done. The General first called for the movement of troops in other areas to get them to the site in California where the decontamination was to take place.

The next day the Presidents of all the major powers appealed to their citizens to cease actions against the aliens and told them that a cease fire had been negotiated. The word got to the majority of the vigilantes and all the government troops.

Within a week the scientists had decided what chemicals to use and a plan had been accepted to send the decontaminated ships to the Arctic above Russia to make sure they didn't have anyone infected aboard the ships.

It was a slow process but progress was made daily.

## Chapter 11

Since it was a simple matter for the alien space ships to travel it was decided that all the decontamination would be done in America at the site on the Colorado River.

Scientists had been sent with decontamination suits and microscopes. Nick wanted the aliens to see the evidence that the germs did actually exist.

The procedures for the actual decontamination were refined once they were speaking with the aliens. Decontaminations suits had been brought that would fit the smaller aliens and they were tutored about how to use them.

The concoction they decided upon was a combination of insecticide and anti-bacterial agents. They had not tested it but knew the qualities of each component and the mixture had been sprayed on areas and checked to see that they had performed as they thought they would. The regimen was not really scientific. They just hoped that what they were using would be long lasting.

Because the ships were so large it took half a day to properly do just one. They then had to check to make sure the disinfectant had done what it was supposed to do. After that the spraying samples were taken from different areas and checked for any bacteria that might still be present.

Once the procedure was implemented Adam was released back to his parents' custody. He had not been mistreated and the aliens now felt that the humans were really going to live up to their promises.

There were a few incidents of vigilantes still trying to get close enough to kill some of the aliens. For the most part these were people who had lost loved ones to their attacks. More troops were brought in for security and the defensive perimeter was layered so that if someone should slip by the first line they would not be able to just move unconcerned to the location of the space ships.

It took them five days to decontaminate the first ship and certify it free of germs.

Nick and the head scientist had a conference with Nur and told him what to do and where to go. "If anyone on the ship exhibits any symptoms of sickness remove him immediately from the confines of the ship. I know it sounds inhumane, but you can't afford to have any germs aboard when you leave the planet."

Nur assured them that he understood and the first ship left for the northern ice fields.

After the first one the procedure was more familiar and the process was speeded up. It still took two months to get all the ships decontaminated. They were receiving reports from the ships as they went north. The first ship had four people infected with some disease and instead of putting them off the space ship used the accepted method of getting rid of corpses to take care of them. It was apparent that the aliens looked at death a lot differently than did humans.

Once the decontamination procedure had been instituted the world leaders emerged from their shelters and tried to get their countries back on the road to recovery.

The world population had been reduced by half during the hostilities. The problem was exacerbated by the fact that the African continent had not been subjected to the onslaught as had the more advanced countries. England, Russia and the United States, the big boys on the block, had suffered the greatest number of casualties. That was seen by some of the more populated countries as an invitation to expand their own influence. Even though most were ill equipped to do what they wanted it didn't keep them from trying.

Several regional conflicts broke out even before the aliens had left. Mexico was almost untouched by the alien presence, other than one settlement in the northern part of the country. Militia units started to cross over into the United States and the President presented an ultimatum to Mexico's President.

Mexico ignored the warning and continued with the northward expansion until a nuke obliterated a large part of Mexico City.

On the other side of the world the Chinese saw the weakened Russians as easy prey. Russia tried to combat them conventionally but after the U.S. nuked Mexico City the Russians did the same to China, only they targeted six of their largest cities. The Chinese had nukes as well and their response took care of what the aliens had left in Moscow, plus three other cities.

Fortunately the Africans did not have the weapons and means of transportation to do much against any of the former leaders of the world, but they did take Saudi Arabia, Egypt and some of the smaller oil rich nations. Syria, Jordan and Iraq joined Iran in trying to obliterate Israel. Israel, once they saw what was coming didn't hesitate. They targeted each of the capital cities of the nations arrayed against them and sent conventional forces to repel the invaders. Israel used tactical nukes as well and held their own.

It was almost six months after the aliens left before the world settled into any semblance of peaceful co-existence.

Nick, Adam and Irene had gone back to the house in Malibu, which had been ransacked by burglars in their extended absence.

It would be years before the infrastructure was once again even marginally adequate to the needs of those who had survived all the calamities.

Adam had kept Myrth and Myrth had taught him how to alter his programming to incorporate those things of earth that had not been pertinent to his old planet.

Nick often wondered how the invasion would have gone had he not happened upon the robot in the desert. For one thing they would not have been able to down the craft that they had with the LASERs. Did it make a difference? Yes, but in the final analysis maybe some of the damage might have been avoided without the opposition.

In hindsight it was obvious that the aliens could not have lasted long even if they had gotten a substantial toehold.

Nick didn't believe for a minute that we were alone in the universe except for the avian that had come to earth. What would happen when the next group came? The thing that bothered Nick most was that they had not even gotten the design of the anti-matter system the avian used.

He and Adam were discussing that subject when Adam smiled. "I've got that covered. Myrth and I know how to design the system. I am not going to let anyone know until the time is right. I think the introduction of the anti-matter weapon will only foment another situation like we had with the nuclear weapons."

"Everyone needs time to rebuild and get on with their lives. Another thing we have is the design for the force field. That we will work on for our own protection. I think we can design a system similar to what Myrth uses that will fit into a pocket like a cell phone."

Nick said, "Well, I hope we are around when the next species tries. I am very proud of you for what you did, and for your capacity for compassion."

The President invited the family to the new White House and presented them all with medals. It was a very fit ending to a situation that could have been a lot worse except for a chance encounter with a rock in the Sierra Nevada Mountains.

The End

# 9.0

By John Buckner

# Chapter 1

Laura Griswold was a geologist by training but a seismologist by profession. She had majored in geology with the thought of working in the oil exploration industry but the lack of female positions open to her caused a change in her professional focus. She had, in fact been on her way to a job interview when fate intervened.

She was staying overnight in Los Angeles prior to a job interview the following day with a major energy company. She was awakened in the middle of the night by a moderate level earthquake. It was her first experience with that particular phenomenon and she was terrified by the shaking and eerie sound of the fractured earth moving beneath her.

Her fear was not rational. She had studied about such events during her college years and didn't understand why the event struck such terror in her. In any event she was still not her usual self when she went for the interview, which might have affected the outcome. She was not offered the job for which she had applied and truthfully didn't want to live in California anyway.

She had another interview set up with an energy company in Oklahoma just after the holidays. She was a basketball fan and flew to Oklahoma City to spend some time with a friend and catch a couple of Thunder games. The friend lived in the city of Edmond, just north and east of the capitol.

In the early morning hours on her first night there she was subjected once again to the whims of Mother Nature when another earthquake struck. It was not very strong by seismic standards, only 4.2 on the scale, but it was enough to rekindle the terror she had felt in California.

Her friend came into her bedroom to check on her and found her cowering in the bed. The earthquake had not lasted more than a few seconds but it had seemed an eternity to Laura.

Nan, her friend, said, "It's nothing to worry about. We have them quite often, though most are not as strong as that one."

Just then another loud noise was heard and the house shook slightly. For the next few hours' aftershocks occurred with the intensity getting weaker with the passage of time.

Laura's interview was in Tulsa and she planned to drive the rental car there from Edmond. She and Nan attended the game that night, which was December 28th. They were going to another game on New Year's Eve. She would then drive to Tulsa on the first and do the interview on the second of January.

The two attended the game on her last night and went to bed. The night was apparently a replay of the night of her arrival because another earthquake occurred at precisely the same time as the previous one, 5:39 a.m. Now how was that for coincidence?

Having experienced two previous quakes in the last week she thought she should now be an old hand but the same unbridled fear took hold the moment the earth started shaking. The motion was bad enough but the sound was what really got her. It was not like anything she had ever heard, sort of a crack and rumble.

Again Nan came in to check on her. "You must have brought these with you from California. We haven't had any quakes this strong in a long time."

"I don't know why they terrify me so badly. I studied about seismic activity in school and I know what causes them but I had never been near one until the one in California. Now these two and I am a basket case," Laura said.

Nan laughed. "These were pretty minor compared to some they have in other parts of the world."

"I know. I am being totally irrational. Maybe if I had been outside when it happened it would not have scared me so badly," Laura said.

"That's probably true. I don't think you feel the movement as much if you are outside or in a car."

"I wonder how frequently they occur around the world," Laura said, more to herself that to get a response from her friend.

"Pretty frequently from what I know," Nan said.

"Well, since I am awake I am going to do some research and find out," Laura said.

She got on her laptop and spent the next hour studying seismic activity over the years. She was amazed at the amount of activity. Hardly a day went by without detected seismic activity somewhere. The advances in measuring instruments and record keeping during the last century had gone a long way toward helping laymen to understand the frequency and destructive capability of earthquakes. Nan was right about the ones they had the last few days being weaker ones.

While Laura was on the web site for the National Earthquake Information Center, or NEIC, she looked at the make-up of the organization and happened across an appeal for qualified people to work at the center in Golden, Colorado. That was near Denver and wouldn't be a bad place to live, she thought.

She filled out an on-line application then and there without much thought to actually being invited to come for an interview.

Nan fixed breakfast for them and Laura was on her way to Tulsa before noon. The drive was only a couple of hours and she had most of the day free after checking into her hotel. She did some more looking at the NEIC web site. She was intrigued by the amount of data contained there and wondered how they collected so much information.

Her interview the next day was in the late morning. After she had breakfast she whiled away the time on her computer. While doing this her cell phone rang. She looked at the caller ID and didn't recognize the area code, much less the caller. She answered the call and was surprised to learn that it was someone from the NEIC.

"Is this Laura Griswold?" the caller asked.

"Yes."

"My name is Sam Watkins. I work at the National Earthquake Information Center. I looked at the application you filled out on-line and was wondering if I could get a little more information about your academic background."

"What do you want to know?"

"You indicate that your degree is in Geology. Do you have any area of specialization?"

"Well, I thought I would go into the energy exploration field and sort of geared my curriculum to that end. Now I find that is pretty much an old boy network and they are not at all interested in females to work in the field. I had my first experience with an earthquake just last week and it frankly scared the crap out of me. I was doing some research on your web site and saw the request for applications so I filled one out."

"Are you serious about wanting to work in the field?"

"Yes I am."

"When would it be convenient to come to Golden, Colorado for an interview?  The government will pay you for the travel and put you up in a hotel if you have some free time in the near future," he said.

"I am supposed to interview with another energy company today but if you are serious I will reschedule this interview.  That's just in case this doesn't work out with you," Laura said.

Sam laughed.  "I won't hold that against you."

"In that case, when is it convenient for you?"

"Could you be here tomorrow?"

"I don't see why not. I will call the other company and check on airline reservations as soon as I hang up with you.  Can I call you on the number on my caller ID?"

"Yes.  Let me know when you are getting in and I will meet you at the airport, or if you'd prefer you can check into a hotel and call me from there."

"I believe the second option is best.  I will call you when I get into Denver."

Laura called the company she was supposed to interview with and asked if she could reschedule.  The receptionist told her they could do it if she would give her some time sort of time frame.

"Is it all right if I call back and do the rescheduling later?"

"Yes just call at least a week before you want to do the interview."

She next called the airline and arranged a flight from Tulsa to Denver.  She had to route through Dallas and went ahead with the reservation.

She also made hotel reservations.

During the flight she tried to analyze why she had made the spur of the moment decision to study earthquakes as a profession.  She finally arrived at the conclusion that her fear of the things had been the catalyst.  Though she still didn't know where the interview would lead she felt the impulse had been a good one.

Only time would tell.

## Chapter 2

Laura had grown up in the eastern part of the country where earthquakes were generally someone else's problem. She had been born in North Carolina, near Asheville, and had grown up in Virginia Beach, Virginia for her formative years.

When she graduated from high school she had no idea what she wanted to do with her life. She had always been a rock hound as well as a frequent visitor to the sea shore to look for shells and such. She hiked in the mountains a lot and always looked for strange rocks or Indian artifacts.

She had developed the habit of cataloging her finds as to location and type of rock. The hobby had remained with her and she decided that geology might be a good way to make a living. When she was ready for college she chose a school with a good geology program. She had looked at the lesser known institutions of higher learning with solid academic reputations. The Colorado School of Mines had been on the list, as were Texas A&M and New Mexico Institute of Mining.

In the end she decided to stay close to home and enrolled at William and Mary in Williamsburg, Virginia. She was a straight A student and had no trouble qualifying for whatever school she should choose. Her family was well off financially so she would not have any financial constraints no matter where she chose to go to school. She qualified for an academic scholarship which took care of the bulk of her expenses and didn't need to work part time to make ends meet.

William and Mary was a very good school but was not geared to any one career field as far as degree programs went. Laura took all the geology courses they offered but was not able to specialize in any one sector of the field.

It was late when she arrived in Denver and she checked in to the hotel and slept for a few hours before calling Sam Watkins.

When she called at 9:30 a.m. he told her he would meet her at the hotel. She provided a room number and waited for his arrival.

He was not long in arriving and drove her to Golden, a suburb of Denver. Sam was in his thirties Laura guessed and had an easy going manner.

Once they arrived at the center Laura realized that it was actually on the campus of the Colorado School of Mines, one of the schools she had been interested in attending and commented on the coincidence.

"They teach a lot of the subjects that go along with our mission and the location makes sense. The center is part of the U.S. Geological Survey and has moved around a bit since it was established. It originally started in Maryland about 50 years ago and has migrated to the current location in three or four moves over the years," Sam said.

When Sam gave her the tour of the center she was vastly disappointed and commented that she didn't think she would care much to be tied to a desk all the time.

She made this comment when she saw the administrative nature of what the center produced. There were seismic graphs and other measuring instruments and the place looked more like an academic environment than anything else.

After the tour Sam took her into his office and got down to business. "Why did you fill out the application for our organization?" he asked.

"I had gone through a small quake in California while there for a job interview. It scared me silly. I had of course studied earthquake theory and the effect geology has on their occurrence but I had never experienced one. It shook me up so much that I was not myself at the interview and that didn't work out. I had intended to go into energy research, looking for oil and natural gas for companies in that business. I set up another interview with a company in Tulsa and stayed in Edmond with a friend for a few days. They had two earthquakes while I was there. They were only in the low four range but we were close enough to the epicenter that they shook the house pretty good. Again I felt the terror associated with the quake. I decided to do some on-line research and that's how I came across your web-site and filled out the application."

"What was the reasoning behind that?"

"I thought it might help me to get over the absolute terror that an earthquake awakened in me," Laura said truthfully.

Sam chuckled. "Not the best of reasons for going into a profession," he said.

"I figured geology has to play an important role in generating earthquakes so there might be a fit," she said.

"And you don't think you would like a desk job," Sam asked.

"I realize that any job in the technical fields is going to have a certain amount of work that has to be done at a desk, but I don't want that to be the primary workplace. I envisioned something like being out doing research and then producing reports on whatever data I had been gathering."

"I have been toying with the idea of bringing a couple of people on as field representatives of the center. I will need to write the job descriptions to get them approved but my thought was to have someone do actual geological studies of areas that experience significant increases in the incidence of earthquakes over time," Sam said.

"Can you explain that a little better?"

"I can give you a good example. You were in Oklahoma over the past few days and during that time you experienced two earthquakes above 4.0 on the seismic scale. How often would you think that happens there?"

"I had not heard of Oklahoma being an earthquake prone area ever before I was there to experience them."

"You are almost one hundred percent correct in that assessment. Until 2007 there were so few earthquakes in that area that none shows on the records prior to that time. Suddenly in 2007 and beyond we have a significant increase in seismic activity in that area. There has been a steady increase in the number and intensity of quakes in Oklahoma since 2007. We have recorded a total of 770 seismic events there since then, some in the 4.0 and above range."

"That sounds unbelievable. From zero to 770 in nine years?"

"Yes. And the culprit might be the fracking process they use now to extract oil. The evidence is circumstantial but Kansas, which is just to the north of Oklahoma and produces some oil instituted strict regulations for the use of the fracking process and the injection of the by-products back into the ground. The number of earthquakes had been on the rise along with Oklahoma. After they enacted laws against the process their earthquake incidence has decreased while at the same time Oklahoma's has increased."

"Let me guess, 2007 was the time when the oil companies started to use the injector wells?" I asked.

Sam smiled. "At least you can put two and two together. Even if we can establish fracking or the injector wells as the cause of the increased earthquake activity we will have a tough time doing anything about it. Oklahoma is so closely tied to the oil revenues for their livelihood that there will have to be some major calamity in order to get them to change the system."

"If it is that dangerous it should be a no-brainer," Laura said.

"The main problem is that we know so little about the area that we cannot unequivocally identify fracking as the primary cause. We don't have enough geological data and the stakes are too high for the oil companies and the state as a general entity to force the issue. The oil companies pay a majority of the taxes that go into the coffers of the state and employ a lot of people who pay additional taxes."

"So how do you get enough data to cause them to change the procedure?"

"You're the geologist. You tell me."

"I'm not even sure what the fracking process entails," Laura said.

"Basically they drill into an oil field and extract what they can from the major pool. When it starts to run dry they drill horizontally and pump the byproducts back into the area they have already exploited. Theoretically they can pump the oil from as much as three or four miles from the area where the well was sunk without having to move the operation. That means they get more oil from the same well head at a cheaper cost. Theoretically pumping the waste back into the hole replaces what they took out, and mathematically that makes sense. But somewhere in the process something is not working as it should. The oil companies don't know what if anything is to blame and until we can prove to them that the process is causing the increased earthquake activity they are not going to make any changes," Sam said.

"Do you think there is any other possibility for the cause of the increased activity?"

"I don't know, nor does anyone else. That's what makes it such a tough problem to deal with."

"So if I come to work for you I will be in the field doing the geologic studies to try to get to the bottom of the problem?" I asked to make sure I was reading this right.

"Among other duties. You will still have to spend some time here learning how our reporting system works and the kind of data we produce. I feel pretty sure I can get approval for the positions I mentioned but it is going to take as much as three months to get the paperwork approved. Do you think you might be interested in the position?"

"How much will it pay?"

"I'm going to write the positions for GS-12, which is just under $70 thousand annually but I might have to accept a GS-11 grade which will be about 10K less than that. The time you are on the road you will be paid per-diem for your food and lodging and either the government will provide a car or will reimburse you for the mileage you put on your own car."

"It certainly sounds intriguing but do you think I am qualified for the job?" Laura asked.

"If you majored in Geology you will have taken the courses that will come into play. Most of what you will be doing will be based on your own knowledge and observations and the biggest hurdle will be getting the cooperation of the oil companies. If they will allow you access to their wells and data it will make the job a lot simpler for you."

"It certainly sounds like something I would be interested in."

"Can you hold off that long to start?"

"Yes. I will go back home and mooch off my parents until I hear from you," Laura said.

Laura went back to Virginia Beach and told her parents about her change in career choices.

Her dad said, "It seems unusual that you would go to work on the very thing that scares you so much."

"I think that's part of it. If I can understand the mechanics of the things better maybe I will look at things differently."

"Is the job going to be in Oklahoma?" he asked.

"No, not from what I understand. I will actually be based in Golden, Colorado, just outside Denver, but will be working in Oklahoma for as much time as I need to be there."

"So what are you going to do while waiting for the paperwork?"

"Do some studying about earthquakes and try to get a historical background if possible. I never paid much attention to the phenomena since we didn't live in an area where we had to worry about them."

Laura did what she said and spent a great deal of time on her computer during the waiting period.

As it turned out it didn't take as long to get the paper work through as Sam had thought. Apparently others were worrying about the situation in Oklahoma and the positions were approved without much debate or foot dragging. It only took 63 days according to Laura's calendar.

When the call came she was ready to go. She loaded her goods in a small U-Haul trailer, bade her parent's farewell, and hit the road.

## Chapter 3

Laura asked Sam about the best location to live and he gave her a map of the area with his recommendations marked on it.

She looked around some and found an apartment nearby that would suit her purposes and was not terribly expensive.

Between all the paperwork and physical examination it took her three days to process for the job. In her slack time she got set up in the apartment and tried to learn her way around the area. Even Virginia Beach, which is quite spread out, had more area than Denver and she found it relatively easy to find her way around.

Once she finished the paperwork Sam called her into his office and gave her a folder. "This is about all we have on the area in question. Some of the energy big wigs are listed so you will have a starting point. We have not devoted a lot of time to actually studying the results of fracking because it is somewhat afield from our normal functions. Most of the information in this folder comes from phone calls, except for the statistical data, and that comes from our sensor observation during actual earthquakes. I will leave the approach up to you, but if you need anything such as someone to vouch for your project just have them call me."

"You can't even give me some direction to use as a starting point? Laura asked.

"You're breaking new ground so you will have to make it up as you go along. I put a lot of money in the budget request to take care of your expenses for a considerable time. I think you should try to get back here at least once a month to brief us on what you are doing and any results. I will expect you to call at least weekly to let me know what the project yields," he said.

"I want to drive my own car from here. Will that be a problem?"

"No. The government will pay you mileage based on the accepted formula, which is more than enough to take care of your expenses. You will be paid the standard per diem rate. I would suggest looking for an extended stay motel and working from there."

Laura made notes of the names in the folder and asked about data access.

"You can find most of the data sources on-line. All our data is published as soon as an event occurs and the historical stuff is in the best format we can devise for continuity. Nothing we do is classified so you should be able to get anything you need from Oklahoma," Sam said.

"Am I going to be working alone or will the person filling the other position you requested be working with me?"

"I haven't filled that position yet but I had envisioned having one of you in the central area and the other on the west coast. California has much more frequent events and they tend to be more severe out there."

Laura packed her bags with most of the clothing she had brought, at least the summer part of the wardrobe. It was still spring so she did take a couple of sweaters along. She had two large suitcases and a few odds and ends that all fit in her car with no problem.

She was up early the next morning and headed for Oklahoma.

She stayed overnight in the Oklahoma panhandle and did some more research on the NEIC data base and charted the quakes that had occurred in the last ten years. Earthquake activity in the area prior to 2007 was practically non-existent. The incidents seemed to have started then and built gradually for the next several years. In 2015 there had been 283 quakes recorded in the central Oklahoma area.

The first thing Laura wanted to do was get a better understanding of what fracking actually entailed. She could get an explanation of the fundamental process from someplace like Wikipedia, but in order to really understand she would need to talk to some people in the oil business. That she established as her first chore.

Laura called her friend with whom she had stayed during the holidays in which she experienced the earthquakes and asked if she could intrude for a few days until she decided where she was going to work from.

The answer was yes of course and she found her way to her friend's house.

The two talked about Laura's new job and what it would entail. Her friend kidded her about her reaction to the quakes they had experienced when she was there. She also wanted to know if the NEIC thought the oil industry was responsible for the high incidence of quakes in recent years.

"I haven't the foggiest idea. I know that one camp feels that the oil people are responsible, but on the other hand I am told that the practice has been going on since around the middle of the last century. If fracking is responsible then it sure took a long time to catch up to them."

"Do you have some set formula to look at to try to get to the bottom of the matter?"

"Not a single page. I was told to study the geological aspects and exactly what I looked at was up to me. I guess I have a blank check to look into anything that might impact the process," she said.

"How are you going to get data on geological formations underground?" her friend asked next.

"I hope to get a lot of the stuff from the oil companies. If I approach them in the right manner they should cooperate with me. That is unless the industry has been hiding factual data for a very long time."

"Well I wish you luck."

Laura started making phone calls the next day. She wanted to find out which company worked the area near the epicenters of the recent quakes.

After several phone calls she learned that different companies operated wherever they could find oil and negotiate with the property owners for a lease.

None of the companies she talked with were willing to give out the information she wanted over the phone. She decided to just drive to the area and see what she could determine in that fashion. The NEIC had charted earthquakes long enough that they could determine the epicenter of a quake to within a very close tolerance. The data they provided was based on seismic sensor input from all over the world. Within the United States there are approximately 7,000 Earthquake Sensor Systems and the telemetry allowed cross referencing from the shock points to pinpoint the quakes.

Having said that, there is no way to actually gauge the validity of the data since you can't actually see the epicenter. Most people take on faith that the NEIC does a good job of locating the quakes. The stronger ones felt in Edmond over the last few years seemed to be centered just to the north of the town and on the eastern side of Interstate 35, the north/south highway between Oklahoma City and Tulsa.

In the afternoon of her first day of actually working Laura drove up Interstate 35 until she started seeing oil wells. She was in the area of interest and started looking for an exit that would allow her access to both the eastern and western sides of the highway.

Most of the wells she saw were individual ones and from what she had learned were probably tied into a network of pipelines to get the oil to a refinery. She stopped at the first house where she could identify a well on the property.

She went to the door and knocked. When the lady of the house answered her knock she asked who the well belonged to.

"We sold the mineral rights through an agent and I don't rightly know who owns the equipment. I think it is Phillips, or maybe Chesapeake. It don't bother us none and really isn't of much concern to us."

she talked to several other people in the general area and got pretty much the same story from all of them. The oil company bought the mineral rights and took care of everything to do with the well. The money was like manna from heaven and they could care less what the oil companies did, just as long as the grazing land was still available to them.

Sam Hunter called her that evening and suggested that she might want to look at a report he had run across on the internet about a study in central California that had linked a series of minor quakes to fracking by the oil companies in the area. The report stated that the quakes were definitely linked to the reinsertion of the fracking residue that was put back into the earth.

Several geologists from different universities combined to do the study. The article didn't say anything about their methodology but stated unequivocally that the reinsertion of a large amount of the residue from previous drilling had triggered the quakes.

She traveled between Oklahoma City and Tulsa for the entire week. While in Tulsa she talked with several people who were involved with the oil industry.

She managed to get an interview with a pretty senior person from Phillips and the same with Haliburton. Both had made data available to her that dealt with the strata encountered during the drilling process. This should be helpful to her in some ways.

During the drilling process the residue that comes up when the well is sunk can be used to tell what kind of medium is being drilled into. There's a lot of pressure at the location of the drill head and the process becomes easier or harder as the strata becomes porous or solid.

Laura met a man who was retired from the oil business. He had worked on the off-shore platforms along the California coast. He told her that they had been using the fracking process since he had been working and that dated back to the 1960 decade.

"I'm no expert," he said, "but I don't believe fracking in and of itself causes earthquakes. Shucks if that was the case we would have been having them constantly throughout Oklahoma, Texas and California 'cause we have used the process in all those places. Now you might be able to make a case for California. They have them often enough that I reckon it is possible. The earthquakes only started in the Midwest since they started reinjecting the residue into the holes."

"You didn't put the residue back in the holes when you were working?" Laura asked.

"No, we pumped it into a ship at the off-shore sites and they hauled it someplace. I have no idea where but we definitely did the horizontal drilling. That's what they call fracking. It was just more cost effective to drill horizontally since it was such a headache and expense building the platforms."

"What did the oil companies do with what they took out previously?"

"They either had it hauled to a holding tank or built holding ponds near the drill site. Basically they just used earth movers to hollow out a large depression and line the hole with plastic and pumped the stuff into the pond."

"How did they get rid of it then?"

"I have no idea. That wasn't part of my job. By the time I would be sent to a site the well would already be in the ground."

"Why did the oil companies start reinjecting the residue into the ground? There must have been millions of gallons of the stuff at all the different location where they sunk wells. Was it causing a problem in other ways?" Laura asked.

"You got me. I know very little about that part of the industry," he said. "I think it might have had to do with forcing the oil out of the shale into the oil line. You know oil floats to the top of water. By injecting the liquid below the shale strata it would force the oil to the top and it would enter the drill pipe above the liquid they had reinserted. I guess the same principle applies to natural gas."

"That makes sense."

"The biggest reason though was the money they would save. They would avoid having to build holding tanks or ponds, which would save money, then the increased productivity of the wells also added to the profit margin."

"Are they pumping the residue back into the off-shore wells?"

"I imagine so. It works on land so it stands to reason that it would work off the platforms as well."

The man didn't seem to be in any hurry to get anyplace and Laura talked to him for almost half an hour.

"I have heard some people advance the theory that the shale layer is what actually lubricates the plates under the earth's crust, sort of a cushion and a smooth layer that prevents the strata underground from violent shifts. Have you heard anyone in the industry mention anything like that?" Laura asked.

"I haven't heard anything like that and I don't think I would believe that anyway. During regular drilling we are pumping oil from the same strata so over time the regular drilling should have the same effect if that were true," he said.

After the conversation Laura gave some serious thought to the method she would use to try to assess the situation as it applied to the oil industry's possible contribution to earthquakes. It was known that earthquakes occurred as a result of the plates along geological fault lines moving, either vertically or horizontally but what actually caused the plates to shift was a matter of conjecture. That it happened so often in given areas had allowed those who studied the phenomenon to chart the fault lines and geological data also contributed but what actually triggered a shift could not be unequivocally stated.

With the incidence of significant events occurring in Oklahoma since 2007 and the beginning of the reinsertion of the drilling residue back into the ground at that time it certainly pointed to a correlation of the events.

Laura had charted all the earthquakes reported since 2007 on a chart of the state. Most of the quakes were north of Oklahoma City and south of Tulsa. There were however, a number to the north of Tulsa, toward the state line with Kansas, where the practice of reinjecting the drilling residue was the normal procedure.

Another thing that Laura noticed from the data provided by the NEIC, was that most of the quakes in Oklahoma were not nearly as deep as those in other parts of the world. While the majority of quakes worldwide were deep underground, some as much as 200 miles deep, the ones that did the most damage were those nearer to the surface of the earth.

The ones she charted in Oklahoma were as shallow as 1 mile in some cases, but were normally between the three and ten mile depths. This coincided with the depth at which the drilling slag was reintroduced into the ground.

Laura's father had told her about the big quake in California that occurred in 1989 during a World Series telecast. That was probably the most famous earthquake in American history, though it was far from the most devastating. It had been measured at 7.3 and the television cameras had caught the impact on live TV. Bridges and freeways collapsed and were recorded either live or just after the fact and the entire nation knew about it immediately. The pictures of mangled automobiles and entire sections of elevated freeways collapsing burned indelible pictures into the brains of those watching.

That one was called the Loma Prieta earthquake and didn't even make the top seven in California history.

All the historical data was interesting but didn't help Laura with the task of determining what was causing the Oklahoma quakes. The data she had charted helped her to get a better feeling for where the quakes occurred and if she could tie them to the actual drilling process it might help her more.

The maddening element of her task was that even if she could show that the earthquakes occurred near where drilling was taking place that would still not provide conclusive proof that the two were tied together.

From the charts it appeared that the majority of the earthquakes in Oklahoma were to the north of Oklahoma City. Did that mean that a fault line lay along that area? Surely oil was pumped from the ground to the south of the Capital just as it was to the north. That was an element that would mitigate against the fracking process causing the quakes, although it was possible that they didn't reinsert the residue in wells to the south.

She simply didn't know enough about the local geology to even make a guess as to the validity of that premise.

One thing she did notice was that the quakes to the north of Edmond formed a very rough circular pattern toward Fairview and Cherokee, then to the north just inside the Kansas border and to the east of Interstate 35 back toward Oklahoma City.

There was a fault line visible on satellite maps called the Meers Fault, which ran southeast to northwest and almost bisected Oklahoma City. From other fault maps Laura concluded that most of the earthquake activity had been located within what was called the Cherokee Platform. This was an area where very little earthquake activity had been detected prior to 2007.

Laura knew enough about the geological formations which cause fault lines that she could reason that the area to the southern part of the state might be very different from the area to the north. That was the major problem with what she was attempting to do. The data was simply not of the quantity and quality that would allow her to draw unvarnished conclusions.

She had been checking in with Sam at least weekly and planned a trip back to Golden after a month in Oklahoma.

John Buckner

Chapter 4

Laura had acquired a mountain of data since her arrival and wanted to talk it over with Sam when she got back there. She had charted the locations of the injector wells and at the very least could show the proximity of recent earthquakes to the area in which the injector wells were located.

She didn't know where the project was going. She was still in the data collection mode of operation. It was possible that even with all the data she would not be able to draw any real conclusion, other than projections based on the data. She had experienced several earthquakes in the area since returning. Fortunately she had been outside for most of them and had not experienced the fear that had gripped her while inside for the others.

The large oil companies were starting to become a bit more concerned but they didn't allow the concern to become public knowledge. The practice of reinjecting the drilling residue was quite profitable to them and if there was any way to continue the practice they were certainly going to take that direction.

The report by the geological study group in California that had tied earthquakes to the practice unequivocally was a matter of concern but not greatly so.

All of them had provided drilling data to Laura Griswold. They had also provided data on the injector wells noting the depth of the reinsertion points.

They were not concerned about the data. It was in accordance with state requirements and was provided to the state authorities routinely.

When she got back to Golden she sat down with Sam and reviewed what she had been doing.

"There's a lot of data from the oil companies. They don't seem overly concerned about the practice. They are working according to state guidelines and provide data routinely to the state. I think the recent article from the geologists in California might have got them to take a step back and look more closely at their practices, but nothing is going to come of it until something drastic happens," Laura said.

"You don't think the incidence of more earthquakes is drastic?" Sam asked.

"Not enough to get them to change the practice. I have charted all the injector wells and the operational fracking wells. There is no doubt that the injector wells are responsible for the rise in earthquakes but they are minor enough that no one takes them seriously. Let me show you something that might be a possible consequence of injecting the residue back into the ground."

Laura took out the chart.

"Look at the way they plot with regard to the Cherokee Platform."

The Cherokee Platform is an elliptical section of earth which lies between Oklahoma City to the south, the Kansas line to the north, Tulsa to the east, and the small town of Cherokee to the west.

"The injector wells are located almost along the outward boundaries of the Platform. There have been hundreds of earthquakes along the outer edge of the boundary over the last several years. They have gradually increased in intensity with the strongest to date measuring at 5.1."

"What conclusion do you draw from that?" Sam asked.

"I don't have any hard references to point to anything but I believe it is possible that the continued use of injection wells where they are located now might contribute to a complete fracture of the Cherokee Platform. If that happens it could cause that entire section of the earth to rise dramatically," Laura said.

"How did you arrive at that hypothesis?"

"I read somewhere that the injector wells put the water back under very high pressure. That is necessary to cause the gas and oil to rise to the pumping wells. What it also does is create tremendous upward lift on the area above the injection point. I believe it is possible that with enough waste pumped back into the ground it will create sort of a cushion for the entire Platform. If that happens then that entire section of earth could rise several feet. If the fracture is nearly clean it could create the granddaddy of earthquakes for that area."

"What range are you talking about?" Sam asked.

"I don't have the slightest idea, but I expect the earth could show a vertical lift of as much as ten feet, maybe more in some areas where the pressure is greatest. If the horizontal movement is present to a larger degree you have the makings of one of the most damaging earthquakes in history. It would make the Great Basin quake seem mild by comparison," Laura said.

"I can see where you would arrive at that conclusion, but detractors would suggest that with almost daily earthquakes they are causing the movement at a slower pace and therefore not likely to cause a cataclysmic event," Sam said.

"I can see the logic of that line of thinking, but with the quakes getting stronger by the day the question is not if we will have a large event, but when."

"How much waste do they pump back?"

"The best estimate I heard was that if the Mississippi River was flowing underground in the area that it would have to flow consistently for eight hours to equate to the amount of waste pumped back," Laura said.

"So your theory is that the waste pumped back will eventually exert enough upward pressure to cause some cataclysmic event?"

"Yes, but they don't inject as much to the northern area and that area might not be subjected to the same stress. Still, the outward boundary of the rest of the ellipse will receive more pressure than the northern sector."

"Most of the faults in Oklahoma are to the south of Oklahoma City. It would seem to me that area should logically be having more earthquakes than the norther part of the state. Don't they pump the residue back into the ground in that area?"

"The only thing that makes sense to me is that the southern part of the state is permeated with more fractures and the waste naturally fills in the fissures and keeps the surface pressure from building up. Keep in mind that I have no data to back that up but they have had far fewer quakes in that area and they pump almost as much oil and gas from that area as they do in the norther part of the state."

"What do you want to do now?" Sam asked.

"I can't see much to do other than keep gathering data and hope something shows up to give us a better indication as to what is going to happen in the future," Laura said.

Laura only spent three days in Golden and she was ready to go back to Oklahoma.

"I want to take a portable motion detector back with me if we have any available. I want to chart the movement near where they are pumping the residue back. Maybe I can get some idea about how any motion translates while they are actually doing the pumping."

"Have you talked to any state officials?"

"You mean the ones who control the quotas on how much waste can be pumped back?" Laura asked.

"Yes."

"I have talked to a couple of them but they get together with the officials from the oil companies and together they arrive at some figure which satisfies both parties. They haven't made any meaningful changes since the practice started about ten years ago. They add chemicals to the water they use for drilling and most of that comes back with the waste. When it is pumped back in below the drill level nobody has any idea about what effect it has on the strata layers underground."

"Your hypothesis is that if they use it to break down rock while drilling then just sitting there static at some level it will still have some residual effect?"

"It seems logical to me that would be the case."

"It will be interesting to see what you come up with," Sam said.

"Am I doing what you had in mind when you offered the job?" Laura asked.

"Pretty much. I told you that we have no blueprint for the type work you are doing. At some point in the future we will have to come up with a more detailed job description."

"I feel so inadequate. I have no idea if my approach will yield anything worthwhile or not. I don't even have any way to measure the effectiveness of what I am doing."

"Just keep plugging and we will see what the first year yields," Sam said.

Laura headed back to Oklahoma. She was still staying with her friend in Edmond when possible. She spent some time in motels but Edmond was close enough that she spent more than half her nights there. She had insisted on paying rent and helping with the food bill. It was only fair and she enjoyed at least having someone to talk to about her work.

The motion detector she acquired was designed to detect movement beneath the earth. She didn't know how effective it would be for what she had in mind but anything was worth a try.

What she wanted to do was move the instrument around to different quadrants from the actual injector well to see if she got any indication as to how the dispersal of the waste occurred. The logical assumption was that the end of the pipe used to inject the waste would cause it to move in the direction in which the pipe was oriented but there was no guarantee of that.

If there were nulls in the geology it would create open space similar to caverns on the earth's surface, or just beneath the surface.

Laura also suspected that there would be minute movement that wouldn't register on normal earthquake detection devices. Just the sound of the waste moving through the pipe should show up on her instrument if she was close enough to the source. She imagined the result to be akin to a sonogram.

She spent the next three months charting the sounds of movement near the injection wells. She also continued to chart the earthquakes that were measurable throughout the area. Most were still at the 2.0 level or below but almost once a week something larger would happen. Most of those were in the 3.0 to 4.0 range.

The largest quake that anyone knew about in the area happened in February of 2016. It was a 5.1 and was centered near the Fairview area which seemed to be more prone to earthquakes than any other area where the injector wells were located.

Laura wondered if there was some feature of the geology in that area which contributed to this problem.

She spent more time there than in other areas and had a lot of data as a result.

She had detected what she thought of as deep caverns in the area. Some were as much as eight miles deep. Of course the data was only her interpretation of the sound produced by the pumping of the waste back to that level.

This started her on another train of thought. What if the combination of depleting the oil above the waste injection well and the upward pressure between the two operations caused only the movement of that segment of strata to move enough to come in contact with each other?  That might very well be the source of the larger quakes that had been observed.  There were obviously no rifts in the earth's crust at the location of the quakes so the movement causing them had to be subterranean.

One thing that had happened as a result of the 5.1 quake was that the state officials and the oil companies had started to talk seriously about reducing the level of waste allowed to be pumped back into the earth.

Nothing had come of the talks yet but it was a good sign that they were starting to worry about the long term results of the injector wells.

Laura managed to get an appointment to talk to a geologist who worked for the largest oil company.

She showed him her charts compiled by the data available from the NEIC and from the readings she had taken at the sites of the injector wells.

She sketched the boundaries of the Cherokee Platform and told him of her premise that all the activity in the area might cause the entire Platform to lift a significant amount.

"Another hypothesis is that the oil taken from above the level of the injector wells might cause a shift to make the two areas meet below ground.  If this happens there will be a significant quake below ground level and who knows what will result from that," she said.

"I appreciate all your effort but there is nothing to substantiate such a claim.  While I will admit that there might be some small effect from the injector wells I don't believe it is anything to worry about.  The small quakes are mother nature's way of keeping equilibrium."

"This data doesn't make you think that there might be some truth in my hypothesis?" Laura asked.

"I just can't imagine anything like that happening in this area," he said.

Laura thanked him for his time and left Tulsa in a high state of agitation.  What was wrong with these people?  Were they so interested in their profits that they could ignore facts that might very well result in a major catastrophe?

It had been almost a month since the 5.1 quake and the state of concern immediately after the quake had started to abate.

All she could do was continue to gather information and try to make people see where the current course of action might lead them. As time passed Laura became more convinced than ever that a major event was on the horizon. The quakes that had been below the 2.0 range had inched upward toward 3.0. She developed graphics to show the gradual increase in intensity of the routine quakes. About twice, maybe three times a year a larger quake would happen.

The period since 2015 had seen a significant increase in events reading 4.0 and higher. Earthquakes in that range were not very destructive in terms of lost property or lives but damage could be seen in minor ways. Cracks in drywall, brick walls crumbling and minor foundation shifts had been reported. Again the damage was not significant so not a lot of attention was directed to those minor things.

Laura was far from alone in her fears that a major Earthquake would occur. More people had purchased earthquake insurance specifically to cover them under that circumstance. The environmental groups were still applying pressure to curtail the injector well limits but without much success.

The Earth First Society, one of the groups had learned of Laura's work and asked her to meet with them. She agreed and had lunch with two of the group leaders.

They met at a restaurant in Bricktown, Oklahoma City's equivalent of 'chic' area. Over lunch they discussed the oil business and their contribution to the state coffers and how that affected the way public officials dealt with them.

One of her lunch companions said, "The state is so dependent on taxes from the oil industry that they are not willing to take any significant action without first clearing it with the heavies in that field. We have been telling them for years that the injector wells are responsible for the increase in earthquake activity but nobody listens."

The other party said, "We were hoping to get some information from your research that might add some weight to our concerns with the state. It is perfectly clear to our group that the state is headed for big trouble if they don't take some action to curtail the amount of waste pumped back into the earth. You would think that just looking at the difference it made in Kansas when they did away with the practice would be enough. The incidence of earthquakes there showed a downward trend almost immediately. The ones they still have in the southern part of the state are probably due to the injector wells located in Oklahoma near the border."

"I have noted the same thing," Laura said. "The oil companies are not willing to even concede that the injector wells are to blame. They point to the southern part of the state, which has had fewer events, and say that they inject just as much of the waste there and can see no effect, ergo the earthquakes in the northern part of the state cannot be blamed on the injector wells."

"And is that a valid argument?"

"It might be to those who want to continue the practice, but to me it simply means that the subterranean areas are very different. There are a lot of fault lines in the southeastern part of the state. Prior to 2007 that was where the majority of earthquakes were felt in the state. My theory is that because of the number of fissures beneath the earth's crust in the south that the pressure from the injectors forces the effluent downward. The pressure is distributed more evenly and doesn't result in any significant movement of the earth."

Laura had brought her briefcase into the restaurant with her and now broke out some of the graphs she had compiled. "You do understand that I am not stating a government position in any way?"

"Yes, and we will not bring your name into any action on our part."

"The area I am most concerned about is what is called the Cherokee Platform. It is this area which is bordered by a couple of fault lines. I don't have any geological data on the area, other than the makeup of the soil in the entire region. The oil companies have provided drilling data on a lot of wells in the area that helps to get an idea of strata at different levels," Laura said.

"What does that mean?"

"It means that you can get a general idea about how the earth is composed in the area of the well. When they start drilling they might drill through dirt and rocky soil for the first hundred feet, then they hit water, which is where most of the aquifers are located. That is the drinking water for a lot of people and is the area of most concern to the majority of everyday citizens. They worry that the drilling will pollute the drinking water. The truth of the matter though is that there is not much danger in that regard. The oil and gas are found at a greater depth with layers of solid rock and other layers of compacted shale and then even more solid rock. What the drilling data does is provide the depth at which the different strata were encountered."

"How does that help with the problem?"

"I don't know if it does but the majority of quakes since the injection process started are within the area defined as the Cherokee Platform. I believe that entire area is sort of like an island resting on the more substantial layer of earth below. Within this Platform lies the strata where oil and gas are located. In the past the oil was pumped out without any great impact on the makeup of the strata. Even the horizontal drilling had no great impact on the earth. Once they started using the injector wells it changed the equation. Now oil and gas was being pumped out of the ground, creating voids where the minerals were found. The injected fluids are then pumped back at a much greater depth and pressure and the tendency would be to exert pressure in the path of least resistance, which in this case would be upward. Because of the voids where the oil had resided previously the upward pressure from the injector fluids would cause upward movement of that section of the earth."

"And that is what causes the earthquakes?"

"I believe that is true. You can see from the charts that most of the earthquakes since 2007 have had epicenters very near to an injection well. While that is not conclusive proof, high percentages cannot be discarded. Even of greater import, at least to my way of thinking, is that eventually the upward pressure from the injector wells will distribute itself with enough uniformity to move the entire Cherokee Platform upward. This will cause a major earthquake if that happens."

"How would you predict a time for something like that?"

"I don't know of any way you could, other than to keep monitoring the intensity of the quakes and look for upward trends. This you can see already over the last ten years if you chart the intensity of the quakes that have been detected."

"How large would the earthquake be if something like that happened?"

"There's no way to predict something like that in terms of how strong the quake would be but it would be much greater than anything this area has ever experienced," Laura answered.

"Is there anything we could say that would cause the public, and more importantly state officials, to take the problem more seriously?"

"I have no idea. I can see a bit more concern from the average citizen just in the short time I have been here. I think the fact that the quakes have begun to strengthen over the last couple of years has had some impact in that thought process. The step the state Corporation Commission took to reduce the amount of salt water the oil companies can pump back should have some impact in reducing both the number and the severity of the quakes but I have no idea how that will play out. The sheer numbers come into play to a large extent. If the oil companies are saddled with a reduction in the amount each well can inject it is possible that they will just place more wells into operation. I am not in any way intimating that they would do that, but it is certainly an option."

The three spent well over an hour over lunch and talking about earthquake activity.

Laura called it a day after the luncheon and was back at Nan's house before the rush hour traffic commenced.

Chapter 5

The next morning Laura decided she would try to better define the area occupied by what they called the Cherokee Platform. She had charted more than 2,000 earthquakes within her rough outline of that area over the last several years. Outside that particular area there had been fewer than 100 quakes in the rest of the state over the same time period.

She also found that the large majority of the quakes were within a ten mile radius of one of the injector wells. And on top of that the quakes were all relatively near the earth's surface. Most were no more than 5 miles deep. She had a wealth of circumstantial evidence but it would not be enough to convince anyone who really mattered that her data was indicative of a major earthquake in the future.

She was at a point that she simply did not know what to do next. It had been nine months since she started the project and she had exhausted all avenues that she knew about.

She decided to write a paper and present it to her boss, Sam Watkins.

When she sat down at her computer to start the paper she had no idea what her conclusions would be but she wanted to get everything down to show she had been spending her time productively.

Statistics was the best method she could think of to show what she had done to that point and she did a lot of bar-graphs and maps to demonstrate her points.

The first graph showed all earthquakes prior to 2007 and those that had occurred since. The disparity would be apparent to anyone with even minimal intelligence.

Next she showed a map with rough locations of the quakes since 2007, the preponderance of those being north of Oklahoma City.

The third graph charted the rise in intensity of those located over the Cherokee Platform.

Geological maps were added to the mix to show the different layers beneath the earth's surface as well as she could present it.

When she got to the narrative section to pull it all together she found that her certainty that a major event was on the horizon had increased to the point that she could no more omit that aspect of the problem that any of the other points she would make.

The first item she addressed was the fact that most of the quakes in the area were very near the injector wells. Her conclusion was that there was a definite connection between the injector wells and the increase in earthquake activity.

The second point she made was that the majority of the quakes were located within the area known as the Cherokee Platform. She explained exactly what that was and how she interpreted the geology of that feature.

She next explained that the term fracking was misunderstood by many people, including herself when she embarked on her current project. The term simply meant drilling horizontally within the oil source. The actual cause of the quakes was not the fracking but the reinsertion of the drilling residue back to a depth below the shale that contained the oil, she explained.

More than two typewritten pages were needed to explain how the process worked and to give her readers a description of the chemicals contained in the drilling residue and the tremendous pressure at which the slag was reinserted.

She used graphics to explain her theory of the disparity between the area from which the oil was extracted and the area where the residue was reinjected.

She used the same graphic to illustrate her theory on what might happen if the pressure from below became great enough to lift the entire Cherokee Platform to meet the area where oil was being extracted.

Her final conclusion was that a major earthquake was imminent in northern Oklahoma. Even if the state began to cut back on the amount of residue that could be reinserted the pressure would continue to build, only more slowly.

She pointed to the increase in numbers and intensity of the quakes and stated that based on the progression of those figures the big one would happen within the next 7 to 10 years and that it might be as much as a 7.5 to 9.5 in the area occupied by the Cherokee Platform.

The project took her two days and when she finished she asked Nan to look the paper over and give her impressions.

Nan did more than look the paper over. She read it thoroughly and then went back and double checked some of the graphs and charts.

"This is unbelievable," she said.

"Yeah, that's my problem. I am not going to get anyone to believe it," Laura replied.

"I didn't mean that the way you took it Laura. I just mean that the information is right in front of us and until I read this I had no idea what had really been happening. Are you sure about all this?"

"I am sure of the data. I compiled it from public records and from my own readings in the field. The epicenters for the quakes charted there are a matter of record and unless the NEIC is completely incompetent, all that is factual. The only part that is not are my conclusions arrived at from the looking at the data. All the indictors point to a major catastrophe and I really believe the conclusion I have drawn from the study," Laura said.

"All of these quakes are near injector wells?"

"Not all, but the great majority are."

"What do the oil companies say about that?"

"The geologists I have talked to, who work for the oil companies incidentally, seem to think that if there is any connection to the injector wells that the smaller quakes are dissipating the material they are injecting and that my suggestion that the pressure will build over time is not valid."

Nan thought that over for several seconds. "But you believe it is valid?"

"Yes, even more so now. I didn't realize how strong the evidence was. Just the fact that the quakes have grown in number and intensity since they started the injection, and the fact that all the quakes are shallow and near the injector wells is enough to convince me that we are playing with fire."

"Who is this for?"

"For my boss in Golden, Colorado at the NEIC. I don't know what he will do with it but I believe he is on my side. The last part of the report, the actual prediction of a major quake, is going to be difficult to get anyone to acknowledge, but I feel very strongly that it is going to happen."

"How far away will it be felt if it happens as you believe?" Nan asked.

"It will be strong enough to create extreme damage within the actual Cherokee Platform area. This area, and probably as far away as Dallas could receive very heavy damage. To the north, probably at least to the northern border of Kansas will see the same. I can't tell you how bad it will be but I think it is going to be a real killer when it hits."

"It sort of makes me want to find someplace else to live," Nan said.

"That's going to be my biggest obstacle to selling this."

"What do you mean?"

"I mean that my boss is not going to be able to sell this to his superiors. They know that it is almost impossible to predict earthquakes with any degree of accuracy. That includes both time and intensity. I have done both those things in this report and I don't believe it will see the light of day until something happens to force them to act. If this report were published tomorrow in the media there would be a mass exodus of Oklahoman's to other parts of the country."

"What are you going to do if they simply ignore you?"

"Find another job I guess, but it won't be in Oklahoma," Laura said.

"How did you arrive at the time estimate?"

"I looked at the rate of increase in the intensity since 2007 and projected that to arrive at the time frame. I also factored in the steadily increasing subterranean pressure under the Platform and used applied mathematics. I know the area that the Cherokee platform occupies, and I know the rate at which the oil companies are reinjecting the slag. I also know the approximate volume of earth above the level at which they are injecting the residue. Mathematically you can determine how much pressure it will take to move the amount of earth above the injection level. It's not very precise but provides at least some ballpark figure."

"Boy that's too complicated for me," Nan said.

"Break it down into something you can relate to. If you want to build a house, or even a large building the engineers have to determine how strong the foundation has to be to keep the structure stable. The weight of the house or building will exert a given amount of stress downward at the foundation of the structure. The people figuring that out have to know the density of the soil and the weight of the building to calculate how deep and strong the foundation needs to be to keep the structure stable. Now reverse that process and figure out how much upward pressure has to be applied to push the structure upward. Then extrapolate that to an entire geographical area, such as the Cherokee Platform. Two things come into play for the situation I am dealing with. First the material taken out of the earth, the actual oil and by products, has a weakening effect on the area above it. There can be downward movement from the earth above because of that fact. Then you inject the residue a couple of miles below where the oil was depleted and you have a section of earth being pushed upward to the void where the oil was located previously. I think that is what is happening now, and has been for a few years."

"If you can figure this out then why can't the state officials, or even the oil companies injecting the stuff?"

"I can't answer that, except to say that a lot of money and the livelihood of a large number of people are at stake. Then too, I have been looking exclusively into the problem for almost a year. Other people may look at portions of the problem but get involved with other things and have no continuity studying it as I have."

"You really don't believe you are going to be taken seriously, do you?"

"My boss will take it seriously, but he has other people to answer to and I don't believe he has enough horsepower to take a stand. I think this is my swan song with NEIC."

"When are you going to submit the report?" Nan asked.

"As soon as I get back to Colorado and have a chance to talk it over with Sam. He has really been a good boss to work for. He doesn't try to micromanage my efforts and has been supportive in getting the things I needed for the work. If he tells me the report will not fly then I will not even submit it."

"Even though you feel pretty sure of your conclusions?"

"You have to remember that I am just a year out of college and the people at the center have been doing this sort of thing a lot longer than I have. There's a chance that I could be way off base, but the data supports my conclusions. That's all I have to hang my hat on. I don't even know if Sam will bring anyone else in on the evaluation of the report, but if he does their word will carry a lot more weight than mine."

"Well you have me convinced. I don't have any close ties to the state and I am going to start looking for a job someplace else," Nan said.

"I am sorry I showed you the report now. I would really hate to have you move away because of my conclusions, which are in no way official."

"I have been following your efforts closer than anyone at the NEIC and I know you have been thorough in your research. I can plainly see what you are talking about and I agree with your conclusions. That's enough for me."

"I hope against hope that you faith is misplaced. I don't really want to be right on this but I fear that I am," Laura said.

On that note she put the report in her briefcase and went to bed.

John Buckner

Chapter 6

Laura had breakfast the next morning and then called Sam.

"I'm coming back to see you within the next couple of days. I have put together a report and I want to get your reaction. I don't feel that there is much more I can do here."

"When are you leaving?" he asked.

"Probably tomorrow morning. There are a couple of things I want to do today."

"Call me when you get here," he replied.

Laura still had the business cards of the two people from the Earth First luncheon and she called one of them and set up a luncheon appointment.

The same two people met her for lunch.

Laura was not overly sure about what she was preparing to do but wanted someone on her side in this issue. She told them that she had put together a report on her work over the past year and that it was not a rosy picture.

"How unrosy is it?" one of them asked.

"Doesn't even smell like a flower by any name," she replied with a chuckle.

"So what's the bottom line?"

"The report will probably never make it to anyone who has any say in the matter. I think my boss will be supportive but he is not very high on the totem pole for his organization. He's probably going to tell me that it is good work but that it will be buried and I will be asked to find other employment," Laura said.

"What is so controversial about it?"

"I predict that this area will experience a major earthquake within the next 7 to 10 years, possibly sooner."

"Define major earthquake?"

"7.0 to 9.0, but that's only guesswork. It will depend on how close my math is to being accurate."

"You're serious! That's more than a major quake, that's a calamity in the making."

"First of all, you can't make any of this public. You can use the data because it is all available if you just take the time to search it out. The way I arrived at the conclusion is going to be the sticking point. The minute any of that comes out people will know

148

where it came from. I don't want to get my boss into trouble because he has been really supportive of my efforts and has done everything I have asked of him. Let me go over the data with you and explain my methodology. If you agree that the reasoning is sound then you can start your own effort to validate my findings. Are we agreed on that?"

Both nodded affirmative.

Laura took the graphics from the report and spread them out as best she could in the limited table space. One of her luncheon companions called a waitress over and asked her to slide another table closer to theirs.

The extra space allowed enough room to lay the material out. Laura explained each graphic and asked if they understood what they meant.

Both nodded. She then explained that her conclusions were based on her knowledge of geology and her understanding of the features of the Cherokee Platform, which she could not substantiate scientifically.

"Look at the epicenters of the events plotted. Those are directly from the NEIC data base. The location of the injector wells is accurate because I plotted those myself. The boundaries of the area in question is based on NEIC estimates and known fault lines. From that point I used my own methodology to arrive at the conclusions in my report."

Laura spent a few minutes explaining her theory about the null area where the oil was pumped out and how she believed the injection of the residue below that level was actually causing the earthquakes that had been increasing since 2007. "Now there is absolutely no proof of that. It is simply my theory of what is happening, but if you look at the depth of the majority of the recent earthquakes you will find them all in the area I mentioned. I know that is not conclusive, but the data supports the theory."

"Now look at the locations of the injector wells. Most are within the area defined as the Cherokee Platform."

"What is that supposed to tell us?"

"I don't know, but it tells me that the biggest portion of the reinserted residue is taking place within that geographic area. The pressure at which they reinsert the waste is very high. Somewhere in the area of 4,000 psi. I used math to estimate the mass of the area above the injection sites. I came up with a figure and calculated how much upward pressure it would take to move that much mass. Now I have no idea how stable the area beneath the injection sites is, so there's a lot of room for error. I also obviously can't plot or measure the density of the material between the areas where oil had been pumped out of the ground and the injection sites, so the figures are only estimates at best."

"What does that have to do with your projection of a major quake?"

"Take this building for example. If you had a small area right at the center point underground exerting pressure upward it would have little effect on the structure. Even in you increased the pressure at that point enough to drill through the concrete the very worst that would happen would be a hole in the floor eventually to relieve the pressure. That would not be a good thing, but it would not affect the structure substantially. Now if you exerted the same amount of pressure across the entire area on which the foundation is laid eventually the pressure would move the building upward, or would erode the foundation area enough that the building would sink. If the building sank at an uneven angle then you would have a collapse of the structure. My theory is that is what is going to happen to the entire Cherokee Platform area."

Both of them looked at her in amazement. "You can't be serious. An area that large would move at the same time?"

"I don't expect it will be at the same time, but once enough of the pressure is released at some point then there will be a chain reaction across the entire area. I have no idea how much movement there will be but it will be significant enough to put the quakes to this point to shame."

"And we can't use this to make people aware," one of her companions said with resignation.

"If I am wrong you would lose a lot of credibility for your cause, and you would also place me on the hot seat for planting the idea. I just wanted you to know that I personally think there is going to be a lot of blame placed if and when this happens. You can access the same data in those graphs on the internet. I suggest you do so and draw your own conclusions from the data. That way you can have some ammunition to fight with."

"What are you going to do if they fire you?" one of them asked.

"Look for another job I suppose," Laura said.

"Would you consider working for our organization?"

"If the job is here probably not. I don't want to live in this area."

"It they do fire you would you give us a call?"

"I can do that much," Laura agreed.

They parted company and Laura went back to Nan's to pack her gear.

The two went out to dinner that evening. Laura hated to be leaving without much hope of continuing her work but that was the way it had to be.

She left early the next morning and drove straight through to Denver. It was a long and tiring journey. She had called Sam and told him she would be late getting in and would probably sleep in for a bit.

She was up by 9:00 and went out for breakfast on her way to the NEIC.

When she arrived Sam invited her into his office and closed the door. "I know you have something heavy on your mind. You want to give it to me all at once or a bit at a time?" he said jovially.

"I think the best method is to use the heavy artillery first." She removed the report she had compiled from her briefcase and laid it on the desk.

He just lifted an eyebrow in question.

"That is the result of my work since I started. I tried to put it together in a way that made sense, but the fact is that none of it makes sense. I just took everything I had gathered since starting and stated what I believed that indicated. You need some time to absorb it, but I don't believe you are going to like the conclusions."

"How long did it take you to put it together?"

"The data is what I compiled from day one. I have been adding to the input daily. It took me more than two days to pull it together and another day to frame my conclusions in the least inflammatory manner I could," she said.

"What's the bottom line?" he said, still not touching the report.

Laura took a deep breath. "I think there is going to be a major event in northern Oklahoma within the next seven to ten years," she said.

"How major?"

"7.0 to 9.0, maybe larger."

He whistled. "I hope you have some good data to support that claim because it's going to take a lot of convincing to get anyone other than me to believe it."

"Look at what is there and tell me if you think I am wrong," she said.

"Take the rest of the day off and catch up with your personal stuff. I will look at it this afternoon and we will talk tomorrow," he said.

Laura did as he suggested, suspecting that he didn't want her talking to any of the others who worked at the center. He wanted to get a feel for just how far out on the limb she was so he could give her some guidance, which she figured was a nice gesture on his part.

She didn't really know anyone in the area and didn't have anything to do so she went back to her apartment and dug into her file copy of the report again. She was trying to poke holes in the report as she was sure Sam would do. After another three hours with the data she was still convinced that her reasoning was sound and that the data supported her conclusions.

She had barely replaced the report in her briefcase when Sam called and asked her if she had any dinner plans.

"No. Just going over the report again myself," she said.

"Would you mind having dinner with me so we can discuss your report away from the office?"

"That will be fine. When and where?"

"I will pick you up in about half an hour if that will give you enough time."

"What kind of place do you have in mind?"

"Nothing dressy, but not a McDonald's either. I thought someplace like a steak house might fit the bill."

"Okay, 30 minutes."

When he arrived Laura was watching from her window and instead of having him come in she went outside and locked the door behind her. She got into the car and he backed out and headed into Denver. "That was quite a job you did on that. I especially liked the way you organized the data to support your conclusions."

"I hear a but in that?"

"The but is that nobody in our organization will sign off on it," he replied.

"I figured as much. I do not see much more I can do from Oklahoma. The data is simply going to keep building in the same framework as in the report. The quakes are going to continue on a daily basis, getting stronger with time until either the state curtails the injector wells or the big one occurs," Laura said.

"You feel very strongly about this don't you?"

"Obviously. I had my friend with whom I was staying in Edmond read the report and she asked me why other people couldn't see that. I told her that if something like that became public knowledge there would be a mad exodus from the state. I probably overstated that a bit, but I think it would happen to a lesser degree. Having said that, I still believe I am pretty close to the mark on my conclusions," Laura answered.

"Unfortunately I am in full agreement with you. You did a very good job putting the data together and even some of our more stubborn colleagues will have to buy into the methodology and what is concluded from that part of the report. The thing that is going to be a real bitch to sell is the prediction of the big one in the time frame you estimated. I want you to explain to me in detail how you arrived at that conclusion," Sam said.

"That part is pretty iffy. First of all I had to accept the accuracy of the NGS estimates on the area identified as the Cherokee Platform. I also had to rely on a general description of the geological characteristics of the area. I had the drilling data from the oil companies on the soil makeup where there are wells. That is not nearly accurate enough to extrapolate across the entire area, but that is what I had to do."

"Tell me how you calculated how much pressure from underground it would take to move the entire area you are talking about."

"Much of this is theoretical and I knew I would have trouble getting that point across, but I believe that entire area is sort of like an island sitting in the middle of an ocean. The lower part is resting on a solid base of geological elements underneath. That is fine as long as nothing happens to upset the balance. My theory is that the residue injected under the strata where the oil is being pumped out is exerting pressure upward. I believe the quakes happening now are a result of that pressure forcing the voids where the oil was pumped to close. There are no open fissures at surface level anywhere in the area and the quakes are no more than five to eight miles deep for the most part. That is the area in which the oil companies are working. I believe as long as they continue to reinject the residue this will continue to happen. If you look at the graph of the location of the injector wells you will see that all the junk is being reinjected in the area occupied by the Cherokee Platform. When the pressure from underneath becomes great enough across the entire area there will be upward movement to relieve that pressure. I had to do a lot of estimation as to the weight of that area. I estimated as closely as I could the surface area, then figured the mass of the area down to ten miles. Because I don't know the exact composition of the area below ground these are estimates as well. I then arrived mathematically at the amount of upward pressure it would take to move the entire area. It is a mind boggling figure, but is achievable if the pressure of the injected material is evenly spread over the entire area."

"That's the area that is going to cause the most problems. Some will say that it is just wild guesswork."

"That certainly is a valid point. I wouldn't characterize it as wild guesswork, but there is certainly a lot of room for error. The key is that if they continue to inject the residue the amount of pressure needed to lift the area will eventually be reached. It may not be within the time frame I suggested, but I firmly believe that it will happen. They currently inject about 1.3 million barrels of waste back into the earth each month. Some of that is at lower pressure, but they use however much pressure is needed to force the waste back into the earth."

They arrived at the restaurant and Sam parked the car. They went inside and were shown to a table.

Nothing more was mentioned about the report until they had placed their orders.

While they were waiting on the food to be delivered Sam broached the subject again.

"You do understand that if you submit the report officially that you become an outcast within the government?" Sam asked.

"Yes, I figured as much. I don't see any more I can do to address the situation back there, and I really do believe events will unfold exactly as I outlined them. The only question in my mind is the timing."

"There has been enough publicity lately that establishes the linkage between the earthquakes and the injector wells. I don't think you will have any problems with the majority of the report. If it were not for the last prediction I would tell you that you did an outstanding job and forward the report onward. I don't want you to ruin any chance you have to advance within your field, so consider the consequences very carefully before you give me the official version," Sam said.

"I have thought about little else since I put it together. I realize that it torpedoes my chances to remain with your organization but I believe I would be remiss in my obligation to the public if I don't bring this to their attention," Laura said.

They discussed the report throughout the meal but the major items had already been covered. Most of the talk related to the cooperation from different entities dealing with the problem in Oklahoma.

"Actually after the initial cold shoulder even the oil companies became more cooperative. They are in compliance with all state and federal regulations so they had nothing to hide. Everything in the report is available in open sources and the only thing that makes it stand out is my conclusions," Laura said.

"You are right about that, but not many have your education and drive to address the problem. I have had similar reports from the person I have in California doing what you were doing in Oklahoma. He is more bureaucratic in his reports but his conclusions are very close to yours, with the notable exception that he doesn't predict a cataclysmic event. I expect what will happen when I submit your report is that they will say thank you very much and eliminate your position as having fulfilled its purpose," Sam said.

"In other words I can start looking for another job."

"I can probably buy you thirty days, possibly more, but they will not accept the final conclusion you presented."

"I sincerely hope I am wrong, but I don't believe I am."

"I will give you a good recommendation whomever you find employment with," Sam said.

Laura didn't think it was the right time to tell Sam that she might become part of his opposition but she was not willing to let the situation play out without a fight. She realized that Sam was not the enemy but his allegiance was to the organization he was running, which was the government. "I appreciate that," she said.

After they finished eating and were on the way back to Laura's place Sam asked, "Do you want me to consider the report I have as the final product?"

"I have to Sam," she said.

After he dropped her off she went inside her apartment and threw herself down on the bed and cried for a long time. Once the tears stopped she started to think about what she would do next. She really had no wish to return to Oklahoma but she had promised the contacts with Earth First that she would get back to them and decided that she would do that the following day.

She had breakfast and made the call. She told the person with Earth First that she had presented her report and would probably be looking for a job within the month.

"You definitely don't want to come back to Oklahoma?" he asked.

"No way."

"Well give me a call if you change your mind."

When she went to work Sam called her in and told her that he was endorsing her report and forwarding it to NGS. "I am going to have to give them a heads up by phone."

"What do you want me to do in the meantime?"

"How do you feel about a week in California working with your counterpart out there?"

"Sounds good to me."

"I will set it up and you can leave tomorrow morning. You probably want to fly out and rent a car."

It was a method to get her out of the office until the report got to Washington but it didn't bother her. She had made her decision and was content that she had made the right one.

The week in California was uneventful for the most part. She liked the man doing the same job out there and they spent some time going over his work. She showed him a copy of her report and told him it was going to get her fired but that she had submitted it anyway because she felt very strongly that it was the right thing to do.

"The same thing could very well apply to this area. I have found the same thing here that you found in Oklahoma. Eventually the injector wells are going to be responsible for more earthquake activity. I don't think I will be able to tie it as closely to the wells as you have, but the effects will be very nearly the same."

On the day before she was to return to Colorado she got a call on her cell phone from a number with which she was not familiar. It was a reporter from Washington, D.C.

Someone had leaked her report and he was calling to interview her about her prediction for a major earthquake in Oklahoma. She told him that she really couldn't discuss an official government report with him and hung up.

When she got back to NEIC the first thing Sam told her was that someone had leaked the report, probably intentionally, and that they were trying to discredit the report. In the meantime the position she had filled had been eliminated and she would have 30 days severance pay. "They didn't even go along with keeping you on for the 30 days."

Laura turned in the government property she had in her possession and cleared out her desk. She called the property manager and told them she would be vacating the apartment. She had very little in the way of personal possessions and managed the entire process in two days.

She got a call from the Earth First people and they offered her a job in Oklahoma City.

"What does it pay?" she asked.

"Probably more than you were making working for the government," she was told.

"Give me a figure," she said.

"I think I might be able to get you in the neighborhood of 100K, but don't hold me to that," he said.

That would be more than she had been making with her other job, including the per diem payments. "Is all your work in Oklahoma?"

"No we have causes all over the world but this is one of the major efforts we are currently working on. I read where your report had been made public. They are truly attempting to make you look like a fortune teller."

"As I said, I really don't want to come back to Oklahoma. If nothing turns up within a month I may get back to you."

Chapter 7

Laura got a call from her mother the next day.

"Well you have become famous," her mother said.

"What's that supposed to mean?"

"You have been in the papers for the past couple of days. Seems a report you produced found its way into the media and you are being painted as a doomsayer," her mother said.

"You are talking about the local paper?"

"Yes, and of course the internet news sites."

"I haven't even looked at any of it."

"Maybe you should. The government 'spokesman' refused to comment about the report but denied that anyone in his organization within the government gave any credibility to the report."

"I knew that would happen. They eliminated my position and fired me."

"What are you going to do now?"

"I don't know just yet. I have been offered a job with one of the environmental groups. I think it is a non-profit, but the pay is almost twice what I was making with the government. I didn't take the job though because I would have had to stay in Oklahoma. I don't want to be there when the big one hits," she said with a chuckle.

"You really believe that is going to happen?"

"Obviously or I wouldn't have submitted the report that cost me my job," Laura said a bit petulantly.

She talked with her mother for a few more minutes and hung up. It was time to get on the road.

She had her cell phone on a Bluetooth hands free device and always used it when she was driving. She had barely cleared Denver when she got a call. She didn't look at the caller ID but simply said, "This is Laura."

A pleasant sounding man's voice said, "This is not a telemarketing call, although I am trying to solicit business. I am a personal agent and I want to discuss the possibility of representing you. My name is Calvin Burkhardt."

"Mr. Burkhardt, why on earth would I need a personal agent?"

"You're kidding, right?"

"Not in the least. I have no idea what you are talking about."

"Don't tell me everyone and his brother from the major networks have not been trying to schedule you for an interview."

"I don't have a regular phone and I am on the road but no one has called me. What is this about?"

"About a lot of money. I read your report about the coming earthquake in Oklahoma and I could see that you are well educated and had the fortitude to go against the government position for something you believed in professionally. I represent people in different career fields as a personal agent to schedule their time and work. I work for a flat ten percent and I am really good at what I do."

"What has that to do with me?"

"I think I might be able to leverage you into a regular on the news networks. Your appearances will be compensated at a pretty good figure I think. You can probably make half a million to a million in a year if we play our cards right."

"You're serious! A million dollars for doing interviews?"

"Maybe not quite that much. It will depend on how you come across on camera and how well versed you are in your subject matter but I think that is a realistic figure."

"Who do you work for?"

"I work for myself. I have a limited liability corporation, but it is basically me and my accountant."

"Where are you located?"

"I live just outside Washington, D.C. but I travel a lot."

"What exactly are you proposing?"

"That you and I enter into an agreement for me to represent you in negotiations with prospective employers."

"I don't know about all that," Laura said.

"Where are you right now?"

"On the road just outside Denver."

"How about I take a plane to Kansas City and have you meet me at the airport. I can ride with you and we can discuss the proposition. I will make a couple of calls to gauge your worth and will be able give you some firm money figures."

"How did you get my number?" Laura asked.

"Trade secret, but nothing illegal."

"When will you get to Kansas City?"

"I will call you after I make reservations. Deal?"

"I suppose so. I don't have any idea how long it will take me to drive there, but I probably won't make it that far tonight."

"I will call you back within the hour, all right?"

"I guess."

After she hung up Laura gave some thought to the conversation she had just finished. If she had understood what Calvin said he was talking about a million dollars for a year's work. That simply blew her mind.

When her phone rang just short of an hour later it was Calvin again. He didn't waste much time on preliminaries. "Would you believe I already have your first two jobs set up?"

"What on earth does that mean?"

"It means that CNN and FOX News want to do an in-depth interview with you to the tune of 25K each," he said. "I didn't talk any specifics, just a general idea of what they were willing to pay."

"This is happening too fast. Let's wait until you get to Kansas City," Laura said.

"I have reservations to leave in three hours. I will be there later today. If you are not going to get that far tonight let me know and I will tell you where I will be staying," he said.

"Okay. Talk to you later," Laura said and disconnected the call.

$25,000 for an interview? That was ridiculous. The next time Laura stopped for gas and food she spent some time on her laptop. She had not paid much attention to what was being said about her or her report and was surprised by the amount of attention she was getting in the news and social media.

Her yearbook picture from college was there and she read some of the comments made by government officials and even some analyses of her report. The comments were mixed. Some thought her report made a lot of sense, while others, mostly government spokesmen dismissed the report as a bunch of hogwash. She was amused by the whole thing.

She did get some idea as to why Calvin Burkhardt was willing to meet her in Kansas City though. The articles implied that Laura was in hiding, unwilling to face the music created by her report. She decided that talking to Calvin would be a good thing and got back on the road. She would push on and try to make it to Kansas City by that night, though it would be very late when she arrived if she managed to get that far.

She had just gassed up again and had a sandwich when Calvin called and told her he had landed in Kansas City.

"I think I am about three hours out. Where are you staying?" she asked.

"I'm at the Holiday Inn near the airport. My room number is 345. Give me a call when you get up in the morning. The place looks like it might be kind of tight for rooms. Do you want me to reserve one for you?"

"That would be nice. I will call you sometime tomorrow morning."

It was after midnight when Laura arrived and the place did look almost full. She checked with the desk and found that Calvin had indeed made a reservation for her. She signed in and went to the room where she quickly showered and went to bed. She thought she would sleep late but was up by 7:00 a.m. She called Calvin's room and they agreed to meet in the restaurant in half an hour.

Laura got there first and realized that she had no idea what Calvin looked like. She need not have worried because he knew what she looked like and showed up shortly after she had been led to a table.

He introduced himself again and sat down.

They ordered breakfast and once the coffee was poured he got right down to cases.

"I put out some feelers to CNN and FOX like I told you. Both are anxious for an in-depth interview. What that means is a segment dealing strictly with your report and an explanation from you about how you came up with the information and what it all means. The segment will not be longer than half an hour. I believe I can drive the fee up for the first interview."

"Why are they so interested in me?"

"Well you wrote the report that has the government trying their best to discredit you. They feel that there has to be some truth to the report or the government would not be going to such extremes to squash it. I don't really know how their thought processes work but the report has gotten national attention and an interview with you will certainly up their ratings, especially if they can get a bit of notice ahead of time so they can publicize the interview."

Calvin was younger than she thought he would be. He was not much more than a few years older than her. He was clean cut, clean shaven, and had brown hair that was over his ears but not long.

"How long have you been doing this agent thing?" she asked.

"Since college. I knew a couple of the jocks and broached the subject with them in their junior year. They agreed to give me a shot at it and I worked very hard to project a positive image for them over the next year. That also meant giving them advice about staying out of trouble and cultivating their public images. I got both of them good contracts and went on from there. It's sort of a dog eat dog profession, but I have done all right so far. What's your background?"

"I grew up mostly in Virginia Beach and went to William and Mary in Williamsburg, Virginia. I majored in geology, though I didn't specialize in any particular area. I went to work for the National Earthquake Information Center, which is under the US. Geological Survey umbrella. The director of the center wrote the job description specifically for someone to look at the uptrend in earthquakes in Oklahoma and California to see if they could be tied to the injector wells that put the drilling residue back into the earth below the level at which they are pumping oil. I did that for a year in Oklahoma and wrote the report that is getting all the attention now. I knew they wouldn't like it but I had to go with the conclusions that the data suggested. The Director of NEIC told me what would happen to the report and asked if I wanted to modify it before giving him the official version. I told him to take it as I had written it because I had very strong convictions that the report was as accurate as I could possibly make it."

"The following week I was told that my position had been eliminated and given 30 days severance pay."

"Well your report created a firestorm. Someone leaked it to the media and it immediately became national news. The fact that the government then tried to discredit it made it even more newsworthy to the newshounds. All the major networks have been trying to line up interviews with you, so your value is at its peak right now. I don't know much about your subject but I looked closely at the report and the data seems to support your conclusions, except for the last prediction. Nobody seems to doubt that what you predict could happen, but they want to know more about how you arrived at the conclusion."

"So tell me what you will do as my agent, and what I have to do."

Their breakfast came and they suspended the conversation until the waitress left and they buttered their toast. While they ate Calvin explained that his job would be to contact the potential employers, that is the news outlets, and negotiate contracts with them based on availability and timing. "Basically I will manage your time and travels to get you the best rate and have you appear where and when we contract for. I will be legally allowed to negotiate on your behalf and sign the contracts as legally binding. In return I take ten percent deducted from your fees and the remainder is placed in a bank account for you."

"And my part of this deal?"

"Show up where and when I contract for you and do the interviews. If certain people want more in-depth work then I contract with them as a separate issue. I am talking something like a series, maybe three or four interviews to thoroughly explain things. It's sort of nebulous, but I'm breaking new ground here," he said with a light chuckle.

They talked through breakfast and Laura told him she was ready to hit the road again. Calvin grabbed his one small suitcase and checked out at the same time Laura did. They barely had room to fit Calvin and his bag into the car and were soon on the road toward St Louis.

Calvin continued the sales pitch and at the same time got a general explanation of how Laura arrived at the conclusion that Oklahoma was going to have a major earthquake in the future.

He was impressed with her presence and ability to think on her feet, so to speak. He thought she would come across very well on television. She was attractive, articulate, and sincere. In other words she was a winner for what he had in mind.

Before they got to St Louis late in the day they had agreed on the contract for a one year period, with clauses for renewal and for ending the relationship after that time.

Laura dropped Calvin off at the airport in St Louis and continued on her way. Calvin had made several phone calls and had CNN lined up for the first interview. Laura told him to wait until after the weekend coming. That would give her time to drive the rest of the way home to Virginia Beach and at least say hello to her parents.

By the time Laura got home on Saturday she had talked with Calvin several times.

CNN was very anxious to get the first interview with Laura and Calvin negotiated the fee at 35K. They didn't want to compete with Monday night sports on competitive networks and set it up for Tuesday evening.

They started their advertising campaign during the weekend using the yearbook photo and to Laura's surprise she was recognized in a restaurant where she stopped for lunch on Saturday.

A lady at the next table said, "Excuse me, but aren't you Laura Griswold?"

"Do I know you?" Laura asked.

"No but I saw the program announcement on CNN this morning. Is Oklahoma really going to have a major earthquake?"

"I believe so, but if you are traveling west you won't have to worry about it this trip. It's somewhere in the future," she said.

The lady laughed. "Seriously, is it really going to happen?"

"That's my theory based on some pretty good data. The problem is that other people don't interpret the data in the same manner I do."

"And nobody knows who's right?"

"That's the crux of the issue. I really hope I am wrong but I don't believe I am."

"Well I wouldn't miss the telecast for anything now that I have met you."

"Thank you, I think," Laura said with a smile.

When she arrived home later that day she found her parent's house staked out by reporters. She pulled into the driveway and upon opening her car door was confronted by two cameramen snapping pictures. "Can I have a moment of your time?" a reporter asked.

Laura turned to him. "What do you want?"

"Just to ask a couple of questions. I've been sitting in my car for three days hoping you would show up here."

"Well I applaud your tenacity, but I have no comment," she said.

"Just tell me if it's true that you are going to do an interview on CNN?"

"I will confirm that much," she replied.

By this time her mother had opened the door and came outside to greet her. They left the reporter and cameramen standing there and went into the house.

"They've been around for several days," her mother said.

Once inside the house she told her parents what was going on.

Her father said, "What's the big fuss all about. People have been predicting earthquakes for ages. What makes this one so different?"

Laura tried to explain the overall implications so he would understand. "The oil companies are pumping a lot of oil out of the ground using a technique called fracking. That is a term that simply means horizontal drilling. They use the initial well and drill laterally when the oil pocket starts to play out. They inject very high pressure through the pipes and it fractures the rock, actually shale, through which they are drilling freeing more oil and gas to be pumped to the surface. The drilling residue is then injected back into the ground at a greater depth. The government regulates the amount of sediment that can be reinjected. The practice ensures that the oil producers get maximum production from the well sites and also saves them a lot of money because they would otherwise store the drilling residue because of the chemicals they use. The overriding concern about the practice was that the drinking water might be polluted by the technique. For that reason the program establishes procedures for applying for well permits and regulates how much residue can be reintroduced."

"After the practice began the earthquakes started. They are not real jolters for the most part, but the incidence in the area where I was working was dramatic. I charted all the oil wells and the injector wells in the area and charted all the earthquakes that have occurred since 2007. You would not believe the number. Most of the quakes were very near injector wells and the depth of the epicenters was less than ten miles deep. The majority of the quakes happen between the areas where the oil is taken out and where the residue is reinserted."

"So there is a definite connection?"

"The data certainly suggests that as being the case."

"Then what is the great controversy over your report?"

"I looked at all the data and concluded that if the practice continues there will eventually be a huge earthquake in the area."

"People have been saying that about California for decades."

"And there have in fact been some major quakes in California over the years, but my theory for a major quake in Oklahoma is in an area that has no major fault lines."

"What are you going to do now?"

"I signed up with an agent, who is lining up interviews for me. The first one is to be on CNN on Tuesday night."

"I saw that advertised. Why do you need an agent for that?"

"Because I am being paid 35 thousand dollars for the interview."

"Why are they willing to pay that kind of money to interview you?"

"My take on the situation is that if the government had just buried the report nothing would have come of it. The fact that they tried to discredit the report made it newsworthy. Now the news people are wondering why the government would go to those extremes."

"Well never look a gift horse in the mouth, I always say," her dad said.

The three talked all afternoon about Laura's time in Oklahoma. The phone rang incessantly but nobody bothered to answer it until the recording came on and they could determine if it was someone they knew.

Reporters still hung around outside but none bothered to approach the house. They had been given orders by the police to not bother the Griswold's.

Calvin called on Sunday and told Laura that she had reservations on a flight out of Norfolk the following day to Atlanta. Someone from CNN would meet her at the airport and take her to a hotel in their headquarters area.

Chapter 8

Laura's parents took her to the airport on Monday. She arrived in Atlanta in the mid afternoon and was driven to the hotel, which was right on the grounds of the CNN building.

She was told that someone would call to escort her to the appropriate area the following day.

That evening in her room she worked on the graphics, hoping they would be compatible with whatever system they would use for the interview.

When she met the news staff on Tuesday they explained how they would do the interview.

She asked about the graphics display and was told that the images could be downloaded from her laptop and she would have a controller to manipulate them during the interview.

The people who would be conducting the interview wanted a briefing beforehand so they would know how to direct their questions and approximately how long her explanations would take to fit the program within the time frame they had allotted.

The entire operation was state of the art. They even gave her a laser pointer to make it easier to reference her graphics. She practiced with the graphics and the pointer until she felt comfortable with the process.

The make-up people told her they would not need to do much but would need her a half hour before the segment aired. It was to be a live interview, probably because that would give the commentators more chance to surprise her with their questions without any time for preparation.

She felt comfortable with the material. She had lived with it for so long and had gone over the report thoroughly to the point that she knew every nuance of the entire package.

She told them that she was going to have trouble keeping her answers short enough to address all the issues so they would need to take that into consideration during the interview.

When all was ready and everyone was on the set Laura didn't feel nervous or apprehensive. The interview commenced and the first curve ball came from the newsman conducting the interview. He said, "Tell us why Oklahoma is going to have a major earthquake."

Laura just looked at him. That had not been the way they had indicated the interview would start.

She gave it a couple of seconds thought and replied, "Sorry but I can't do that without exposing you to the data that supports the statement."

The newsman had hoped to get her flustered but the ploy was not going to work. "You put together a report that predicted a major earthquake in northern Oklahoma. Could you tell us why you think that will happen?"

"I can show you with data that I gathered over a period of a year in the area. The prediction of the major earthquake is the final conclusion and a lot of other things are going to be happening that will lead up to that. If I just make a blanket statement that it is going to happen without showing how I arrived at that conclusion I will appear to be the crackpot that certain people think I am."

"Then how would you convince us that your prediction is accurate?"

"May I?" Laura said lifting the controller slightly.

"Be my guest," he said.

Laura called up the first graphic, which dealt with the number of quakes and pointed out the marked increase since 2007. She stated that was the time when the state really started using the injection well technology. She used the laser to point out the salient features. She then went to the graph which showed the location of the producing wells and the injector wells. She pointed out the epicenters she had plotted and made the point that all were very near injector wells. She next went to the graph which dealt with the severity of the quakes and pointed out the rise in the severity over the same time period.

The newscaster said, "That is really startling data. How did you get it all?"

"It is all open source data and can be accessed by anyone who takes the time to look at it. The first point to these graphics is that you can see a definite link between the time the quakes started and the use of injector wells."

They were almost 15 minutes into the segment and Laura told the host that the allotted time was not going to be adequate to do justice to the amount of data she had.

"Just do the best you can with the time we have," he replied.

"I am going to take this in sequence, and chances are that we will not get to the final part of the report. People need to understand how all this ties together to see how I reached the conclusion I did."

"So like the Saturday morning serials you will leave a cliff hanger?"

"If necessary. I refuse to make a statement that cannot be substantiated with some amount of reference data. If after I present my case people choose to disbelieve my conclusions then they are at least basing their beliefs on the best data available."

During the next commercial the newscaster came to Laura. "You really need to move it along. We have to get to the bottom line of your prediction by the end of the segment."

"I told you that I would not do that without presenting all the data that led to the conclusion and the explanation of that last part alone will take a lot of time. You can end the interview any way you want but I am not going to make a blanket statement until all the methodology has been covered. Some of that is very theoretical and needs explanation that many of your viewers will not understand without examples of the principles involved."

Unknown to Laura the network switchboards were lighting up. The moderator was aware because he was getting the information from his earbud. He knew there was not going to be enough time to get through it all and resented the barrel Laura had him over. She simply refused to be rushed into the statement the newsman wanted her to make.

During the final segment of the interview Laura started to talk about the fault lines that caused most earthquakes. She pointed out the fact that there were not many of them in the area of Oklahoma where she had been working.

She had just explained that the Oklahoma Corporation Commission had conceded that there might be a connection between the earthquakes and injector wells and they were considering lowering the amount of waste that could be reinjected when the director gave her a sign to cut it off. She made one more comment that she thought was appropriate. She asked a rhetorical question. "How much waste is being pumped back? Imagine the flow of the Mississippi River dumping underground in that area for eight solid hours and you have the volume that is being reinjected monthly. I am told that we are out of time, so I ask you, did the data I presented make sense to you? If so you will want to dig a bit deeper into the subject. I apologize for not doing what I know you viewers wanted, but I want to present all my information before I subject you to the prediction I made and the reasons for that step."

The newscaster said, "Sorry folks, that's all we have time for at the moment. We will be following up on this story and you can bet we will give it all to you at the earliest possible time."

Once the lights were out and the microphones unhooked the director came to Laura. "You came across very well but it would have been better if we could have hit them with your prediction."

"I'm sorry but I don't make blanket statements without the data to back them up. I think your viewer numbers will be up considerably for the program at any rate."

"You are not wrong about that. The switchboards have been going crazy."

"One other thing, I didn't like the way your talking head tried to sandbag me. If we do this again someone needs to have a talk with him," Laura said and turned away to get the makeup off her face.

Before she left one of the network executives cornered her. "I must compliment you on your performance. You really come across good on-camera. I think we might want to schedule you for some follow-up work."

"Give my agent a call," she said and walked away.

Laura had not even gotten out of the offices when Calvin called. "That was really great. You just ooze sincerity and competence. Your presentation couldn't have been better. I think the majority of the people who watched the segment understood what you presented. I detected a bit of friction between you and the newscaster," he said questioningly.

"He didn't follow the procedure for what we discussed before the telecast and tried to get me to just make a blanket prediction. I told one of the executives that someone was going to need to have a talk with him if we worked with them anymore. He hinted that they might want to do some follow-up. I told him to contact you."

"The FOX interview is on Thursday. You will need to be in New York by Thursday morning," Calvin said.

"I will be back in Virginia tomorrow. I can take an early flight on that day," Laura said.

Laura was suddenly a very recognizable face. People pointed her out on the street and in public places. She had not even revealed her reason for the earthquake prediction yet but people were already casting her in the role of an earthquake expert.

Her parents were lavish in their praise for her television appearance.

"Well I have to do it again on Thursday for FOX. I imagine that will simply be a lesson in geology. It's going to take a lot of time to present this in a believable manner," she said.

She flew to New York on Thursday morning and Calvin met her there. "I wanted to be able to run interference for you if necessary," he said.

"Did CNN get back to you?"

"Yes. They couldn't believe the ratings they got for your segment. They want to tie you into a consulting contract exclusively but I told them I didn't think that would work. They called back later and wanted to have you on again during the Sunday morning talk show hour for sure with some possible follow-up. I am negotiating that with them at the moment."

"How is this coming event going to be structured?"

"I have no idea. We will go to their studios and see what they have in mind."

When they arrived they immediately got together with the news director and the newscaster who was going to present the questions to Laura.

They had seen the ratings for her CNN appearance and were salivating at the opportunity they had to take the next step in her presentation. "Did you get along with old what's his name?"

"You mean the newscaster?" Laura asked.

"Well enough. He didn't do as he said he would in the preliminary discussion and tried to change the script. I thought that was very unprofessional and told his boss as much. I feel very strongly that I need to lay the groundwork very carefully before I spring the conclusion on the public. I believe very strongly that what I predict will happen. It might not be within the time frame of my estimates but it will happen. I want to take the time to give some examples to support my conclusion and that is going to take

172

some time. I would suggest that we review very quickly the points I made in the CNN presentation and let me start to explain the methodology. I don't think I can do it adequately in 30 minutes but I refuse to give the punch line before the people know what the joke is. Are you going to be okay with that?"

"I believe we will have the largest audience for a newscast since 9/11 so handle it however you want. Just make sure you and the Elmer Fudd here are on the same page," she was told.

"I have some visuals to demonstrate the area in question. I am going to have to talk some geology, physics and math. All of it is somewhat theoretical. I can't use actual figures because they don't exist so I need to use examples that the audience can relate to. It is going to be time consuming and we might not have time to get through it all."

"What kind of examples?"

"We are talking about a geographical area called the Cherokee Platform in geological terms. It covers a large area in northern Oklahoma roughly between Oklahoma City and the Kansas border to the north and from Tulsa to a small town to the north west of Oklahoma City called Cherokee. Part of it actually extends into southeast Kansas. The Platform is approximately 26,000 square miles in area. There are approximately 10,000 injector wells in Oklahoma. Many of them are in that area. The injector wells are scattered throughout the Platform area. If you can imagine that area as an island resting on a solid foundation you begin to see how the injection of huge amounts of drilling residue might affect the stability of the region. My theory has to do with the amount of oil and gas extracted from the earth between roughly 3,000 feet and 8,000 feet, and the reinsertion of the residue at something like six to eight mile depths. The chemicals used in the drilling process are not neutralized and could possibly have some eroding effect on the strata at that level."

"What kind of example could demonstrate something like that?" the newscaster asked.

"The best example I can come up with is a regular house foundation. Soil samples determine what strength the foundation needs to support the weight of the structure above it. If a lot of pressure is applied over a very small area beneath the foundation it will not have much effect. However if the same amount of pressure were to be distributed over the entire area of the foundation it would either force the structure to move upward or the ground underneath would be eroded and the structure would either sink or topple. I used mathematics to determine the approximate weight of the area of soil above the injection levels of the residue. Without considering any other factors, such as the effect of the chemicals reinjected I arrived at the amount of lift pressure it would take to move that much weight. I then calculated the amount of injector fluids being pumped back into the earth and determined approximately how much time would be needed to reach the critical balance. It is not very precise but I believe the data I have been working with is a good indicator that what I predict is going to happen. First, the incidence of quakes has increased dramatically since the injection started. Second the quakes are primarily centered near the injector wells. Third the quakes are getting stronger with each passing year."

"My theory is that the void created by taking the oil out and the pressure of the fluids being injected below that level work to fill the void from the pressure below. I think that is what is causing the quakes now, but eventually the pressure from below will cause a major shift in the entire Cherokee Platform. I don't know how much movement will occur, or in what given area, but it will create a major earthquake."

"I can certainly understand why you want to present the background. What kind of questions should I ask to get you on the course you want to take?"

"Just the common sense things. Why, what, how; those kind of things that the audience might want to ask but can't," Laura said.

They did the telecast that evening and the half hour went by without a defining conclusion. Like the Saturday morning serials there was another cliff hanger.

FOX wanted more of Laura's time as well. Calvin told them he would get back to them.

He had been on the phone with CNN during Laura's preparation and had arrived at a preliminary figure for the hour long program on Sunday.

FOX's ratings for the segment they did even surpassed those CNN had garnered. Whatever else was happening Laura had gotten the attention of the entire nation with her presentations.

The Sunday show on CNN was again done from Atlanta and was opposite Face the Nation and other similar shows.

The larger time slot allowed Laura to recap the earlier information and finally get to the bottom line about her conclusion. Many people had seen the report that was leaked and knew what was coming but the fact that she presented the data so well and her conclusions seemed logical with regard to the other aspects of the events that she had an audience ready to believe her before she actually vocalized the foregone conclusion.

"I believe the data I have presented supports the conclusion. I know that there are a lot of professional people watching this who will scoff at the unscientific approach but there are times when you have to go with what you have and I believe this is one of those situations. There is no way to get accurate data to do what I have done. Hydrogeological modeling is about the closest you could come and there's no model available to do that. I like to think that I used a logical approach based on the data available. I know there will be those who do not agree with my conclusions and especially the prediction for a large earthquake in that area. My immediate superior said as much when I presented the report. I am not trying to convince Oklahomans to leave their homes but I had to express my beliefs in the report I produced. I want to thank the public for being patient with the manner in which I presented this data. I also want to remind everyone out there that I am not an earthquake specialist. I have only worked in the field for a year and that certainly doesn't qualify me as an expert."

They had a couple of minutes of air time left and the host asked about what could be done to avoid what she predicted.

"Cutting the amount of fluid reinjected would be a good first step. They could then gauge the effects of that action by a decrease in seismic activity in the area concerned."

After the segment was finished Laura and Calvin went back to their respective homes.

She got a call from the Earth First group in Oklahoma City. They thanked her for helping their cause and offered the job again, which she refused.

Calvin called at least daily. He had lined up several more interviews and talk show appearances. He had also gotten calls from others outside the scientific community offering speaking engagements.

Her report had really brought the injector wells into the public eye and more people were questioning the practice than ever.

The government had given up on the plan to discredit her and had indicated publicly that they would conduct further studies to either validate or discredit her theories. That most of the points from the early part of her presentation were valid could not be denied.

The Oklahoma Corporate Commission, which regulated the wells in the state had decreed that a forty percent reduction in the amount of residue allowed to be reinjected would go into effect immediately.

During the next two years the number of earthquakes in Oklahoma decreased by about one third. The intensity of the quakes also remained steady rather than increasing as had been the case earlier.

The subject was still in the news constantly but over time the debate raged on. Even with the reductions enacted by the state the only change was in the frequency of the seismic activity.

Just when the controversy over the question of the major earthquake was beginning to die down a magnitude 6.0 quake occurred in the same area, near Fairview, Oklahoma. That one was strong enough to do significant damage. Even the larger buildings in Oklahoma City and Tulsa experienced movement. Many of the single family homes nearer the quake experienced substantial damage. Foundations cracked and walls crumbled. In the Fairview area nearest the epicenter some houses collapsed completely. The interest in Laura's prediction was rekindled and she spent the next three months doing the talk shows again.

There were a couple of smaller aftershocks from the bigger quake but no more substantial damage. There had been several fatalities because the quake had happened at night and the houses that collapsed with people sleeping resulted in some deaths.

The dollar figures that Calvin predicted had not been reached but Laura had become a millionaire during the three years immediately following the initial flurry of activity. She had been kept very busy with the schedule Calvin kept her on. She averaged a couple of appearances a week.

As a result of the latest seismic activity the state again reduced the quota on liquids that could be injected by another ten percent. From Laura's viewpoint the state was in a no win situation. They depended heavily on oil revenue for their livelihood and hated to do economic damage to the state, but also had the public's safety to consider. They were attempting to find a middle ground that would satisfy everyone and that was an impossible task.

During the next couple of years the earthquakes continued but at a slightly lower level than previously. The severity also began to edge downward. Seldom did they experience anything greater than 3.0. Things seemed to be leveling off and the public outcry had abated.

John Buckner

Epilog

Laura had kept in touch with Sam Watkins at the NEIC and they spoke on the phone regularly.

The study being done in California when Laura had been with them had reached the same conclusions that Laura had relative to the injector wells causing the quakes but had not concluded that the practice would cause significant seismic activity in that area.

The state corporation commission in Oklahoma called Calvin and asked if Laura would be willing to come to Oklahoma City for a meeting to review the situation with them before they produced their next annual report.

The date and time was set and Laura returned to Oklahoma. She stayed in a hotel downtown. Nan had long since moved out of the state and was now working in Philadelphia, Pennsylvania.

During the first day of the meetings she was asked to go over her theory again for their benefit and to comment upon the probability of her prediction coming to pass and whether or not their earlier actions in limiting the amount of residue pumped back into the earth was having the desired effect.

It was 9:30 in the morning while Laura was telling them that she had no way to know if their actions were enough to override her theory. She was standing in front of the group in a conference room in the state capitol building when the lights suddenly went out and the building started to tremble and sway.

Laura's final thought before the building collapsed was that she had indeed been right about the major earthquake, and regretted with her last breath that she had agreed to come back to Oklahoma.

The End

# The Thirteen

## By John Buckner

## Chapter 1

Lemuel Burgess was an auto mechanic in a small town just outside Boston, Massachusetts. He had lived in the same house since birth almost forty years in the past. He had no siblings and had taken care of his mother for more than five years after the death of his father just over ten years ago. He had been born when his parents were in their late forties and both were well up in their years before they died.

Lemuel's father had died as the result of an automobile accident just short of his 85th birthday. His mother had died of natural causes, in her case kidney failure, when she was 91.

Lemuel was really an oddity in many ways. He had never been farther away from home than New York City, and then only once. Boston was only a short distance away but Lemuel couldn't even tell you how the city was laid out. He had only been there an average of once a year and paid little attention to the geography, or for that matter the scenery.

He owned his own repair shop, which was located on the same property where his house stood. He was strictly a one man operation and spent as much as 12 hours in the shop on some days. Cars had been his love since high school. He had taken an auto shop class in school and never looked back. He knew that he wanted to be a mechanic for a livelihood.

He discussed the idea with his dad and started saving money to build the shop from that point forward. He and his dad did a lot of the work on the shop and it was well built. On the day he graduated he put the sign up. Burgess Mechanical Repair, it said. He didn't take out an advertisement in the phone book or newspaper. He did have a phone installed in the shop and the number listed in both the white and yellow pages.

His classmates knew that he was a very good mechanic and came to him to solve problems they had with their cars that were beyond their own ability to resolve. His customer base started out with his own age group. They of course told their parents and soon he had more work than he could handle.

He refused to hire any help and simply scheduled the work as he estimated he could get it done. He never overcharged for his services. If anything he undercharged. He made enough money to keep the business going and to help his parents with the bills. The family was not very well off financially, but managed to get along fine on what the father made at his city job in Boston.

Lemuel had gone to school after the advent of computers in cars and could run the diagnostics to locate a problem in most cases. He actually relied on his innate ability to recognize problems from the symptoms more than on the computer.

To say Lemuel was a bit slow mentally would not be an untrue statement. He was not autistic, nor did he have any other mental problem that could be pinpointed, but his IQ was below the average and his brain seemed to process information much slower than normal. He had been the odd man out in almost all situations in school when sides were chosen for teams in the games that children played. He didn't date much because of his shyness and the way the girls perceived him.

He just went along with the flow, knowing at times that he was being discriminated against, and guessed at the reason. Still, he was large enough that he could hold his own in any scuffle that broke out and didn't have any problems in that regard.

He knew about sex, and had even tried it once with a girl pretty much on his mental level. While the experience was okay he didn't look at it as something to waste a lot of time on.

He prepared most of his own meals and got along just fine.

He had no living relatives that he knew about and was happy with his lot in life.

That was the situation the day he received the letter. There was no return address and he didn't make any connection with anyone he knew or did business with. The letter was in a plain white business sized envelope.

He didn't even open the letter when he picked up the mail, as he did with others that had some meaning to him. Had it not been for the handwritten address and plain envelope he might have discarded the piece of mail without ever opening it.

That evening when he called it a day he prepared himself a simple meal of left over roast and a salad.

As he ate he was looking through his mail again and came across the unopened letter. He used his knife to slit the flap and took the contents out of the envelope. It contained a single sheet

John Buckner

of paper, folded twice, and when he unfolded it he discovered a $100 dollar bill.

He fingered the bill and wondered what this could all be about.  His curiosity was now aroused to the point that he stopped eating to read the letter.  It was pretty simple and to the point.  It said:

Dear Mr. Burgess,

You don't know me, and I hope you will not think me too forward for contacting you in this way.

The $100 is for your time, and to let you know that this is not a joke or scam of some sort.  You may keep the money as a token of my thanks for reading the letter.

I am a rather wealthy person and some think I am somewhat eccentric.  I enjoy helping those less fortunate than myself and have more money than I could ever spend.  I am about to conduct an experiment for which I need a group of people with certain characteristics.  My associates have been doing research to find those individuals for more than a year.  You happen to possess the qualities I need for the experiment.

I know that you must be curious, but this letter was sent to determine if you might like to participate in the program.  It will not take a lot of your time, only 30 days to be precise.

In return you will be paid one million dollars.  There are some stipulations, and they will be explained to you at a face to face meeting if you are interested.

Please give the matter some thought and call the number listed here if you think you might be interested.

A toll free phone number was listed but there was no signature.

Lemuel thought the whole thing very curious.  The hundred dollar bill looked real, but it might be counterfeit.  He would take it to the bank and have them look at it tomorrow.

The letter didn't even hint at what the experiment would be, nor where it would be conducted.

Lemuel thought that he could certainly use a million dollars, but what would he have to do for it?  Usually when something like this came in the mail it was only a lure to encourage you to follow-up, at which point you find out what the scam was about.  He would of course keep the hundred dollars.

He laid the letter aside and thought no more about it until he went to bed.  As he lay there waiting for sleep to come he thought about the letter again.  What kind of experiment could it be to pay him one million dollars for thirty days of his time?

It must be something illegal he thought, otherwise they would have contacted me in person.  The letter didn't identify any institution or organization for which the experiment would be conducted.  It had said that it was a wealthy individual.

Lemuel was thinking about what he could do with a million dollars when sleep overtook him.

## Chapter 2

Nathaniel Grimes, called Nate by his friends, lived in a suburb of Kansas City. He was 38 years of age and lived alone in the house he had inherited from his parents.

They had perished in a plane crash three years before. Both were of social security age when they died. They were on a trip to celebrate their 50th wedding anniversary when the accident happened.

They had flown to New York and then on to Europe. The plan was to visit London, Paris, Rome, and possibly Oslo, Norway, where his father had been born.

They got Paris and London out of the way and were on the way to Rome when the plane crashed in the mountains of Switzerland.

They didn't find enough of the remains to ship back to the states so there was no funeral.

Both had taken out flight insurance and told Nate what to do if anything happened to them. The policies were for $100,000 each, and with the regular life insurance there was enough to pay off the house and buy a new car with some left over for a rainy day that he put in the bank.

Nate was the produce manager for a major grocery store. He had worked at the same job since he dropped out of college in his first year.

Nate was of average intelligence and was just over six feet tall. He had dirty blonde hair that he got from his father's side of the family. He didn't drink, ate healthy food, and didn't smoke. His health was excellent.

His job didn't pay a lot but was adequate to meet his needs.

He had thought off and on about looking for a better job but never pursued the matter beyond the thought process.

Nate had been something of an athlete in high school. He played basketball and football. He thought that he might try to play at the college level but quickly discarded that idea when he saw the size of the players on scholarship. He weighed less than 200 pounds and had no scholarship offers so if he played it would have to be as a walk-on, and the chances of making the team were remote at best.

Most of the new students were more interested in partying than in classes and before the first semester was over so was Nate's educational ambitions. The main reason he had enrolled was to have a shot at sports, so he really didn't miss anything about the experience.

He had landed the job at the grocery store and been there ever since.

He came home from work on Thursday evening and went to the mailbox as was his custom. He removed the mail from the box and carried it into the house. He separated the legitimate mail from the junk as was usual and almost threw the plain white envelope away with the junk mail.

The address was hand written and there was no return address so he opened it first to determine if it was in fact junk. He was surprised when the $100 bill fluttered to the floor as he unfolded the paper inside.

He picked up the bill and held it up to the light to see if it was real. He had enough experience at the grocery store to know how to tell the real from the phony. It looked like a real bill. He read the letter, which said exactly the same thing as the one Lemuel Grimes had gotten.

He read it through a second time. Yes, the letter had said a million dollars.

Like Lemuel, Nate was struck by the fact that it was an individual rather than some institute. What kind of experiment could be worth that kind of money to an individual? Nate had no clue, but if the letter was on the level that was more money than he could even dream about. With it he could get rid of the house in Kansas and move to a better location.

It might be some sort of scam but he would call the number the next day and see what happened. He could take some vacation time from his job. He got three weeks per year and had not taken much since his parents had been killed. He had to have more than a month built up.

At the very least it was worth a phone call.

Nate had been married while in his early twenties but it didn't work out and they divorced after two years. There were no children and his ex knew he didn't have anything worth going after in court so they just went their separate ways to fend for themselves.

Nate had dated some after that but never got serious about anyone. If whomever he was dating started to get serious he broke off the relationship right away. No way did he want to get tied down to the situation he was in before. Sex just wasn't that important to him.

A million dollars! Why he could live on that for 20 years if he was frugal, maybe even longer. It was certainly something to dream about.

# Chapter 3

William Carter was a teacher.  He taught creative writing at the university in Columbia, South Carolina.  He had been at the job for just over ten years.

He grew up in South Carolina and had been in the army during the trouble in the Middle East.  As a matter of fact he had been in two of the wars, one during the younger Bush's tenure, and the second when Obama was President.

He had survived both deployments but not without some souvenirs.  He had been near enough to a roadside explosion to catch some shrapnel and lose some of his hearing.

The injury happened on his second tour and he decided he had enough after that.  When his enlistment was over he got out and went to college under the GI bill.  He already had a couple of years before he went into service and had enough of the eligibility left to complete a master's program.

Bill, as his friends called him, was an average guy.  He was 5'10" and weighed 180.  He had brown hair and gray eyes.  He still walked with a bit of a limp from his war wound.  He had gotten a Silver Star and a Bronze Star along with the Purple Heart and 'I was there' medals.

His wife had divorced him when he elected to go back to Iraq for a second tour of duty.  He really didn't blame her for the divorce.  She came from a moneyed family and the divorce was uncontested.

Bill had PTSD, or so the VA doctors told him.  He didn't have a lot of the symptoms he thought were associated with the ailment but he did get very nervous in a crowded environment, especially public events.

All in all his life was moving along as always when he received his letter.  Like the others it had a $100 bill in it and the same message.

Bill smelled a rat right away.  There was no way some individual was going to offer a million dollars for 30 days of his time.  This had to be a scam of some sort but he didn't have any idea what it might concern.

His first thought was to take it to the police and let them run it down.  Since there was nothing but a phone number they probably wouldn't have much luck with it, and if they did manage to find out who sent it they had not committed a crime. In the end he decided to call the number and run it down himself. If it wasn't kosher he could always go to the police after the fact and tell them what he had learned.

The writer in him thought that it might provide a good plot for a book. He had started several but never got beyond a few chapters before he discarded one idea after another.

He thought that he didn't have the temperament for writing, even though he taught the subject at the college level. He knew all the mechanics but didn't have the drive necessary to stick with one project.

He took the letter out again and started to analyze the writing style. It was short and to the point. The letter didn't give any indication whatsoever as to the subject of the experiment.

Was it an experiment or a study? There was a world of difference in the meaning of the two words. The letter did say experiment. In Bill's experience an experiment usually involved some amount of risk, depending on the experiment. Maybe that was why the offer of so much money was there.

The letter was certainly thought provoking if nothing else.

He wondered if the experiment would involve others or if it was a one person sort of thing.

A lot of questions but no answers.

In addition to the three mentioned, ten others received the same letter within a day of those. The wording was identical in all cases.

None of the recipients were very well off financially and the money would certainly be an enticement.

Mel Gibbons worked for a building contractor near Houston, Texas. He was 32 years old and had a high school education. He was 6'2" tall and weighed just over 200 pounds. He had black hair and brown eyes. His parents were Mexican immigrants and had changed the family name from Gonzalez to Gibbons after they became legal.

He had grown up in the Houston area, one of three children. The other two had left the area. One lived in Los Angeles and the other in Albuquerque, New Mexico.

His parents were elderly, though both still worked. His father worked at an upholstery shop and his mother worked for a cleaning company. His mother's parents, both in their upper eighties lived with the family as well.

Mel had tried to make a go of it on his own as a contractor but didn't have much success. He had the skills but not the business know-how to get the jobs. He made pretty good money, $15.00 per hour, and didn't have the headaches of dealing with taxes and building permits.

When he came home from work that day his mother handed him the envelope. He looked at the address and opened it. The $100 bill was there with the cryptic message.

He thought that the money might be counterfeit and would have it checked at the bank the following day.

His first thought was, scam. The money however gave him pause. Why would someone send that much money if it was a scam. Five or ten dollars would be more likely. He decided that it wouldn't hurt to call the number the next day and see what it was all about.

His mother asked and he told her he had no idea what it was all about.

Ted Walters lived in a suburb of Los Angeles. He was forty years old but looked much older. He had prematurely gray hair, which he kept that way with gray coloring. His face was lined from so much time in the outdoors and he had a perpetual dirty look. Even after a fresh shower he still looked dirty. Perhaps it was because of the image he wished to portray.

Ted was a professional panhandler. That was his job, at least in his eyes. He had a relatively nice home that he kept in meticulous shape. The yard was always trimmed neatly and the trim paint on the house was fresh.

Ted's schedule called for him to work in the mornings one week and in the afternoon the next week. He scouted for likely areas and set up a schedule for the times when his area of choice had the most traffic. Shopping centers he usually worked in the afternoons and public transportation locations such as airports and bus stations he worked in the mornings.

Since it wouldn't be seemly for a fat person to be panhandling Ted kept his weight down and dressed in baggy clothing. His actual weight was just under 175 but he looked thinner.

The good part about his activity was that he didn't have a lot of taxes to worry about. When he was a kid he loved to surf. He lived near enough to the ocean to get there daily. If he couldn't bum a ride with one of his friends he would walk to the beach, some two miles, carrying his surfboard on his shoulder.

He didn't have much growing up and started his career at a very young age. He would hang around the beach restaurants and ask for a handout until someone ran him off. He was surprised at the number of people who would pass him some change, and in some cases folding money.

He would even get propositioned by an occasional homosexual, which he thought of as easy money.

The only drawback to Ted's situation, at least in his eyes, was that he couldn't use a bank to keep his money. He did have a bank account but if he deposited the kind of money he made questions would be asked.

As an alternative he had devised several hiding places within and around his home to stash the cash. He didn't have an accurate count but estimated that he had more than half a million dollars in ready cash.

He sometimes cleared as much as $500 a day at his chosen profession, and the work was very easy on the muscles.

He would clean up somewhat before going home for the day. He kept a wash rag and water in his car and it didn't take much to make himself more presentable after a shift. He always parked his car at least two blocks from the area he was working and made sure none of his marks saw his direction of travel.

His neighbors had no idea what he did for a living. He was reclusive and the only time the neighbors saw him was when he was doing the outside work.

When he arrived back home that evening he took the mail from the box and went inside. He popped the top on a beer and went through the mail quickly. He laid it on the table and took the cash he had accumulated that day to one of his hiding places, a loose board in the hallway closet.

He came back and opened the mail. When he came to the letter he thought it strange that there was no return address.

He used a letter opener and slit the flap. When he withdrew the single sheet with the $100 bill it caught his attention.

The letter he read and thought about who could possibly be doing something like this. He thought the bill was legitimate and decided that he would look into the matter further the next day.

Both his parents were in a nursing home and he visited them at least two or three times a week, usually after the evening meal, and always brought them treats of some kind, usually candy bars, or sometimes the fried pies that fast food restaurants sold.

Both were near 90 and strangely enough, both had their mental faculties pretty much intact. They had been in the assisted living facility for three years and seemed perfectly happy. They shared a room, though each had their own beds. That didn't prevent them from sharing each other's beds when they wanted though.

All in all it was the best solution to providing for their care. The best part was that the state paid for it.

Adam Rathman was a long haul truck driver. He was 34 years old and was the sixth of seven children born to his parents. All the siblings were either dead or lived in other states. He had two sisters who had perished in a house fire when he was a pre-teen. He didn't even have many memories of them. An older brother was killed in Iraq several years before and he had two sisters and a brother who lived out of state with their own families.

Adam still called his parent's place home, though he spent little time there. It was simply a place to unwind from the many long road trips he took in the eighteen wheeler. He was an independent trucker. He owned the tractor, which was equipped with a sleeping compartment that mostly served to catch the required sleep mandated by law during his deliveries.

He barely made enough money to keep the rig in shape and provide for his bare necessities. He contracted with a booking company to arrange his loads and he never knew what he would be hauling or where he would be going from day to day.

He only averaged a few days each month at his parents place in College Park, Georgia. His parents were in their upper eighties and lived on small pensions. He helped out with the bills when he was around and they seemed to both be healthy and enjoying their later years.

His mother usually kept his mail in a grocery bag between trips.  When he arrived home this time he went through the mail and came across the plain white envelope without a return address and opened it.

He held up the $100 bill and asked his mother if she recognized the handwriting on the letter.  She didn't, so he read the letter that came with the money.  It didn't make a lot of sense to him, and though he was not well educated he did discern that whoever sent the letter was offering a million dollars for a month of his time for some sort of experiment.

That was a no-brainer to him.  He could endure anything for a month for that kind of money.  That is assuming that the offer was on the level.  He would call the number in the morning and find out what it was all about.

Thomas Cochran was a farmer in the panhandle of Florida, not far from Pensacola.  He had been raised on the same farm he was now working.  He made very little money with the venture.  He did grow enough for himself and sold some at a roadside area from his truck.  The farm was not large and he managed to work it on his own.  His parents had lived there until last year when they had gotten frail enough that he didn't like leaving them alone.

He had applied to the state for assistance to get them into a home for the elderly and the state picked up all the expenses in exchange for their social security money, which was less than $2,000 per month for the two of them.

The home was about an hour's drive away and he only managed to visit once or twice a week.  His mother was beginning to have trouble even recognizing him and it was breaking his dad's heart to see her in that condition.  There was not much either of them could do about it so they both endured.

He had spent a long day on the tractor and when he came in for the night he picked up the mail from the box just up the road.

The letter with which we are all now familiar was in the batch of mail he laid on the table.

Thomas was rail thin, only packing 150 pounds on his six foot frame.  His skin was like leather.  The sun and wind from his constant exposure made him look more like a Native American than the average white man.

Thomas had graduated from high school and read a lot, so he was fairly intelligent. When he opened the letter and found the money he had the same initial thought some of the others would have, 'this sounds too good to be true'.

The offer was so enticing that he might even participate in something illegal if it was not a capital offense. He laid the letter aside with the thought of calling the number the next day.

Lloyd Wheeler was a real estate agent. He lived in Seattle, Washington and worked out of Tacoma. He was close to 40 years old and had lived in the Pacific Northwest most of his life, excluding a two year stint in the army. During that interlude he had spent a year in Afghanistan.

He was the fourth of four children born to his parents and was what he thought of as an accident, which usually happens when the female forgets her birth control remedies or thinks she is past the child bearing years.

In his case his mother had been in her mid-forties and his father near fifty when he was born. Both were still living at home and he hired a nurse/companion to stay with them while he was away. Both were near 90 and seemed to be in good health.

When Lloyd came home from work that day and saw the envelope lying on the table he wondered who would send a letter without a return address. He opened the letter and took out the $100 dollar bill. He read the letter and turned it over to see if anything was on the other side. The theme of the letter was really out of the ordinary to his way of thinking. What kook would offer that kind of money for a 30 day experiment?

He fingered the bill. It seemed real but nothing about the letter made any sense. Not even a signature. The money seemed to be the real thing though, and if that was the case then maybe there was more to this than what he could determine.

At the very least he could call the number they provided and see what it was all about.

Mick Langston was a 36 year old nursery worker in Elmira, New York. He was the foreman of a crew that did landscaping work on private homes in the spring through summer. In the fall he did tree work and leaf clean-up. The winter was pretty much dead time and he spent most of that at home.

Mick was of Irish descent and had never been married. He lived at home with his parents and a younger brother, who, if truth be told, wasn't worth the powder it would take to blow his brains out. He was lazy, used drugs and was a constant concern to their parents. Mick had several discussions with his brother about his lifestyle without much success, even when he beat the living crap out of him.

Mick wasn't a mental giant, but he was a physical one. He stood at six and a half feet tall and tipped the scale at nearly 300 pounds.

Mick's parents were getting on in years and his dad was no longer able to work. Still, with the house paid for and what Mick brought in they made things work. Social security covered the food and utilities. Mick took care of everything else from his salary.

It was not the life of Riley, but it was a comfortable arrangement for them.

When the letter came Mick was just as baffled as others had been. He held up the hundred dollar bill to show his parents. "Somebody wants me to participate in an experiment. The letter says they will pay a million dollars for one month. How's that for good money?" he asked his father.

"There's a saying in the old country, and I suppose it is just as applicable here. If something sounds too good to be true, it usually is."

Mick laughed. "I've heard that one and I agree, but this looks like a real hundred dollar bill. I will have the bank check it tomorrow and if it is real then I will call the number they give and find out what it is all about."

Elizabeth Owensby, Liz to her friends, lived in Denver, Colorado. She was 5'6" tall and had a shapely figure at 130 pounds. She had brown hair and green eyes and worked as a clerk at a chain clothing store in the local mall.

She didn't make a lot of money but had regular daytime hours and not a lot of responsibility. Her grandparents had emigrated from Scotland just after WWII. Both had lived long lives and had not been dead long. Her mother and father, who was an invalid, lived with her, or rather she lived with them since they owned the house.

Her father had been in an industrial accident at the plant where he worked making car parts. One of the robotic arms the company used to move the parts down the assembly line went haywire for no apparent reason while he was at his work station very close to the machinery. The arm didn't stop when it was supposed to after performing its function and pinned him to the housing for the unit. He had broken ribs and partial paralysis in his back as a result. He had three surgeries to try to correct the problem but without success. A lawyer from his union contacted him while he was in the hospital and told him he thought he had a good case to get some money out of the company and came to talk to him about it.

He agreed to the law suit and it was settled out of court in a few months. He got a small pension and a lump sum settlement as well. The lawyers got a good chunk of the money but he did have enough to pay the house off.

He could get around with the aid of a walker but had to move slowly because he drug his left leg.

He was in his late seventies now and Liz's mother was a year older and in good health. She did some of the light house work while Liz was at work and the family had a decent life style.

Liz was 43 years old and had never married. She thought she might be a lesbian since she had no interest in men. The thing was that she had no interest in women either. If anything she was asexual.

When she arrived home from work she always looked at the mail before she started preparing dinner, or supper if you are from the south.

She looked at the letter with no return address and her name and address handwritten on the front. She opened the envelope and saw the $100 dollar bill. She fingered it and thought that it was real. She read the letter. She then sat down and read it again.

"This is really strange," she said to her mother.

Her mother came to the table and read the letter. "It is indeed strange. Was that a hundred dollar bill?"

"Yes and the letter says to keep that for the trouble of looking at the letter. Someone has more money than brains."

Her mother was still holding the letter. "This says they will give you a million dollars to participate in a month long experiment. It must be really dangerous to offer that kind of money."

"Well for the prospect of that kind of money I will at least call and find out what the experiment is,'" Liz said.

Her dad came into the dining room and sat down at the table. His wife handed him the letter and asked, "What do you make of this?"

He read it and didn't say anything for a couple of minutes. He was apparently trying to decide how to respond. Finally he said, "You should be very careful with this. There are so many scams going around that this might just be another one. The offer of a million dollars has a ring of falsehood. That's probably an enticement to get you to call so they can really fleece you."

Liz laughed. "I wasn't born yesterday. I will check the money to see if it is real, then if that checks out I will call them and see what they have in mind. I will make the call after work tomorrow so you and mom can hear the conversation."

Liz had dreams that night about what she could do with a million dollars.

Sharon Longwell was a nurse at a hospital in Raleigh, North Carolina. She was an LPN, as opposed to a RN. They basically did the same job but the RN had more educational requirements for certification than did the LPN. There was a difference in the pay scale as well.

Sharon had been in the health industry most of her life. She had started taking courses in her early twenties and it took her almost ten years to complete the curriculum going to school part time. Because she worked shifts it was difficult at times to arrange classes so she could attend. She switched shifts with others to manage her class load and was very proud of the LPN certification.

Sharon had been married and divorced twice, once in her early twenties and again when she was thirty. She had not had children and didn't really want any. The first marriage had ended when she caught her husband cheating on her. They had not dated long before they decided to marry and that was probably a mistake on her part in retrospect. Anyway it was water under the bridge.

The second time she was in her early thirties. She had gone slower that time and the two seemed very compatible. The problem was her work. Her husband was somewhat possessive and when she thought about it after the divorce decided that he was an egotistical ass. He wanted everything his way and couldn't handle the shift work she had to do.

They had only been married for nine months. There was no alimony or settlement from either divorce, so Sharon continued to work at the hospital.

She lived in an apartment near the hospital and could walk to work. She had a car but used it sparingly. She didn't have many outside interests and visited her parents at least once a week in a convalescent home in Durham. Both parents were in their eighties and had no major health problems that she knew about.

When she opened her letter she first couldn't believe what she read. Having been in the health care business for so long she knew something of the way medical experiments were conducted. They didn't use humans until they had tried the drugs out on animals, and it took a long time to get to clinical trials for new formulations. For that reason alone she almost dismissed the letter out of hand.

Certain drugs, such as chemotherapy treatments, had looser guidelines, but to participate in one of those programs you had to have cancer.

There were surgical techniques that had to be tested, but that was mostly done in hospitals under pretty strict guidelines as well.

She could not think of any medical or drug experiment that would fit with what the letter was suggesting.

Possibly the experiment was not related to the medical profession.

She could not come up with any experiment that would fit into her understanding of the letter.

The money was real enough and that alone would give her the incentive to call the number and find out more.

Mary Washington worked for the federal government in Washington, D.C. as a clerical assistant to a Senator from West Virginia. She had grown up near the town of Charleston and had gotten the job when she graduated from junior college. She had since finished her requirements for a BA degree and had gotten several promotions during her time in Washington.

She was now a GS-9, which was a government pay grade for civilian workers. She made a decent wage but not enough to afford anything upscale, either housing or clothing. It took most of what she made to provide for the necessities of life and she lived from one paycheck to the next.

Her parents were elderly but both still alive and in reasonably good health. They were in an assisted living facility in Charleston, West Virginia and she had a sister living there who looked in on them at least weekly. Mary herself only got back about once every three to six months.

Mary did not have much of a social life. She was not what one would call attractive. It was not that she had any physical flaws. She was just not very attractive. Her teeth were a bit crooked and her features were very plain. She used very little make-up and could have done a better job choosing her wardrobe. She was colorblind and some of the combinations she wore to work provided her co-workers with a topic of conversation for the entire day. She was very competent at her work and for that reason gained acceptance. Her tenure with the Senator was longer than most others in the office.

When she got her letter she simply read it and decided to call the number to see what developed.

Marie Alvarez was the final person who received one of the letters. She lived in Phoenix, Arizona and worked as a hotel maid. She was in her mid-thirties and crossed the border from Mexico almost 20 years previously.

Maria was soft spoken and had a much better grasp of English than she acknowledged. She found it convenient at times to pretend that she didn't understand a question asked in English if she didn't want to provide an answer.

She lived in an area of primarily Spanish speakers and shared a house with three other women in similar circumstances. Between the four of them the rent was kept at an acceptable level.

Maria was a bit on the heavy side, though by no means fat. She didn't date much and sent what she could afford back to Mexico to help provide for her aging parents.

When the letter came to her she read it silently and didn't speak of the matter to her housemates. It was not something that concerned them and if it worked out word would get out about her coming into some money and she didn't want that to happen. If she should get a million dollars the first thing she would do is hire a lawyer to make her presence in the United States legal, then try to arrange for her parents to come north. She would definitely call the number.

# Chapter 4

Robert Thorley was an attorney at least that is what his diploma from the University of Virginia said. He was in his mid-fifties and had never set foot in a courtroom as the representative of any client. When he graduated at the top of his class he had limitless possibilities and had been contacted by some of the most prestigious law firms in the nation.

He was trying to decide which offer was the most lucrative when an unrelated event took his life in another direction. He received a letter asking for a meeting to discuss employment. The letter didn't give any indication as to the nature of the employment but stated that if he agreed to accept the employment he would be compensated to the tune on one million dollars per year.

The missive related that he could show his acceptance of the offer by showing up at 1:00 p.m. the following day at a shopping mall on the north side of the town. He was told that he should go to the information booth and someone would contact him.

The offer had just enough intrigue and mystery to pique his interest. The other offers he had did not pay nearly what this party was offering but he had no idea what the employment entailed. He had about decided to take a job that paid only about a fourth of what this job offered.

Robert was not from a wealthy family and had to scrape and scratch to earn his degree. He was something of a child prodigy in his younger days and had an IQ that was almost off the charts. He had a near photographic memory and absorbed knowledge the way most folks absorb the calories they ingest.

He was somewhat bothered by the methodology of the meeting arrangements but figured it might be some eccentric whim. Another possibility was that the job was related to the intelligence business. At any rate it was enough to entice him to the meeting.

He drove to the shopping center the next day just after noon and had lunch at the food court. He kept an eye on the information booth to see if he could detect anyone hanging around obviously waiting for someone, maybe him.

During the hour that he sat eating and watching he identified a couple of people that might be the person who was meeting him.

Both had entered the area within the fifteen minutes before 1:00 p.m. but not together.  One sat on a bench nearby, ostensibly reading a newspaper, and the other was window shopping close enough to keep the booth in his vision.

It really didn't matter which of them was the man he was to meet.  He just thought he could score some points by introducing himself to the person before they had a chance to identify him.  They obviously knew what he looked like, otherwise they would not be able to recognize him.

At two minutes before the hour he made his way toward the information booth.  He walked directly to the man reading the newspaper and said, "I'm Robert Thorley.  I think we were to meet."

The man laid the paper aside and looked up.  "I have no idea what you are talking about," he said.

Robert had been fairly sure this was the man but his response indicated otherwise.

Another man, whom he had not noticed before tapped him on the shoulder and said, "I am the person you are supposed to meet.  Would you follow me please?"

He had not offered a name and Robert meekly followed him out of the mall and to a stretched limousine with smoked windows.  He opened the rear door and motioned Robert inside.  He then closed the door and went to the driver's side and got behind the wheel.

A diminutive figure sat in the back seat of the limo, a blanket covering his lower body.

"Just drive around for a while," he told the chauffeur.

The limousine started and exited the parking lot.  The driver drove north on highway 29 and Robert turned his attention to the man in the seat beside him. The two were sizing each other up, but for different reasons.

"My name is Elijah Worthington.  It is possible that you have heard of me, though I try to keep a very low profile.  Not to brag, but I am extremely wealthy.  I have had my people keep an eye on you for almost two years now and I think you and I will be able to work together," he said.

"Work together has an entirely different connotation from working for you.  Can you clarify that point?" Robert asked.

The man laughed. "While you will be working for me, if we reach an agreement, we will be required to work together to accomplish anything worthwhile. You are the most intelligent person I could find, and unlike most geniuses you have a good grasp on reality. You don't exhibit animosity toward the lesser fish that swim around you and you are socially adept."

"What does the job entail?"

"I guess you could call it private secretary, or even personal advisor. My thought was to bring you into all my business affairs and use you as a sounding board for actions and investments. I never enter into any business agreement until I have all the facts, and you will in many cases obtain those facts for me. Everything I do is within the law, but if the situation calls for some dirty work I am not above authorizing that."

"How much are you actually worth?"

"It's in the billions. I can't give you a definitive answer. In addition to the million dollar a year salary you will receive a percentage of any investment return exceeding some percentage that I haven't decided upon as yet."

"Why me?"

"I told you. I have had you investigated from your birth to now. I have had people evaluating you for the past two years. I am talking about head doctors, behavioral specialists, even your doctors, though they don't know that I obtained the information from their personal records. There's not much about you that I don't know. Having said that, there are always secrets that don't want to become known. Do you have any such secrets?"

Robert gave the matter some thought. First of all this man told him he had him followed for two years, just on the off chance that he might be able to offer him a job upon graduation. That took a lot of time and money. He now admitted that there might be things about Robert that he didn't know and wanted him to fill in the blanks.

"I haven't killed anyone and buried the body, or committed any other felony. That would be an obstacle hard to overcome in my chosen profession. I have done things that do not make me proud, but nothing against the law. Will my lawyer training come into play with what you want me to do?"

"It is possible, though I have a piss-pot full of lawyers already. I do not have a personal relationship with any of them. They are there to take care of legal work. You on the other hand will be by my side more than not. That was the primary reason you were investigated so thoroughly. I don't have to worry about you trying to enrich yourself because I will be paying you more than you will ever need. In addition to the money, you will be provided living quarters in whatever location we find ourselves, and all other living expenses will be provided. What do you think?"

"What are the terms of employment? Will there be a contract for a specified time or otherwise?"

"Otherwise. This is the kind of relationship that can't be put on paper. I propose that if you accept the position that we just go from day to day until either of us decides that we have had enough of the other, or our paths diverge."

"The deal is certainly better than anything else I have been offered. I suppose you want an answer right now?" Robert said.

Elijah laughed. "You really are quite intelligent."

"When do I start?"

"Just as soon as you can pack your bags and get to the airport. My plane is there. If you can get that accomplished this afternoon I will hold the plane for you. If you need another day I will send them back to get you."

Robert was taken back to the shopping mall and picked up his car. He drove to his apartment and packed his clothing in less than 30 minutes. He penned a note to the apartment manager that he had vacated the apartment and that he could have the furnishings to do with as he pleased. His rent was already paid through the end of the month. The deposit Robert told him he could keep for his troubles cleaning the apartment.

He called a female acquaintance and asked her to drive him to the airport. On the way he passed the title to her and told her that she could have the car, which was several years old. He would not need it wherever he was going with a limousine available whenever he needed to get to someplace.

He was at the airport within two hours of the time he had left Elijah. He didn't know where the plane was located but found the chauffeur waiting for him at the small terminal.

He was delivered to the business jet and they were in the air within a very few minutes.

That had happened in 1988. Now, more than 30 years later he was still with Elijah, and was independently wealthy from the money he had made with the man.

Most of the things he did were strictly legal, but there were obstacles that needed to be removed from certain playing fields before they could take the action upon which they had decided. The minor stuff was accomplished through cut-outs that could not lead back to them. Breaking and entering, strong armed activities and bribery were just some of the things that were required to reach their goals.

As Elijah had told him, he would be working with him rather than for him and he was a lot more intelligent than Elijah, a fact which they both recognized. The partnership seemed to be a match made in heaven, or in their case hell. At any rate they were very compatible and enjoyed each other's company.

It was almost a month after Robert hooked up with Elijah that he asked him about the blanket he seemed to always have across his lap, even when he was behind his desk.

"I have a circulation problem brought on by trauma. The lower extremities always seem to be cold and the blanket helps."

"What is the nature of the circulation problem?" Robert asked.

"I will tell you the story sometime after we get to know each other better," was the reply.

Robert did not pursue the matter any further and it was almost a year later before he got the story from Elijah.

"When the Russians were fighting in Afghanistan I went to Kabul to negotiate a business deal. Our government had asked me to provide some munitions and other hardware to the Mujahedin and I was there to negotiate the price and delivery details. The Russians stopped my vehicle, killed the driver and took me captive. I still don't know where they took me, but I was tortured because I had been seen with one of the rebel leaders and they thought I knew a lot more about their command structure than I actually did. They first tried to starve the information out of me, and when that didn't work they started pounding on my limbs with truncheons. Both my legs were broken in multiple places, as were the bones in my feet. I couldn't give them information I didn't possess and after almost a month they dumped me on the street in Kabul. I was taken to a local hospital and once I became coherent enough to contact the Americans they got me out. I spent almost a month in military hospitals trying to repair the damage. The bones healed properly but there was nerve damage as well as damage to the blood vessels. I was happy to even be able to walk for the first few months."

"Did you manage to deliver the munitions?" Robert asked.

"Not only that but I gave them stinger missiles to help take care of the Russian helicopter gunships. I didn't even charge them for follow-on orders."

"I suppose you have had a grudge against the Russians ever since," Robert said.

"I avoid their company whenever possible, which is all the time. I wouldn't do business with them even if the deal would make a lot of money for me. I try to stick it to them in any way I can."

"I guess that's what you call holding a grudge."

Elijah laughed. "One of these days I might decide to really make them pay. I am not sure how yet, but the idea is always near the surface of my mind."

The relationship had held for the long term. Robert did most of the planning for their financial activities. He would identify businesses that were on the verge of bankruptcy and buy the notes on them. Once the mortgages were in hand they would entice the owner to sell for less than the business was actually worth and take over the business. The right people would be brought in to get the concern on its feet again and they would sell for considerable profit.

Robert was very adept at finding what was needed.

Once it became apparent that Robert had a flair for picking winners Elijah allowed him to do as he wished, supplying the money for each endeavor.

Over the years Robert built a considerable data base of people he could rely on for shady dealings. He never had direct contact but had several people he could count on to find the skills he needed for some chore.

Even if they should be investigated no evidence would be found.  All transactions of that sort were paid for in cash and no direct reference to Elijah's companies was ever made.

Elijah was only 5'7" tall and weighed 150 pounds.  He ate healthy food and had a gym at the estate in the mountains of Colorado, where they spent most of their time.  He used the equipment regularly and encouraged Robert to do likewise.

They traveled together at times to investigate some issue they were interested in, and other times Robert traveled alone in the private jet.

There was a road to the mansion in the mountains but it was never used by Elijah or Robert.  There was a helicopter pad behind the main house accompanied by a complete workshop, tools and spare parts for the helicopter.  Elijah had two helicopter pilots, one on call at all times.  He had a small house built for the pilots and repair crew. A pilot and mechanic were at the house at all times.

He paid them well for the inconvenience and nobody complained.

The jet was kept in Colorado Springs and was available around the clock.

Elijah's headquarters was in Chicago, though he was only there a couple of times each year.  It was basically an office staff where the paperwork was kept for his many holdings.  He had a very competent office manager and he took care of all the paperwork.

Elijah was in his seventies before he encountered a problem that he could not solve.  He and Robert were sitting at the table, having just finished breakfast, when he experienced chest pains.

At first he thought it was indigestion and took a couple of antacids.  The pain did not go away and by late morning he told Robert that he thought he might be having a heart attack.

Robert immediately got on the intercom and told the pilot to prepare for a flight.

They went to Colorado Springs since it was the closest and the hospital had a helipad.  He had the pilot call ahead and arrange to land at the hospital and have the emergency room standing by.

When they landed Elijah was taken into the cardiac care area and treated.  All the tests were done, including EKG, MRI, and the next day, a stress test.

Elijah had blockage in the major arteries and they surgically implanted stints in the blocked areas.

He was in the hospital for three days. When he was ready to be released the doctor talked to Elijah, with Robert present at Elijah's insistence.

"Although we placed stints in the arteries that were partially blocked that was not the crux of the problem. The arteries were pliable enough that they should have been able to handle the necessary blood flow. The major problem is that your heart is simply not strong enough to pump the quantity of blood needed to supply the body."

"What exactly does that mean?" Elijah asked.

"It means that your heart is about worn out. The muscles of the heart are just not strong enough to do the job. We can put you on blood thinners which will help the problem somewhat, allowing more blood to be pumped with the same amount of effort on the part of the heart. Other than that there is not much that can be done. There are no methods to rejuvenate the heart muscles."

"So you're telling me there's nothing you can do?" Elijah asked.

"We can implant a pacemaker to keep your heart in rhythm but that doesn't deal with the root cause of the problem, which is that your heart is just wearing out more quickly than is normal."

"Is there nothing at all that can be done?" Elijah asked.

"The only solution I can think of is a heart transplant. That procedure has been perfected in the last few decades and with the anti-rejection drugs patients who have undergone the procedure have lived for as many as 20 additional years."

"How do I go about getting a transplant?"

"You put your name on the national register and when they come across a match it will go to the person most compatible and who has been on the list the longest. The list is quite lengthy right now and I don't know how to evaluate your chances for a compatible donor."

"Thank you for your time and efforts doctor," Elijah said.

Elijah was taciturn for the entire flight back to the estate.

Robert knew him well enough by this time to hold his peace and let Elijah work the problem through his mind.

He thanked the pilot and went into the house with Robert following along behind.

"What can I do?" Robert asked.

"Nothing.  I need to think this situation through.  I will talk to you tomorrow," he said and headed for his bedroom.

# Chapter 5

The next morning at breakfast Elijah said, "I have been giving my health problem some thought. Since the waiting list for transplants is so large it might be a good idea to find a donor on my own."

"You are talking about someone with a fatal disease?" Robert asked.

"Not necessarily."

"You will still have a problem with the health authorities jumping ahead on the list."

"I believe any problems in that regard can be resolved."

"What, exactly do you have in mind?"

"I'm going to let you find me a donor. The person will need to have the same blood type as a starting point. It will have to be someone who doesn't have much in the way of material possessions and a history of longevity in the family would be desirable. The approach will need to be worked out but there will be enough time for that while I have a hospital built," Elijah said.

"You are going to build your own hospital to have the surgery done?"

"Yes indeed. It will be a benevolent act as it will benefit many people other than me. I think a two year time line will work out. That will give me time to have the construction done and you time to take care of the other chores."

"You are talking about a willing live donor I assume. That is going to be a tough nut to crack. No person in their right mind would consent to giving up his life, even for a lot of money, unless there are extenuating circumstances."

"What if you gathered the proper group together and offered them, say a million dollars to participate in an experiment. Make the number of potential candidates large enough that the odds of survival will be great enough that they will take the chance. It would simply be a gamble with very good odds and most poor people would jump at the opportunity if it is presented properly."

That conversation had been the catalyst that set the plan into motion.

Within the week Elijah identified what was needed in the way of a hospital. He put Robert to work finding the right doctor.

It would have to be a person who was foremost a qualified heart surgeon, and one who could deal with the moral dilemma that the project would entail.

The hospital would have to be in an area that really needed one, and that didn't have a real large population base. He might even consider building the hospital in a foreign country where the rules were a little more lax than those in the United States.

Robert actually came up with the best solution in that regard.

"Why not someplace like an Indian Reservation where there are not many people and they still need health care?" he asked.

"That might be a good solution. We will look into that as a first choice."

They found two locations that would meet their needs. One was in Arizona and the other in Utah. The Navajo reservation in Arizona and the Ute reservation in Utah. Both were sadly deficient in health care facilities and either would probably fall all over themselves if someone offered to build a facility at no cost to the tribe.

Robert researched the physical aspects of the proposed project to determine size and capability.

They settled on a 100 bed facility, which was not terribly large for a health care facility. It would be equipped with the latest in technology as far as capability went. It would have four operating rooms with the latest in surgical equipment and an emergency room that could handle 10 patients simultaneously.

Robert and Elijah visited each of the areas and talked with tribal officials. The offer was tendered to the Ute tribe in Utah. They were ecstatic over the situation and called a special tribal council meeting to vote on the offer. The result was as they had expected and Elijah had the legal department of his company draft the documents necessary to meet legal requirements.

Once that was done Robert started investigating all known doctors who did heart transplants. Strangely enough the majority of those were located in Europe.

Once they decided on the doctor they had to make the approach.

The doctor was Swiss and his track record was pretty good for survival in the procedures he had performed.

Robert went to Switzerland and talked to the doctor.

"What we offer is the opportunity to run your own hospital, albeit a small one.  It will have all the latest equipment and we will consent to a research function that will allow you to try to perfect new procedures.  The hospital will be governed by our national health laws but you will be the man in charge.  You can name your own salary, within reason, and if you run the facility at a profit you will receive a share of the profit."

"What's the catch?" he asked.

"Your benefactor is in need of a heart transplant.  By the time the facility is up and running we hope to have a donor.  You will perform the surgery and care for the patient through his recovery," Robert said.

"Why do I think that the donor will not be a volunteer?"

Robert said, "The donor will be a volunteer.  It's just that waiting to go through the normal routine might be longer than your patient has.  Since he has so much money he decided to try to stack the deck in his favor.  The only ethical issue involved is jumping the waiting list that the national health authorities maintain."

"Would my benefactor balk at one million dollars a year in salary?"

"No, and he will also have you a nice house built near the facility.  It is in a rather remote area and housing will be provided for the hospital staff.  Basically it will be like your own small town."

"May I have some time to think it over?"

"No.  I need a decision right now.  If your answer is no then I will have to go the second best transplant surgeon."

The last was said to stoke the man's ego.  Everyone wants to think that he is the best at his chosen profession and doctors are no different.

"What if I give you a tentative yes and confirm tomorrow?"

"I suppose I can wait that long," Robert said.

When the two met the following morning, the doctor, whose name was Hans Schefter, agreed to the proposition.

"Something I didn't mention earlier is the fact that the hospital will have its own helicopter.  We will also build an airstrip long enough to handle smaller jets.  That way you can travel when necessary.  A smaller prop plane will be made available to you and the maintenance will be provided by us."

"That is very generous. Is this someplace my wife will like?"

"Probably not. I would suggest that you maintain a second home in someplace like Salt Lake City, Las Vegas, or even Phoenix. Your wife will probably find one of those cities more to her liking. You could fly home a couple of times a week."

The doctor nodded in agreement.

"I will have a contract drawn up for you by our lawyers. The period for which you commit will be five years. After that we will see where we stand."

"When will I start?"

"That's up to you. If you want be involved in the building project you can start any time after next month. Your accommodations will be rather primitive until we can get the house built. We are using the plans from an architect who did the original design for someone else. He will make sure it meets all the building codes for the area. If there are specific ways you want the operating rooms laid out then you need to review the plans. There will probably be enough to keep you occupied from about thirty days on. It will give you the chance to meet some of your future patients at the small clinic they have now. You will also need to work on the staffing requirements and give me numbers and qualifications so I can line up the people for you," Robert told him.

By the time Robert got back to Colorado the plans were completed and the contract with the builder had been executed. The construction would be started right away.

With that part of the plan underway Robert turned his attention to finding the right donor.

He and Elijah talked about it at length.

Elijah was unmarried and had no close relatives. Robert was probably closer to him than anyone else in his entire sixty plus years.

"How are you going to go about identifying potential donors?" Elijah asked.

"Use your criteria to do the initial identification. I am talking about blood type, health issues, and that sort of thing. The first list will be quite lengthy. I will probably use the computer to winnow the list, adding more criteria as the list gets smaller. I will have to get a computer program designed for that purpose. Once the list is more manageable I will start looking at individuals."

"What sort of criteria will you use?"

"Blood type is the obvious first criteria. Then I will look at age, race, gender, marital status, and determine any health issues. I think family longevity will also be an important factor. When I get the list under 2,000 I can start to apply socio-economic criteria. I don't want to contact anyone who has close ties to someone. They need to be on the lower rung of the economic ladder. In other words I will be searching for people who have few if any ties to others, and who really could use a great deal of money. Their current health will also be a factor and if necessary I will have them examined by our own doctor."

"How long do you anticipate before you have a good list of candidates?"

"It could take as much as a year to do it right. As long as your health holds up the time line is good. It will take at least that long to get the facility built anyway. Once I get the list to under 100 I will put some people doing background and surveillance on those. I hope to end up with at least 20 but less will work," Robert said.

"Another factor which will come into play is your blood type. You are AB NEG and less than one percent of the population has that blood type. That means that our initial number is going to be lower and the elimination process will go faster," Robert continued.

"Doesn't that mean that there is a better chance to move up the national list with so few people having the blood type?"

"Yes and no. It means that there are probably a lot fewer people with your blood type needing transplants, but it also means that the number of compatible donors will be fewer."

Dr. Schefter got the necessary visa and arrived in the country as they were excavating the foundation for the hospital. Since there was no ready supply of water the builder had to search for water. The hospital would have its own well and sewage treatment facility. The utility company would bring the necessary power to the location, for a price of course.

Robert hired a different contractor to erect the housing for hospital workers. Robert asked Schefter to come up with an estimate of the needs so they could get that part of the project started.

When he was satisfied that the building work was on track he turned his attention toward finding a donor.

He instructed the people who would gather the data to screen medical records for blood type. He hired a computer hacker to find a way to access medical records electronically.

The hacker knew the company that provided the software for medical record keeping and told Robert that the best way to get the information was to bribe one of the software engineers to provide a path into the data bases. It only cost $100,000 to get access to all patient records from facilities who used the software, which was a large percentage of the population.

The engineer simply made a change to the software that was sold and initiated an automatic upgrade to add a way into the data. He was told that he would only have to leave it in place for a month and that he could then change back to the previous software.

The engineer wanted assurance that they were not going to use the data for any illegal reason. Robert gave the assurance but thought that the man must be an idiot to think that someone asking for access to data illegally would not use it for unlawful purposes.

He had his hacker set up an office in Dallas, Texas to compile the data. He would use half a dozen people to methodically scan the data bases of all major medical facilities in the country. Once that was done they would go on to clinics which used the same software.

During the month they mined the data they found over four million people who had the right blood type. Their data base was huge with data they had stolen. Now they would have to narrow the list down using other criteria.

The first factor applied was an age range. Robert figured anyone over fifty might have already gotten the best days out of his heart so that was the cut off. That took care of almost half the list. Younger people didn't tend to visit the doctor or hospital as frequently as the elderly.

He dropped the age ceiling to 40 and eliminated a couple of hundred thousand more.

Next he eliminated all those married. That took care of a lot more.

He wanted to use a monetary range to find the poorer candidates but there was not any data in the medical records that dealt with income, unless the patient was a welfare recipient.

He asked the hacker if he could find those with longevity in the family.

"They have sections of the initial questionnaire asking if the parents are still alive. We will have to screen manually for that information but it can be done. It will not be totally accurate because we won't know the time differential between now and when the form was filled out unless we do that manually as well."

"Just do the best you can with it. I need to move the project forward soon," Robert said.

Just six months after he started the project, Robert had the list narrowed down to 200. He screened the records of all those himself and chose 20 from that list for follow-up investigation.

He then called a security firm that he had used in the past and put them to work building complete dossiers on each of the 20 people he had identified. They were scattered all over the country and it was expensive to do the surveillance. Still, the expense was necessary.

He asked for weekly updates so that he could stay on top of the situation. Anytime something turned up that was unfavorable for his purposes he eliminated that person from the list.

After six months of surveillance and digging the list was down to thirteen.

Robert spent a lot of time with the surveillance reports on the remaining potentials.

The panhandler's activities had come to light during the time they watched him and Robert thought about eliminating him. The scheme was innovative enough that he decided to keep him among the group that he would talk with eventually.

In the meantime the hospital was coming along at a satisfactory pace. The builder was a bit ahead of his schedule and the living quarters for the employees had been completed. There was a single family dwelling of almost 4,000 square feet for the Director, and a four sided apartment building with an open space in the center. The apartments were two bedrooms with large living rooms.

The building was three stories and had 40 apartments on each level, ten to each side.

The staffing included nurses, assistants, doctors, lab technicians, cleaning crews, cooks and administrative staff. Some of the single nurses might have to double up in the apartments but it was a problem that could be dealt with easily enough.

Most of the cleaning crew would come from tribal members. That would cut down on the need for housing.

Things seemed to be coming together rather well.

# Chapter 6

Robert got a toll free number to use specifically for the follow-up with the thirteen on his list. He wanted to do the first interviews privately. Later he would get them together and explain some of the aspects of the program that might influence them to pass up the deal.

He used mathematical probability theory to arrive at the chances of survival for the group. Twelve of the thirteen would survive. That was a probability of nearly 93 percent. With the million dollars each on the table it would be difficult for the people on his final list to turn the deal down. Choosing to participate would be a bit more difficult than placing a bet with a bookie on an almost sure winner because their lives would be on the line.

Much would depend on how persuasive he was when explaining the project. He thought that no more than two of the thirteen would refuse the money.

The letters had all been mailed from the area in which the recipient lived so they would have all gotten them on the same day. Robert had thought very carefully about how much money to use as a lure to get them to call. More than the hundred would have made the pitch seem more like a scam. Anything less would not have caught their attention to the degree that he wished.

The one flaw that he saw in his plan was that none of the potential subjects had any close relatives to leave the money to. Would that influence their decision? He thought it possible, but with the chances for survival at better than 90 percent maybe it wouldn't make a lot of difference.

He stayed close to the phone on the day after the letters went out. Some would probably put the call off until the next day, depending on when they opened the letter. He only got one call on the first day, that from Marie Alvarez.

She wanted to know what the experiment entailed. Robert told her it was not something he wanted to discuss over the phone but he would call her back within the next couple of days to set up a face-to-face meeting if she would provide a phone number where she could be reached.

She gave him the cell phone number and asked that he call after 5:00 pm when she got off work.

Robert had always been self-assured in all things he took on.

This was the first time that he could remember having any trepidation about a task he undertook. It wasn't the fact that one of the participants would die as the result of his actions, rather it was the unknown vagrancies of the human mind that concerned him.

He would have to interface with all the subjects and the odds of one or more of the finalist talking about the experiment after the fact could cause him a lot of grief if they spouted off to the wrong people.

As he lay in bed that night he tried to analyze his current situation. Most of the others he had sent letters to would probably call the next day and he was unsure about following through with the plan. His misgivings about what he was about to do simply would not go away.

What if Elijah didn't survive long enough to get the transplant, he thought. He was in his seventies now and had almost constant care. Robert had brought in a nurse to care for him full time. He could still get around on his own, but he was easily fatigued and spent most of him time either sitting in a recliner or lying in bed. He had lost weight and his appearance reminded Robert of the pictures he had seen of the concentration camp Jews who had been repatriated after WWII. He was that skinny.

He had no living relatives and Robert knew that he was listed in his will as the sole beneficiary. His death would solve the problem in more ways than one. First he would come into a fortune that he had helped build over the years, and second, the people he was pretty sure would opt to participate in his experiment would all live. Robert was very rich in his own right. The money he had helped amass over the years made him a millionaire many times over. What he had was a drop in the bucket to what Elijah Worthington was worth.

That would all be his when Elijah checked out.

He thought about ways to lengthen the project to give Elijah more time to die, but Elijah knew the time table too well to extend it more than a few days.

Robert was somewhat ashamed of himself for even having the thoughts that were running through his mind on that night.

He tried to push the thought from his mind but had no success. The more he thought about it the more he liked the idea of Elijah not living to receive the transplant. He didn't know how he would make it happen, but the idea had taken root and he somehow knew that he would get rid of Elijah before the experiment came to an end.

He would then tell the experiment participants that it was an experiment designed to measure their reactions to stress, or some such drivel. Since that would assure the survival of all the participants there should be no repercussions from any of them.

He would still have to tell them the original premise of the plan, just in case things did not go as planned.

The next day he received calls from most of those he had sent letters to. He took the same tact as he had with the first caller and told them that he would need to meet face to face to give them more details.

Only a single individual had not called back. He would give it one more day and then have the telephone disconnected.

The lone holdout was Adam Rathman, the trucker, and he had not called because he was on the road and had simply forgotten about the letter. He called on the third day.

Now he could start setting up the appointments to see them individually.

That was going to take the better part of two weeks because they were scattered across the United States.

He started with Marie Alvarez in Phoenix. He rented a suite in one of the nicer hotels and called Marie at 6:00 pm and asked her to come to the hotel.

She showed up at the appointed time and accepted a soft drink when offered some refreshment.

Robert had a folder on her, which he removed from his briefcase after they were seated.

He said, "So how would you like to earn a million dollars?"

"I would love to, but what do I have to do to earn it?"

"Agree to participate in an experiment for no more than thirty days. You will need to come to the location I choose as part of a group of thirteen. The group will include three other women and eight men. There is some risk because one of the thirteen will not survive. The odds are right at 93 percent that you will survive to spend the money, which will be deposited to your account before the experiment starts.  The money is yours and can be verified with your bank before you leave Phoenix.  The taxes will be paid on the money and the million will be free and clear.  I know that you are in the country illegally and that you would like nothing better than to have your parents join you here.  A million dollars will help you accomplish those things."

"What sort of experiment is it?"

"It is statistical analysis to learn what impact a large amount of money has on making a decision that might cost you your life," Robert said.

"Are you saying that one of the group will die?"

"Exactly.  You need not concern yourself with the mechanics of the experiment.  You will not be harmed during the course of events, unless you are the unlucky one of the group."

"Only one out of thirteen will not survive?" she asked.

"That's it.  Only one."

The mental wheels turned as Marie weighed the odds.  One of thirteen was not bad odds, and if she didn't survive she could leave the money to her parents.

"I will do it," she said.

"Do you have a check book so I can get the account number and routing data for the deposit?" Robert asked.

Marie took out her checkbook and Robert copied the numbers he would need.

"I will be in touch with you again within two weeks.  The money will be deposited to your account the day I have someone pick you up to take you to the location of the experiment."

Since he was in the western part of the country he decided to catch the one in Los Angeles and the one in Seattle next.

He flew to Los Angeles and got a suite at a hotel near the airport.  When he placed the call to Ted Walters he asked if he could come to his house for the discussion.

Ted was more than agreeable.  If this turned out to be some sort of scam he would at least be on his own turf.

Robert hired a chauffeured limousine and arrived on time.  He told the chauffeur to come back for him in one hour as he exited the car and walked toward the front door.

Ted had apparently been watching for him as he opened the door before Robert could even ring the bell.

Robert introduced himself and they sat at the dining room table. Robert noticed that the house was immaculately clean, quite the opposite of the public man.

Once again a folder came out of the briefcase. "Let me start by saying that I probably know more about you than you do yourself. I know that you make a living panhandling, and I know where you stash the cash. I also know that you have not paid taxes on over half a million dollars. Having said that, I am not here to threaten you with exposure, but to offer you the opportunity to make a million dollars, tax free, I might add. The taxes will be paid on the money before it is deposited into your bank account."

"How do you know all that?"

"I have had you observed for almost a year. I have keys for the locks on your doors and my people have discovered where you stash the money. You are very resourceful, though somewhat on the lazy side. You do visit your parents regularly, and that is your one redeeming quality."

"Why would you give me a million dollars?" Ted asked.

"Because there is some risk involved in what you will be doing. Thirteen people will participate in the experiment but only twelve will survive. The odds are just short of 93 percent that you will survive. So are you a gambling man?"

"What sort of experiment is it?"

"One to see how people handle stress when they know they might be doing something that could cost them their lives," Robert said.

"Just one of thirteen will not survive?"

"That is correct."

"How will the money be paid?"

"If you provide the bank account and routing number I will deposit the money on the day you are picked up. You will be able to verify the deposit before you leave L.A."

"Suppose I tell you I will go along and change my mind after you deposit the money?"

"Then I guess I would have a talk with the IRS and probably the local law enforcement people to make them aware of your shortcomings."

"I thought you said you weren't here to threaten me?"

"I did indeed, and if you decide you don't want to participate in the experiment without trying to con me out of a million dollars my lips are sealed. However if you lead me on with the intention of scamming me, all bets are off," Robert said.

"One out of thirteen?" Ted asked.

"That is correct, and you will not be subjected to any procedure that will harm you."

"Okay, count me in," Ted said. "When do we start?"

"Within two weeks. I will send a plane for you. I will call and give you the details at the proper time."

The interview had not taken more than thirty minutes and Robert had to wait for the limousine to return, so he had a drink with Ted.

Robert thought his hardest sell would be the professor in South Carolina so he had the pilot fly to Columbia. He had slept most of the flight and after he checked into a hotel and had dinner he called the professor, William Carter and set up a time to meet. He agreed to talk to him in his office at the university the next day.

This one was no stranger to death, but would he take the chance that he might be the one facing the grim reaper?

When they met in Carter's office it was obvious that Carter thought he was about to be scammed in some way.

Robert took out the folder with Carter's information in it. Instead of regurgitating what was in the folder he simply handed it to Carter for his perusal. The folder was rather thick and documented Carter's activities from a very early age.

He spent almost 15 minutes going over the information, then handed it back to Robert.

"Well, I will say you are thorough. Now what's the catch?"

"There is no catch, but there is some risk," Robert said.

"Okay, lay it out for me."

"I am conducting an experiment to gauge how people react under extreme stress. I am not talking about torture, or even manipulation of the mental process. I have thirteen subjects, including you if you care to participate. They will be together for a month. Each will be paid a million dollars, tax free, and up front. The experiment dictates that one of the thirteen will not survive.

That makes the odds something short of 93 percent that you will survive."

"What happens to the one who does not survive, and what is the criteria for selecting the one who is unlucky?"

"It will be sort of like the lottery. I will assign each a number and put them in a hat and draw one. The entire process is totally random."

"What happens to the one you select?"

"That need not concern you, unless of course you are the one selected. If that turns out to be the case the situation will then be explained. You would be entering the lottery with a 93 percent chance of walking out a winner. Those are pretty good odds no matter how you look at it."

"Well a million dollars is a pretty attractive incentive. When is this going to take place?"

"Approximately two weeks from now. I will send a plane for you at the appropriate time if you choose to participate," Robert said.

"How do I get the million dollars?"

"Give me your bank account and routing numbers and the money will be electronically wired to your account. You will have time to verify the deposit before you get on the plane."

"May I think it over?"

"I will be in town overnight. Call me before 9:00 am with an answer one way or the other."

When he left Carter's office Robert was not sure if he would accept or not. He would stay overnight and wait for the phone call the next morning.

When morning arrived Robert had breakfast and was back in his room before 8:30. He had about decided that Carter was not going to call. He packed his bag and was ready to walk out the door when his phone rang.

Carter agreed to participate and gave Robert the bank information.

The next seven days were a whirlwind of activity. Robert flew from Columbia to Atlanta, then to Pensacola. He then headed north to Washington, from there to Elmira, then on to Boston.

On the way to Seattle he stopped in Kansas City. In every case the individuals had agreed to participate. It looked like he would have all thirteen to choose from.

Robert had given the premise of getting rid of Elijah a lot of thought over that time period and decided that was the best solution.

He had purchased a small ski resort in the Colorado Rockies a few months ago. Since it was not winter there would be no other guests to worry about. All his subjects would be housed at the resort.

They could do their own cleaning and cooking.

He now had to decide how to get rid of Elijah without leaving any clues. Since he was so weak and frail it should be a simple matter to place a pillow over his face until he suffocated, or he could fall down the stairs, maybe even fall down onto the rocks below as the house was on a hilltop with rugged terrain on three sides.

There were enough options to choose from.

Robert spent half a day making arrangements for the money to be deposited into the thirteen accounts. After paying the taxes on the money for each of the individuals the total cost came to almost 20 million dollars.

Once that was out of the way he briefed the pilot about what he was to do. It would take a couple of days to gather all his participants but that couldn't be helped. He chose the following Monday as the starting time.

# Chapter 7

When Robert returned to the mansion on the hilltop he went to Elijah's bedroom. If anything, Elijah looked worse to Robert than he had when he left for the interviews. He was so weak he could hardly hold his hand out to Robert.

"You'd better hurry Robert, I don't believe I have much time left," he said.

"Everything is set up. The pilot will start picking them up over the weekend. Is there anything I can get you?"

"Just a new heart," Elijah said with about all the mirth he could manage.

"I will have the doctor do physicals on all of them to be sure all is as it is supposed to be."

Robert went to the office in the house and tried to catch up with the correspondence that had accumulated in his absence. Elijah was too weak to even make the effort to deal with business matters and left everything to Robert. He spent the rest of the afternoon in the office. He dealt with financial matters but his mind was partly on Elijah as he weighed the moral aspect of killing the old man.

He had decided that the most painless method would be to simply place a pillow over his face until he stopped breathing. With the state of his health he felt sure that no questions would be asked by the authorities. Unless the circumstances were suspicious the authorities wouldn't even perform an autopsy. He, as the heir, would not authorize an autopsy unless doing so would look suspicious. All they would find was that he stopped breathing in any case.

The ski resort had a couple of buses to transport guests to and from the lodge. The buses were the 20 passenger variety and he could have the chauffeur meet the plane when they arrived and bring them to the lodge.

Robert got in touch with the doctor in Utah and told him to use the small plane to come to Colorado and that he would have someone meet him and bring him to the lodge.

"Be sure you bring the necessary equipment to give them all complete physicals. I am particularly interested in the health of their hearts," Robert told him.

Everything went as planned and the entire group arrived at the lodge before lunchtime on Monday.

Robert had assured that the kitchen was well stocked. There was a walk-in freezer and a commercial sized kitchen so the only thing to worry about was fresh bread and fruits.

He would have the chauffeur make a grocery run at least once a week.

The doctor arrived that afternoon with a lot of equipment. During that afternoon and the next day he examined each of the thirteen. All were given clean bills of health.

After the doctor left he got the group together and explained what the project was about.

"All of you are healthy, and rather well off financially at the moment. At the end of thirty days twelve of you will be transported back to your homes. One will be selected to donate a heart to someone who is in need of a transplant."

This brought gasps and statements of incredulity.

"That's what this has been about from the start?" Mick Langston asked.

"Yes," Robert answered.

"I'm not sure I like the sound of that."

"You can opt out of the program, but the million dollars will have to be returned. I must remind you that your chances of survival are about 93 percent. The selection will be random, and twelve of you will be free to enjoy the million dollars you each have now," he said.

None offered to return the million dollars.

Robert left them alone. They would no doubt discuss the situation, but he had set the hook firmly and expected all of them to agree to stay until the end.

When he had gone discussion broke out among the group.

The women tended to band together and Ted Walters and Bill Carter moved outside to talk. Bill told Ted that he wouldn't put it past Robert to bug the place and he did not want Robert privy to his conversations.

"Do you think this is legal?" Ted asked.

"I have no idea if it is or not. If the donator is volunteering it might make some difference, but I just don't know. He sure went to a lot of trouble to get us all together. The million dollars is a powerful aphrodisiac," he said.

"We will all be basket cases before this is over, wondering which of us till be the sacrificial goat," Ted said.

"It appears to me that it would be murder to have someone donate a heart while still alive, no matter what he is paying us," Bill said.

"He knows that much money will make it hard give it back, especially now that we are all here. Even with the odds of survival at better than 90 percent I don't want to see this go that far. The group will become close during the 30 days and it will be difficult to know that someone you have developed a relationship with is not going to survive," Ted said.

"Since he is so willing to kill one of us, then we could return the favor," Bill said.

"What do you mean?"

"I mean that before it comes to selecting the donor that Robert might have a fatal accident of his own. I don't believe the proposed recipient will bother to look for any foul play. This place is so rugged and remote that it is entirely conceivable that he could suffer a fatal fall onto the rocks below the lodge."

"You really think so?" Ted asked.

"It would take some planning, but yes I think so," Bill said.

"Are you going to say anything to the others?"

"I think we have to. All of us will have to be in on it to assure success without any legal repercussions."

"How are you going to tell the others?"

"In ones and twos. I don't trust that Robert didn't have the lodge bugged and I don't want to take that chance. I will get them out in ones and twos and try the idea out on them."

While the volunteers were plotting to get rid of Robert, he was plotting to get rid of Elijah.

Over the rest of that day and part of the next, Bill talked to all the volunteers and told them what he proposed.

"Morally, I believe that killing Robert is no worse than him having one of us killed for the purpose of donating an organ for someone we don't even know. With Robert out of the way I don't see anyone else pursuing us for the money we were paid. I assume you all checked that the money had been deposited before you came here."

Lloyd Wheeler and Sharon Longwell were the only two that voiced any resistance to the plan. Both said they wanted some time to think it over.

"Well we have about three weeks, but in the meantime I am going to do some planning. If you have arguments on the morality of getting rid of him, just remember that he is going to do the same to one of us unless we act first," Bill said.

Robert didn't spend much time at the lodge. He left them pretty much to their own devices and except for the scepter of the death of one of their number hanging over their heads, it was like a paid vacation.

The group interacted quite a bit and friendships blossomed during the next three weeks.

It was getting near the end of the third week that Lloyd and Sharon came around to Bill's side of the issue. They had been sleeping together for most of the time and the relationship seemed pretty strong. Neither could imagine the other becoming a heart donor. Together they approached Bill and told him they were in on the plot to do Robert in.

The problem now was how to do the job.

Ted, Bill and Lloyd walked the property looking for a good place for Robert to have his fatal accident. The area just behind the lodge was very rugged and a rail fence had been erected to keep people from falling down the incline.

"This looks like a good location, but how are we going get him out here?" Ted asked.

"That shouldn't be too hard. One of us will ask for a word in private and get him out here. Others can them follow him outside and do the job," Bill said.

"I think a blow to the head with a large rock would make the job easier, and would be consistent with an accidental fall," Lloyd said.

"Then that is what we will do. Stash a couple of large rocks nearby so we don't have to go searching at the time we choose," Bill said.

# Chapter 8

On the same day Robert was plotting the demise of Elijah. He was so weak and wasted now that he could barely get out of bed to use the restroom.

The nurse didn't stay with him constantly. She had a bedroom in the house and mainly made sure he got his medications as prescribed and helped him exercise.

Robert knew her habits and waited until she was ready for her afternoon nap. He double checked to make sure she was asleep and moved to Elijah's room. He was not hooked up to any machines so there would be nothing to indicate that he was dead until after the fact.

Robert walked silently into the room. Elijah might have been sleeping, or could have just had his eyes closed. His breathing was even but labored. Robert made his way to the left side of the bad, lifted the pillow and placed it over Elijah's face. Elijah struggled feebly for about a minute. His efforts ceased but Robert kept the pillow firmly in place for four minutes. He then leaned down and checked for a heartbeat and found none. He lifted the arm and checked there as well.

He then replaced the pillow and exited the bedroom. He went back to the office to work on business matters. It was almost two hours before the nurse called out to him that she thought Elijah was dead.

Both of them went into the room and the nurse checked for a pulse again. Finding none she suggested that they call an ambulance.

"It would be easier to fly the body to the hospital, but the authorities might not like that," Robert said.

"I will take the responsibility for moving the body. That way the doctors at the hospital can certify the death and the authorities won't have to get involved."

"If you are sure that's the best way to handle it," Robert said.

He called the pilot and told him to warm the helicopter up and then come help him load Elijah into the helicopter. The body was delivered to the hospital in Colorado Springs where the nurse explained what happened.

She told the emergency room doctor that he had been having difficulty breathing for the past couple of days.

The doctor certified the time of death as the time they delivered him to the emergency room. The death certificate was filed and that was the end of the matter for the time being.

Robert decided to hang around the house until the authorities called and that happened the following day. They were not calling as part of an investigation but because the hospital wanted to get rid of the body. The death certificate listed the cause of death as heart failure. Robert was listed as the next of kin and would have to make arrangements for the funeral and burial.

Robert figured if he had a funeral that he would be the only attendee so he called the mortuary and asked them to pick up the body and cremate it.

He would also have to have the will probated and that would take a very long time due to the diversity of Elijah's assets.

It was two more days before he returned to the ski lodge.

Most of the group was in the recreation room of the lodge when he arrived.

He said, "Ah, you're all here I have some news for you."

Bill said, "Before you get into that might I have a word with you in private."

"Certainly," Robert said.

Bill led him outside by way of the patio door. When he walked down the steps toward the railing Robert followed. The two were standing near the rail looking toward the mountains when the blow to the back of his head was delivered by Ted. Mick Langston had accompanied Ted, just in case his strength was needed. When Robert fell to the ground the three of them quickly picked him up and threw him over the railing. He bounced off rocks all the way to the flat area some 100 feet below.

"I suppose someone should have a look to be sure he is dead. I can't negotiate the terrain, so you two are elected," Bill said.

Micki and Ted climbed carefully down the rocky hillside and went to the body. Mick checked for a pulse, while Ted checked to see if he was still breathing. Satisfied that Robert was no longer among the living they climbed back up the hillside and reported the fact to Bill.

Bill took out his cell phone and called the local sheriff's office. It was almost an hour before a sheriff's car pulled into the drive way.

Bill explained what had happened, at least what he thought the deputies would believe, and took them outside to the railing and pointed to the body below.

The two climbed down the rocks and checked the body.

They then climbed back up to report that he was indeed as dead as a doornail.

"Who owns this place?"

"I assume Mr. Thorley did. He invited all of us here to participate in some stress studies. None of us really knew him," Bill said.

"I will need to get the coroner out here to retrieve the body. I suppose they will want statements from at least part of you who saw what happened," he said.

"We were scheduled to be here for a few more days, so we will all be here as long as you need us," Bill said.

While the deputies were outside on their car radio's Bill broke out a bottle of wine (there was no champagne) and poured about half a glass for each of them. He raised the glass and said, "To Robert Thorley our benefactor," he said and they all had a sip of the wine.

The moral of the story is that the best laid plans sometimes go awry for the slimmest of reasons, not the least of which is bad timing.

The End

# 1551

## By John Buckner

# Chapter 1

Once upon a time in the medieval ages, there lived a young lad in the Scottish countryside, not far from Glasgow. The lad was nothing special according to the measuring stick of that day and time. He was the son of a man who tilled the land and tended cattle and sheep on their small tract of land which had been granted them by the Monarch some thirty years previously.

It was a time when there was little formal schooling for the poor, and it was not uncommon for parents to sell their children into a life of servitude, believing that would be better for them than what they could offer. Times were hard, and a portion of everything they raised had to be set aside for the King's taxes. For the family of three to survive they toiled from sunup until sundown, every day of the week. The lad's name was Kevin McEwen and he had only recently had his sixteenth birthday.

His parents were in their late thirties and only had the one child. They adored the lad, and wanted better for him than they could provide, but alas, their lot in life was hard and they had little opportunity to better either their situation or his. What they had done was to insure that he learned to read and do his numbers. They had even tried to get him enrolled in the school for squires, thinking this would be better than farming and raising sheep. That had not worked out, and so they sought to get him into the clergy through their local Vicar. The Vicar turned out to be a sexual deviant, and once Kevin became aware of this he abandoned the scheme outright, not telling his parents the reason.

Kevin had grown up with hard work and his musculature was well developed. He did not look like one who lifted logs as his countrymen did for sport, but he was deceptively strong. He was also very agile and could run for hours at a time. His skill with a longbow or crossbow was well above average, as he used these to supplement the family food supply with any game he could kill. He had to be very careful because of the King's decrees against hunting, and learned stealth out of necessity. His family did not often venture off their land, and he knew very little about the outside world, or for that matter his own world in the Scottish Highlands.

He had little time for outside activities, and though he was of an age when even the thought of a beautiful maiden made his loins ache, he had no female acquaintances of his age. He often day dreamed of situations where he was a knight and rescued damsel's in distress.

Kevin had been taken to church when he was younger and the family could find the time away from the work, and had listened to the sermons by the Vicar, not the sexual deviant, but one he liked and respected. The art of writing and reading had started to take hold in Scotland for the poor folk during the previous three or four generations, and as a result there was a smattering of literate people in the area.

In church Kevin listened intently to the sermons, which dealt with subjects with which he had no familiarity. The concept of good and evil was firmly imbedded in the sermons. Whatever God did was good, and those who opposed Him were the evil ones. This was a time when the Bible was still in Latin, and the Vicar's and Priest's had to translate for the benefit of their flock. Sad to say, some translated for their own benefit, and it was rare indeed to have a caring and honest Vicar.

Nonetheless, Kevin grasped the primary tenets of the Bible. When he heard the same verses from two or more people, then to him this gave it more credence as being what the Bible really said. He accepted the concept of God as a single Deity who made the earth and ruled over it. He had also heard enough of the New Testament teachings to accept that Jesus had come to earth to die for our sins, and that salvation for the soul was available through a belief in Him. He did not conceptualize these beliefs, nor did he talk about it a lot. Much of his work was done alone and was hard enough without trying to carry on a conversation.

Kevin accepted his lot in life, but naturally wished for better. The choices were minimal. In the village there were merchants, but their lot in life did not impress him as being much better than his own. The life of the Knight, or what he thought that life would be like, was beyond his reach as well. The Knights came from the higher classes and he discarded that line of thought as being beyond his station in life. There were simply no avenues open to him that he knew about. He had heard tales of sailors who went to sea, but that life held no promise for him. For one thing, he didn't think he would like being cooped up on a ship for long periods of time, and with his luck he would be prone to seasickness. On top of that, he had heard that the sailors were treated badly by the Captains.

He had even dreamed of going to one of the big cities to live, but he did not know what he would do to make a living. He would need a place to live, and food would not be easy to obtain either. He would be giving up one back breaking life for another of the same ilk.

This was Kevin's frame of mind as he tilled the soil for the new planting with a broken down mule, and a furrow blade that had seen better days. With the reins around his neck and his head down he wrestled the blade along the furrow. The blade struck something hard that sent a shock up Kevin's arms. It didn't appear to be a large rock, but the sensation was unlike anything he had felt before. It was almost like the feel he got when he was struck behind the elbow. Except that this made both his arms feel the same way.

He stopped the mule and looked to see what he had hit. There were no large stones in the furrow and he was puzzled. He dug around in the furrow at the point where he thought the object should be, but could not see anything. As he raked his fingers through the soil a last time he saw the glint of light off a rock, at least he assumed it was a rock. He picked it up and it gave off a brighter glow. He turned the object over in his fingers to see if he could tell what it was.

The object was elliptical, and was about five inches long and three inches wide. As he gazed at the object it seemed to change colors, from white to yellow to orange to blue. He was totally baffled. His first thought was that the object was very strange and that he should put it down before something bad happened, but he could not release the stone. His mind was saying one thing, but his muscles were doing the opposite.

He must have stood there mesmerized for quite some time, because he sensed that it was getting dark. He looked to the sky and saw that it was indeed getting dark, but the darkness was storm clouds boiling in all directions. As he watched it got darker and darker. Soon the clouds were so thick that it was like the middle of the night.

The mule had bolted, dragging the plow behind and Kevin made no effort to stop her. It was almost as if he was rooted to the place and he could not move even if he made the attempt. The object in his hand continued to glow, morphing from one color to another. The changes became so rapid that Kevin could not keep up with them. He became dizzy and disoriented. His head felt as if he was spinning in circles and he began to feel a touch of nausea. It was at this point that his mind went completely blank and he fell to the ground.

He did not see the shape that slowly moved earthward from the dark clouds, nor did he see the door that slid open on the apparition to allow his body to float upward and into the craft.

The craft stayed within the clouds and rose straight up. Within seconds the clouds started to dissipate, leaving windy and rainy conditions in the area. To the average person the entire event seemed nothing more than a summer storm that had blown in quickly and was dumping a large amount of rain over the landscape, which the farmers welcomed.

The only oddity was the mule that had bolted away, still attached to the plow with no human in sight.

Kevin awoke in a strange environment indeed. He found himself lying on a metal table, with some contraption on his head, his legs and arms shackled to the table. Oddly, he felt no fear or apprehension. He gradually became aware of other presences, though he could not move his head to have a closer look. He could hear voices, but they were speaking in a language that was not familiar to him. Still he had no fear. He managed to croak out a few words, the essence of which was, "Where am I?"

The owners of the voices did not come into view, but seemed to be trying to answer his question, though he still did not understand what they were saying.

Finally he could discern a few words. The voice asked, "Can you understand me now?"

Kevin managed to reply, "Aye."

"I suppose you are quite disoriented and wondering where you are about now," the voice said.

"Aye, ye got that right," Kevin replied.

"We mean you no harm. You happened upon one of the sensors we placed on your planet a long time ago. We have been studying your planet for many of your centuries, and you are only the fifth earthling to come upon one of our sensors."

"I'm still confused," Kevin said. "You are not from here?"

"No, we are from one of what you call stars, at a distance you could not even comprehend. Our civilization is well advanced and we are an expedition whose purpose is to study your planet and make reports to our leaders."

"Why am I here? And how is it that I can understand you?"

"The device on your head allows us to discern your language and communicate with you. As to why you are here, that is because you unearthed the sensor and held it in your hands. That is the method we use to study the specimen of earthly life forms."

"You mean I am a specimen for you to study?" Kevin asked. "I was trying to think of some way to better my lot in life, but this is not what I had in mind."

There came a sound much like a laugh, and the voice replied, "Still, it could be that your fortunes will take a turn for the better. I told you that there had been five earthlings before you to make contact with us. One you may have heard of was Alexander, who conquered much of your known world. Another was a lady named Cleopatra."

"Those names mean nothing to me. I have spent my entire life on the farm where I picked up your stone. I can read, but barely, and I know a little about numbers, but what I know best is tilling the soil."

"That will change. We are expanding your ability to use your brain, that you will be better able to communicate with us, and so you will better understand your own abilities and where we fit into the situation."

"Is that the reason for having me bound and the contraption placed on my head?"

"The bindings are for your safety more than to hold you. You are on our ship, so if you got away where would you go? Our appearance is apt to startle you the first glimpse you have, and that is the reason for the bindings. Those will be removed shortly. As to the device on your head, that is what allows us to converse."

The alien who had been speaking moved slowly into Kevin's view. Kevin's first thought was that the alien had been right about their appearance startling him. The figure looked nothing like a human. His head was shaped more like an animal. Something like a cross between an ape and a dog, though Kevin had never seen an ape and could not make the comparison. The mouth and jaws were somewhat elongated, but the nose was much higher. The eyes were more widely separated and they didn't have any ears that Kevin could see. They were also completely hairless, with very smooth skin. The pupils of the eyes were a bright orange.

"You were right about your appearance being startling. How is it that you are able to understand me?"

"We communicate in a different manner. Our thoughts are transmitted directly to you."

"Where is the light coming from?" Kevin wanted to know. "It is a source with which you are not familiar. Most of the things on our craft will not be familiar to you. I am going to release your bindings, but you must keep the band on your head in order to communicate with us. Do you understand?"

"Yes," Kevin replied.

The bindings suddenly fell away from Kevin. He was able to sit up on the table and look around. The sight left him completely paralyzed. The room was not like anything he had ever seen. The walls were covered with lights, buttons, and geometric shapes that were almost as dazzling as the gadget he had picked up in the field. There were also four more of the aliens in the room.

Kevin had no knowledge of any of the things he was viewing. His mind was so overloaded that he thought he must be dreaming. He longed for the simplicity of following behind the mule in his father's field. He closed his eyes tightly, hoping that when he opened them again the surreal scene would be gone. Alas, such was not the case. When he opened his eyes again the aliens were still there, and all the gadgets that he knew nothing about were there as well.

To grasp the depth of the shock to Kevin you must realize that many of his acquaintances still believed the earth to be flat. Kevin had not strayed more than a very few miles from his homestead in his short life. The primary concern of those he knew was food and shelter, and 90 percent of their time and effort was devoted to the provision of those two necessities.

Kevin had heard tales of Knights on holy quests, and on very rare occasions members of the royal court would visit their small village to collect taxes or post royal proclamations that few of them could read, but that was about the extent of his worldly knowledge.

The alien, who seemed to be the spokesman for the group, addressed Kevin again. "What we will do, with your consent, is enable you to function at a higher level."

The aliens didn't have a lot of experience dealing with humans but knew that a simple explanation was necessary to help Kevin understand that they would not harm him but make his life better. The chore was akin to trying to explain abstract concepts to an infant. The vocabulary and understanding were just not there. It was even difficult to settle upon an approach that he could understand.

"What do you mean by that?" Kevin asked.

"Well, to put it in terms that you can relate to, have you noticed the difference in the yield from crops planted on new ground and old fields that have been used for some time?"

"I have noticed that, yes," Kevin replied.

"Did you ever wonder why that is true?"

"No, I just know that virgin land yields more crops."

"It is because the elements that cause the crops to prosper are depleted over time. When you till the soil you stir them up somewhat, helping to a degree, but there is still not enough to cause a good crop. The better crop comes from new soil. Think of your mind as a field that has been overused. We are going to make your mind like an unused field. Your thoughts and actions will be that much better."

"In what way?"

"You will understand things more quickly, and you will probably have ideas and wonder why someone else has not thought of them sooner. You will be able to read and write better within a short time and be more intelligent than anyone in your village."

"I have long dreamed of having a better life. Will this help me to do that?"

"Definitely. You will be able to do anything that you desire."

"And what am I to do to repay you?" Kevin asked.

"You don't have to do anything, but we would like to stay in touch with you to monitor your progress," the alien spokesman said.

"I will do that, and I agree to cooperate."

Kevin was led back to the table and a different band placed around his head. This one had several wires leading to some contraption whose function Kevin couldn't not even begin to guess.

He lay back down on the table at the urging of the aliens. He was stationary for a few minutes. During this time he did not see or feel anything happening. When the bands were exchanged again he asked what that had been about. Since he had felt no sensation, he could not imagine that anything had happened.

"That is all we have to do. You will see changes immediately when you are back among your people. We will return you to your land. You should keep the band that is around your head. If you need to communicate with us you can do so with it.

The spaceship moved into the dark clouds created for the purpose of obscuring it and returned Kevin to a location near his farm. He was told to stand inside a tubular enclosure and suddenly found himself back on solid ground. The spaceship rose into the clouds and disappeared.

The rain was coming down very hard, but dissipated rather quickly after the spaceship left. Kevin got his bearings and made his way back to his home. He didn't know how much time had passed, but assumed it was the same day. Someone, probably his father, had taken care of the mule. The ground was still wet and he deduced that not a lot of time had passed while he was aboard the spaceship.

Kevin was like someone in a dream. How was it possible for something like the apparition he had seen to stay in the air? What held it up? If he told anyone else they would not believe him, he still hardly believed it himself, and he had experienced it.

His dad asked him about the mule and he told him that a bolt of lightning scared her and he sought cover in the woods knowing she would return to the house.

Kevin noticed changes right away. He seemed to look at things he had taken for granted more analytically, but the first thing he noticed was in his studies. His parents had set aside time each evening after supper for him to study, though they didn't call it studying. Kevin used a couple of candles for light to see by. It was simply a way to expose him to self-education. Kevin had a hard time with numbers. He could add single numbers without any trouble, but when the numbers became complex he had no clue how to go about it. Basic division and multiplication were so foreign to him that he had never even heard of those functions.

On the first night as he practiced with addition he realized that he could add complex numbers; that is numbers with two or three columns. The method simply came to him as he looked at the numbers. He spent a good deal more time than the normal half hour or so. He was intrigued with the concepts in his head. Before a week had passed he could manage the basics of simple math and was beginning to delve into geometry, though he didn't know what that was.

His reading skill increased dramatically, and in church the following Sunday he found that he was trying to translate the Latin the Vicar was speaking into English.

Kevin had always been content to walk behind the mule plowing the fields. Now he found the chore tedious and started to search for ways to make the job easier and faster. Why couldn't the mule pull a harness with two blades attached he wondered?

That night he sketched his idea for a two pronged plow. There was a rudimentary forge in the barn where they heated the

242

metal to shape blades and such. After he had finished his work in the field he went to the forge and stoked the fire. He gathered enough metal for his purpose and got the fire as hot as he could. With hammer and anvil he shaped the metal into two plowshares.

It took him the better part of the week, working in the late evening, to fashion the framework for his new plow. By the end of the week he had it finished. His father had wondered what he was doing but had not interfered.

The first time he hitched the contraption to the mule he found it was very hard to lift the weight of the plow to transport it to the work area. He made something similar to skids to ease the burden of moving the plow. These he could put in place under the plow and the mule could drag it easily without his having to take the weight off the plow. Once the plow was in the field he removed the skids and the mule pulled the two pronged plow as she would a single blade. The effort it took was greater, but the added efficiency meant that the mule didn't have to work as long.

His father was amazed at what he had done, and the fact that the work went twice as rapidly. "How did you come up with this idea?" he asked.

"I don't know," Kevin replied. "It just popped into my head as I was walking behind the mule. I believe I might be able to sell these to other farmers."

With the increase in efficiency plowing the fields Kevin had more time in the evening. He spent this time working the forge, making two furrow plows. When he had four completed he took one to the village and asked the local merchant from whom they bought staples if he would try to sell the plow. He did not ask a great deal for it; only enough to buy materials for additional projects and to pay the merchant for handling the sale.

The first plow sold the very next day, and after the farmer had a chance to use it he extoled its virtues to his neighbors. By harvest time nearly every farmer within their community had one of the plows and Kevin had more money than he had ever dreamed of.

After the experience with the plows Kevin spent more time with a copy of the Bible, which was of course in Latin. Just through basic memorization of verses he had gained enough knowledge to start to translate the Latin to English. He didn't do it on paper, but in his head. He mouthed the Latin words, at first almost inaudibly. As he became more confident in the pronunciation he spoke them aloud. His parents heard him at first mumbling the words, then speaking clearly as he gained more confidence, and wondered what on earth he was doing. His mother asked, "Kevin, what are ye about?"

"I am learning to speak Latin," he answered.

"And who is to explain what the words mean?" she asked.

"I know the meaning of the words."

"How could that be?"

"The Vicar always reads the Bible in Latin and I know what the English version means. That gives me enough of the basics to deduce the meaning of other words. Soon it all comes together for me."

"You mean you can read the entire Bible in Latin and know what you are reading?" she asked.

"Yes mother. I don't know why I can do this now when before it was just gibberish, but I know that I am right."

Almost a year after his encounter with the aliens a new Vicar came to the village. He was a much younger man than the old pervert, and one of the first things he did was to visit all the farmers in the countryside.

His visits had a twofold purpose. His salary wasn't much, and he figured the farmers would make gifts of the fruits of their labors. It was during his visit to the McEwan farm that he met Kevin. He stayed and talked for quite some time. During the course of his visit he learned that Kevin could speak Latin. At first he was disbelieving. How could a simple farm boy know Latin when even the clergy had to spend in some cases years learning the language.

He addressed Kevin in Latin, not expecting him to understand a word he had spoken. When Kevin replied, answering the question, he had to revise his thinking. Not only could Kevin understand him, but his response was succinct and grammatically correct.

He wondered if Kevin would be willing to work with him at the church on a part-time basis. He couldn't pay much, but thought that he might be able to solicit translation work with Kevin to help. Glasgow was within a day's journey on horseback and the city offered many more opportunities for that type work.

Kevin agreed to work with him and during the next few months the two handled a lot of translation work translating from English to Latin or vice versa. Kevin was making enough money to help his parents and they hired a worker to do what Kevin had previously done. Kevin of course paid the salary and still had money left over.

In his spare time Kevin studied Greek and French. He quickly became proficient in both those languages and the translation business increased in scope.

It was not long before word of Kevin's linguistic prowess came to the attention of the English throne. An emissary was sent to entice him to move to London and work for the King.

Kevin still had the headband the aliens told him he could use to communicate with them but had not used it since his weird encounter. Part of his mind still could not accept what had happened. His increased intelligence was the single thing that convinced him that he had not been dreaming. Before he made a decision to go to London he wanted some greater degree of assurance that he had not dreamed the entire thing up.

He begged off on going to London immediately and decided to use the headband that night.

In his room he put the headband on. Aloud he said, "Are you there?"

The response was immediate. "You don't need to speak aloud, we read your thoughts."

Kevin thought about what he wanted to ask them. "Am I meant to go to London to work in the king's court?"

"That is entirely up to you. That it would be a step up in your society is self-evident though, and the move will open other doors of opportunity."

"Then you think I should go?"

"The decision is entirely up to you. We have no influence on your actions. The only stipulation is that you must only do that which is morally right."

"And who is to judge that what I do is right?"

"Why you of course!"

"I don't understand."

"Your intelligence gives you the ability to discern right from wrong, or that which is moral and that which is immoral. If you act in a manner that is not consistent with that which is good, then the outcome will not be in your best interest."

Kevin could think of no rejoinder to this and took the headband off. If he understood them correctly, which he obviously did, then his own views of right and wrong were what really counted.

The prospect of leaving his mother and father was worrisome, but he was now almost nineteen years old and most others had started their own lives by that age. He thought that he would be able to take care of them if they would agree to accompany him to London.

The following day he broached the subject with them. "I have been offered employment in the king's court. Would you like to go to London with me?"

His father fielded the question. "Your mother and I have discussed the matter at some length. It is obvious that this area no longer holds much to interest you, and sooner or later you need to get on with your own life.  However, your mother and I are happy here and would as soon stay right where we are.  Take the position offered to you and go with our blessings and prayers."

The Scots still had a nominal ruler, who served at the pleasure of the English king, but the real power was in London.

The year was 1544. Not too many years after the 'black death' outbreak in England in 1535 the weather seemed to change for the better for a number of years.  The temperatures began to inch upward and crop yields edged upward with the longer growing seasons and more favorable conditions.  One result was an increase in the population, though this could by no means be considered a result of a higher birth rate.  Rather it meant that fewer people died from starvation or other diseases caused by unhealthy or inadequate diets.  This was perhaps Mother Nature's way of assuring equilibrium in the order of things. There was a further outbreak of the disease in England in 1543 which had an impact on those on the lower rung of the general population.

# Chapter 2

Kevin traveled to London in a carriage belonging to the throne. He even had an escort consisting of four horsemen from the king's court. England and Scotland had been to war as recently as the previous ten years. King Henry VIII was in power and after the tragedy of the Black Death not many years before, and the loss of half the population of the kingdom to that scourge, had divorced his subjects from the Roman Catholic Church. The monarch was now head of the Church of England, which was the official religion.

King Henry VIII had a long and contentious reign. His early years saw his emphasis on siding with whomever was opposing the Roman Catholic ruler of the time. He switched allies often and was not hesitant to engage in wars on the continent if he saw the possibility of gain. This led to two very real problems. First, he depleted the surplus of funds left to him by his father, and second, he left the everyday management of his subjects to advisors.

To add to his woes he had suffered a leg injury in the middle part of his reign when he was thrown from a horse and, probably due to the lack of physical activity, gained considerable weight. To partially solve the first problem, although that was not the primary reason for the action, he broke away from the Roman Catholic Church. This ushered in what history calls the protestant reformation. His annexation of the monasteries and their holdings that had paid taxes to the Pope meant that that money now went to King Henry.

The second part of the problem was that with King Henry on the continent, fighting someone else's war, the King of Scotland decided it was a good time to break away from the throne. Catherine, Henry's wife of the time, sent an army to oppose the breakaway and the Scottish king was killed at the battle of Flodden.

The King, in the latter days of his reign, could be likened to a beach ball with arms and legs. From historical reports he was quite chubby to say the least.

Though Kevin was not aware of any of this, the situation to which he was about to subject himself was wrought with many possible pitfalls. Henry was very moody and was prone to dealing with those who displeased him by simply having them beheaded. He had even used this tactic on a couple of his wives. The cousins to the north were almost considered second class citizens in any event.

The trip to London was very educational to Kevin. They traveled along the roads at a pace that did not overwork the horses pulling the coach, stopping at intervals to give the horses a blow, or when someone needed to answer nature's call. There were side curtains that could be closed, but Kevin didn't bother. He wanted to see everything possible during the journey.

At night they stopped at inns along the route or occasionally a castle. Apparently the king had stables in every hamlet and town because they changed horses frequently.

As they exited the Scottish Highlands and left the hills and forests behind the scenery changed to rolling hills and high grass. Some of the areas near the road were cultivated but there was still a lot of vacant land. Kevin idly wondered why this was so. As they continued the southward trek he found the answer. Much of the area in what he learned was called the moors was swampy and not well suited to agriculture. Not many towns existed along that particular road, and he thought he detected a bit of apprehension in his traveling companions.

When they stopped for the night he mentioned this to one of the escorts.

"It's a bit dangerous through this stretch if you know what I mean," he was told.

"I don't know what you mean. Why is it considered dangerous?"

"Lots of highwaymen you know. They are as likely to attack a carriage in midday as toward evening."

Fortunately the carriage was not attacked during the journey. Kevin had a lot of time to think during the trip. He wondered what he would be doing upon his arrival. The king's emissary had not given him much detail, simply said that he would be employed in the king's court.

When he finally arrived in London after almost two weeks in a carriage, Kevin was happy to be done with the jostling and tedium of travel. His clothing, though serviceable, was not exactly the fashion in good old London town. This was immediately pointed out to him by the stodgy old codger who met him.

Far from sitting at the foot of the throne, Kevin learned that his planned employment was to be one of the court scribes. In essence, he would be one of several who did nothing but prepare correspondence for the king and translate any documents which were in a foreign language. He would be housed within the castle in rooms set aside for both work and sleep. These he would share with others engaged in similar work.

He was taken the next day to a tailor who would prepare three sets of clothing for him, for which the throne would be billed. The bill may or may not get paid, but that was not Kevin's concern. One of the other scribes was assigned to show him about the castle and grounds. Kevin's first thought was that this was not going to be the bed of roses he had been promised. He, like the others doing the same kind of work, were expected to work from very early morning to late evening. The pay was not all that good either. The only redeeming feature was the food. There was as much as he wanted, and the quality was very high.

Kevin's linguistic expertise became obvious right away. He could translate documents much faster than anyone else in the section. He very seldom had to use what passed for a dictionary. This was a very crude list of words others had trouble with and they copied them down with explanations for what they thought they meant.

Within two weeks instead of trying to look something up the others weren't sure about, they simply asked Kevin.

One of the most abominable chores, as far as others were concerned, was to take dictation from the King. He moved about talking, as if to someone in the room, and the scribe was expected to transcribe what he had said. This would be similar to a secretary taking dictation in today's world. Unfortunately Mr. Gregg had not invented shorthand yet, and all of the scribes had trouble duplicating what the King spoke in this fashion. The accepted procedure was to immediately come back to the work area and try to reconstruct with the help of the other scribes. Even the overseer of the group participated in an attempt not to exacerbate the ill feelings of the King.

Upon learning of this custom, and witnessing the flogging of a scribe who had not apparently gotten the gist of the King's dictation, Kevin decided that he would go into the self-protection mode. He did something similar to what Mr. Gregg had done centuries later. He devised symbols for commonly used words and phrases. He didn't produce a document, he simply committed them to memory.

The King was something of a scholar himself. He had been schooled in Latin, French, and Spanish at a very young age. This obviously furthered his cause when communicating with those on the mainland during the early days of his reign. He tended to test those who came to be scribes of the court, whether to show his superiority, or to decide that they were adequate to the job is anyone's guess.

The stage is now set for Kevin's introduction to the King as one of his new scribes. He went in with one of the more experienced of the group to learn the ropes.

Upon learning that a new scribe was being broken in, the King decided to see how competent young Kevin was. He addressed him in French. "Combien de temps a-t-il fallu à apprendre le Latin?" he asked. (How long did it take you to learn Latin?)

"Il ne tarda pas à tous. J'ai récemment commencé à s'intéresser aux langues," Kevin replied. (Not long at all. I have only recently taken an interest in languages.)

In Italian he asked, "Parli pure italiano?" (Do you speak Italian as well?)

"Ho qualche piccola possibilità in quella lingua," Kevin replied. (I have some small ability in that language.)

The King was obviously impressed. "Where do you come from?"

"From Scotland, not far from Glasgow Sire," Kevin replied.

"And how did you become educated?"

"I learned all I know on my own, and through interaction with others."

"How old are you?"

"I am 19."

"I am particularly interested in how you learned Latin," the King said.

"I listened to the verses the Vicar's quoted and compared them to what the English translation said. By comparing the two I could deduce the meaning of many words. As to the modifiers, they became self-evident, even in the stilted language of the Church. Since the English Bible is now available it is a good way to refine the meaning of certain words. I seem to have a gift for languages is the only explanation I can give, Sire."

"And is your hand as fast as your tongue?"

Not sure what was meant by that question Kevin looked at his companion for help. His companion avoided his gaze.

"I am not sure I understand the question Sire."

"Can you write as quickly as your mind hears my words?"

"I do not know Sire. You will have to be the judge of that," Kevin said.

The King laughed, shaking all over. "Well, we will see how you measure up. You will write down what I say in English, then translate it to French. I would see both copies if you please. When can you have the documents ready?"

"That will depend on the length of the document. If it is no more than two or three pages then I can have it ready by this afternoon," Kevin said.

The King looked at him incredulously. "And when I send them back for corrections?"

"Certainly by the end of the day Sire."

Kevin did not know that the normal time for this process was at least a day, sometimes two.

"Then I shall put you to the test. Take out your parchment and pen." When Kevin was prepared he dictated the letter. As was his custom, he strolled back and forth before the throne as he talked.

His voice was strong enough that Kevin could hear him well and he was thankful that he memorized the symbols for common words and phrases. It also helped that he had an almost photographic memory since the encounter with the little people, as he had come to think of the aliens.

When the King was finished he asked Kevin, "Is there anything you are not sure about or that needs clarification?"

"No Sire. I believe I have it all, and it looks to be no more than two pages. Shouldn't take more than an hour or so," Kevin replied.

The King smiled. Those who really knew him did not read the smile as a symbol of satisfaction with Kevin. Rather they all believed that the young man was soon to be subjected to the King's wrath, as had many of them.

Kevin and the other scribe went back to the work area. On the way the scribe who accompanied him said, "You might have been better to err on the side of caution. If you are not back in the

King's presence with the documents as you predicted, then you will be given a flogging that you will long remember."

"I don't see a problem having them ready by then. I may even have time for a cup of tea as well," Kevin replied.

His companion went straight to the head man with the report, while Kevin went to work on the documents. He sat at his desk and did the English version first. The chief scribe didn't say a word. The young man would have to learn the hard way.

The English version went very quickly, for that was Kevin's first language and came more natural to him. The French version was a bit slower because of word choice when two or more words could convey much the same meaning. He made note of those instances on a note sheet and provided the other choice or choices of terminology.

In Just under an hour the task was completed. Kevin went to the head man and asked what the procedure was for presenting the documents to the King. It was obvious to Kevin that the King had intended him to personally present the documents, but he did not want to make a fool of himself by presuming as much.

"Are you sure the document is as the King dictated it?"

"In every respect sir. I have even provided additional word choices for the French version."

"Last chance. Are you absolutely sure this is what you want the King to see?"

Kevin looked at him with a puzzled expression. "Why would it not be?"

"What I meant to say was, are you really confident that this is essentially what the King dictated?"

"It is exactly what he dictated," Kevin replied indignantly.

"Very well. Let us see how well he remembers his own words," the boss said.

He led them to the King's chambers and discretely knocked on the door.

One of the doormen on the inside opened the door and the two were motioned inside.

The King was lounging on a large couch, apparently especially made for him, as it was half again as large as the normal couch. "Well my fine young Scotsman, let me see how well you have done."

Kevin handed over the documents. He kept his note pad, but explained that in the French translation he had noted other words that would convey the same meaning with a shade of different inflection.

The King scanned the document quickly, then obviously read it more slowly. "Did I really say that?" he asked, pointing to a particular sentence.

Kevin thought about it for a few seconds. "Yes Sire that is exactly what you said."

The King laughed and took up the French version of the letter. "Which words have you alternates for?"

"These sire," Kevin said, handing the notepad to the King. After what seemed a very long time the King looked up and smiled. "I doubted that you could accomplish this in such a short time and was even prepared to allow you time to make corrections, but you truly do have a calling to this kind of work. How could you so exactly duplicate what I dictated as if in normal conversation?"

"I cannot explain sire, except to say that I seem to remember all that I hear," Kevin replied.

"That is a skill that cannot be taught. I feel I am wasting your talent in such a menial role. Let me give the matter some thought and I will surely find some better method to use your talent."

Kevin and the head scribe went back to the work area. Everyone looked up as they entered.

"Well, how did it go," one of the brave souls asked.

After giving it some thought the chief scribe said, "Well, at least he didn't let the side down. But before you start to celebrate

I must tell you that the King has other plans for Kevin as soon as he decides what those plans are. In the meantime, I suggest you stay in Kevin's good graces as he may soon have the authority to have any of you flogged." The last he said tongue in cheek, though everyone was not so sure about the method of delivery.

Kevin continued with his translating chores for the next two weeks. He had not been in the presence of the King since delivering the translation and had almost forgotten the King's comment about finding a better use for his talents, so it came as a surprise when the chief scribe came to him and told him that the King desired his presence immediately.

Kevin couldn't change into better clothes, since what he had on was the best he had. He slicked his hair back with water and followed the boss to the King's chambers.

When they knocked and went in the King thanked the chief scribe and dismissed him. He also sent one of his senior advisors, who was within hearing distance, on a meaningless chore.

The guards were still at the door, but otherwise as far as Kevin could tell he was alone with the King.

"Tell me young Kevin, have you any other hidden talents?"

"I do not understand what you are asking sire."

"Can you do other things better than others? Do you analyze the things you see around you?"

"I suppose I can do some things better than others. I am not so sure about the other part of that question sire," Kevin responded.

"What can you do better than others?"

"I suppose I can use a bow, either a longbow or crossbow, better than most. I can lift more weight than most men my size, and I can outlast most men at any physical feat. I can plow a field quicker than most, and I always look for better ways to accomplish any task."

"That last part is what interests me. You say you always look for better ways to accomplish a task. That is what I mean by analyzing the things around you. To what do you attribute these traits?"

Kevin thought about the encounter in the field on his father's farm but knew better than to even consider telling that. "My upbringing I suppose. My parents always taught me to look at alternatives to anything I did. I devised a two pronged plow head to double the work output of the farm animals." Kevin chuckled. "I even sold those to the nearby farmers."

"What I had in mind was to make you my personal envoy. We can come up with some title if you would like, but basically I want you to travel around the kingdom and identify what doesn't work the way it is supposed to. Then we will find a way to fix it, unless the solution is so simple that you can implement it without my interference. Do you think that is something you could do?"

"That is a lot of responsibility for one so young," Kevin said with a touch of amazement.

"You will need someone to travel with you who will teach you the finer points of the nobility and the way things really work in this messed up world of ours, but you are exactly what is needed at this particular time. We will start you off locally. By that I mean that you will not be more than a day's travel from my presence until I am satisfied that your progress is such that you should go on to bigger and better things. I propose that you spend a fortnight or so with our warfare people, and if that goes well I will make you a Knight and that will insure that you are paid the proper respect when you need it. Does that sound acceptable?"

"I don't know what to say sire. Who will teach me what I need to know?"

"I will decide about that while you are learning the finer points of warfare," the King said with a laugh.

The King summoned the Captain of the Guard and gave him instructions concerning Kevin. "Take this young man to your superior and tell him that he has two weeks to teach him all about warfare."

"Yes sire," the Captain said and motioned Kevin outside.

There was a large contingent of soldiers within the castle grounds, but the bulk of the training took place outside the city, both for realism and practicality.

Once outside the hearing of the King the Captain of the guard introduced himself as Thomas Fellows. "What is it that His Majesty wants you to learn?"

"I think he just wants to know how competent I am to take care of myself. Bow, sword, and horsemanship are probably the main things."

"Have you any experience with those things?"

"I can use a bow pretty well, both longbow and crossbow. I can ride fairly well, though I have never been in a saddle. I have never even held a sword. I don't think he has in mind my leading a cavalry charge against an entrenched enemy or any of the other battlefield strategies. I think what he wants is to justify his wish to make me a knight," Kevin said.

"That sort of thing is usually a birthright," the Captain observed.

"That was my impression as well, but I suppose there are exceptions to every rule," Kevin responded.

"Just be aware that if that happens you are not going to be welcomed with open arms into that fraternity."

"Ours not to reason why, etcetera," Kevin responded.

The Captain took him to the head of the King's detail and relayed the orders of the King.

The two haggled over exactly what the King meant when he said to 'teach him all about warfare'.

Kevin explained what he thought the orders meant in the context of his conversation with the King. In the end they decided to send him to the training commander with an escort of six soldiers and let him explain what he needed to know about warfare.

"Maybe you had better head the escort so you can explain the circumstances to the training commander, since you got the order directly from the King."

Within an hour they were on the way to the training grounds.

Kevin was offered the option of riding in a coach but opted to ride on horseback with the others. He had not been on a horse or mule in quite some time, and had forgotten how much stress is put on the lower part of the body during long rides. He was feeling the stress long before they reached their destination. It was almost dark when they arrived and Kevin was introduced to the camp commander and assigned a place to sleep. Others took care of the horses.

Kevin arose just after daybreak. Most everyone was stirring at this point and he asked about the mess tent. He had tea and a bowl of mush, along with an apple before the Captain who had escorted him came in and found him.

"I see you are not a slacker. Have you had all you want to eat?"

"Aye. What now?" Kevin asked.

"I will take you to the camp commander and he will decide on a schedule for you," Fellows said.

When they found the commander Kevin got a better look than he had the previous evening in the dim light. The man was tall and had a lot of meat on his bones. He also had enough scars to cover about half his body. "Well my young lad, what do we start you out on first?" he asked more to himself than in expectation of an answer. "How's your strength?"

"Good for my size I should think. I worked on a farm until recently."

"Did you ever fight?"

"An occasional scuffle and in games, but never anything where I was really trying to hurt anyone," Kevin replied.

"Let's take you to the pits and see how you handle yourself," he said.

He then led them across the camp to a cleared area. The ground was grass and dirt and had been encircled in chalk. "This is where we practice our hand to hand combat. The only rule is that you cannot go outside the marked area. You may kick, punch, or use any method within reason to get the best of your opponent. No gouging of the eyes and no biting. Let's see if we can get you paired with someone about your size."

He went to the man in charge of the physical combat and told him what was required.

Soon about half a dozen men roughly the same size as Kevin were gathered around. The trainer picked one of the men and motioned him and Kevin to the combat area.

Kevin walked into the circle. "What is the objective?" he asked.

"To make your opponent cry for mercy, or render him helpless long enough that if it were real combat you could have killed him."

"On my signal," the trainer said and lifted his hand. He didn't hesitate more than a couple of seconds and brought the hand down. Kevin's opponent came at him in a rush.

Caught by surprise Kevin was bowled over and the man was on top of him before he had time to realize what had happened.

His opponent raised his right hand to deliver a blow. Kevin bucked and turned his head away. The fist only grazed his cheek, but it still hurt pretty badly.

While his opponent was off balance Kevin lifted his upper body and got a hand around the other's neck. Instead of trying to free himself he pulled the man toward him. The man was not expecting the move and was tensed to move that way against the pressure he was sure Kevin would exert to rid himself of the burden.

As his head came forward Kevin lifted his own head and butted him in the center of the forehead. It hurt Kevin almost as much as the other, but he was prepared. When his opponent's grip loosened Kevin rolled him off and get shakily to his feet. Both were bleeding from the gashes in their heads the blow had opened up.

The other got to his feet and once again lunged at Kevin. Kevin dodged away and punched the man in the kidney as he went by. The blow was short and powerful and the man went to his knees. Kevin moved in behind him, grabbed a handful of hair and with his foot in the back of his opponent pushed him to the ground. He quickly grabbed an arm and twisted it behind the man's back and placed a knee in the small of his back. Still somewhat stunned and in agony from the blow to his kidney, the man yelled, "I give up, I give up."

Kevin did not release his grip but held until one of the instructors told him that was enough.

He released the other and wiped the blood from his forehead.

The head trainer chose another of the men and motioned him into the circle. "Are ye ready lad?" he asked Kevin.

Kevin nodded affirmative and he raised the hand and lowered it. This opponent was not as hasty as the first had been. He circled Kevin.

Kevin simply turned to remain facing him as he circled. Each was trying to size the other up for possible weaknesses. This one was fairly agile and his feet were a blur as he danced around Kevin. All of a sudden he lashed out with his left hand at Kevin's head.

Kevin knocked the arm aside with his right forearm and kept the fist moving toward the face of the man. The blow landed and had enough power to bring the man to his knees. Kevin then used his left fist to deliver the blow that rendered his opponent unconscious.

Someone brought water and poured it on the man. He shook his wet hair and got to his feet. "Aye, a ringer so ye are," he said.

"Sorry, I don't understand that term," Kevin replied.

"It's someone who would have you think he is less capable than he really is," the man said. "I'm Charles Ashbury," he said by way of introduction.

"I'm Kevin McEwan," he responded.

The two shook hands.

"Where did you learn to fight?"

"I only played with my mates around the farm. I have never had any training," he replied.

"Well, I am happy that you are on our side. I suppose you have never shot a bow or run for miles either."

"I am actually pretty good with a bow, and I run like the wind," Kevin said.

The commander heard the comment and said, "We might as well find out if you need additional training in those areas now." He turned to the physical trainer and said, "Round up the six fastest you have."

Within five minutes the group had gathered. To another of the men the commander said, "Go get a horse." Since Kevin didn't know the route they normally ran he was going to just have them follow the man on horseback until he could judge speed and endurance.

When the man came back with the horse he told him what to do. To Kevin and the other runners he said, "Follow the rider until I give the signal that the race is finished."

The rider set off and without signal the runners started after him. Kevin did not run very fast from the start. His limbs were still not loose and he did not want a strain or cramp. He moved along at a steady pace, feeling his muscles loosen a bit. He added more speed as his muscles responded. The others were almost fifty yards ahead of him before he increased his pace to match theirs. After another five minutes he added more speed and started to close the gap.

The rider took them through the woods, although along a well-traveled trail. Kevin moved steadily up on the others and when they exited the woods he went ahead and continued the pace he had now set. He could hear the labored breathing of the other runners as he passed them.

Kevin was just getting into his element now. He was in a rhythm that he could continue for hours. The rider led them around the circle where the earlier fights had taken place. Kevin was well ahead of the others now and opening the distance with each stride. Three times around the circuit they ran. Each circuit took approximately fifteen minutes. By the time he finished the third circuit the commander waved him to a stop. He was so far ahead of the others that they were not yet in sight.

Kevin continued to jog in place at a slower pace to allow his muscles to relax. He was breathing hard, but was not totally winded, even after a good 45 minutes of steady running.

"Well, that was quite impressive," the Commander said.

"Why did you start out so slowly?"

"Because my muscles were not loose enough to stand the stress. If I had started out fast I probably would have had cramps before the end of the first circuit."

"Are you really good with a bow?" he asked.

"Yes," Kevin said simply.

"What is your best distance?"

"Longbow or crossbow?"

"Does it make a difference to you?"

"No, only the calculations are different. I am probably better at a shorter distance with a longbow. For longer distances the crossbow is better because the smaller shaft does not move as much in the wind."

He led Kevin to the target pits and most of the others followed.

To the archery instructor he said, "I need to find out how well this young lad can handle a bow. Start with the longbow and far enough away to give him a good test. Then give him a crossbow and increase the distance to whatever he feels comfortable with."

While the target was being set up Kevin tested the pull strength of the longbow and the balance of the arrows. He chose half a dozen to his liking.

Once all was in readiness the commander said, "Your show lad."

Kevin stepped to the line and drew the bowstring. He had mentally calculated the amount of drop he could expect during the flight of the arrow. There was a bit of wind, but not enough to make a lot of difference. His first arrow was in the second ring of the target. He loosed five more arrows, all in the center of the target.

The target was moved to half again the distance for the crossbow. Kevin used the first arrow to gauge the wind and movement of the shaft. The results were similar to the Longbow arrows.

"Do any of you fellows think you can best him?" the commander asked.

No one commented, except Charles of Ashbury, who said, "Where did you learn to shoot like that?"

"On our farm. I had to make my own bow and arrows. I never had anything to shoot that was of this quality," he said, indicating the equipment at hand.

It was almost lunch time and the commander led them back to the mess area.

"You say you have never handled a sword?" the commander asked.

"Never even held one," Kevin confirmed.

"If I might commander, I will be happy to work with him on the fundamentals of swordsmanship," Charles said.

The commander visibly gave the matter some thought. "Very well. Start this afternoon and tomorrow let me know how long you think it will take for him to become marginally proficient with the broadsword."

Charles ready friendship somewhat surprised Kevin. It was not usual to become friends with someone who knocked you on your backside and turned your lights out.

After lunch Kevin and Charles went to the armory and drew swords with scabbards. Instead of going to the area normally set aside for swordsmanship training they moved to the edge of the woods.

Charles spent over an hour just talking about the sword and how it was currently used. He explained that there were many different types of swords and the use to which one intended to put the sword dictated what type of sword should be used.

Charles explained the double edged sword, the longer, thinner swords favored by the Frenchmen and the cutlass. He discussed the advantages and disadvantages of each. He explained the parts of the sword and their purpose, such as the handguard and grip, and the different strokes used with the broadsword. The movements felt awkward to Kevin from the beginning. He simply didn't feel comfortable with a sword.

He had Kevin emulate his movements to demonstrate the thrust and parry, and the broad stroke. Kevin absorbed the information like a sponge.

Charles was well educated. His father was a Duke and he had the best of everything growing up. He assumed Kevin was also of his class, but when Kevin asked why the King was so fat he had to rethink his conclusion.

"We don't refer to the King as fat, though that is what he is. The nobility call it plump, or a little on the heavy side. Where are you from and how did you end up here?"

"I am from Scotland, about a day's ride from Glasgow. I grew up on a small farm with my mother and father. The three of us worked the farm for as long as I can remember. A few years ago I was listening to the vicar read the Bible in Latin. I had memorized some verses in English and started mentally trying to translate the Latin into English. It seemed to work and before long I found I could read the Bible myself in Latin. We got a new Vicar and he came around to visit everyone. When he was at our house somehow the subject of language came up and he discovered I could speak Latin. He proposed that we go into a joint venture to translate documents between English and Latin. It paid enough to hire a hand to take care of my chores on the farm and we did that for almost two years. In my spare time I studied French and Italian, even a bit of Spanish. I seem to learn languages rather quickly."

He continued, "One day someone representing the crown came to me and proposed that I should come to London to become a translator in the King's court. I talked it over with my parents and decided to give it a try. On my first introduction to the King he spoke to me in French and Italian. When I responded he said he would like me to take a letter he dictated. I did so and he asked how long it would take to have it ready in English and French. I said maybe two hours and he seemed amused. When I headed back to the work area with the scribe who had taken me to the King he said he thought I should have erred on the side of caution because if I didn't deliver what I had promised that I would probably get a good flogging."

"I did the transcription and translation in about an hour and took it to the King. He was impressed with the speed and correctness of the letter and asked how I could be so quick and accurate. I told him that I simply remembered most of what I heard. He said there should be a place I could be better utilized than as a scribe. He said I should get some training in warfare while he thought the situation over. I mentioned my youth and station in life and he said that after the training if all went well, he would make me a knight and tell me what he wanted me to do."

"So you are going to be a personal emissary of the King?" Charles asked.

"I suppose that is what he has in mind. He mentioned observing to find things that are wrong and fix them, or suggest a way to fix them to him. I really don't know what this will entail," Kevin said.

"Your being knighted in such a manner will not set well with the nobility, at least most of them. They look at knighthood as a prerogative of the noble class. That is to say that they believe all titles should be solely the realm of the nobility."

"This was pointed out to me by the Captain of the King's guard. I really don't have much say in the matter. If it is the King's desire to make me a knight, then I will become Sir Kevin, or whatever."

Charles laughed. "You are certainly smarter than many of the nobles I know, and the King obviously likes you. I would caution you that the King has a very nasty streak if you should fall into his bad graces. His favorite method of dealing with those who displease him is beheading."

"Then I shall attempt to stay on his good side," Kevin said. "When I told him that I was too young for the job he was proposing he said he would have someone along with me to help me deal with the nobility. I think he knows what you just told me, that I will not be accepted by the nobles, knighthood or no."

"Where do you come from?" Kevin asked.

"I am actually from Suffolk on the east shore. My father is the Duke of Suffolk," Charles said.

"And why are you doing this training?"

"The way that works is that as a measure of respect to the throne, the nobility is expected to raise armies for the King's wars. It has been so forever. The nobility collects taxes in their district. A portion goes to the throne, a portion to the noble, and the remainder is used to keep a ready army. The Duke of Suffolk is expected to provide an army tomorrow if the King decrees that one is needed.  In reality I think it is a matter of the King asking how many men can be provided and the provider barters the numbers as far downward as possible.  None of them want to send their best people off to war, but that is the cost of doing business with the King," Charles explained.

"Then when you finish here you will return to your home to run your father's army?" Kevin asked.

"Knighthood is the first step in the process.  From there I would be a titular leader of my father's army, but in reality those who have battle experience will make suggestions, which are really orders about how to deploy the army or how to fight a battle."

"What would happen if you didn't want to become the head of your father's army?"

"Never thought about it.  I guess it could happen, but who would pass up such an opportunity?" Charles asked, what he thought was a rhetorical question.

"I would," Kevin said.

"Why is that?  You would be in charge of hundreds, maybe even thousands of men and live the best of lives."

"Yes but what if the King levied you for an army and you did not approve of the proposed war?"

"Then I guess you would have to fight the King.  That's what they call rebellion," Charles said.

"I guess I have an awful lot to learn," Kevin said.

"You will learn quickly enough.  You are really quite gifted with natural talent, and you are much stronger than you look," Charles replied.

"I don't know how that is going to work with whatever the King has planned for me.  When I was younger I used to dream about what life would be like in the city, or to be a knight.  Now that those things look possible I am not so sure I didn't have a better life back on the farm," Kevin said with a chuckle.

"The grass always looks greener in someone else's pasture until you start to see the weeds," Charles said.

"Well, practice the strokes I taught you and see if you can get a feel for the sword," he continued.

Kevin spent almost an hour duplicating the sword strokes Charles had taught him but the sword never did feel right in his hands.

The following day they staged mock sword fights with wooden swords. Though they were not sharp, a solid blow still left a bruise. Kevin, with the gash on his forehead, which had scabbed over, and multiple bruises from the wooden sword blows was sore all over.

On the third day they moved on to the horses. Kevin had ridden quite a lot on the farm. Not the good quality animals they had at the King's training ground, but the mules they had on the farm. He had to control the mule while plowing, and when riding her. He had a good touch with the reins and could get the animal to do things that others could not. He liked the feel of sitting in the saddle better than on the animal's bare back, but he still had no way to keep his feet in place.

He wondered how the knights in armor managed the feat. It seemed to Kevin that it would be extremely hard to keep one's balance with all the extra weight. It would be much better he thought if there were straps to keep the feet in balance with the rest of the body.

That evening he and Charles went to the stables and talked to the blacksmith. Kevin explained his idea for what would come to be called stirrups. Some people used a single strap on one side to help in mounting the horse, but Kevin's idea was to use one on each side for riding as well as mounting.

He sat with the smith and helped cut some leather to fashion what he envisioned. It took them the better part of the night to get the stirrups sized and mated to the leather of the saddle. Once it was finished Kevin tried the saddle out. It was much better for him. Charles tried the saddle and pronounced his approval. In addition to controlling the animal better it also allowed the rider to make much sharper turns without falling off the horse.

"That's quite ingenious," Charles told Kevin.

"Others have probably tried this in the past. I just wonder that none here have thought of it."

Early the next morning the smith told the camp commander what they had done and he insisted on seeing a demonstration. Kevin mounted the horse without assistance and put it through its paces. The commander was impressed and gave the horse a try.

"That is a much more comfortable ride, and is also a lot safer. I will see about having all the saddles equipped that way."

Kevin practiced with various swords for more than a week. He could not get a feel for sword fighting no matter how hard he tried. "I guess this is one of those things that really does take years of practice," he told Charles. "The sword just seems so unwieldy to me no matter how I hold it or how much I practice."

"Maybe you should think about a shorter sword," Charles suggested. "That will place you at a disadvantage if you have to actually fight someone with it, but at least you will be comfortable with it."

At the end of the two weeks the Captain of the King's guards came back for Kevin. The camp commander had given Kevin a really nice longbow and a quiver of arrows. It was a nice gesture which Kevin appreciated.

"If you should find yourself near Suffolk, be sure to stop in," Charles told him as he got ready to return to London.

"I will do that. How long are you going to be here?" he asked.

"Maybe another month."

"If I get back this way I will stop to say hello."

Kevin and his escort headed back to London.

Kevin stayed in his old quarters with the scribes. The Captain of the guard came for him the next morning and escorted him to the King's chambers.

"I have heard good reports about your training. You apparently impressed everyone with your prowess. I even heard that you suggested a way to improve the saddles for the horses to give the rider better stability," the King said.

"The training was very useful, but I will never make a good swordsman. The things are simply too big to feel comfortable to me. A friend I met suggested having a shorter sword made that would suit me better."

"Who is this friend?"

"Charles, the son of the Duke of Suffolk," Kevin replied.

"Ah he is a fine young man. Mayhap he will be your companion if he agrees. He is the son of a noble and is well educated. I will see if his father feels that he can spare him for some amount of time. He will be ideal to teach you the finer points of dealing with the populace."

"If that is your wish Your Majesty."

"I think we should have a dinner party, a big dinner party, at which I will make you a member of the knighthood." The king turned to his valet. "Take this young man and get him some proper clothing."

During the next two days Kevin spent a lot of time in tailor shops in London. He was fitted for everything a young noble might wear. He had very little money, but everything was at the King's request and nobody balked at providing what was asked for.

Waistcoats, trousers, white shirts, shoes with buckles, stockings; if there was anything they missed Kevin didn't know what it was.

The event was planned for the following Friday evening to give the invitees time to travel. More than fifty riders were dispatched with the invitations. Kevin had been upgraded to private quarters in the castle but still spent time with the scribes.

He also roamed around the other parts of the castle trying to get a feel for the size and how the hierarchy was set up to deal with the King's needs.

Within the castle word had spread about Kevin's forthcoming knighthood, although no one mentioned it in the hearing of the king. Still he was the same old Kevin and spoke to everyone in the same manner he had used previously. In other words he did not let the prospect of becoming a knight go to his head.

When the day of the gala event arrived the king called Kevin in and explained the procedure to him.

"Those coming to the ball do not know the reason for the invitation. They suspect it is just to be an evening of gluttony and debauchery, which it will, but only after I have the chance to perform what I feel will be one of the more important acts of my reign. I have thought long and hard about using someone like you as a personal emissary but until you came along could not find anyone I felt could do the job I wanted. I believe you will more than meet my expectations."

Not knowing what else to say, Kevin said, "Thank you sire. I hope I am not a disappointment to you."

"Perish the thought. I have seen and heard enough about you to know that you will exceed my expectations. Your friend Charles will be here for the ball. Why don't you ask him if he would willingly accompany you on your travels? It will be much more effective to have someone you know and like as a travelling companion, and his doing so will lower the tax rate for his father," the king said.

Kevin became more nervous as time for the ball grew nearer.

Dressed in the finest clothing he had ever worn, Kevin made his way to the ball room. As soon as all the guests had arrived the King called for silence and called Kevin forward. With all the pomp and circumstance of the ceremony Kevin became Sir Kevin.

Unknown to Kevin, and apparently others as well, Charles was also knighted in the same ceremony. After the ceremony when the activities recommenced Kevin sought out Charles and related what the King had said about the two becoming a team.

"I believe the king has already mentioned it to my father because he asked what I thought about the proposition. The king must have offered a sizeable temptation because my father seemed to like the prospect," Charles said.

"He mentioned to me that your father would receive a reduction to his tax rate," Kevin said. "I just hope his expectations are not too great that whatever we do will make a great difference."

"Don't sell yourself short old boy. You are smarter than anyone I have ever come across. I believe we will do just fine, and think of all the fair maidens we will run upon."

"I'm not sure I would know what to do. I have never been with one," Kevin replied.

"Oh, then we will make that a priority in your education," Charles said with a laugh.

There were a number of young maidens at the ball and Charles introduced Kevin to many that he knew from his own social circle. Kevin was not at all bad looking and several showed interest in his company.

Although Kevin did not have much formal education he spoke well and was a welcome addition to various conversation groups. He still did not know much about the upper crust of society, to which he was now being introduced, but knew when to hold his silence and all in all seemed just another of the crowd.

He did drink more wine than he ever had at one time and was feeling the effects when the evening started winding down. He had danced with half a dozen lovely young ladies. Fortunately he had some instruction in dance in preparation for the festivities.

Charles shared his room with him after the ball and they talked well into the morning about what Kevin was expected to accomplish.

Morning arrived much too soon for both of them.

It was almost mid-day before they were summoned to the king's presence. He also looked a lot worse for wear. He had put away more wine than anyone else at the ball. Even with his bulk he had been quite drunk at the end.

"I hope you enjoyed the festivities," he said to them. "Now, some instructions about your coming endeavors; I want the two of you to travel around the city for a while. Your task is to analyze everything around you. Look at the way things are produced, how things are used, even how the barter system works. If you see better methods, introduce them if you can. Keep notes so you can let me know if there is anything that needs to be done by royal decree. Most of all I want you to identify anyone not loyal to the throne."

"Stay within a day's travel for now. I would have a report at least once each fortnight. I have ordered the purser to provide funds for each of you and I will give you a letter designating both of you as my personal emissaries. Plan to leave tomorrow. Take whatever you need from the stables and armory."

After they left the king's presence Kevin asked, "Are you comfortable with those instructions?"

"The guidance seemed pretty broad. What if we decide to do something and he doesn't like it after the fact?" Charles replied.

"I suppose that is one pitfall we will have to watch for very carefully," Kevin replied.

"Well, how does it feel to be Sir Kevin?"

"Not any different than it did just being plain Kevin. And how about you Sir Charles?" Kevin said with a chuckle.

"Same here. I suppose it will matter to others though."

"I want to get a shorter sword made before we embark on our task," Kevin said.

The two went to the swordsmith and Kevin explained what he wanted. The smith measured the length Kevin indicated, and told him it would take a couple of days to complete the task.

"That is fine. I will be traveling around town for a while, so I will check back in two or three days."

Since they were to remain in London they decided to just return to the palace in the evening and not take any baggage. It would be much easier traveling around on horseback without the extra burden.

# Chapter 3

On the day after the kingly instructions the two got horses from the royal stable and embarked on a leisurely journey around the city. They had no plan, except to observe and see what caught their attention.

The city was like any other in that time. The buildings were primarily made of wood, with some stone structures interspersed. The single most glaring deficiency both Kevin and Charles noticed was the apparent disregard for sanitation. Animal droppings were prevalent almost everywhere they traveled. Human waste was a problem as well.

There did not appear to be any structured method for disposing of waste, either animal or human. Kevin mentioned this to Charles. "Have there never been any instructions for dealing with bodily wastes?"

"Not to my knowledge. Most people simply dig a hole and dump it in there until the hole is filled, then cover it and dig another in a different location."

"And the animal waste?"

"I think shopkeepers are responsible for cleaning up in front of their places of business, but they do not always adhere to the rules."

"That might be one of the first things we mention. I hate the smell, and the waste obviously is not good for human health."

"That might be the reason the 'black death' was so devastating. I don't know for a fact, but it would seem that the waste would breed whatever caused the plague," Charles said.

"It will probably take a royal decree to get people to pay any attention to the need to keep things tidy, but we can rough up the instructions and see if the king agrees."

Shortly before noon they found themselves near the market area. The sight was something for Kevin to behold. He had not seen the area previously. The tiny market in his town was pretty orderly compared to what he saw there. He wondered how a shopper could find anything without walking the length and breadth of the market. There were no signs or directions of any sort. The open area was littered with many different items for sale.

There were clothing stores and specialty shops for major items throughout the city, but those who didn't have a storefront location had to use the common market area. Farmers made up the majority of merchants in that area, but there were also things like furs, animal hides, coal and firewood, trinkets of all sorts, and some smattering of crude weapons. The arrangement was also somewhat haphazard. People just set up shop wherever they found a vacant spot.

Kevin observed, "I think this is another area that could stand some improvement. If the market area was divided into sections and like items displayed in the same area it would make it a lot easier for the person to shop for what one needed."

Kevin kept notes on his observations, as did Charles. They tied the horses to a hitching rail and hired a peasant boy to watch them. They then went in search of anyone in authority to discuss the situation. No one could direct them to the party who managed the area.

When Kevin asked one of the farmers who was responsible for assigning spaces to sell the products the man said that he had been coming there for years and knew of no one in charge of the market. It was always first come first served as far as space went, he told them.

They spent half the afternoon at the market. Most of the people who had things for sale also had a makeshift privy behind their displays. When someone needed to answer the call of nature they simply went to an unoccupied area and did their business.

The procedure seemed crude and uncivilized to both Kevin and Charles.

It was late in the afternoon when they left the market. The boy they had hired to watch the horses had stuck to the task and Kevin gave him some coins.

They rode back to the castle and asked one of the maids to fetch supper. They had not eaten much since the morning meal and both were famished.

During the evening they worked on the flyer that would eventually turn into a royal decree about sanitation. While they were at the task they recommended establishing a sanitation crew to enforce the clean-up of waste. The city was divided into 10 sections and one person would have the full time job of policing a section.

Kevin even added a note to charge shopkeepers a small amount to pay the wages of the inspectors. He also established a requirement for every buggy or carriage to carry a scoop and bucket for collecting animal waste. As part of the order he established fines for anyone caught not complying with the decree.

The market area he had mentally measured by breadth and depth. He and Charles created a drawing with lanes from front to back. In each section they identified the type goods that could be found along that lane.

They also recommended a manager's position for the market to control the set-up and sale of goods. A small tax was added to the sale of items so that the manager's salary could be paid. Any additional funds would go to the crown.

As the two traveled about the city over the next two weeks they encountered other market areas and did the same thing as for the first. During their night time wanderings they found that many of the inns sold intoxicants. In checking the origin of the spirits they found that much of it was of the homemade variety. The inexact science of fermenting the spirits made for a wide range in the alcoholic content. Kevin thought this might be something that would bear looking into, not so much for the control of alcohol, but from the safety standpoint. If not brewed correctly alcohol poisoning could result. Kevin didn't have a lot of experience with alcohol, but his logic told him that his assumptions were true.

By the end of the second week Kevin and Charles both had several pages of notes on their observations and recommendations.

The session with King Henry was a long one. He wanted specifics about each item. When the session was over he told them that he was very pleased with their observations and that all the things they had noted would be accomplished.

The first royal decree had to do with sanitation. Not the ten inspectors Kevin and Charles had recommended were placed on duty but fifteen. The district map was redrawn to reflect the areas for which each would be responsible.

The idea for managing the markets was instituted immediately and by the end of the next week they could see the results of that endeavor. The King had not only designated a manager for each market area but assigned soldiers to enforce the edict.

The two spent another week traveling around London and observing the changes. The streets suddenly became cleaner, and the offensive odor was drastically reduced.

The markets were now orderly and signs posted near the roads made it easier for shoppers to locate the items for which they were searching. As they moved about they observed many people lauding the king for finally paying some attention to the lower classes.

The streets of the city were a combination of hard packed clay, paving stones, and loose dirt. The major thoroughfares were mostly paved with stones, but the side roads were mostly dirt or clay. This was fine in dry weather, but when it rained or snowed the travel became something of a problem with wagons and carriages becoming stuck in muck and mire.

The roads in the countryside were even more problematic. Kevin looked at the very rudimentary maps of the country and deduced which roads received the most traffic. These he prioritized by the amount of travel he thought each would receive. He recommended that these roads be paved with stones to keep erosion down and make travel easier in inclement weather. They studied the availability of guest houses and inns along the heavier traveled routes and estimated the distance a coach could travel in one day's time. At each juncture they marked the map and recommended that the king build guest houses at each of those locations. Their plan called for the king to supply the money to build the facilities and hire local people to manage them on a percentage basis.

The king was not only satisfied with their work but overjoyed at their astuteness in observing what needed to be done to improve life for the everyday citizen. That it also brought in money for the throne was an added bonus.

He liked the idea for the guest houses and paving the roads. He decided to use his military to help with the road work. There were no major wars going on at the time, and the work would keep the soldiers in shape and do some good at the same time.

After six weeks the king told them that it was time to branch out to the rest of the country and see what could be fixed in the same manner as London. He would expect to hear from them monthly, though not on a regular schedule. They could send dispatches when necessary, but he wanted to keep track of their whereabouts. He also suggested that they take a small contingent of soldiers along for safety purposes.

When the word was put out to the king's guard for volunteers to accompany the two there was no shortage of those willing to go along. They decided to only take ten. That should be enough to discourage everyday crooks and robbers. If some larger force should confront them they would be better off running away and the smaller numbers would allow them to do so more effectively.

Kevin had a shorter sword now and it felt a lot more comfortable to him.

Charles wanted to visit his folks and they planned the first part of their trip to visit Suffolk.

On the way they stopped at almost every village and town on their route. They did much the same as they had in London with the sanitation problems. Kevin noted bridges that needed repair and kept track of them in his notes.

Another problem they tried to address was lawlessness. In areas where robbery and rustling were prevalent they tried to get an idea of the numbers involved. In cases where there appeared to be gangs at work they sent messengers to the king suggesting a military presence to deal with the problem. In cases where more enforcement was needed they authorized additional billets in the king's name.

In some cases they settled disputes among local inhabitants that were long standing. These dealt mostly with property boundaries or other minor things.

Most towns and villages were structured with defensibility in mind. Some retained walls and gates as in earlier times. The dukes and other nobility near these villages were charged by the king to provide protection for the peasants in their areas. Some were more industrious about this chore than others. Kevin and Charles made it a point to visit the nobility in particular.

For the most part they applied common sense to solve the problems they encountered. The nobility readily accepted them as the king's envoys, especially after being shown the royal introduction they carried with them.

They were almost three weeks making the journey from London to Suffolk.

When they arrived Charles's family welcomed them graciously. Charles spent a couple of days showing Kevin around the family holdings. Much of the cultivated land owned by the Duke of Suffolk was tended by peasants as what became known as sharecroppers in later years. The Duke provided housing and a portion of what was grown for those who tended the land. They were also given a portion of the profits from sale of items they raised.

The first thing Kevin noted was the use of the single furrow plow. He mentioned to Charles that the farms would be more productive with a two or even three pronged plow. The Duke had a full time blacksmith and Kevin and Charles went to him and Kevin showed him how to build the double furrow plow.

Kevin had never as much as viewed the ocean and they were close enough that Charles planned a day's outing to visit the seashore. The soldiers who accompanied them were enjoying the travels as much as Kevin and Charles. Kevin was amazed at the number of soldiers in the Duke's army. There were over 2,000. Most performed the work of modern day law enforcement officials and they carried out everyday chores aside from these duties.

The Duke had a substantial castle, complete with moat and drawbridge. Many of the soldiers lived within the castle confines to provide protection.

The function of the nobility was much different from Kevin's early perceptions. It took a large number of people to handle all the tasks associated with the well-being of the populace under a Duke. Land and tax records were kept much as they are by cities and counties in modern times. All the administrative and court matters had to be accomplished by the ranking noble. Kevin supposed it was the same in his small town, but he had never given the matter much thought.

The visit to the city waterfront was another eye-opener for Kevin. No self-respecting citizen visited the waterfront after dark. The sea-going lot was a rough bunch and fights in the sea side drinking parlors was the rule rather than the exception. Sailors who had been to sea for long periods viewed violence as a way of life. There were daily rations of rum aboard His Majesty's vessels, but the portions were strictly controlled. Once ashore the sailors tended to make up for lost time. The practice of impressing civilians for sea duty was also prevalent in those times.

Captains who needed bodies to fill their crews and could not hire them legitimately simply picked up drunks and took them aboard just before sailing. Once the drunks sobered up they had no choice but to stay on the ship or entrust their fate to their swimming abilities.

Both Kevin and Charles abhorred the practice but it had been a way of life for British seamen as long as anyone could remember. Both made notes to try to change the practice but would have to tread very carefully if they brought that up to the king.

Still, Kevin thought it a good idea to suggest to the duke that he increase the military presence along the waterfront to break up some of the fights and keep some semblance of order. Charles agreed that they should broach the subject so as not to play favorites as they were sure the situation would arise again before their travels were finished.

The waterfront was the only area in which they found fault. Kevin did the talking when they reported to the Duke.

"You are to be commended on your stewardship of your holdings. Everything seems to be running smoothly and the people hold you in high respect," Kevin said.

The Duke smiled. "Thank you for the suggestion about the plows. That will make the work easier and improve the output. I detected a 'but' in your compliment however."

"The truth is that both Charles and I were a bit appalled at the primitive conduct along the waterfront after nightfall. We expect that we might find the same situation in other places and in order to try to deal with the matter we feel a greater military presence might be in order. Arrest those who cause problems and after a while the problem will go away, or at least become manageable. Even a small fine for troublemakers will help pay the wages of the soldiers," Kevin said.

"Those poor souls have been at sea for months in some cases and they need some way to unwind. I agree that it is unseemly, but better to keep them in their own area so other folks aren't bothered," the Duke replied.

"If I might suggest, why don't you start regulating the production of alcoholic beverages and strive for uniformity in the alcohol content. That might help keep some sober and also turn a small profit. I know that sailors are going to drink, and some are going to fight, but I believe that will lessen the sheer brutality of what goes on there," Kevin said.

"Did you try this in London?" the Duke asked.

"As a matter of fact we did. I really believe that those who brew some of the spirits are not as careful as others and many deaths could be attributed to bad drink. Controlling the production of spirits might help to alleviate some of that."

"I hadn't thought about that, but I suppose it is true to some extent."

"I don't see wholesale changes, just steps to show those doing business on the waterfront that they are not exempt from the laws others have to live by," Kevin said.

"I will take the matter under consideration," the Duke said.

Charles and Kevin, along with their escort, headed inland and when they turned north into the Moors Kevin questioned Charles about the area and why there was so much lawlessness there.

"I don't rightly know. I suppose it is because the land is so unhospitable and that makes it easier for the bandits to hide. Why do you ask?"

"When I was being brought to London the leader of the escort said it was common for highwaymen to attack at any time. I just wonder how difficult it would be to exist in such an environment," Kevin said.

Copses of trees were scattered around the landscape randomly, some of them quite large. "What would you say to exploring some of the area off the road?"

"I'm game for anything, but I think we should have a good supply of food before we undertake anything like that," Charles said.

At the next settlement they stopped and got some food to take along. While they were getting the food Kevin asked the proprietor about bandit activity in the area.

"There's not so much near here, but to the north there seems to be a gang operating. Seems like every few days someone comes through who has had a run in with them. Some people have disappeared along that stretch over the years," he said.

"Has no one done anything about it?"

"The Duke has sent people after them but they have never had any luck finding them."

"Let's move farther north and sleep out tonight," Kevin suggested.

They went back outside. The escorts had taken care of the horses and Kevin told them the plan. He had acquired enough food for a couple of meals for all of them. He turned it over to one of the soldiers and they mounted again. There were several hours of daylight left and they rode for almost two hours before stopping to rest the horses and bed down for the night.

They were in a copse of trees near the road. Beyond the trees was nothing but high grass. The horses were tethered to a rope tied to two of the trees. That would allow them to forage for grass but still keep them from running off.

One of the soldiers used his flint to get a fire going and they sat around the fire for the early part of the night.

"We are in bandit country, so we want to post a watch all night. Set it up so you rotate and everyone gets some sleep. I don't believe there will be much danger from the road unless someone should enter the road near us. Keep an ear out for the noise of hoof beats and watch the rustle of the grass beyond the trees. Everyone keep your weapons handy," Kevin told them.

As for himself, Kevin had been raised in the country and was familiar with the sounds and habits of animals. He didn't think anyone could surprise him, but he would not be awake all the time. He told Charles to be sure he had his weapons close by.

All bedded down with the exception of the assigned watch. They would take one hour shifts, or thereabouts, and most would get at least eight hours of sleep.

Kevin dozed off pretty quickly. He had his bow with a quiver of arrows lying beside him and his sword on the other side, unsheathed. It he had to use the cursed thing he didn't want to have to take the time to remove it from the scabbard. He was awakened at what he thought to be just after midnight by the position of the moon. He heard sounds around him but couldn't immediately make out anything. He slid his hand into the sword's handguard and rose to his knees, kicking Charles in the process. They had let the fire burn down and nothing was left now but a few cinders. On the opposite side of the fire a scuffle was taking place but he couldn't see well enough to lend a hand.

Charles roused and also grabbed his sword and got to his knees. Other than the two figures struggling with each other the others were still asleep. Kevin yelled to alert them and within seconds all were alert.

"The horses," Kevin said to the guard nearest him.

The man quickly moved away to where the horses were tied. Kevin grabbed another of the guards and whispered to him to help the other one with the horses.

The first man to get to the horses found someone trying to loosen the rope which held them. He almost beheaded the man with the broadsword. Another man was with him and came toward him with either a knife or hatchet. It was dark enough that he couldn't tell, but he knew it was an edged weapon and swiped at the man with his sword. He felt the blade bite into flesh and heard the man scream. His compatriot was now on the scene and the two of them stood back to back near the horses.

The blood had frightened the horses and they were rearing and neighing. A third guard joined the two and together they quieted the horses. In the meantime three other men had entered the fray where they had been sleeping.

The escort guards were much better trained than the bandits and managed to handle the four without much trouble. Kevin and Charles simply stood by and watched the action as best they could. Nobody attacked them so they simply waited until the action was over and Kevin stoked the hot coals until he could get a flame going. The firelight allowed them to see what had happened. Both men by the horses were dead, as were three of the four who attacked the guards.

"Bring the live one over here by the fire," Kevin instructed.

The man was brought so his features could be seen by the light of the fire. He looked to be somewhere between 30 and 40 years old. He had scraggly hair and a beard down to his chest.

"I take it you are part of the gang who has been terrorizing this area," Kevin said conversationally.

The man did not respond and one of the guards gave him a lick with the flat side of his sword. "The man is talking to you mate."

"We just happened upon you and thought to relieve you of your horses. We had no intention of hurting anyone."

"And how many before us have you done the same thing to?" Kevin asked.

"You have to understand, there's not much of a way to make a living around here. The soil is so marshy that it is hard to find a place where anything will grow. There's no way to make a living so we do this and either eat the horses or sell them if they are any good."

"Have you ever thought about going someplace else to find better land or honest work?" Kevin asked.

"Those of us who do this look upon it as honest work," the prisoner said.

"Do you have a leader?"

"Of sorts. Nothing official but we all gather in a copse of trees and store our goods and sleep there. It is not like an organized gang."

"How many in the group?" Kevin asked.

"More than you want to tangle with," the man said sullenly.

Another stroke with the flat side of the sword caused the man to cry out in pain.

"There's upward of 50, but not all there at the same time," he said, rubbing the location where the sword had landed.

"Bind him and have someone watching him through the night. Have a couple of the men take the corpses to the roadside and let's see if we can get some sleep," Kevin said.

Kevin and Charles had been bystanders to the entire episode.

As they lay back down and the fire started to die out the men were back to their sleeping pads.

In a low voice Kevin said to Charles, "Do you fancy paying a visit to the hideout?"

"It might be a little more than we can handle, but I see nothing wrong with finding the location and assessing the situation."

"Then let's do that at first light."

# Chapter 4

As the sun started to rise the group roused and started to prepare for departure. The horses were saddled and a couple of the soldiers went to where they had taken the dead bandits to see what they had killed.

It was a rag-tag bunch who were mostly dressed in rags. None had been near water for quite some time. Even over the smell of death the odor of their unwashed bodies could be detected. None appeared to be under 30 years of age. The soldiers took what was usable from the bodies and went back to the others.

"We're going to allow our friend here to lead us to their hideout. Make sure your bows are handy as we travel," Kevin said.

Kevin, Charles and the soldiers mounted their horses and prodded the prisoner along ahead of them afoot.

The prisoner led them along a path that they apparently used routinely. There was marshland to both sides of the narrow tract and they rode single file to stay on the dry portion of the land.

After about an hour they spied a large copse of trees in the distance. "That's where we hang out," the prisoner said.

"Shall I end his miserable life before we advance?" one of the guards asked.

"I don't think that is necessary. Tie him up and leave him on the path we will pick him up on the way back," Kevin said.

The prisoner was bound and the rest of the group started toward the trees. As they got nearer Kevin separated the group. "Three of you go around the south side of the copse. You three go to the north. We will give you time to get into position and then ride straight in," Kevin said.

Kevin and Charles both loosed their bows and notched an arrow. After enough time had passed Kevin led the group forward. As they got nearer the trees it was obvious that the area had been used for a long time. Most of the underbrush had been cleared and it was fairly easy to see the area under the trees. Kevin could smell smoke from their cooking fires and a few minutes later could actually see the flames. Some of them might still be sleeping but Kevin could only count 12 up and moving about.

Nobody raised the alarm as they got nearer to the camp. They probably thought it was the group who had attacked them returning. The groups who were moving to the north and south had tethered their horses and were making their way to the encampment on foot. All had their bows out and were ready for battle.

"What do you think Charles? I only count 12 up and about. Figure about half that again still sleeping and I think we can handle them."

"I'm just along for the ride. If you think we can handle them then we probably can."

Kevin rode up to the leader of the guards. "Just ride straight in until they become alert. They probably think we are the group that was out returning. Once they recognize that we aren't who they think we are, let loose with the arrows. I suppose it is possible they will surrender, but I don't believe that is what will happen."

The guard smiled as Kevin turned back to his position at the back of the group.

They were no more than 150 yards from the trees when one of the bandits raised the alarm. Kevin and his group spurred their horses as the men in the camp ran for their weapons.

The soldiers spread out and loosed the first volley of arrows. Kevin and Charles continued forward with their bows at the ready.

Four men had fallen to the first volley of arrows and Kevin dispatched another with his first arrow. By the time the guards who had been circling around the camp got into the fray the outcome was pretty much settled. Only two of the bandits were left alive and both were wounded.

Kevin had one of the guards tend the wounded and another of the guards to go for the other prisoner. When they were all together he said to the prisoners, "Bury the dead and don't be here when we come back."

With that the group left the camp and headed back to the road.

"Well that was very well done," Charles said.

"I don't know how long it will be before another group takes up the call, but probably not long," Kevin said. "What is needed is a small garrison along here someplace to react to reports of bandit activity."

This was far from the only encounter of that type they had in their travels. They went all the way to Scotland and visited Kevin's folks. They were amazed when Kevin told them what had happened to him and his Knighthood.

"I can afford to take care of you in London if you want to come now," Kevin said.

"We are still happy here, and proud that you have done so well."

They stayed a few days and headed back south along the western coastline.

They had sent the king three dispatches so far. They had no idea if they were well received or not. That decision would have to await their return to London.

The trip down the western side of the country took almost three months.

Kevin and Charles discussed whether or not the king had meant for them to go to Wales or whether they were meant to stay within the boundaries of England. They decided that if he wanted them to survey Wales they could take another trip to accomplish that chore.

They traveled all the way to the southern seacoast and followed the coast until they could turn back toward London.

Neither Kevin nor Charles had given any thought to money when they embarked on the journey. Charles had suggested that they just borrow from the nobles and have them deduct the amount from their taxes. That solution worked well. Once shown the letter from the king there were few who would refuse anything they asked for, even if they had no expectation of being reimbursed.

During the last night before they would arrive back in London as they lay on their sleeping mats gazing up at the heavens, Kevin asked Charles, "Have you ever given any thought to what might be up there?"

"Up where?" Charles responded.

"In the sky."

"Stars and the moon as well as the sun," he replied. "Other than that I have no idea."

"What if there is other life out there somewhere?"

"I don't think it is possible. However, I don't know much about the sky, except that seamen can tell roughly where they are by looking at the positions of the stars at night. Do you think the stars are far enough away that they could be the size of earth and look that small to us from here?"

Kevin had carried the headband with him on his person since he had left his home in Scotland. He was toying with the idea of telling Charles about his encounter with the aliens. The two had grown very close during their time together, almost like brothers, and Kevin felt his secret would be safe with Charles.

"I believe so, and there is definitely other life out there," Kevin said.

"You say that with a degree of conviction not natural for you," Charles replied.

"I suppose that is because my belief is strong."

"And what makes that belief so strong?"

"Because I have seen the evidence," Kevin said.

"What sort of evidence?" Charles asked.

"This," Kevin said, taking the headband from underneath his clothing.

"What's that?"

"It's something not made on earth. Look at the design of the material. It expands when you pull on it," Kevin said, demonstrating the elasticity of the item. Have you even seen any material that would do that?"

"No I haven't, but that doesn't mean it comes from someplace up there," Charles said.

"It was given to me by someone not like us."

"And what did he look like?"

"Like a cross between a dog and some other animal, though they are quite intelligent and advanced well beyond us."

"Are you sure you feel all right?"

Kevin laughed. "I have never uttered a single word about what I am going to tell you, not even to my own parents." Kevin handed the headband to Charles and said, "Look closely at the material."

"I can't tell anything in this light, or lack of light. What am I supposed to be looking for?"

"Get closer to the fire and see if you can see the finer fibers in the material."

Charles moved closer to the firelight and bent down close to look at the item better.

He stretched it and watched it conform to its natural state when he released the pressure. "What is it supposed to be?"

"It's a device that allows me to communicate with those from somewhere up there," Kevin said, pointing toward the night sky.

Charles just looked at him, unbelieving.

He moved to get a better angle of the light from the fire on the item he was holding.

"I admit that it is not like anything I have ever seen, but what you say is beyond belief."

293

"I'm going to tell you a story, but you must not reveal what I am going to tell you to anyone," Kevin said.

"Is it about there being life up there?" Charles asked, pointing to the sky.

Kevin nodded affirmatively.

"Nobody would believe anything I tell them about that anyway."

Kevin laughed. "While that's true there might be some who would look at me in a different light."

Kevin then told the story about being in the field plowing and running across the strange rock. He described the situation and how the strange object had appeared in the clouds and he had been taken into the thing. He told of the strange objects and lights inside the craft and what the aliens looked like. He then told them how they had placed the other band on his head and within a short time discovered that he was smarter than he had been before by a magnitude that he could not have imagined.

He concluded the story, "Everything I do mentally is so much better than before that I can't even make a comparison. The band allows me to communicate with the people from the sky."

Charles had been mesmerized by the story. Now he said, "I admit that you are probably the smartest person I have ever known, but I don't see how that gives the story you just told me any credibility."

"I think this band will do that. I have to ask them first," Kevin said, placing the band around his head.

The response was immediate.

"And how is young Kevin today?"

"If someone else uses the headband will they be able to communicate with you?"

"If you wish. If you do not wish us to we will remain silent."

"I want him to know about you. He is a good person and for some reason I just believe it is right to let him know that you exist."

"Then we will communicate with him."

Kevin removed the band from his head and handed it to Charles. "Place this on your head. You will be able to talk to them but you don't need to say anything out loud. They communicate by thought."

Charles did as instructed. Kevin watched the amazement on his face as the mental conversation was taking place.

Of course Kevin had no idea what was being said but it was a lengthy conversation.

Finally Charles removed the band from his head and handed it back to Kevin. "If I had not experienced it I would not believe it."

"I know. Kind of awesome, isn't it?"

"Where are they actually from?"

"Someplace a long way out there," Kevin said waving once again at the sky. "They told me it took them a long time to get here and that they travel at the speed of light, whatever that means."

"How did they come to contact you?"

Kevin related the incident where he picked up what he thought was a stone and how they had shown up in the cloudburst.

"I think they are able to influence the weather in some way to mask their presence because when they returned me to my farm it was in another downpour. What sort of questions did you ask them?"

"First what they looked like. They must have implanted an image in my mind because I saw what you described. I asked them where they came from and they simply said a far distant star. I asked them why you were so intelligent and they said they had enhanced your mental capacity, though they didn't say how. I asked them how long they had been around and they just said a long time as we measure time. The questions just popped into my mind and the answers followed immediately."

"I have only used the headband twice since the incident happened. They told me the item I picked up in our field was a sensor that let them know that someone was in contact with it. They them come to the location and beam whoever is touching the sensor to their craft. I was unconscious when they did it to me. I awoke on a metal table with my limbs strapped and a band on my head. It was this band, which allows them to communicate with me. I could never do justice to the experience with words. It was so different from anything I had ever experienced that I wasn't even afraid."

"How did they give you more knowledge?"

"I don't think it is more knowledge as we use the word. They said they only enhanced my ability to use more of my brain than normal individuals. I don't know this for a fact, but they implied that we humans only use a small portion of our brain. They apparently increased the portion that I use because I noticed a difference right away. They placed a band similar to this one on my head for a short time. I didn't feel anything taking place but it must have because I noticed the difference even that same day. It isn't something I have to think about or even be aware of. It's just that I started to look at everything differently. I was not very good with numbers but I studied each evening. The next time I did I noticed that I could add two or three numbers where before I had no idea how to go about it. That's how I learn languages. I listened to the Vicar in church and in my mind translated his Latin into English for the verses that were familiar to me. When I got home I used the Latin bible and found I could remember most of the words I had heard in church. Within a couple of weeks I could speak Latin fluently. I remember almost everything I see or read."

"Why did you choose to tell me this?"

"I don't know. I just had a feeling that you should be aware of the situation for some unknown reason. When I asked them if you would be able to speak with them they said that they would if it was my desire but otherwise they would remain silent."

"Obviously the King is not aware of this ability," Charles said.

"Nobody is, except you and me."

"I find it fascinating that there could be life out there," Charles said, again pointing to the skies.

"I felt exactly the same way after the encounter. Now it doesn't seem so far-fetched. I guess it is because I understand more about how the earth works."

"What do you mean?"

"I mean that I never thought about the earth turning, but it does so and makes a complete revolution each day. I think each of the points of light we can see that we call stars are simply other locations like the earth. I don't believe there is life on all of them, but surely some would be habitable for people like us, or like the little people," Kevin said.

"Is that what you call them?"

"It just kind of stuck in my mind. They are much shorter than we are. I think about half our height, or maybe a bit taller," Kevin said. "It seems impossible but the contraption in which they travel remains in the air with no noticeable means of support. They must use some sort of propulsion system that is invisible. When they left they just rose straight up in the air at incredible speed. The inside of the craft was the most amazing. On the walls they had things that gave off intense light. You could see everything inside just like it was daytime outside."

"How old were you when you had this encounter?" Charles asked.

"I was 16."

"So it was about four years ago and you haven't told anyone?"

"Not a soul. It just didn't seem the right thing to do. Remember, I was just a farm boy and who would believe me if I did tell them?" Kevin asked.

"Did the encounter have anything to do with your incredible physical abilities?"

"I don't believe so. I believe that is a result of the way I grew up. I worked hard all my life and that kept me in good physical shape. When the last plague epidemic struck about ten years ago my village was quarantined. We stayed on the farm for almost a year, not even going to church, without any contact with anyone other than our closest neighbors."

"Where do you see your life going from this point forward?" Charles asked.

"I don't really know. I suppose what we are doing is important, at least to the king. I learned enough about his actions during his reign to realize that he is selfish and egotistical. He squandered the funds left to him by the previous king and didn't pay much attention to the matters of the people at home. His penchant to deal with problems by execution is not what I would consider a godly quality either. I only know that things have not gotten much better for anyone since he became monarch. The infant mortality rate is tremendously high from what I have been able to gather and I think something could be done about that. Did you know that almost half the babies born in the kingdom do not survive beyond the first few weeks?"

"I didn't know, but now that you mention it that seems to be about right. What could you do about that?"

"I don't know. Study the problem for one thing and find why that is so. Most children are born at home, probably without the benefit of anyone who knows much about the procedure. I think a program of trained people to assist women in childbirth would help to decrease the number of fatalities associated with the birth process. I see so many other things that require attention that I have a hard time knowing what to mention to the king and what to keep to myself. I don't want King Henry to even have an inkling about my real capabilities."

"He is not going to live forever. What will you do when he dies and someone else becomes King or Queen?"

"Try to survive like everyone else I suppose. I have no property, no money, and little of value. My main asset is my mind and I don't know how far that will take me," Kevin said.

"I should think a long way from what I have seen," Charles said. "If all else fails you can come live with me."

It was the winter of 1546 and they returned to London just before Christmas of that year.

Upon their first audience with King Henry they presented their findings relating to the long journey they had just concluded.

The King was very taken with the thoroughness of their findings and listened to their recommendations for improving the functioning of his kingdom. They were with the king for most of the afternoon.

When they were back again in Kevin's quarters he said to Charles, "Did you think the King looked ill?"

Charles replied, "I thought it might be my imagination and was not going to mention the fact, but I believe you are correct. He is definitely out of sorts for some reason."

On the following day Kevin was summoned by the King once again.

He wondered what the summons could possibly mean and had not the faintest idea. When he arrived he was pleasantly surprised to find that he was to be given land and a castle as a reward for the services he had performed during the preceding year.

The land was in the western part of the country, nearer Wales than London, and was a portion of the real estate taken over from the Pope when Henry decided to divorce his people from the Catholic religion. He was encouraged to see to his bequest at the earliest opportunity. Kevin again noted that the king did not look at all well.

"I believe it will be prudent to give you a promotion so to speak. Henceforth you shall be known as the Duke of whatever the place I gave you is called." He told Charles of the news and the two agreed to set off the next day to see exactly what Kevin now owned.

# Chapter 5

The king apparently had the impulse sometime early in their journey because when they arrived Kevin was told that the word had come from the king months ago that they now had a new master.

The castle was not much of a castle as those things went, but it was defensible with high walls and sturdy gates. It did not have a moat, but Kevin saw no need for such at any rate.

Kevin and Charles rode the boundaries along with the head caretaker. The entire property was little more than a couple of thousand hectares. There was a small village near the castle and the population was not more than 200 souls. The village people tended the fields apparently.

The castle staff housed perhaps another 100 people.

The property had apparently been under the care of someone who had displeased the king in some manner. He was not among the living anymore and the population was apprehensive about who the new owner would be.

Charles commented that Kevin would now have the opportunity to put his ideas into practice.

"I was just thinking along the same lines. Do you want to stay a while and see how it goes?"

"I believe I would rather get back to my father's house. I will stay for a few days and help you with the administrative parts of the task though."

"I also have to decide what I am going to be the Duke of," Kevin said.

He asked one of the inhabitants what the area had been called.

"Earldom is what the local folk call it," was the reply.

"Then I shall be the Duke of Earl," Kevin said. (Pun intended)

Charles stayed long enough to help him set up the administrative duties similar to his father's estate. It was a laborious but necessary chore. He started to immediately evaluate those living on what was now his property to find the best candidate to handle the details.

He also put the blacksmith to work turning out double bladed plowshares. He wanted to have everything ready for the planting season before spring.

His next task was to find likely candidates for nursing duties to handle childbirth and other maladies for which he could teach remedies.

To his credit, Kevin didn't just pass out orders. He took time to explain the purpose of his actions and was very popular with the people on the estate.

It was in early February of 1547 when news came of the death of Henry VIII. Kevin had no idea who would replace the King but did know enough about succession to understand that it might be a very contentious time in London while that was being sorted out. He elected to just stay put and see what transpired. He couldn't imagine the successor taking the land away from him but was by no means sure about the conclusion.

As it turned out the King had made provisions for his successor. It was to be his son, who was only ten years old at the time. Others would obviously be responsible for the day to day affairs of the kingdom and a lot would depend on who occupied those positions.

Kevin thought that being far away from London was not a bad thing in his case.

He did not try to initiate a lot of changes simultaneously. Instead he changed the things most pressing in his estimation and waited until he could gauge the acceptance and effects of the changes. He appointed two middle-aged women to learn all they could about childbirth and instructed them to be present at all birthing events from then.

It would be several months before he would be able to judge the impact their presence would have on the process.

The plowshares were something the people would be able to judge the results for themselves, and when time to start breaking up the soil came his actions received overwhelming accolades.

Kevin addressed every issue that he had identified while on the trip for King Henry and soon had what would have passed for a model community in that time. There was very little disease and sanitation issues were scrupulously monitored.

He kept statistics for the births and monitored them to see if he could detect any difference in the mortality rates. It would be at least a couple of years before he could draw any conclusion but thought he could see a difference within the first year.

He fell in love with one of the young maidens and married in his second year on his new land.

No one from the throne had bothered him, other than the usual tax collector.

In the third year he could definitely see an upward trend in the number of babies that survived the birth process. That was a very positive thing for him because he was soon to be a father himself.

He became the father of a healthy baby boy in the summer of 1550.

He had not given a lot of thought to religion. The people who were on the estate when he took over were all Protestants, or at least non-Catholics. They had a small church in the village and a local Vicar to minister to the flock.

Others outside the small village had heard of the changes Kevin made and visited to see for themselves. Of those, a certain percentage desired to stay in the village. Soon more houses sprang up and the population of the village almost doubled. Additional land was needed to grow enough to feed everyone. Kevin negotiated to purchase land from a neighbor and expanded the size of his holdings.

His neighboring nobles learned from Kevin's actions about dealing with especially the childbirth process and the two bladed plows. The entire area of the country prospered while other areas remained as they were.

There is a saying, that success breeds contempt, and that is precisely what happened to Kevin. Others of the nobility heard about Kevin's success and were envious. Had they taken the time to investigate things might have turned out differently, but that did not happen. Instead three influential Dukes who lived closer to London banned together and raised an army large enough to contest Kevin's holdings.

They made the march to the outer reaches of the country and attacked the small village, killing man woman and child.

The commotion was noticed by the keepers of the castle gate and the castle was buttoned up as tight as they could make it. When the sun rose the next day the invaders attacked. Kevin's army held their own, but they were so vastly outnumbered that defeat was a foregone conclusion.

Kevin took a break from the ramparts of the castle long enough to take his wife and baby boy to the area in the dungeon of the castle to secret them in the passage that he had prepared for just such an occasion. He gave the headband to his wife and told her, "When little Kevin reaches six years of age, place this on his head. Do not let anyone know about it."

Though frightened she nodded her understanding.

Whether his wife and child made it to safety he would never know, for when he returned to the battle he had loosed fewer than a dozen arrows before one found him. He knew that the wound was fatal. His last wish as death overtook him was that his son would live long enough to contact his benefactors.

The End

www.ingramcontent.com/pod-product-compliance
Lightning Source LLC
Chambersburg PA
CBHW062123170626
46813CB00002B/552